VOLUME
FOUR

IMAGE COMICS, INC.

Robert Kirkman
CHIEF OPERATING OFFICER

Erik Larsen
CHIEF FINANCIAL OFFICER

Todd McFarlane
PRESIDENT

Marc Silvestri
CHIEF EXECUTIVE OFFICER

Jim Valentino
VICE-PRESIDENT

Eric Stephenson
PUBLISHER

Corey Murphy
DIRECTOR OF SALES

Jeff Boison
DIRECTOR OF PUBLISHING PLANNING
& BOOK TRADE SALES

Jeremy Sullivan
DIRECTOR OF DIGITAL SALES

Kat Salazar
DIRECTOR OF PR & MARKETING

Emily Miller
DIRECTOR OF OPERATIONS

Branwyn Bigglestone
SENIOR ACCOUNTS MANAGER

Sarah Mello
ACCOUNTS MANAGER

Drew Gill
ART DIRECTOR

Jonathan Chan
PRODUCTION MANAGER

Meredith Wallace
PRINT MANAGER

Briah Skelly
PUBLICITY ASSISTANT

Randy Okamura
MARKETING PRODUCTION DESIGNER

David Brothers
BRANDING MANAGER

Ally Power
CONTENT MANAGER

Addison Duke
PRODUCTION ARTIST

Vincent Kukua
PRODUCTION ARTIST

Sasha Head
PRODUCTION ARTIST

Tricia Ramos
PRODUCTION ARTIST

Jeff Stang
DIRECT MARKET SALES REPRESENTATIVE

Emilio Bautista
DIGITAL SALES ASSOCIATE

Chloe Ramos-Peterson
ADMINISTRATIVE ASSISTANT

www.imagecomics.com

BRIAN K. VAUGHAN
WRITER

FIONA STAPLES
ARTIST

FONOGRAFIKS
LETTERING + DESIGN

ERIC STEPHENSON
COORDINATOR

C H A P T E R

NINETEEN

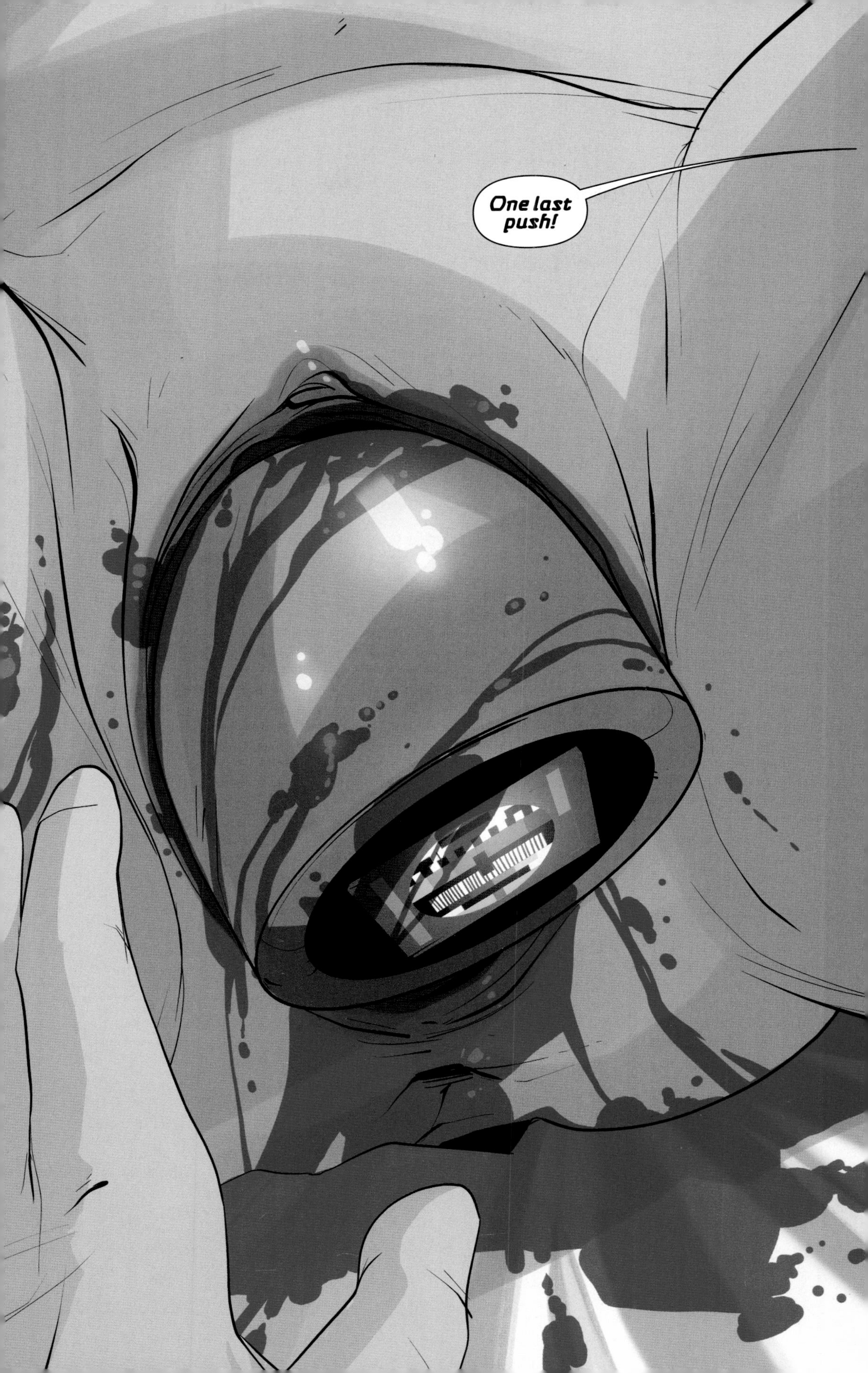
One last push!

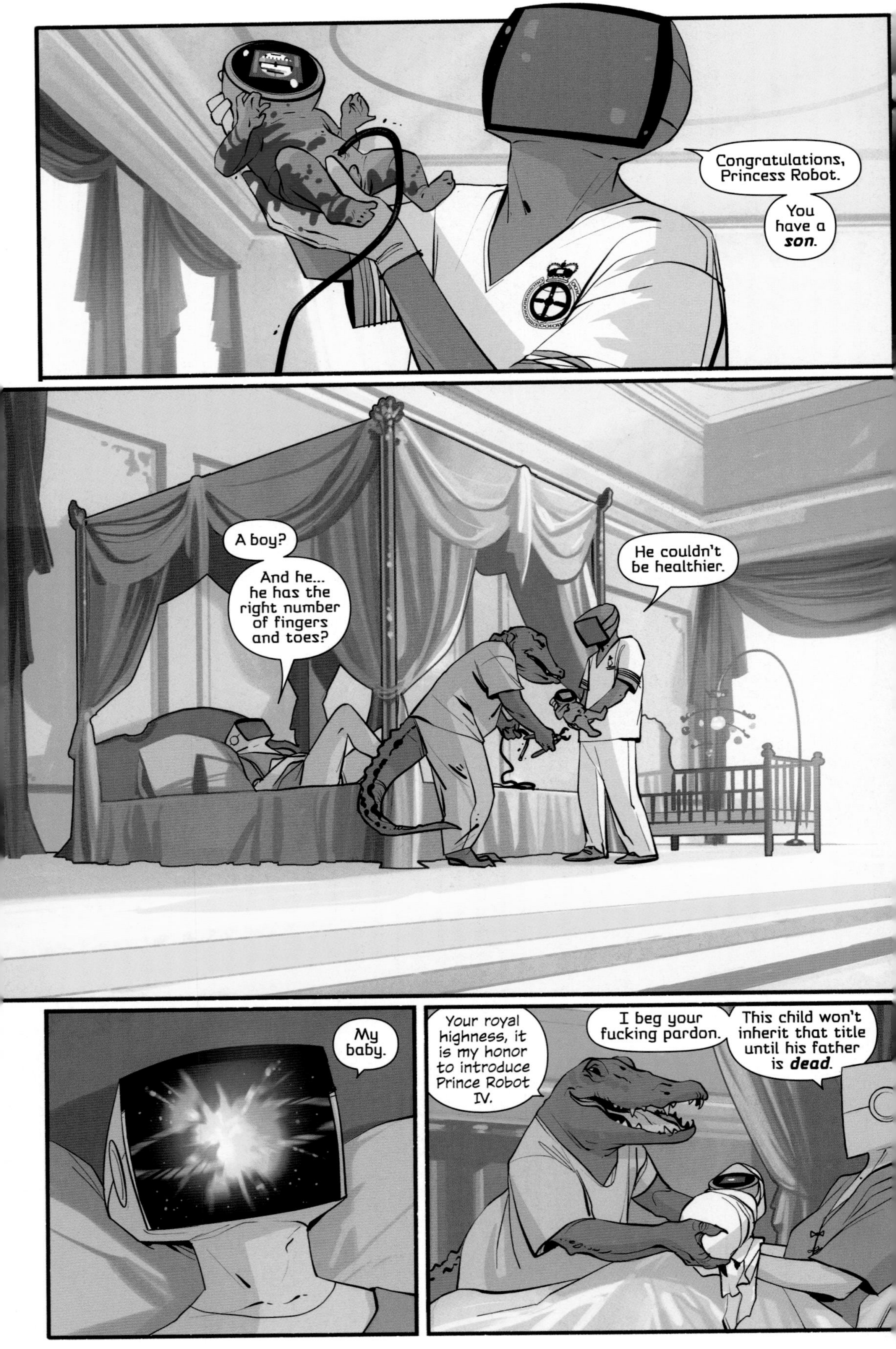
Congratulations, Princess Robot.
You have a *son*.
A boy?
And he... he has the right number of fingers and toes?
He couldn't be healthier.
My baby.
Your royal highness, it is my honor to introduce Prince Robot IV.
I beg your fucking pardon.
This child won't inherit that title until his father is *dead*.

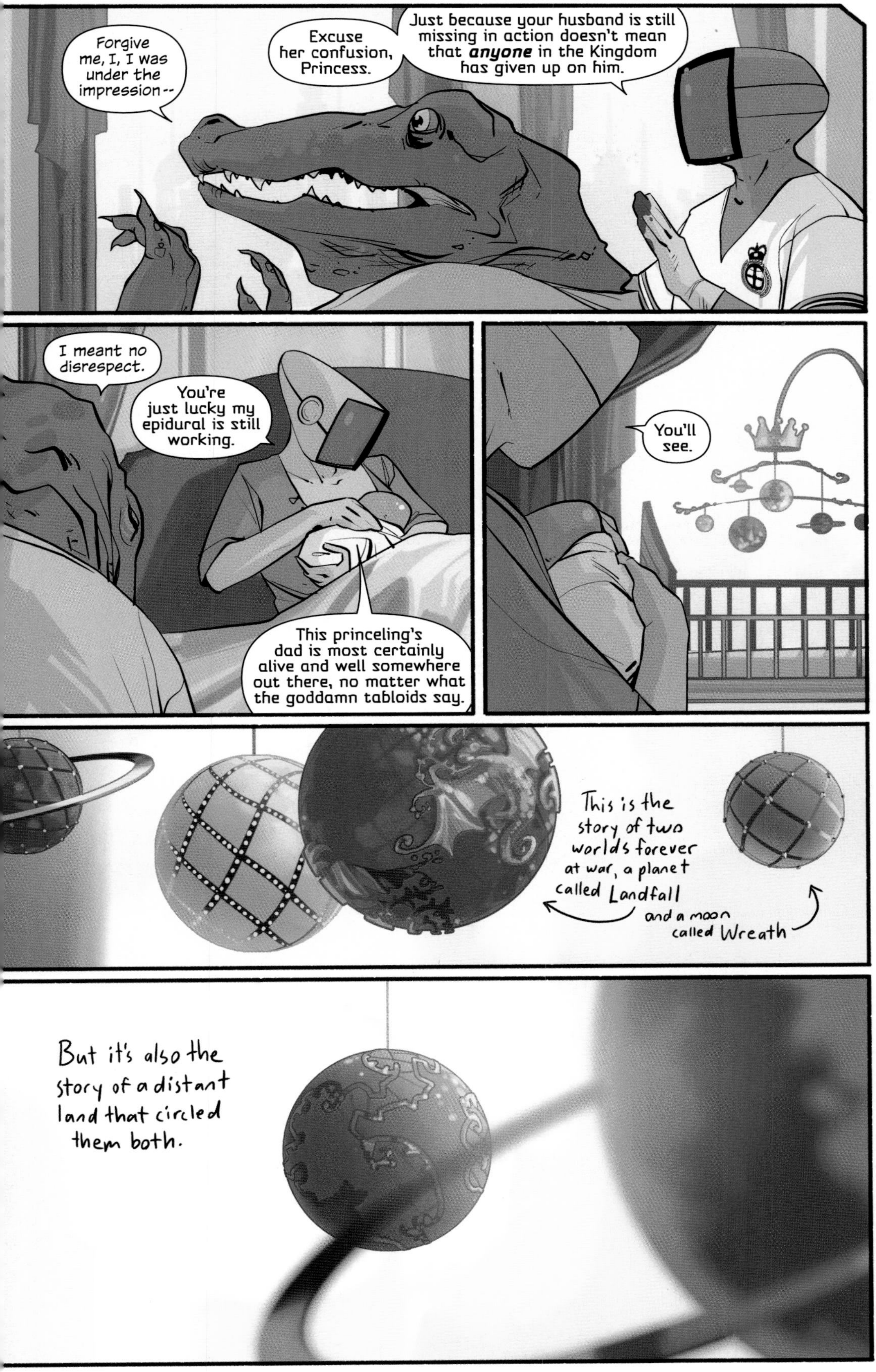

Forgive me, I, I was under the impression--
Excuse her confusion, Princess.
Just because your husband is still missing in action doesn't mean that **anyone** in the Kingdom has given up on him.
I meant no disrespect.
You're just lucky my epidural is still working.
This princeling's dad is most certainly alive and well somewhere out there, no matter what the goddamn tabloids say.
You'll see.
This is the story of two worlds forever at war, a planet called Landfall
and a moon called Wreath
But it's also the story of a distant land that circled them both.

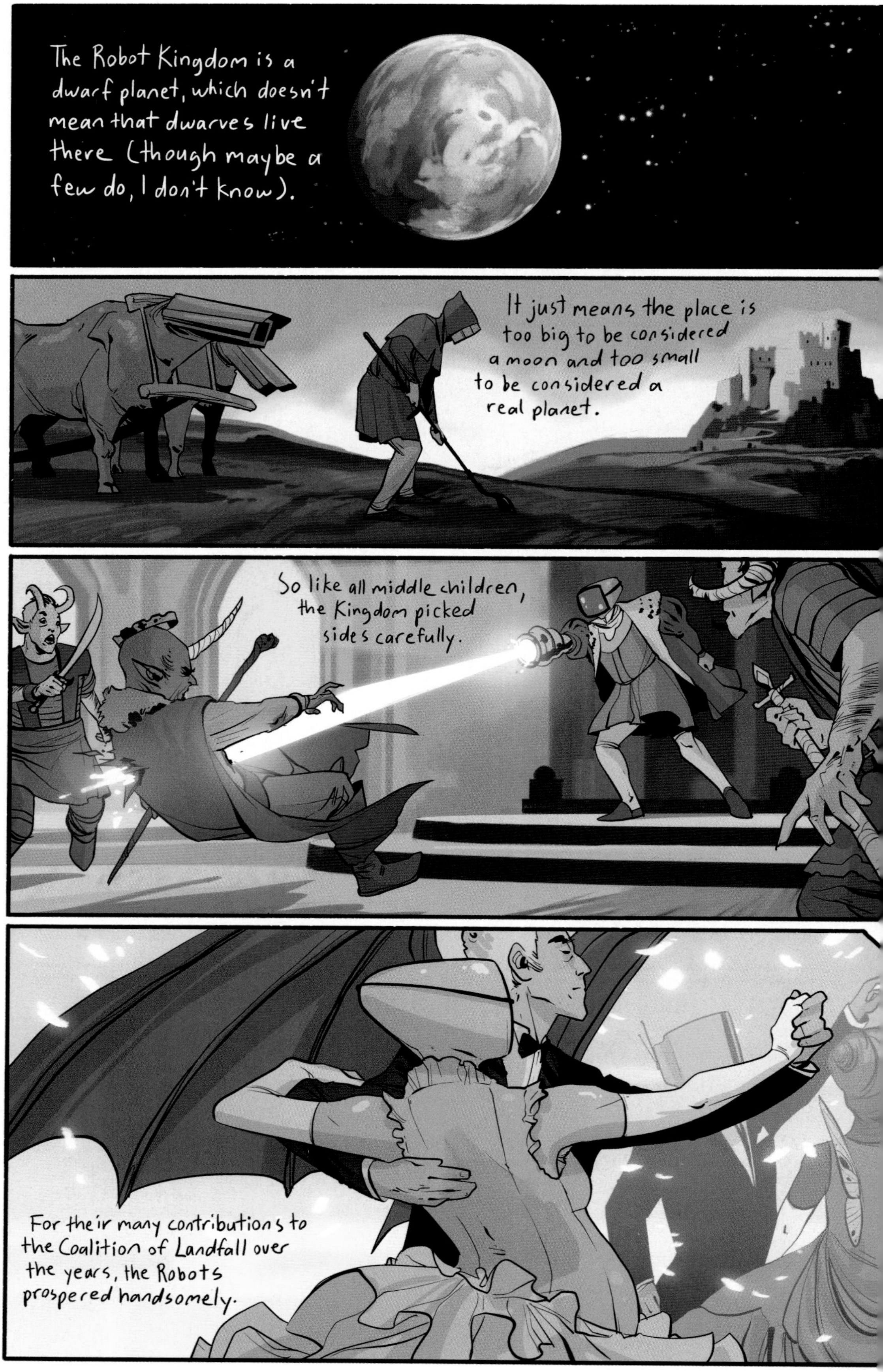
The Robot Kingdom is a dwarf planet, which doesn't mean that dwarves live there (though maybe a few do, I don't know).
It just means the place is too big to be considered a moon and too small to be considered a real planet.
So like all middle children, the Kingdom picked sides carefully.
For their many contributions to the Coalition of Landfall over the years, the Robots prospered handsomely.

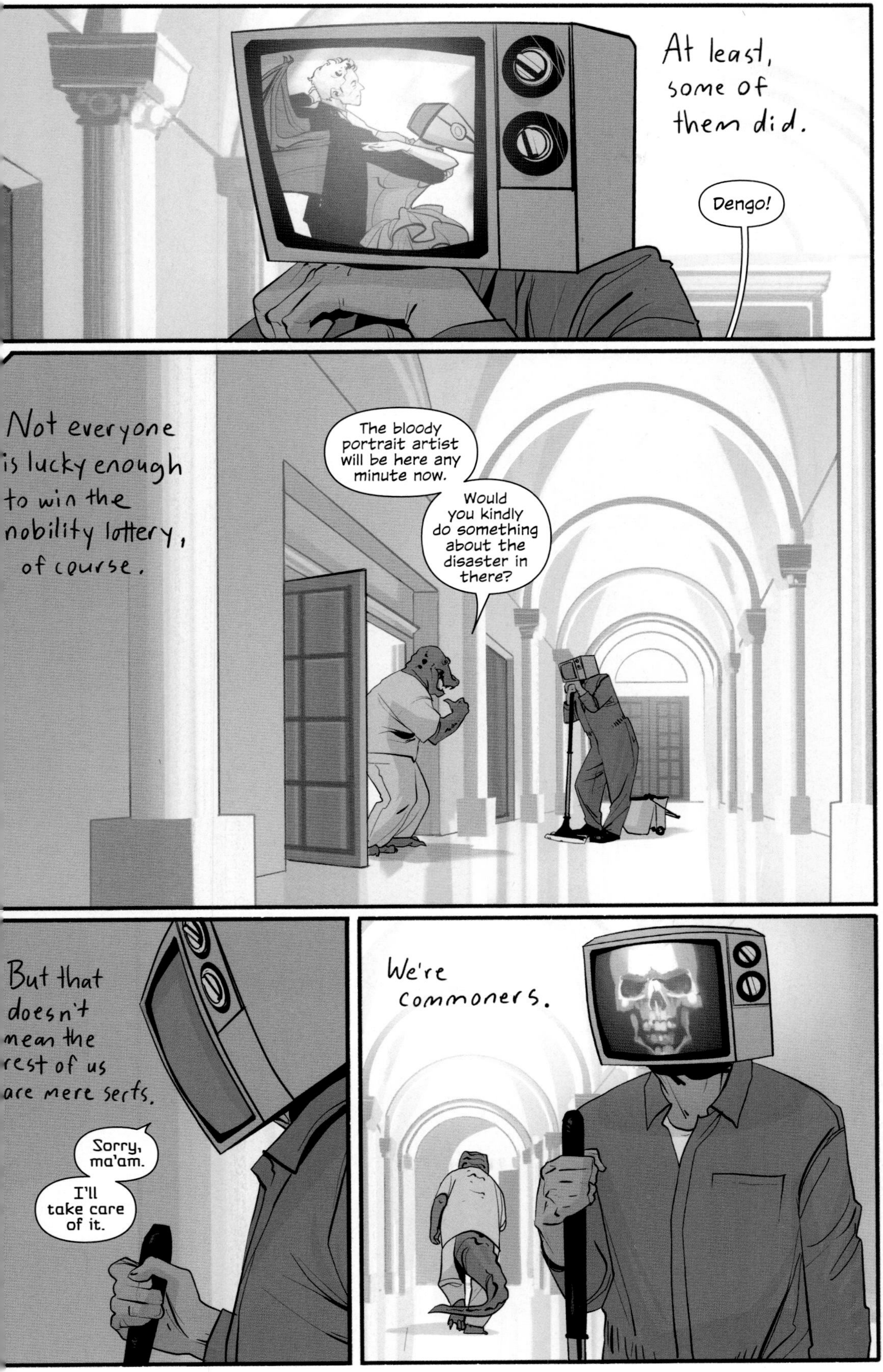
At least, some of them did.
Dengo!
Not everyone is lucky enough to win the nobility lottery, of course.
The bloody portrait artist will be here any minute now.
Would you kindly do something about the disaster in there?
But that doesn't mean the rest of us are mere serfs.
Sorry, ma'am.
I'll take care of it.
We're commoners.

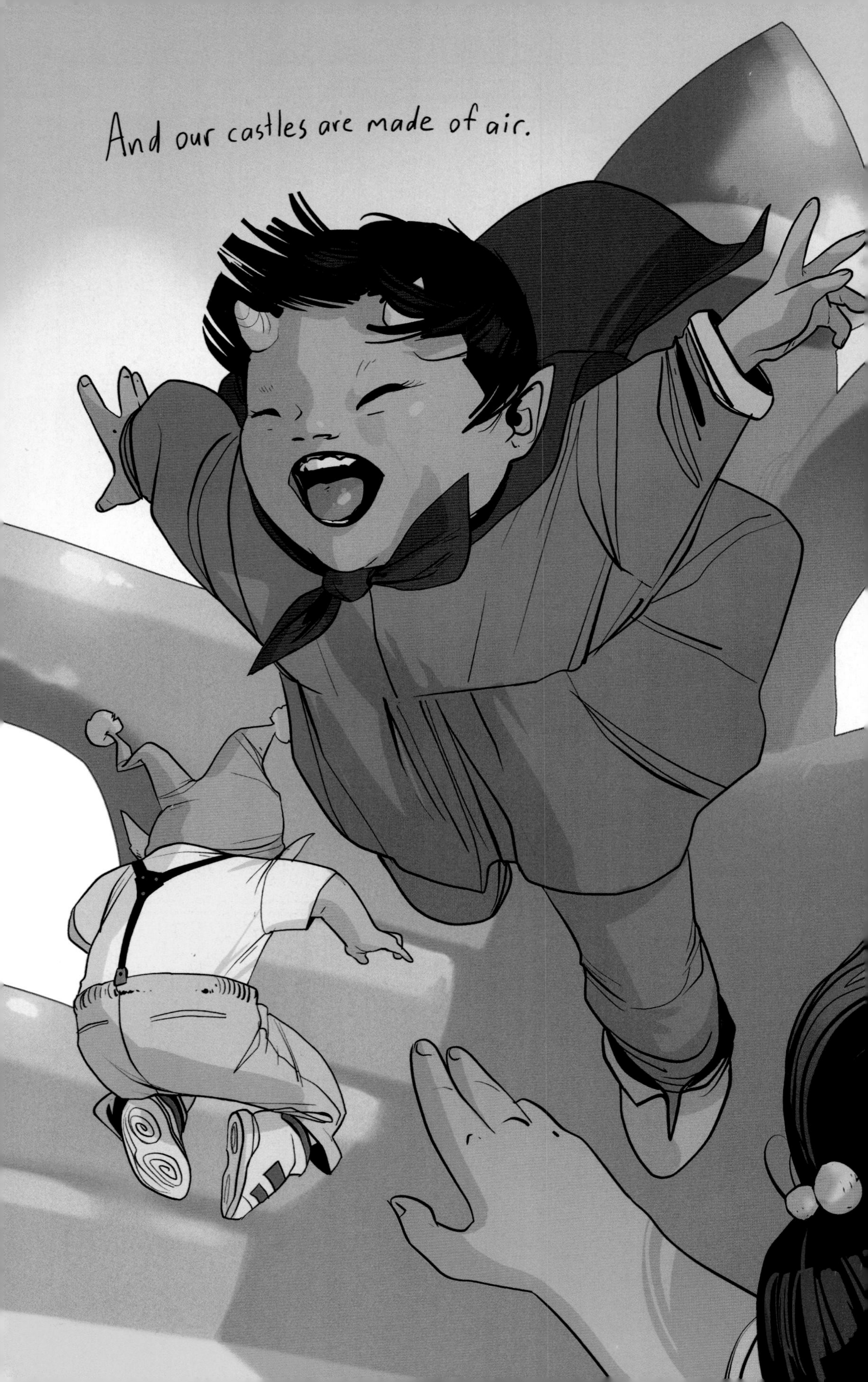
And our castles are made of air.

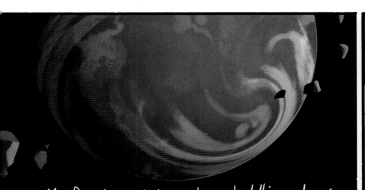

My family and I spent my toddling days on another world altogether, GARDENIA, an ugly planet with gorgeous weather.

FEE, DADDY, FEE!

Soak it up, I'm not always this adorable.

We'd been safely ensconced here for several months, and... you know what, forget it.

You'll catch up.

Bonan matenon.

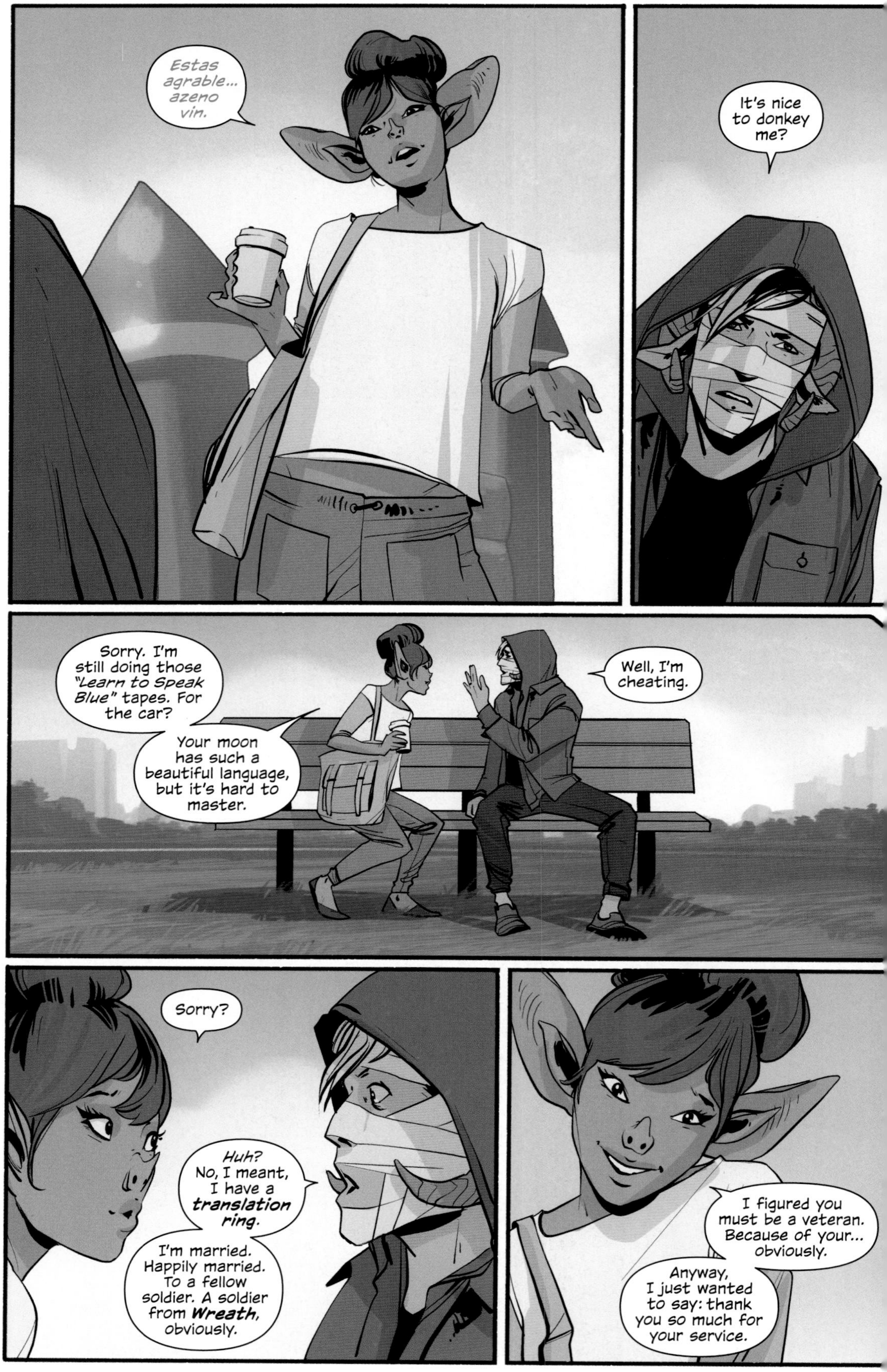

Estas agrable... azeno vin.
It's nice to donkey me?
Sorry. I'm still doing those *"Learn to Speak Blue"* tapes. For the car?
Your moon has such a beautiful language, but it's hard to master.
Well, I'm cheating.
Sorry?
Huh? No, I meant, I have a ***translation ring***.
I'm married. Happily married. To a fellow soldier. A soldier from ***Wreath***, obviously.
I figured you must be a veteran. Because of your... obviously.
Anyway, I just wanted to say: thank you so much for your service.

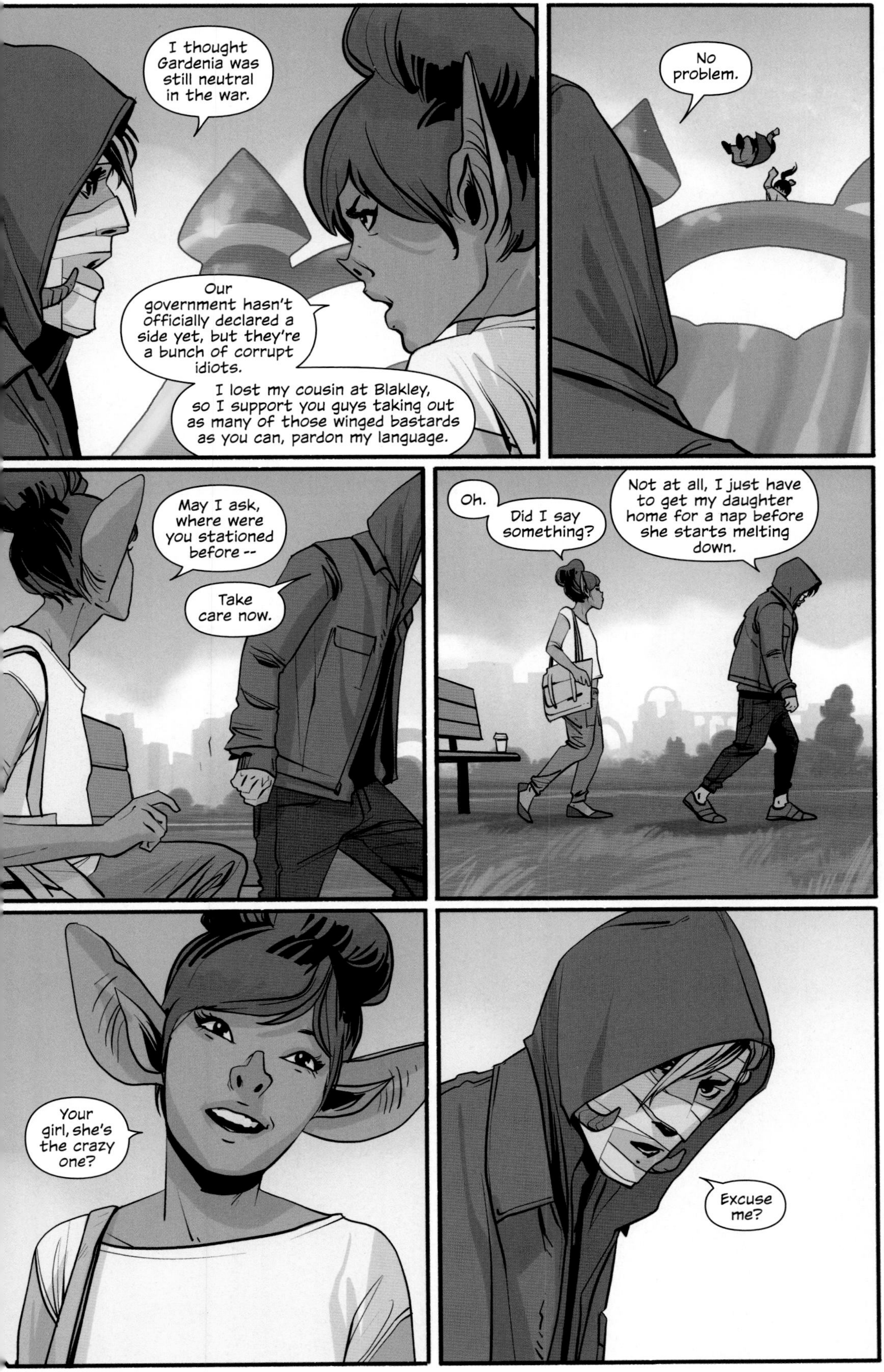
I thought Gardenia was still neutral in the war.
Our government hasn't officially declared a side yet, but they're a bunch of corrupt idiots.
I lost my cousin at Blakley, so I support you guys taking out as many of those winged bastards as you can, pardon my language.
No problem.
May I ask, where were you stationed before --
Take care now.
Oh.
Did I say something?
Not at all, I just have to get my daughter home for a nap before she starts melting down.
Your girl, she's the crazy one?
Excuse me?

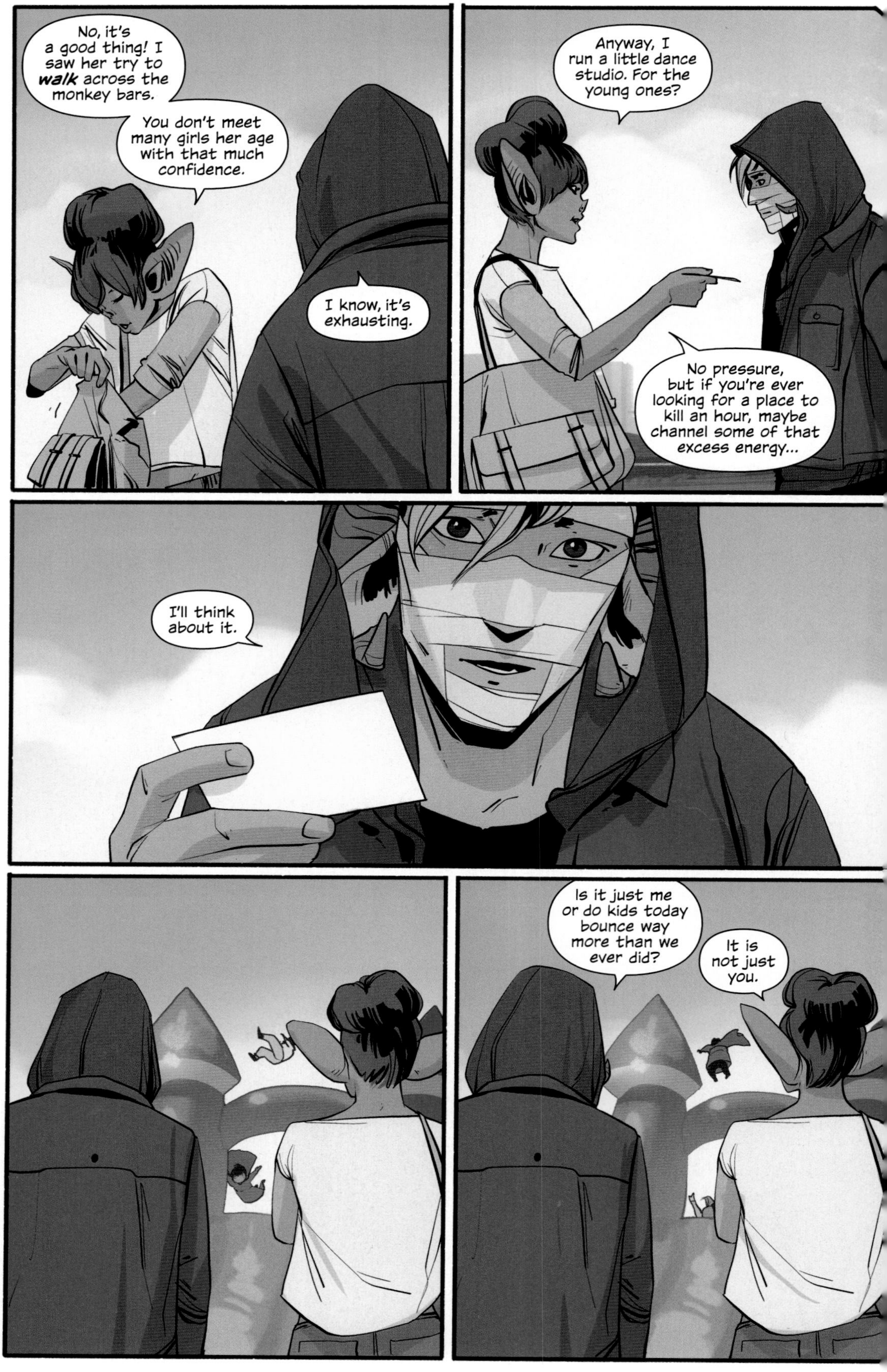
No, it's a good thing! I saw her try to *walk* across the monkey bars.
You don't meet many girls her age with that much confidence.
I know, it's exhausting.
Anyway, I run a little dance studio. For the young ones?
No pressure, but if you're ever looking for a place to kill an hour, maybe channel some of that excess energy...
I'll think about it.
Is it just me or do kids today bounce way more than we ever did?
It is not just you.

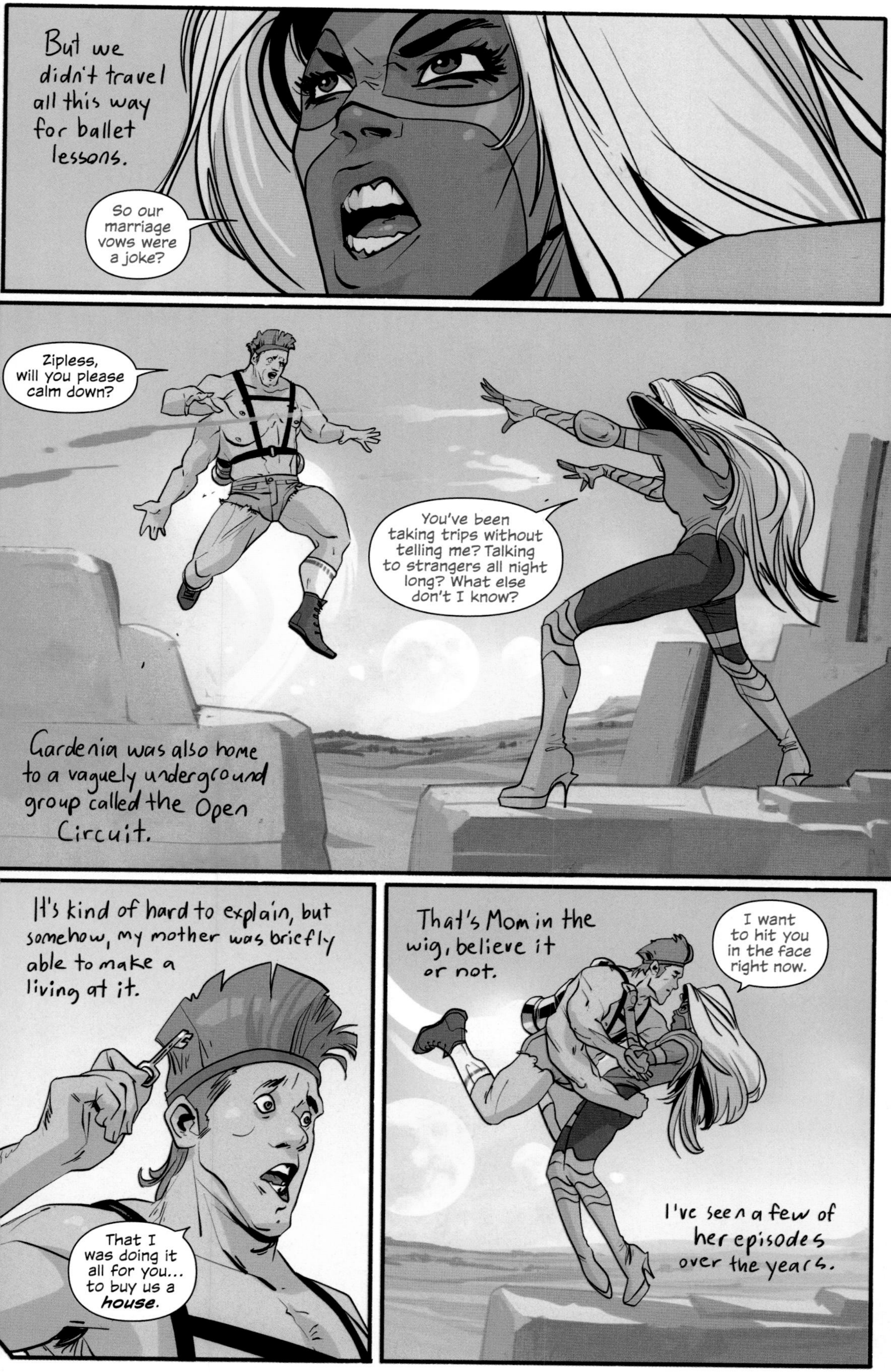

But we didn't travel all this way for ballet lessons.
So our marriage vows were a joke?
Zipless, will you please calm down?
You've been taking trips without telling me? Talking to strangers all night long? What else don't I know?
Gardenia was also home to a vaguely underground group called the Open Circuit.
It's kind of hard to explain, but somehow, my mother was briefly able to make a living at it.
That I was doing it all for you... to buy us a house.
That's Mom in the wig, believe it or not.
I want to hit you in the face right now.
I've seen a few of her episodes over the years.

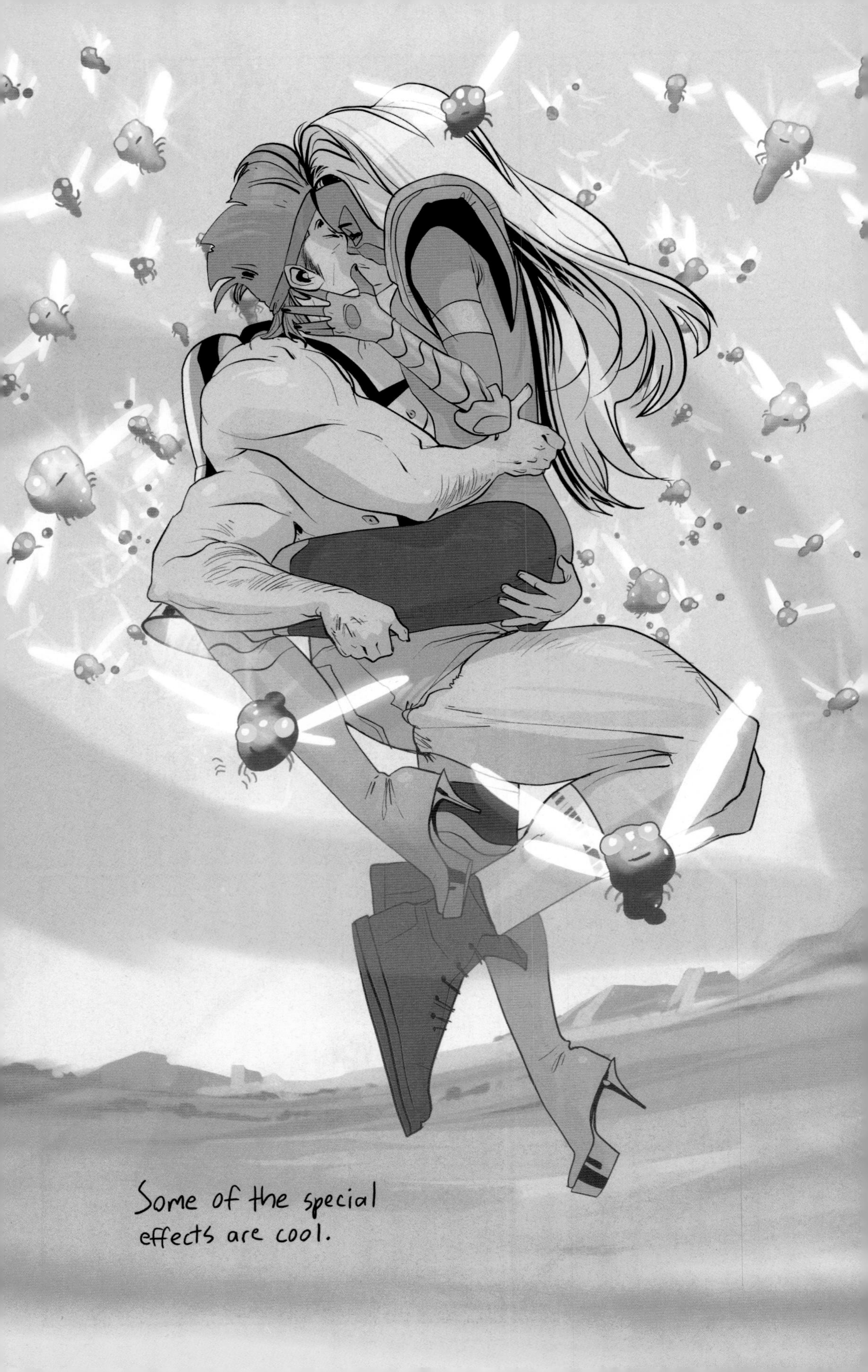

Some of the special
effects are cool.

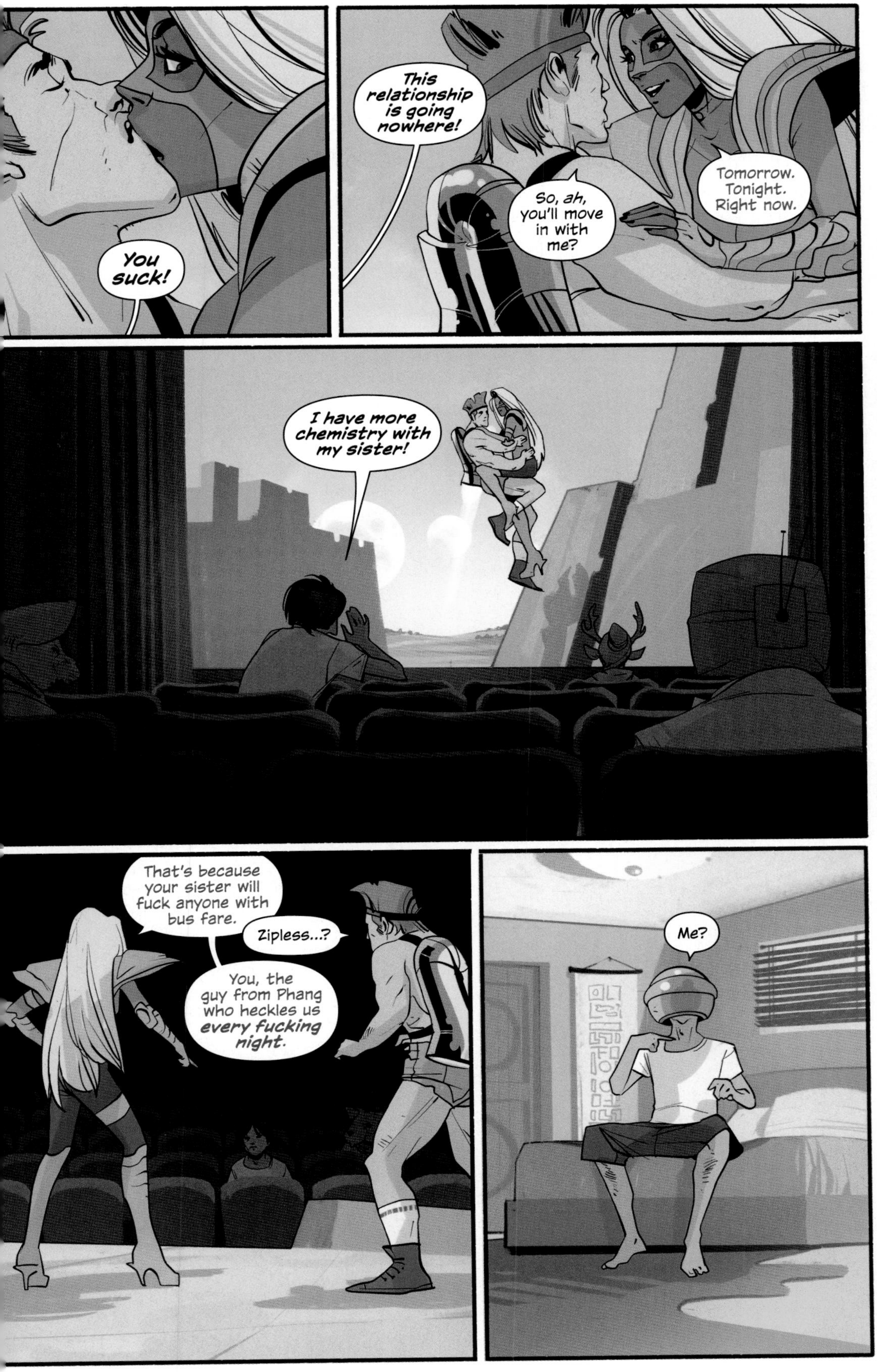
You suck!
This relationship is going nowhere!
So, ah, you'll move in with me?
Tomorrow. Tonight. Right now.
I have more chemistry with my sister!
That's because your sister will fuck anyone with bus fare.
Zipless...?
You, the guy from Phang who heckles us *every fucking night*.
Me?

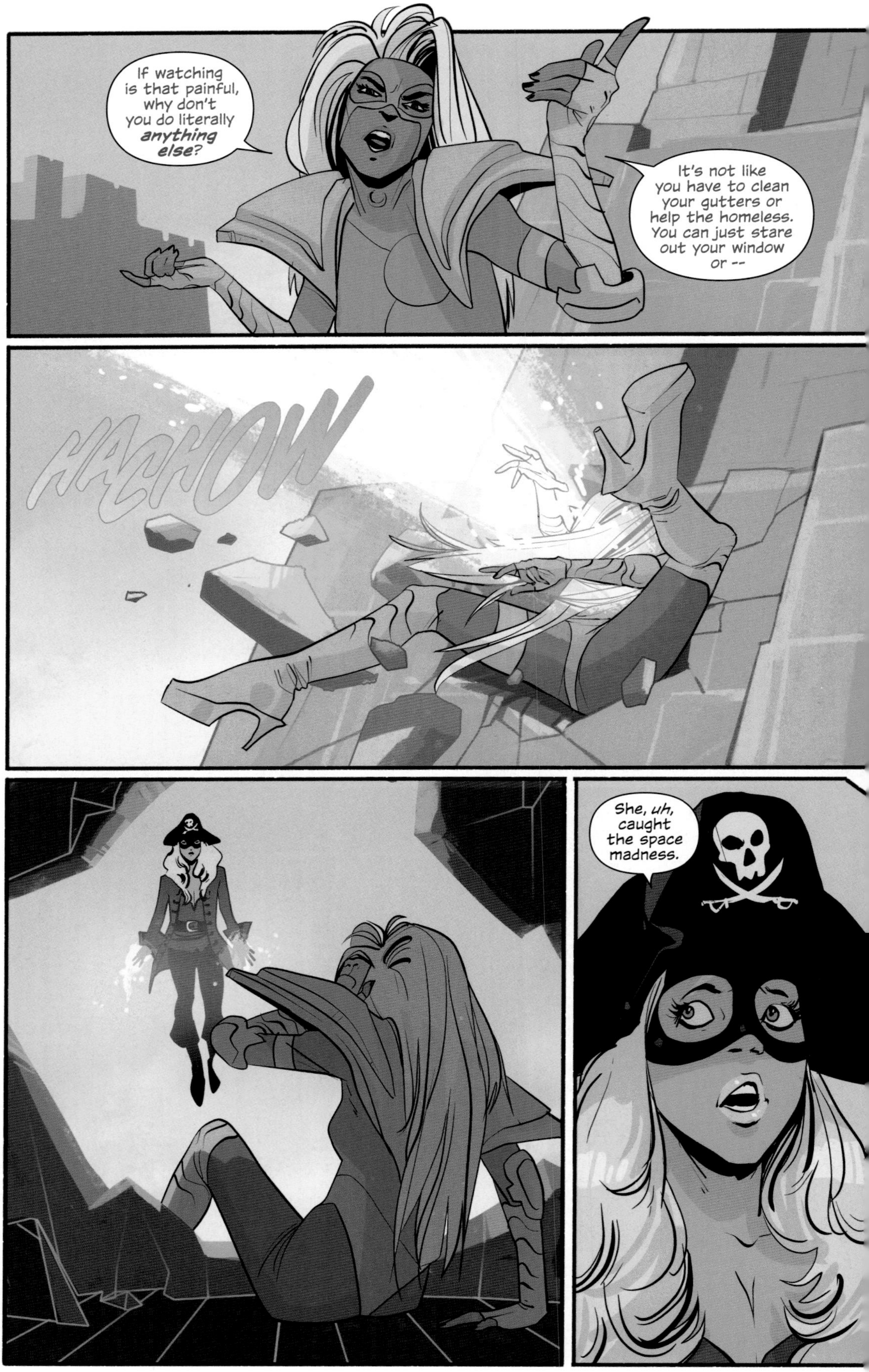
If watching is that painful, why don't you do literally ***anything else***?
It's not like you have to clean your gutters or help the homeless. You can just stare out your window or --
HACHOW
She, *uh*, caught the space madness.

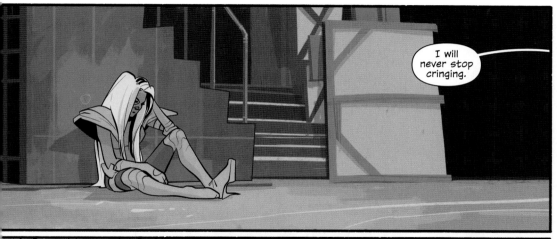

I will never stop cringing.

You encouraged us... just a second...

You encouraged us to respond to the audience more.

No, I told you to be aware of the fourth wall, not to punch a *glory hole* through it.

You're fired.

Please don't do that.

I know it was cheap, but I was just trying to defend the troupe.

You were trying to defend *yourself*, which I have told you a million times never to do.

Right, because we always let the work speak for itself.

No, because you suck at this job and those hecklers are right.

Leave your getup with the understudy.

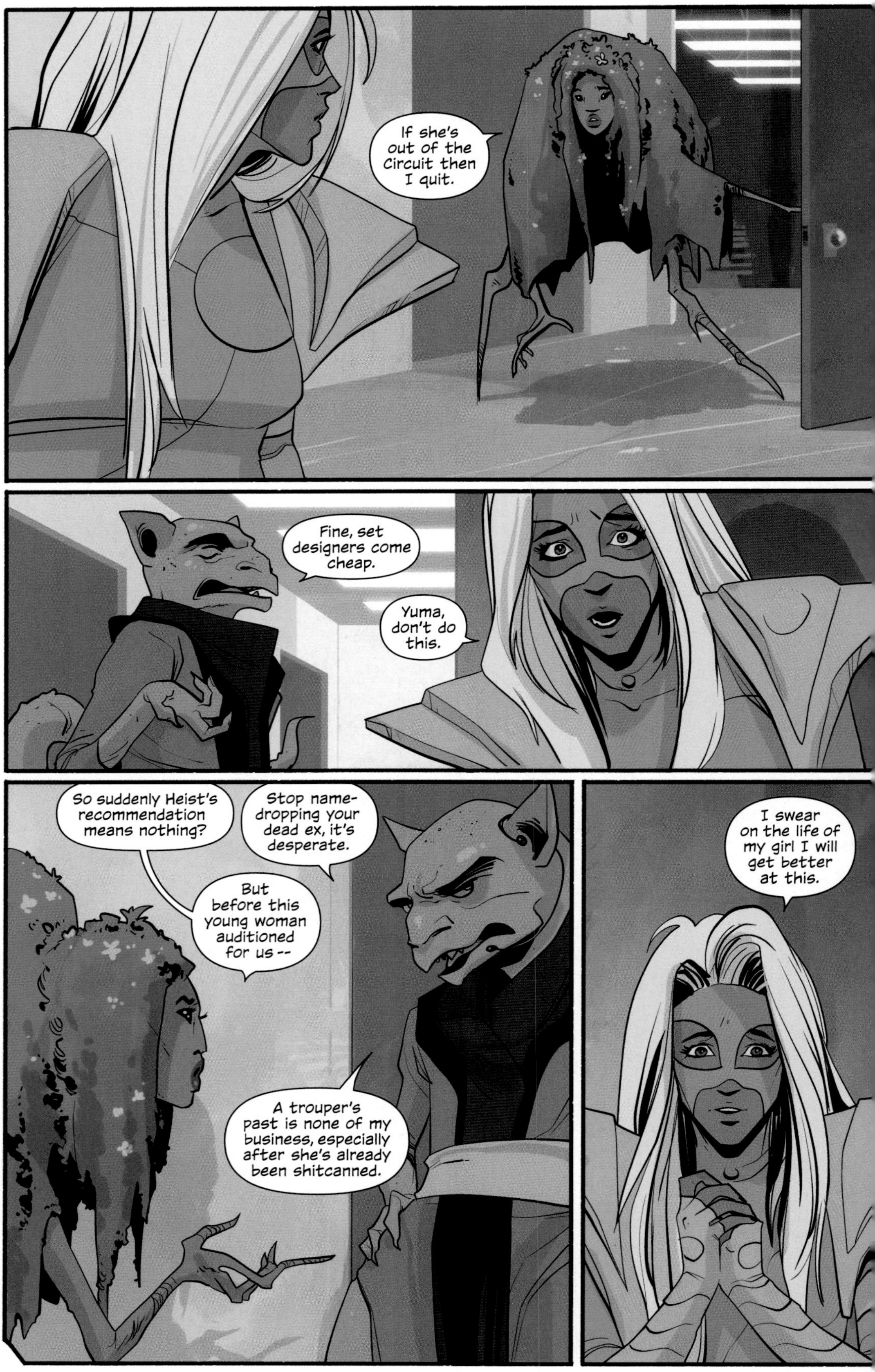
If she's out of the Circuit then I quit.
Fine, set designers come cheap.
Yuma, don't do this.
So suddenly Heist's recommendation means nothing?
Stop name-dropping your dead ex, it's desperate.
But before this young woman auditioned for us --
A trouper's past is none of my business, especially after she's already been shitcanned.
I swear on the life of my girl I will get better at this.

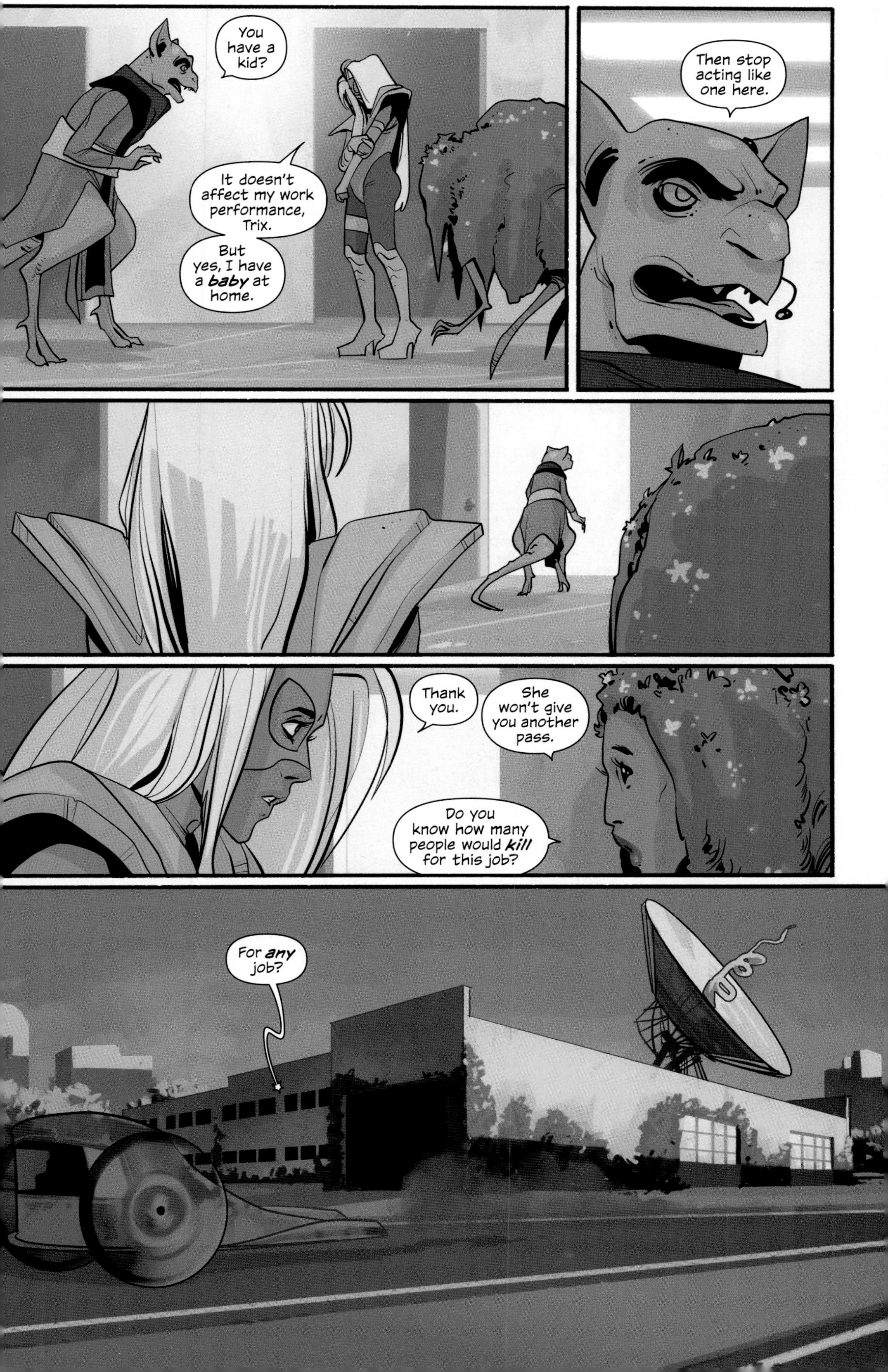
You have a kid?
It doesn't affect my work performance, Trix.
But yes, I have a baby at home.
Then stop acting like one here.
Thank you.
She won't give you another pass.
Do you know how many people would kill for this job?
For any job?

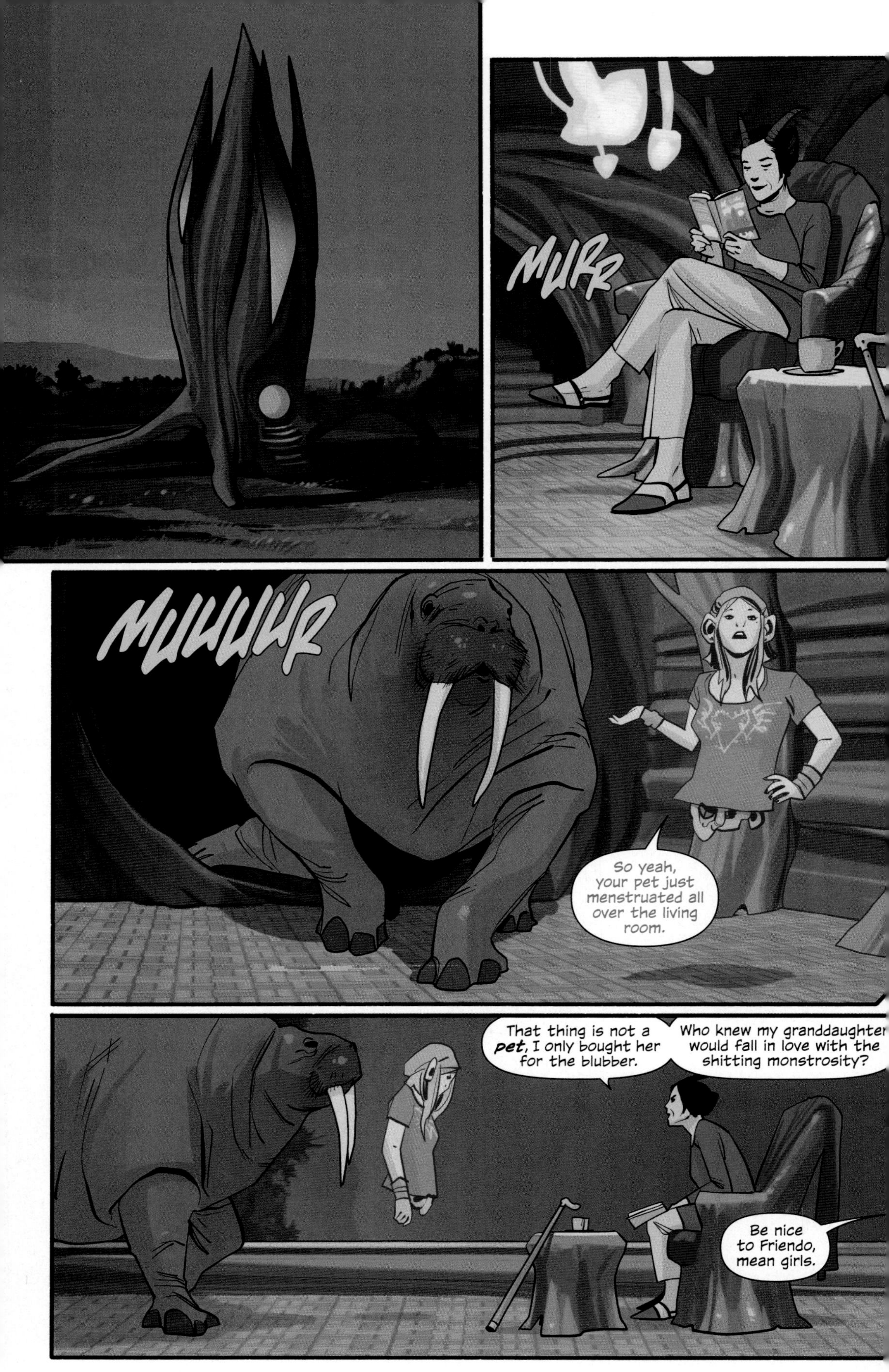
MURR
MUUUUR
So yeah, your pet just menstruated all over the living room.
That thing is not a *pet*, I only bought her for the blubber.
Who knew my granddaughter would fall in love with the shitting monstrosity?
Be nice to Friendo, mean girls.

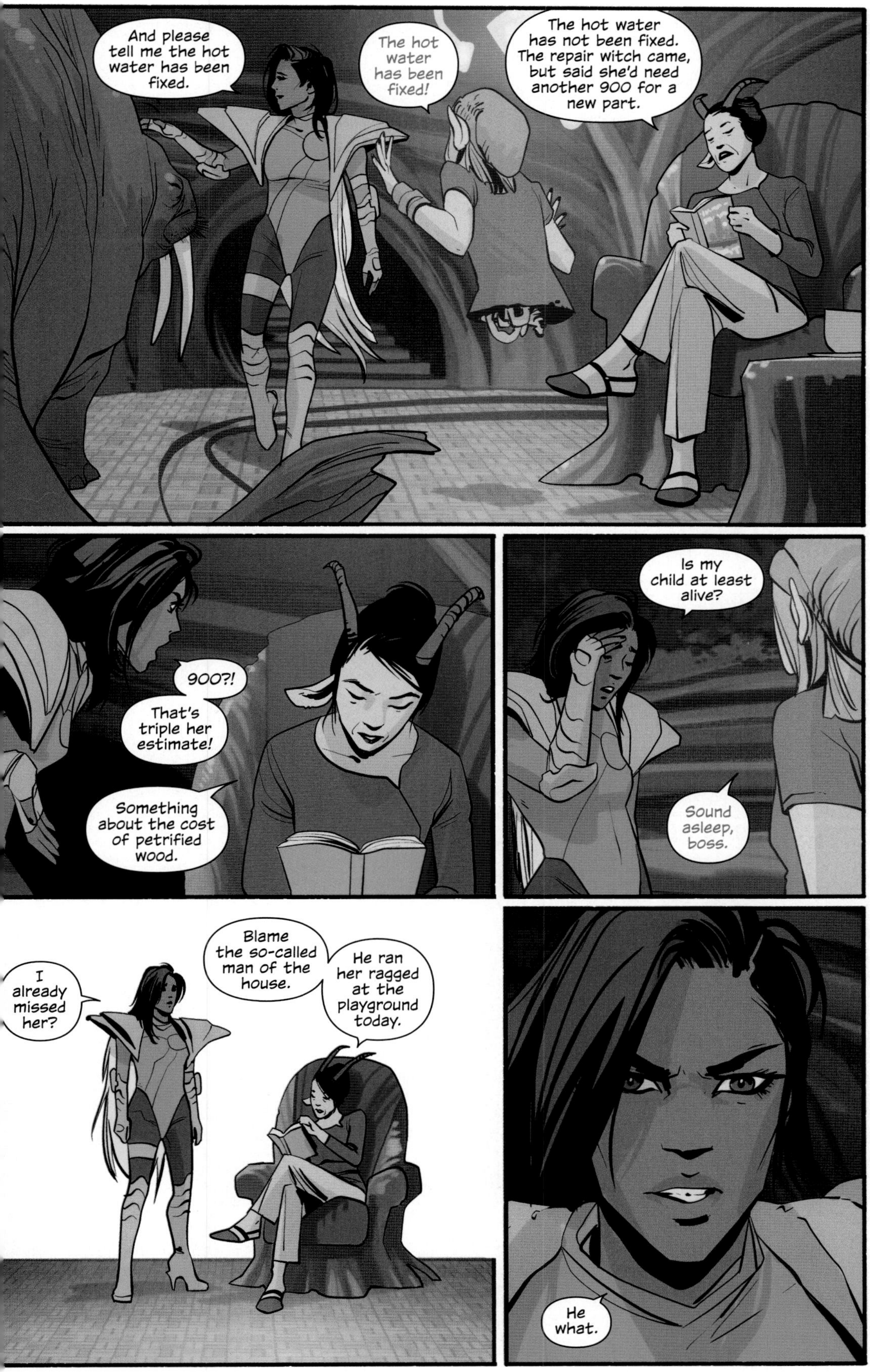
And please tell me the hot water has been fixed.
The hot water has been fixed!
The hot water has not been fixed. The repair witch came, but said she'd need another 900 for a new part.
900?!
That's triple her estimate!
Something about the cost of petrified wood.
Is my child at least alive?
Sound asleep, boss.
I already missed her?
Blame the so-called man of the house.
He ran her ragged at the playground today.
He what.

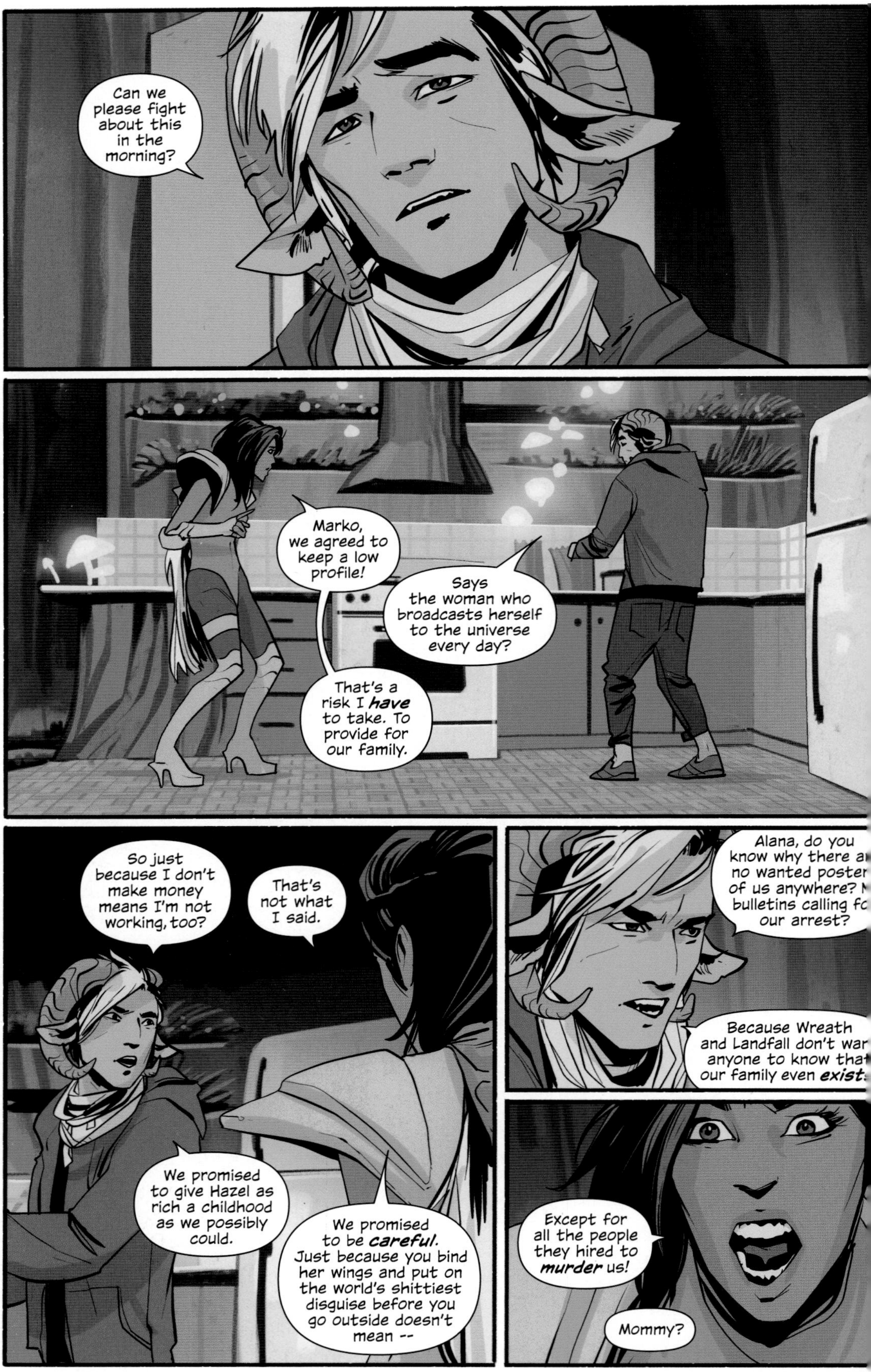

Can we please fight about this in the morning?
Marko, we agreed to keep a low profile!
Says the woman who broadcasts herself to the universe every day?
That's a risk I ***have*** to take. To provide for our family.
So just because I don't make money means I'm not working, too?
That's not what I said.
We promised to give Hazel as rich a childhood as we possibly could.
We promised to be ***careful***. Just because you bind her wings and put on the world's shittiest disguise before you go outside doesn't mean --
Alana, do you know why there a no wanted poster of us anywhere? bulletins calling f our arrest?
Because Wreath and Landfall don't wa anyone to know tha our family even ***exist***
Except for all the people they hired to ***murder*** us!
Mommy?

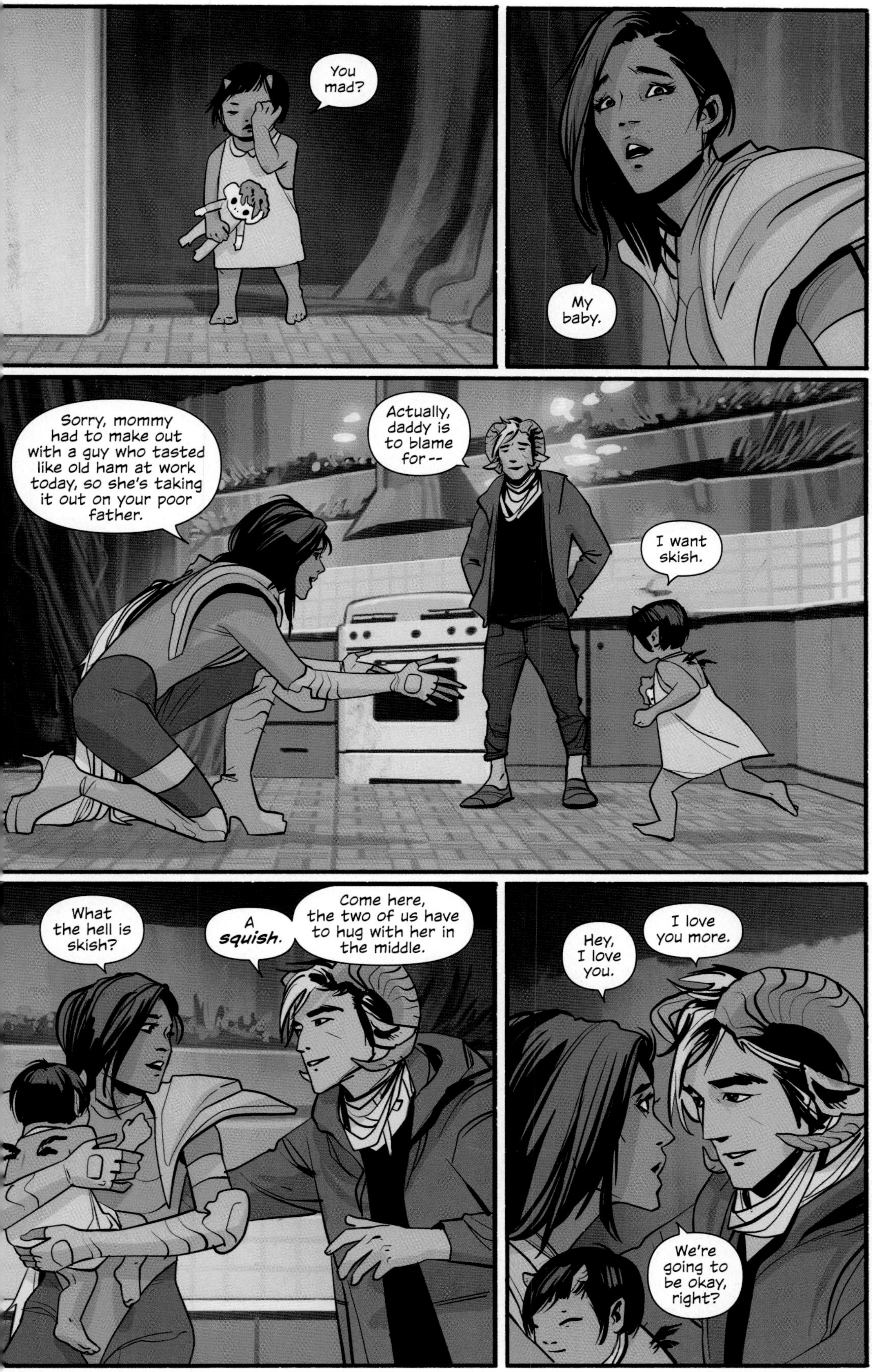
You mad?
My baby.
Sorry, mommy had to make out with a guy who tasted like old ham at work today, so she's taking it out on your poor father.
Actually, daddy is to blame for--
I want skish.
What the hell is skish?
A *squish*.
Come here, the two of us have to hug with her in the middle.
Hey, I love you.
I love you more.
We're going to be okay, right?

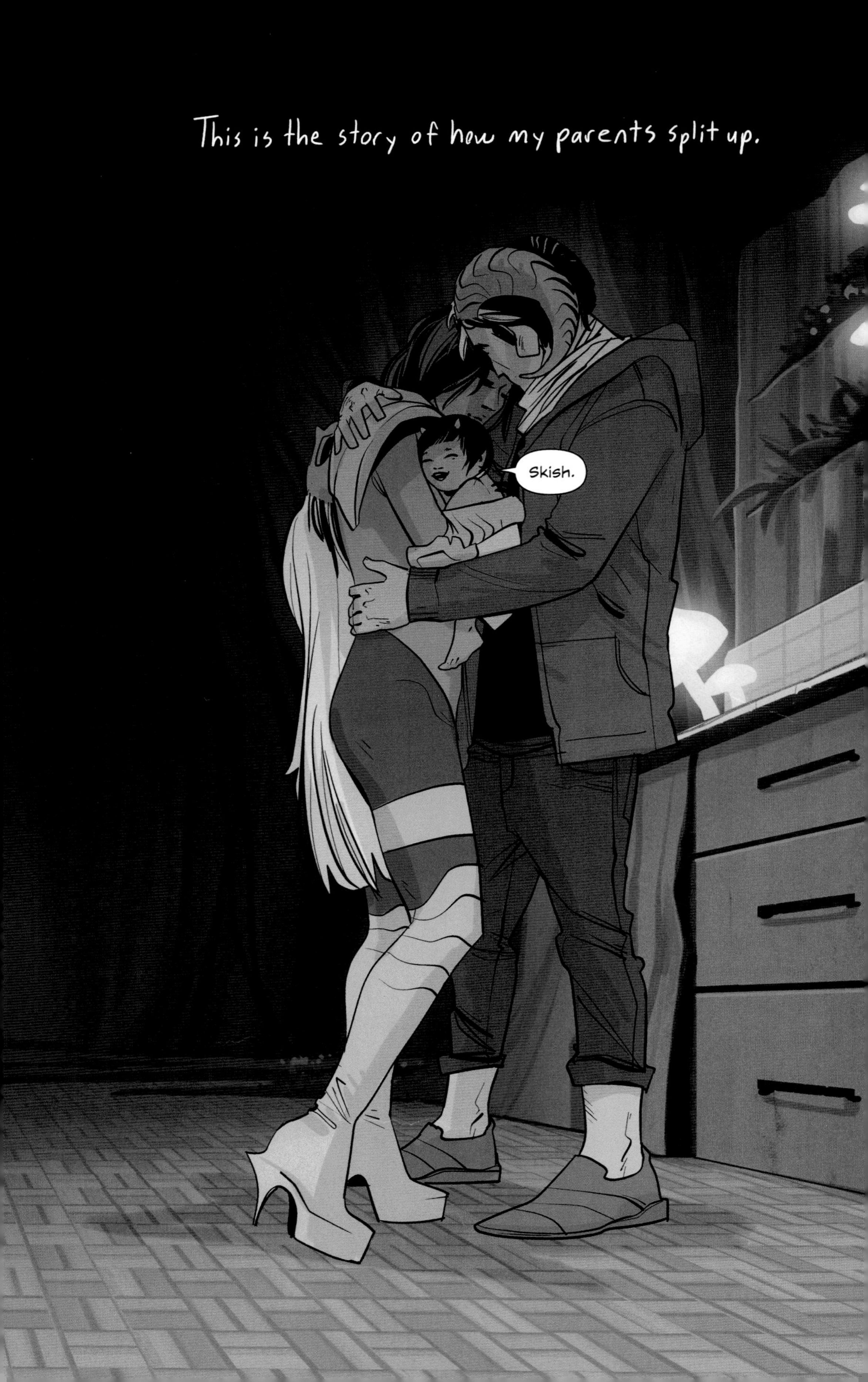
This is the story of how my parents split up.
Skish.

end chapter nineteen

CHAPTER
TWENTY

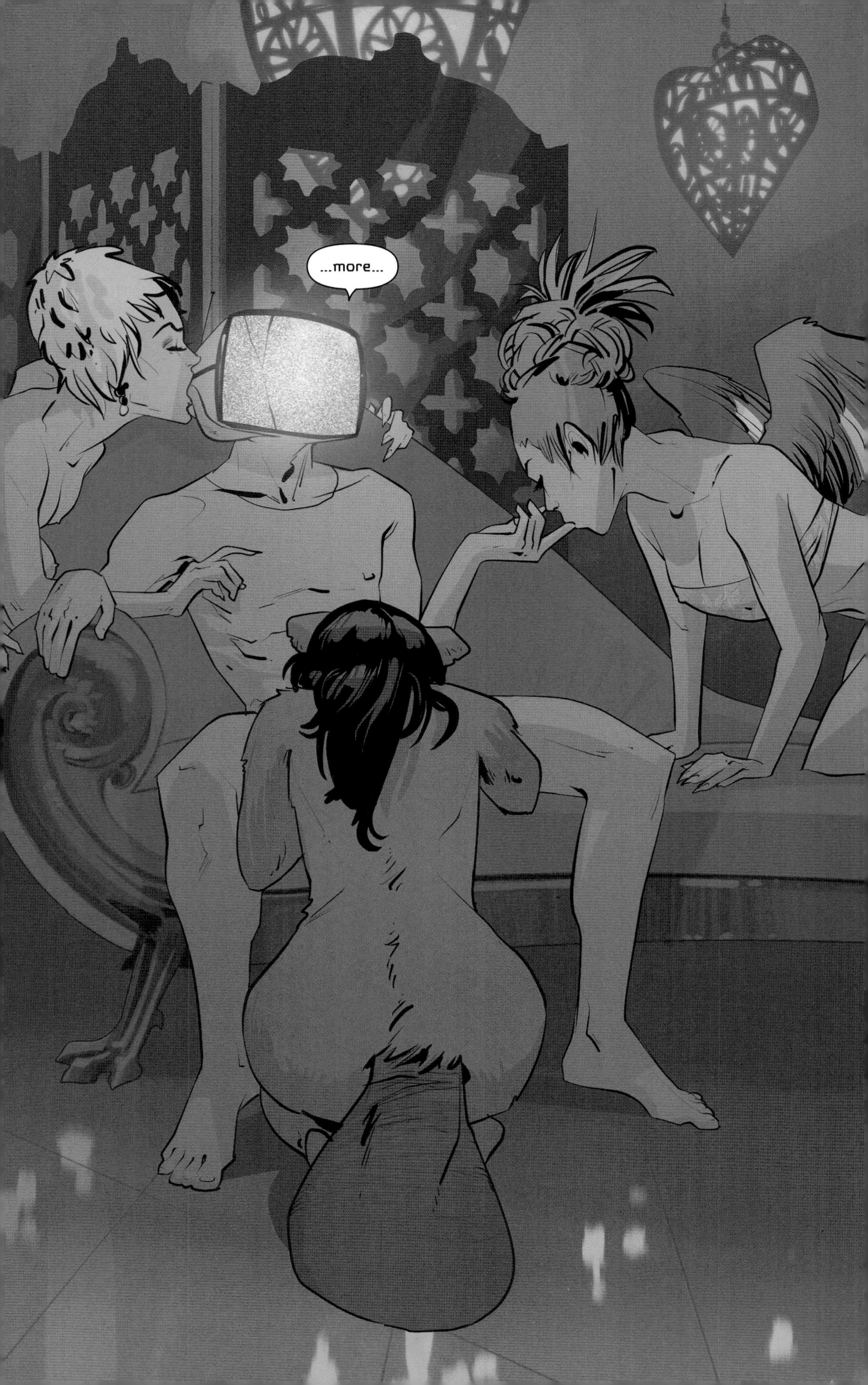
...more...

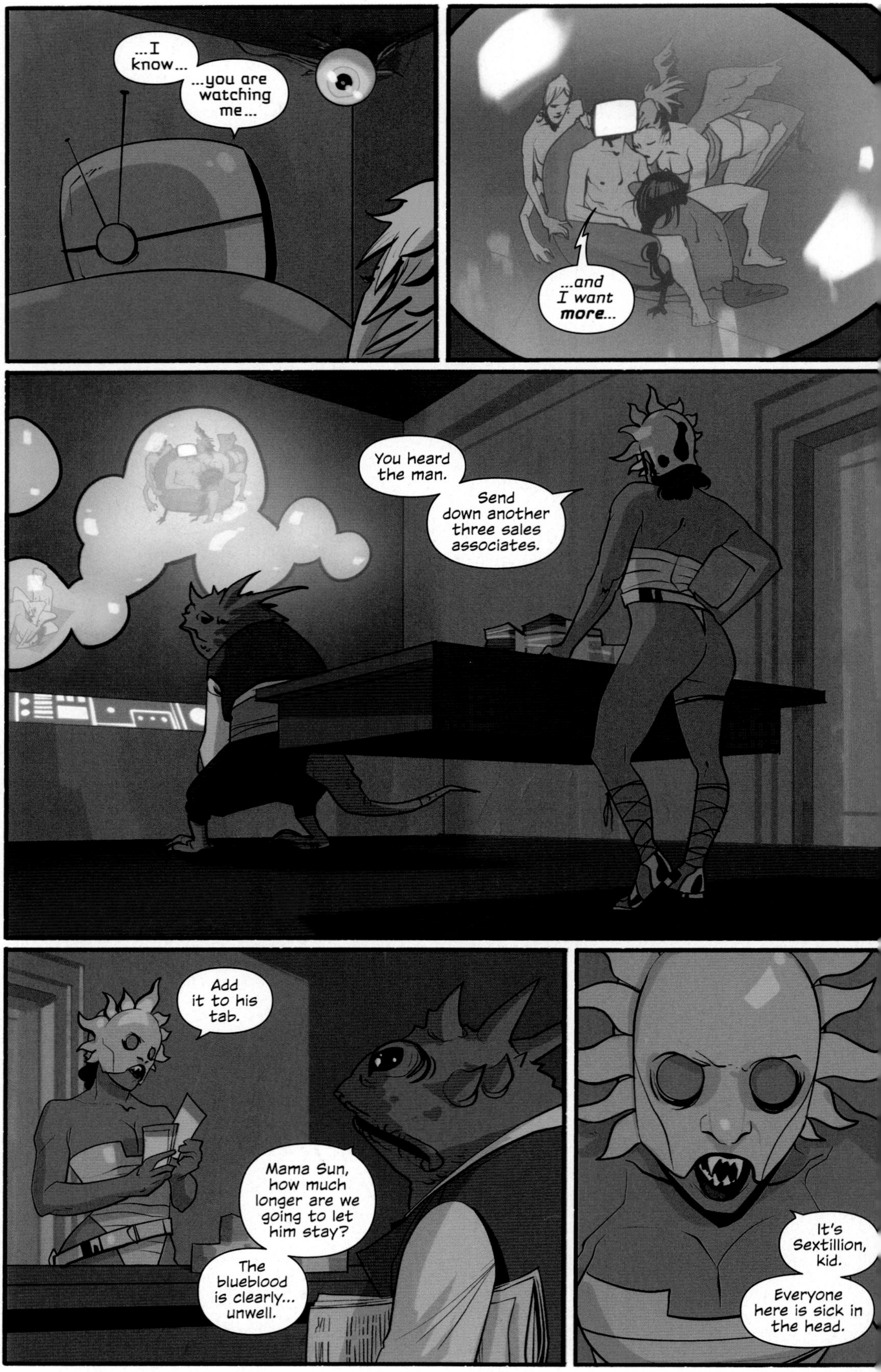
...I know...
...you are watching me...
...and I want **more**...
You heard the man.
Send down another three sales associates.
Add it to his tab.
Mama Sun, how much longer are we going to let him stay?
The blueblood is clearly... unwell.
It's Sextillion, kid.
Everyone here is sick in the head.

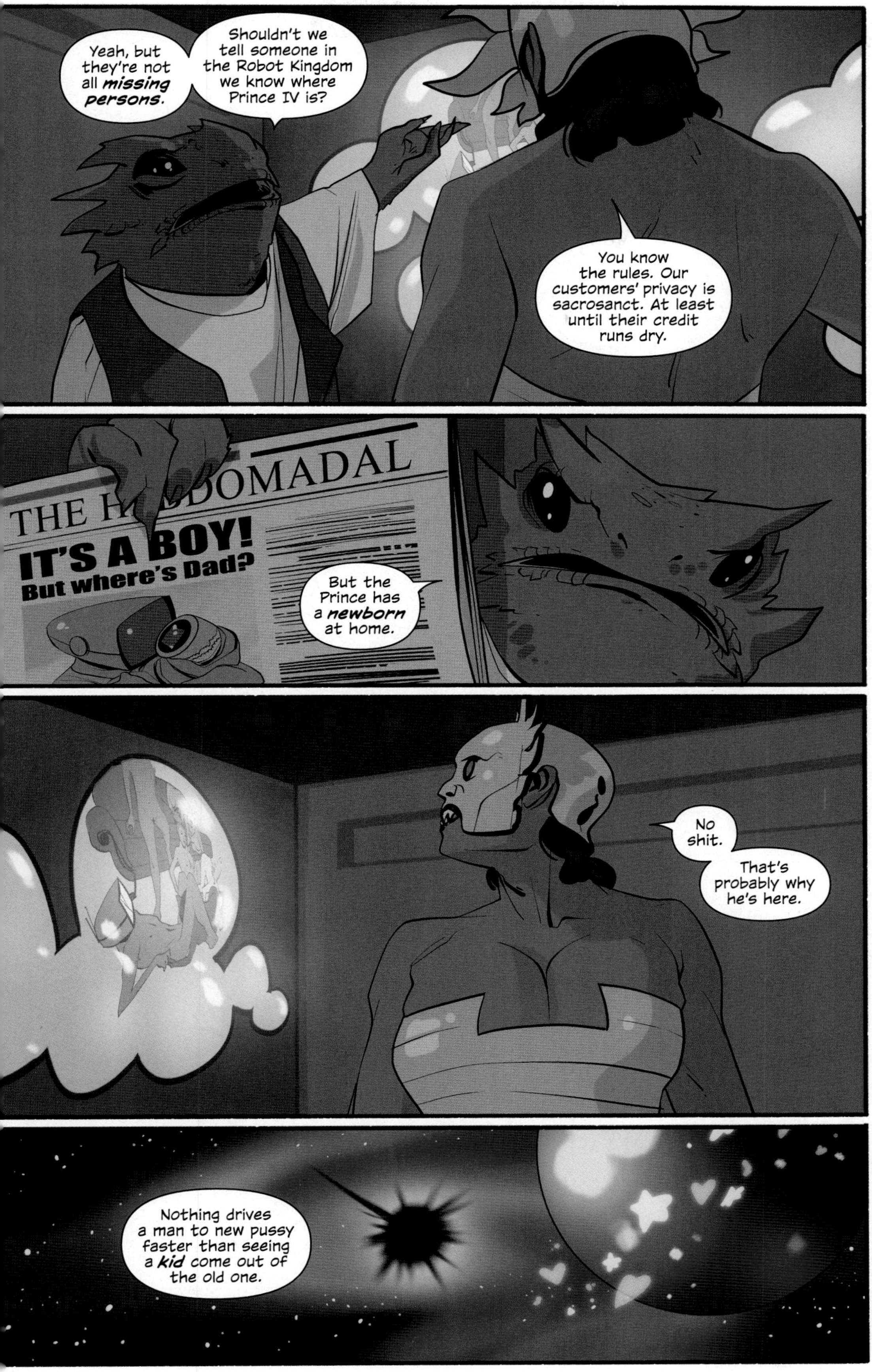
Shouldn't we tell someone in the Robot Kingdom we know where Prince IV is?
Yeah, but they're not all ***missing persons***.
You know the rules. Our customers' privacy is sacrosanct. At least until their credit runs dry.
THE HEBDOMADAL
IT'S A BOY!
IT'S A BOY! But where's Dad?
But the Prince has a ***newborn*** at home.
No shit.
That's probably why he's here.
Nothing drives a man to new pussy faster than seeing a ***kid*** come out of the old one.

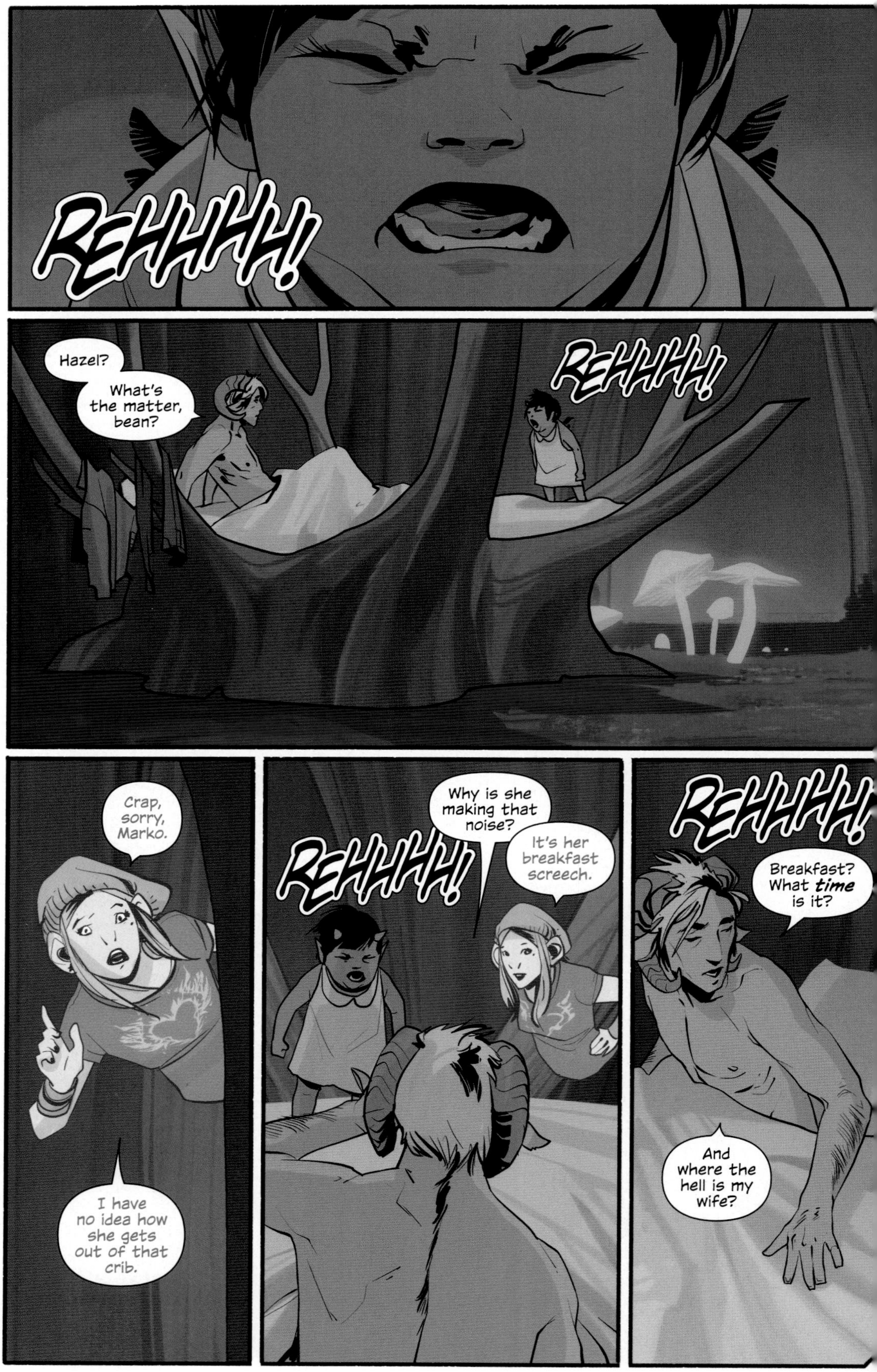
REHHHH!
Hazel?
What's the matter, bean?
REHHHH!
Crap, sorry, Marko.
I have no idea how she gets out of that crib.
Why is she making that noise?
REHHHH!
It's her breakfast screech.
REHHHH!
Breakfast? What *time* is it?
And where the hell is my wife?

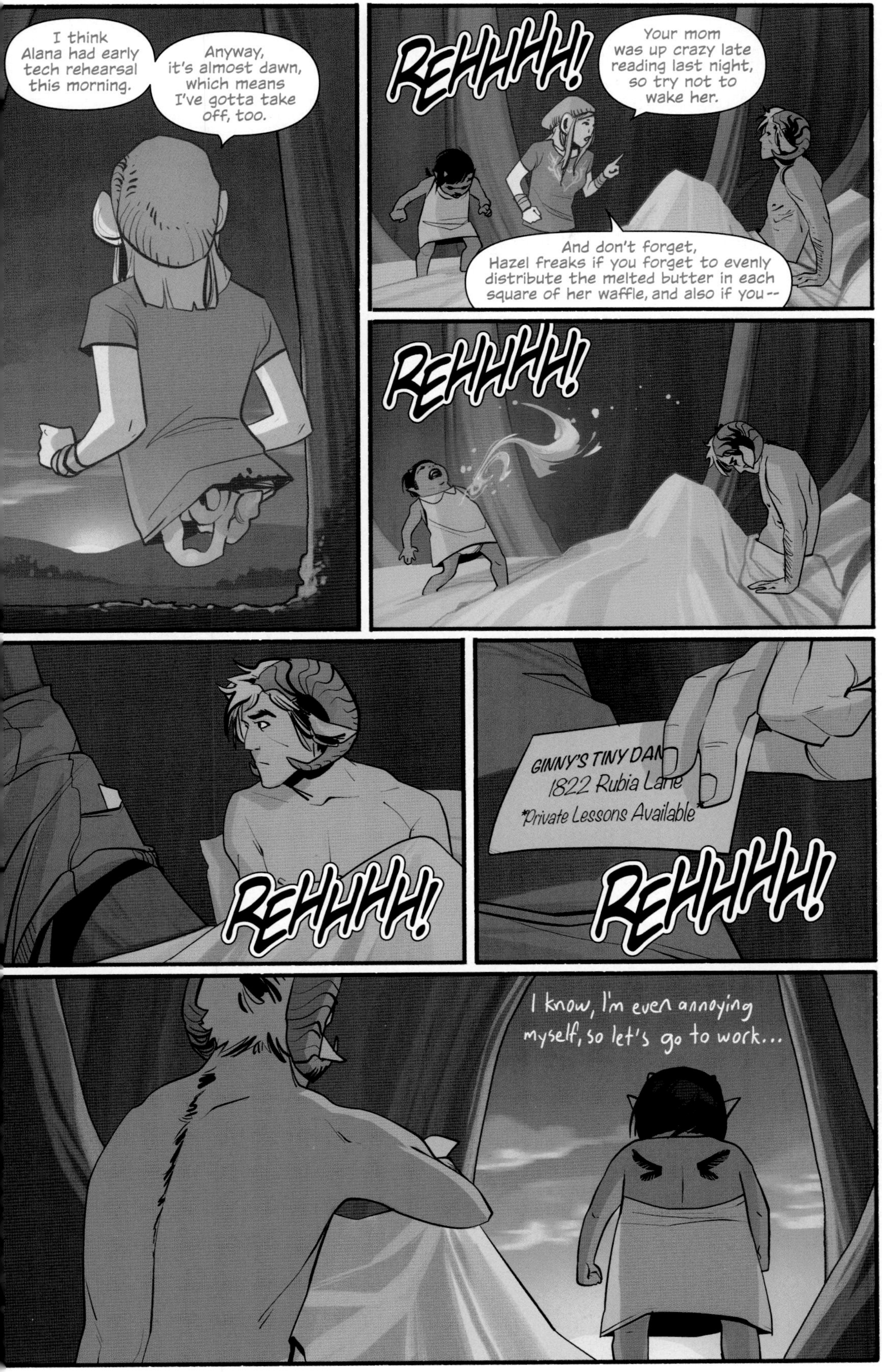
I think Alana had early tech rehearsal this morning.
Anyway, it's almost dawn, which means I've gotta take off, too.
REHHHH!
Your mom was up crazy late reading last night, so try not to wake her.
And don't forget, Hazel freaks if you forget to evenly distribute the melted butter in each square of her waffle, and also if you--
REHHHH!
REHHHH!
GINNY'S TINY DAN
1822 Rubia Lane
Private Lessons Available
REHHHH!
I know, I'm even annoying myself, so let's go to work...

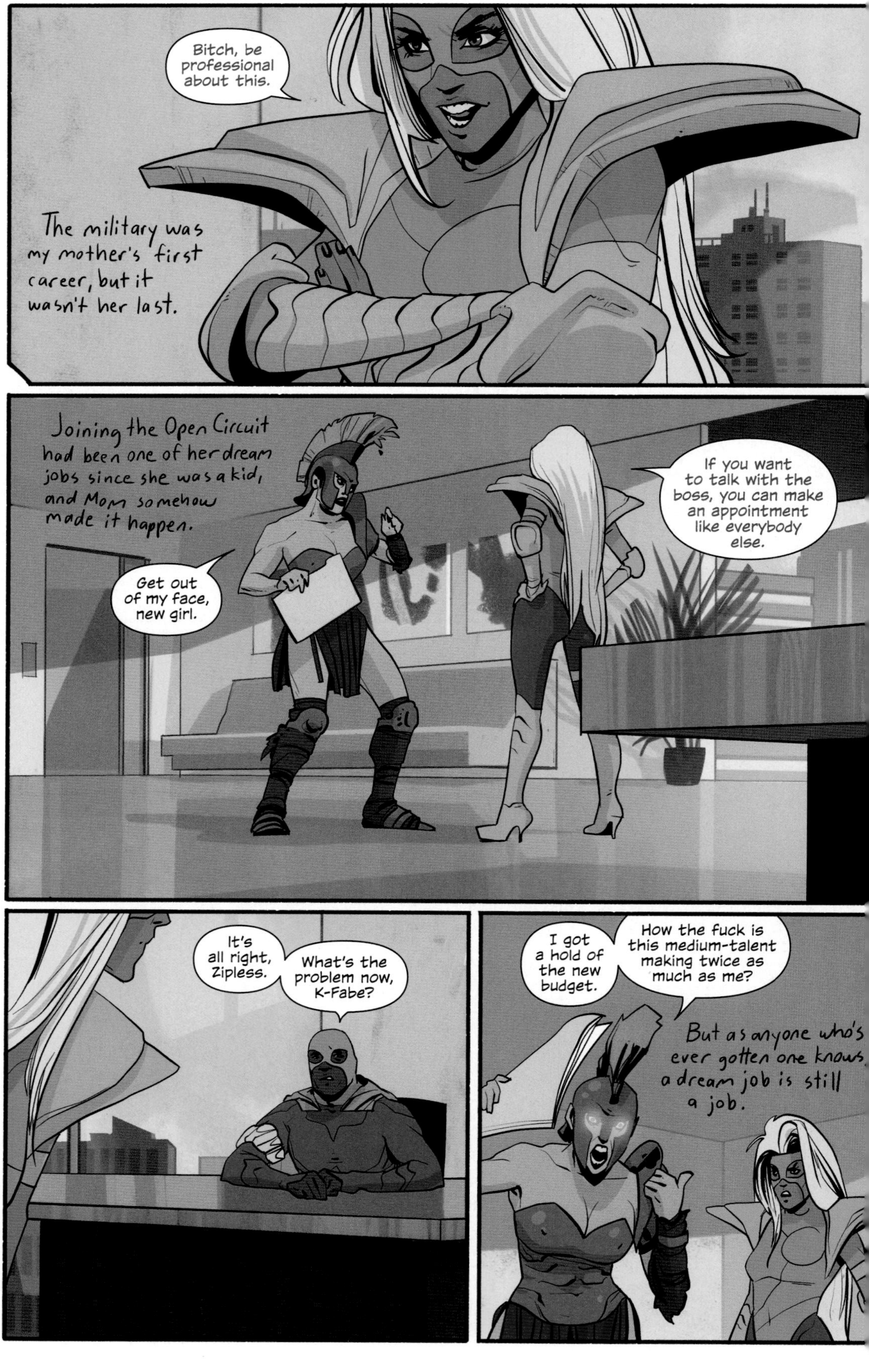
Bitch, be professional about this.
The military was my mother's first career, but it wasn't her last.
Joining the Open Circuit had been one of her dream jobs since she was a kid, and Mom somehow made it happen.
If you want to talk with the boss, you can make an appointment like everybody else.
Get out of my face, new girl.
It's all right, Zipless.
What's the problem now, K-Fabe?
I got a hold of the new budget.
How the fuck is this medium-talent making twice as much as me?
But as anyone who's ever gotten one knows, a dream job is still a job.

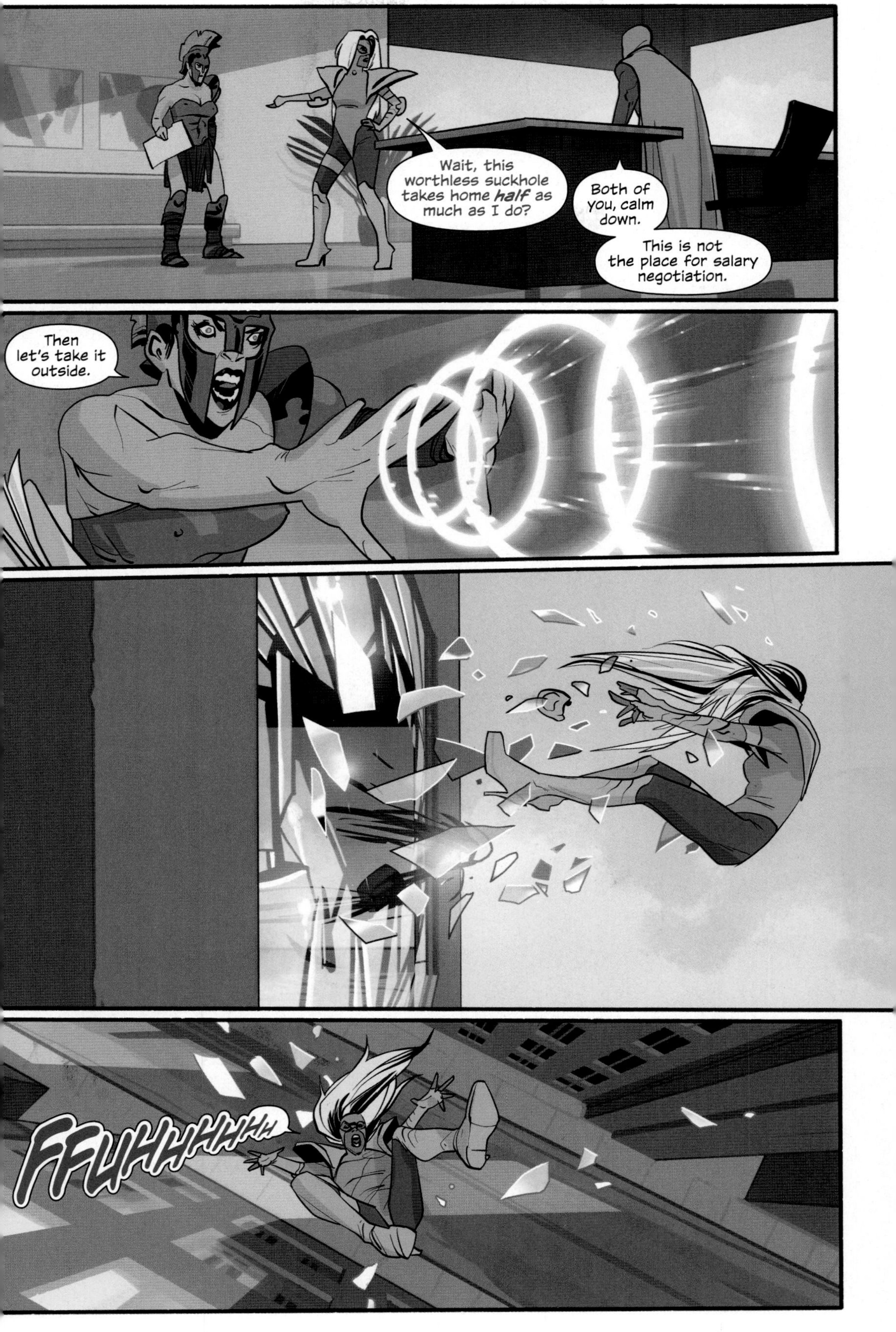
Wait, this worthless suckhole takes home *half* as much as I do?
Both of you, calm down.
This is not the place for salary negotiation.
Then let's take it outside.
FFUHHHHHH

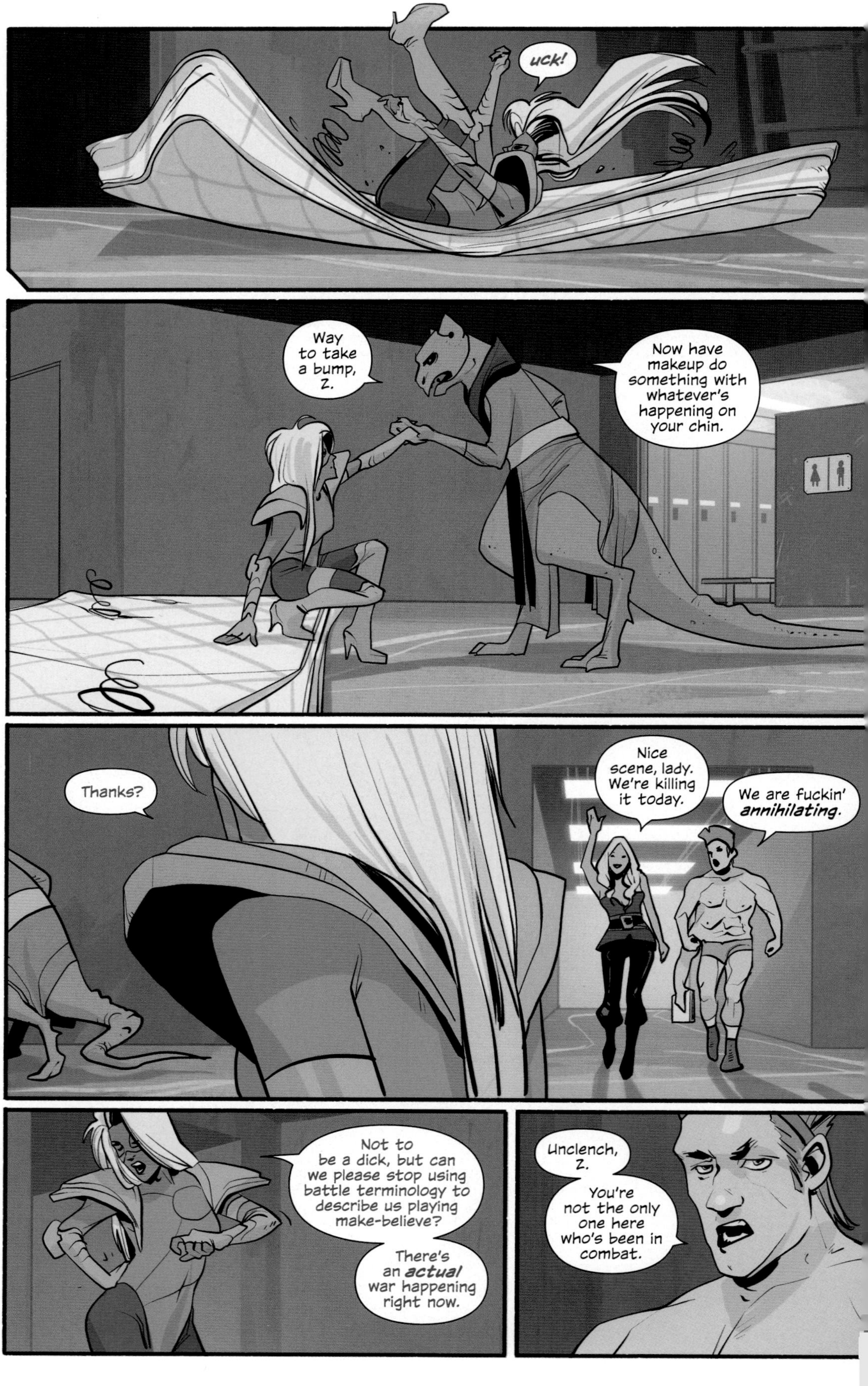

uck!
Way to take a bump, Z.
Now have makeup do something with whatever's happening on your chin.
Thanks?
Nice scene, lady. We're killing it today.
We are fuckin' ***annihilating***.
Not to be a dick, but can we please stop using battle terminology to describe us playing make-believe?
There's an ***actual*** war happening right now.
Unclench, Z.
You're not the only one here who's been in combat.

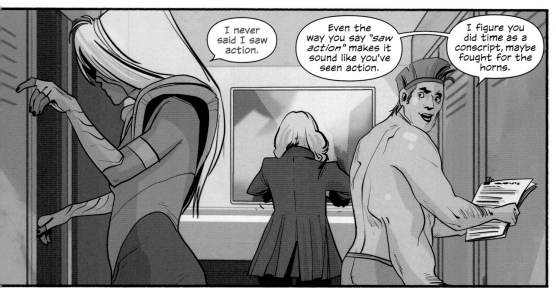

I never said I saw action.

Even the way you say *"saw action"* makes it sound like you've seen action.

I figure you did time as a conscript, maybe fought for the horns.

Nah, she's an ex-*Freelancer*, probably broke her contract after she slit the wrong guy's throat.

That's why Zipless never lets us see her out of getup.

I'm just saying, I respect the craft, but we should quit acting like this is something it isn't.

We're not soldiers, we're *entertainers*.

Like hell.

We're drug dealers.

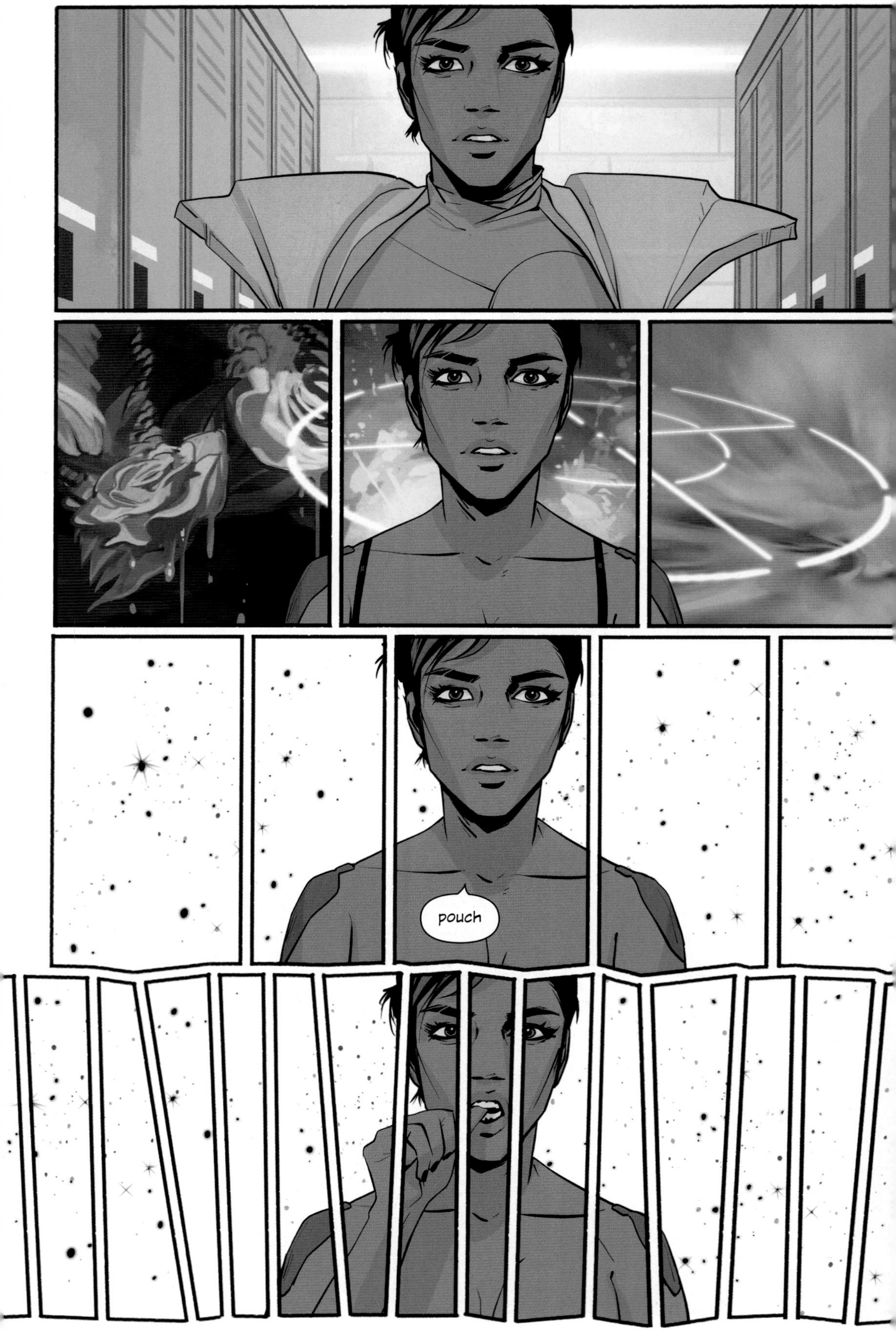
pouch

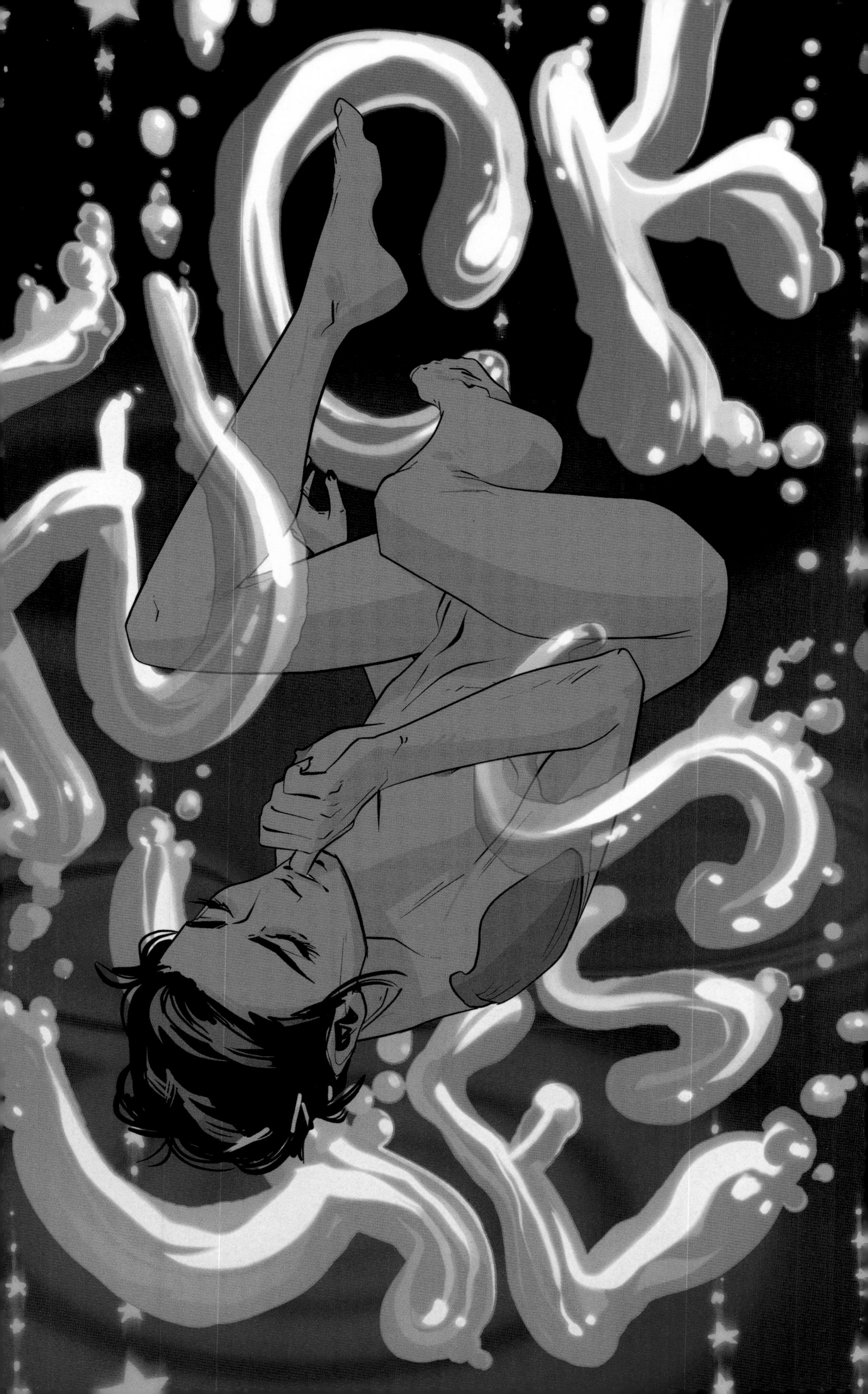

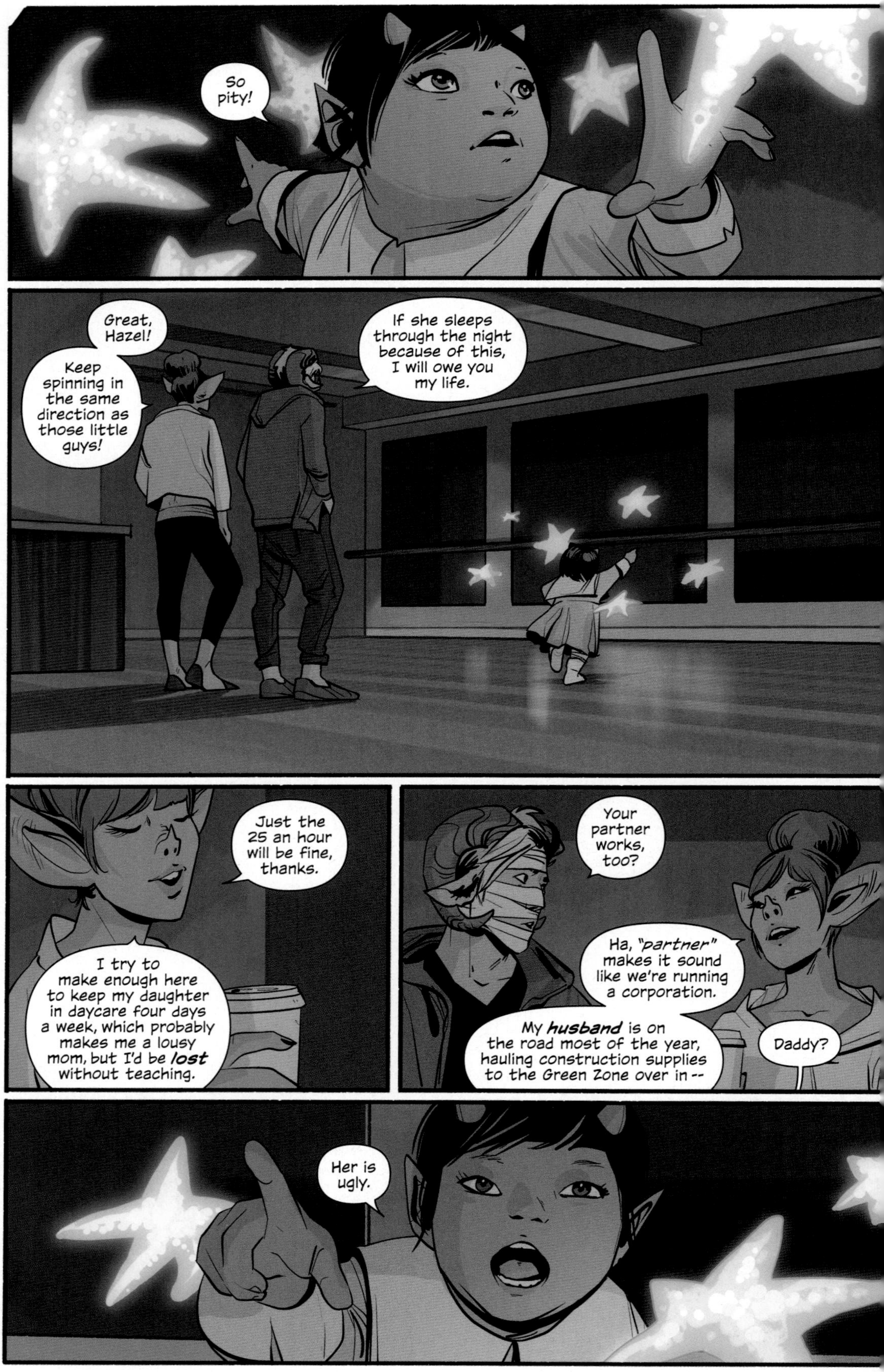
So pity!
Great, Hazel!
Keep spinning in the same direction as those little guys!
If she sleeps through the night because of this, I will owe you my life.
Just the 25 an hour will be fine, thanks.
I try to make enough here to keep my daughter in daycare four days a week, which probably makes me a lousy mom, but I'd be *lost* without teaching.
Your partner works, too?
Ha, *"partner"* makes it sound like we're running a corporation.
My **husband** is on the road most of the year, hauling construction supplies to the Green Zone over in --
Daddy?
Her is ugly.

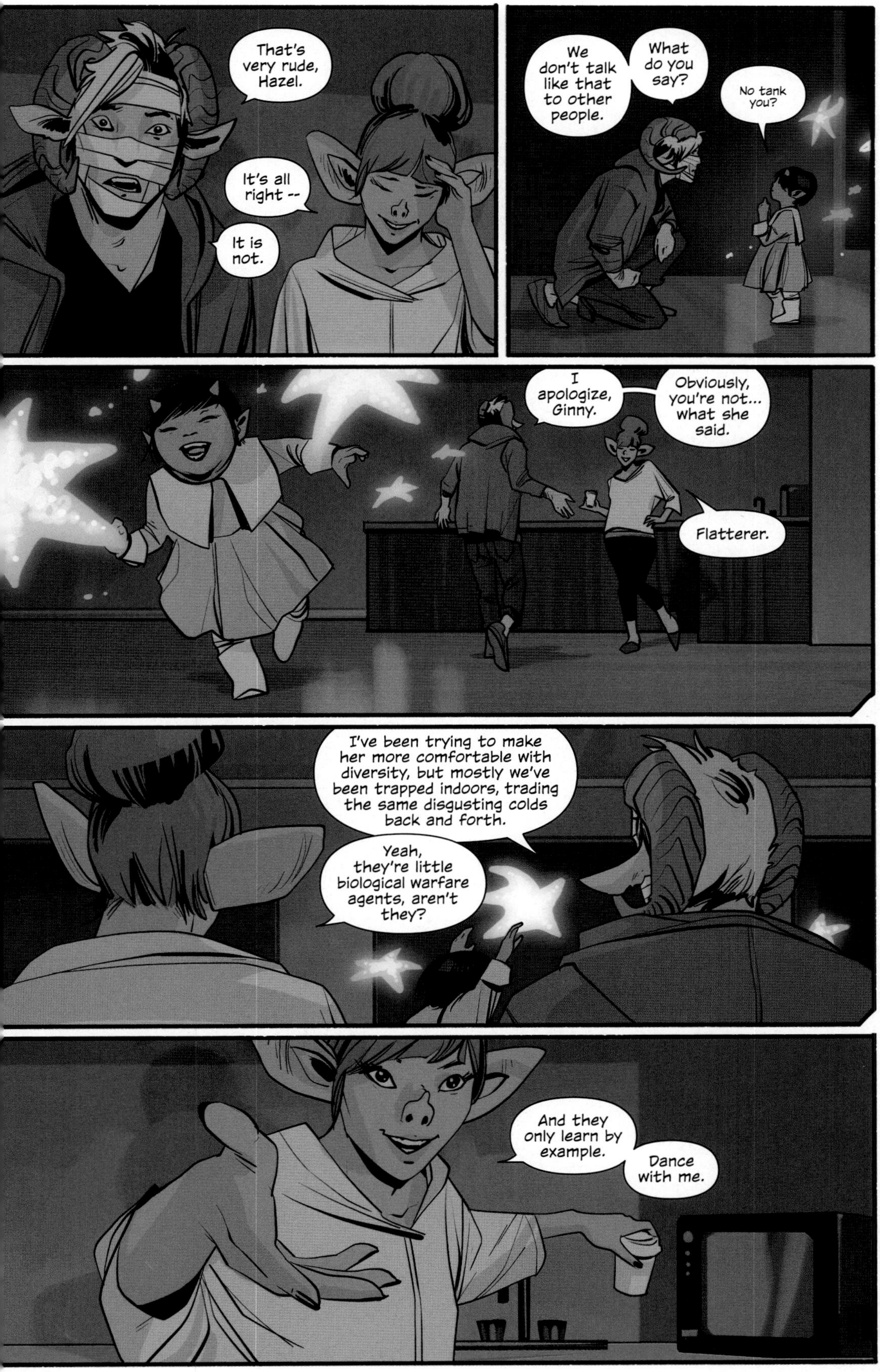
That's very rude, Hazel.
It's all right --
It is not.
We don't talk like that to other people.
What do you say?
No tank you?
I apologize, Ginny.
Obviously, you're not... what she said.
Flatterer.
I've been trying to make her more comfortable with diversity, but mostly we've been trapped indoors, trading the same disgusting colds back and forth.
Yeah, they're little biological warfare agents, aren't they?
And they only learn by example.
Dance with me.

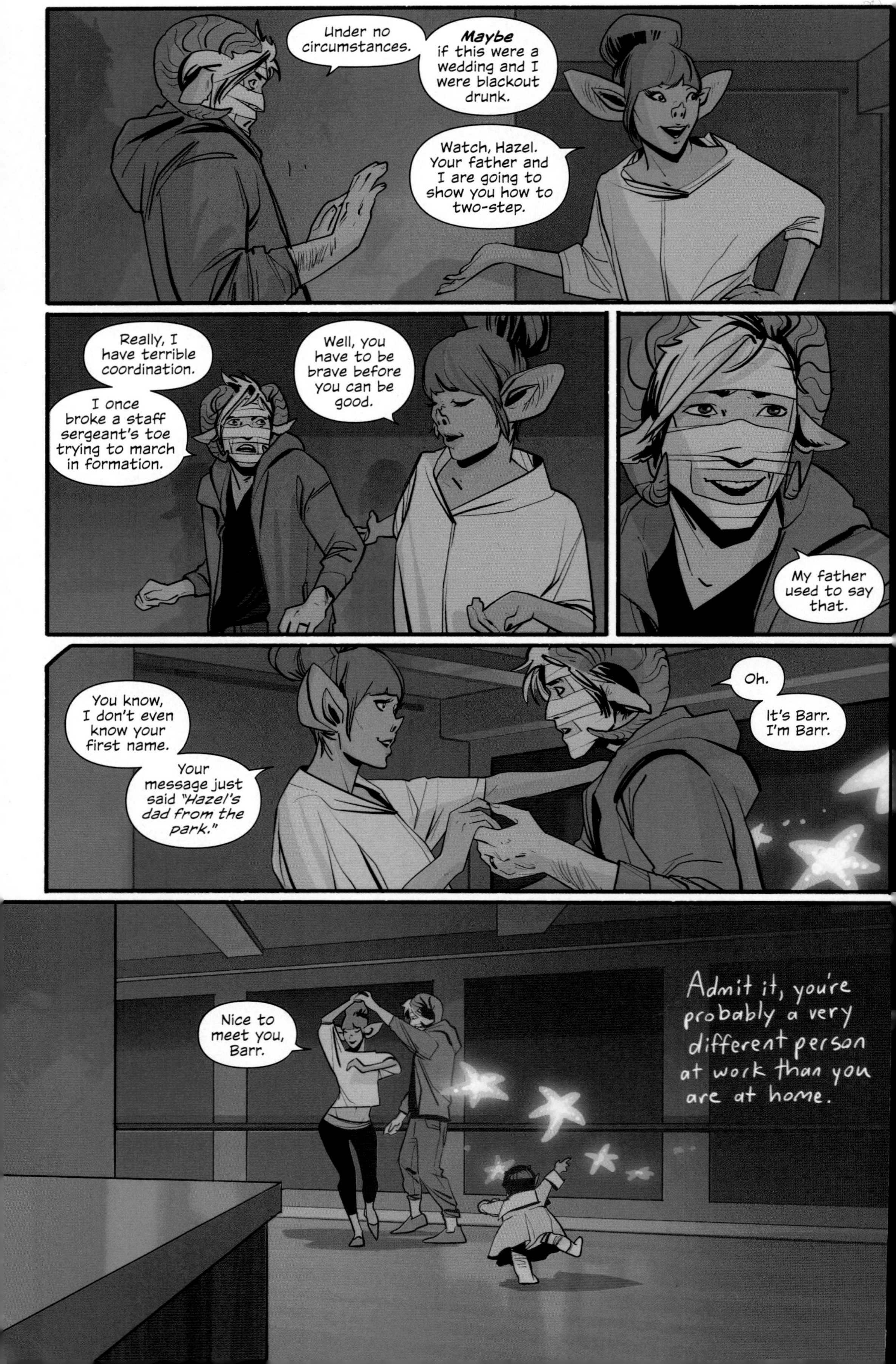

Under no circumstances.
Maybe if this were a wedding and I were blackout drunk.
Watch, Hazel. Your father and I are going to show you how to two-step.
Really, I have terrible coordination.
I once broke a staff sergeant's toe trying to march in formation.
Well, you have to be brave before you can be good.
My father used to say that.
You know, I don't even know your first name.
Your message just said *"Hazel's dad from the park."*
Oh.
It's Barr. I'm Barr.
Nice to meet you, Barr.
Admit it, you're probably a very different person at work than you are at home.

Everyone needs to be someone else sometimes.

Goodnight, goodnight, my little knight. Mummy loves you so...

klick

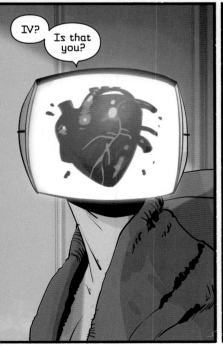

IV? Is that you?

Nah.

Just one of your lowly subjects.

Who the fuck...?
I've been your custodian for nearly two years, and you don't even know my name?
HELP!
No need to wake the baby, Princess.
I gave your palace guards the night off.
Please.
I don't care what you do to me, but please don't hurt my boy.
I would never harm a child. I'm a father myself.
At least, I was for a time.

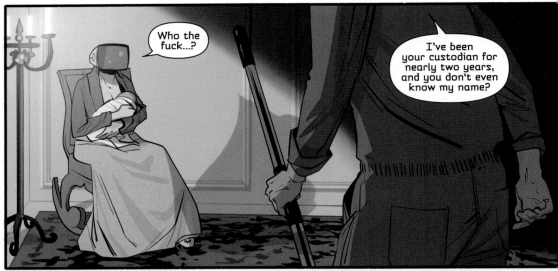

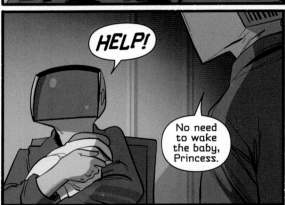

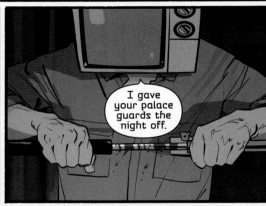

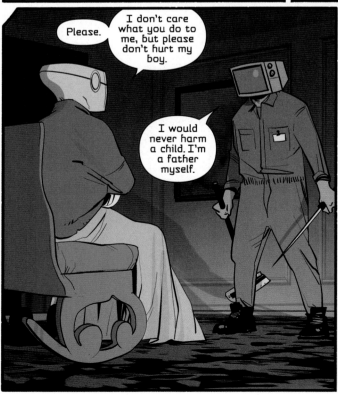

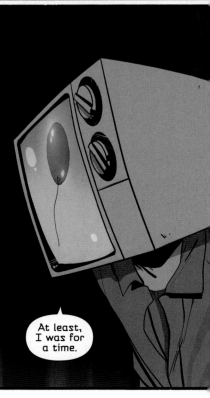

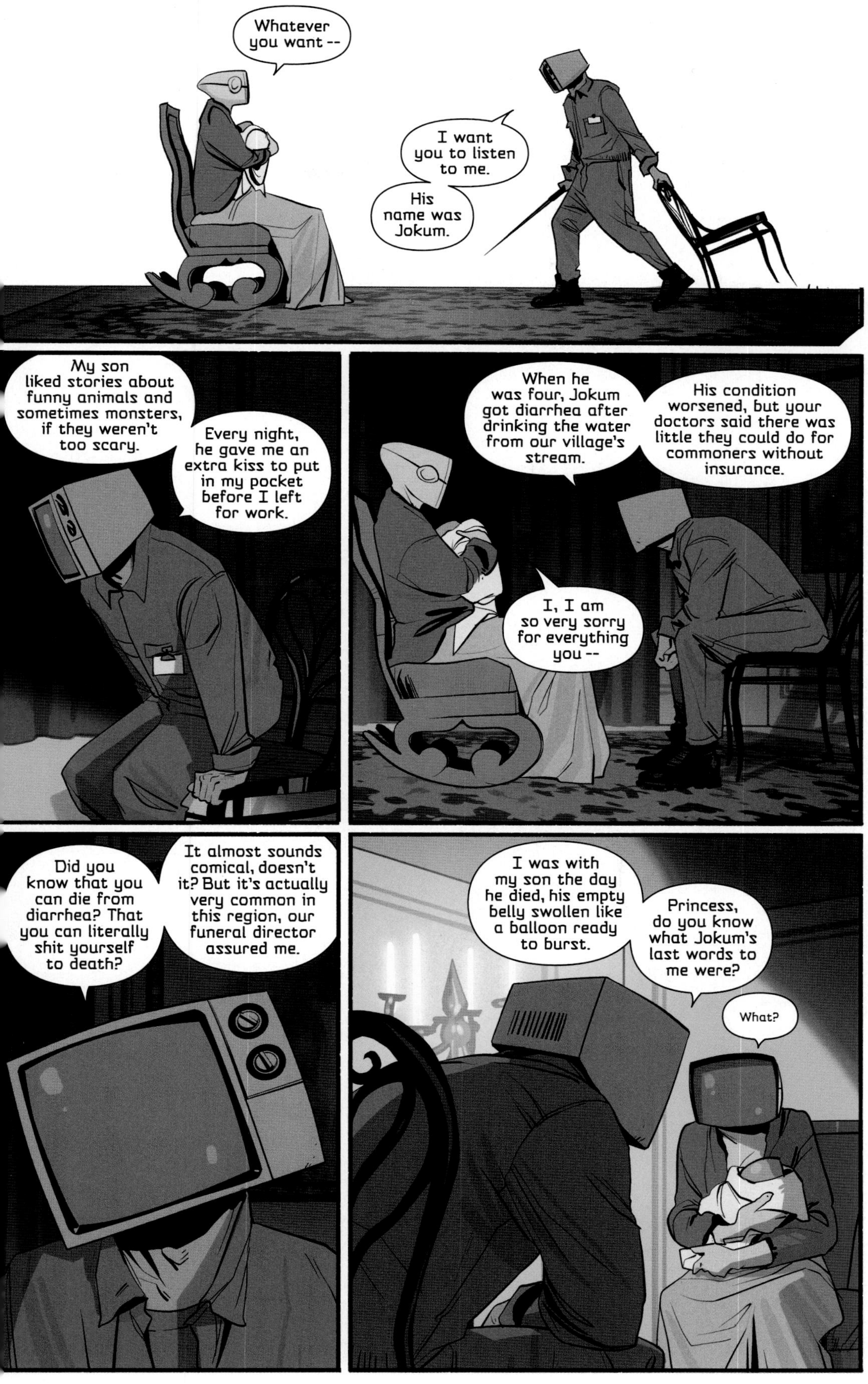
Whatever you want --
I want you to listen to me.
His name was Jokum.
My son liked stories about funny animals and sometimes monsters, if they weren't too scary.
Every night, he gave me an extra kiss to put in my pocket before I left for work.
When he was four, Jokum got diarrhea after drinking the water from our village's stream.
His condition worsened, but your doctors said there was little they could do for commoners without insurance.
I, I am so very sorry for everything you --
Did you know that you can die from diarrhea? That you can literally shit yourself to death?
It almost sounds comical, doesn't it? But it's actually very common in this region, our funeral director assured me.
I was with my son the day he died, his empty belly swollen like a balloon ready to burst.
Princess, do you know what Jokum's last words to me were?
What?

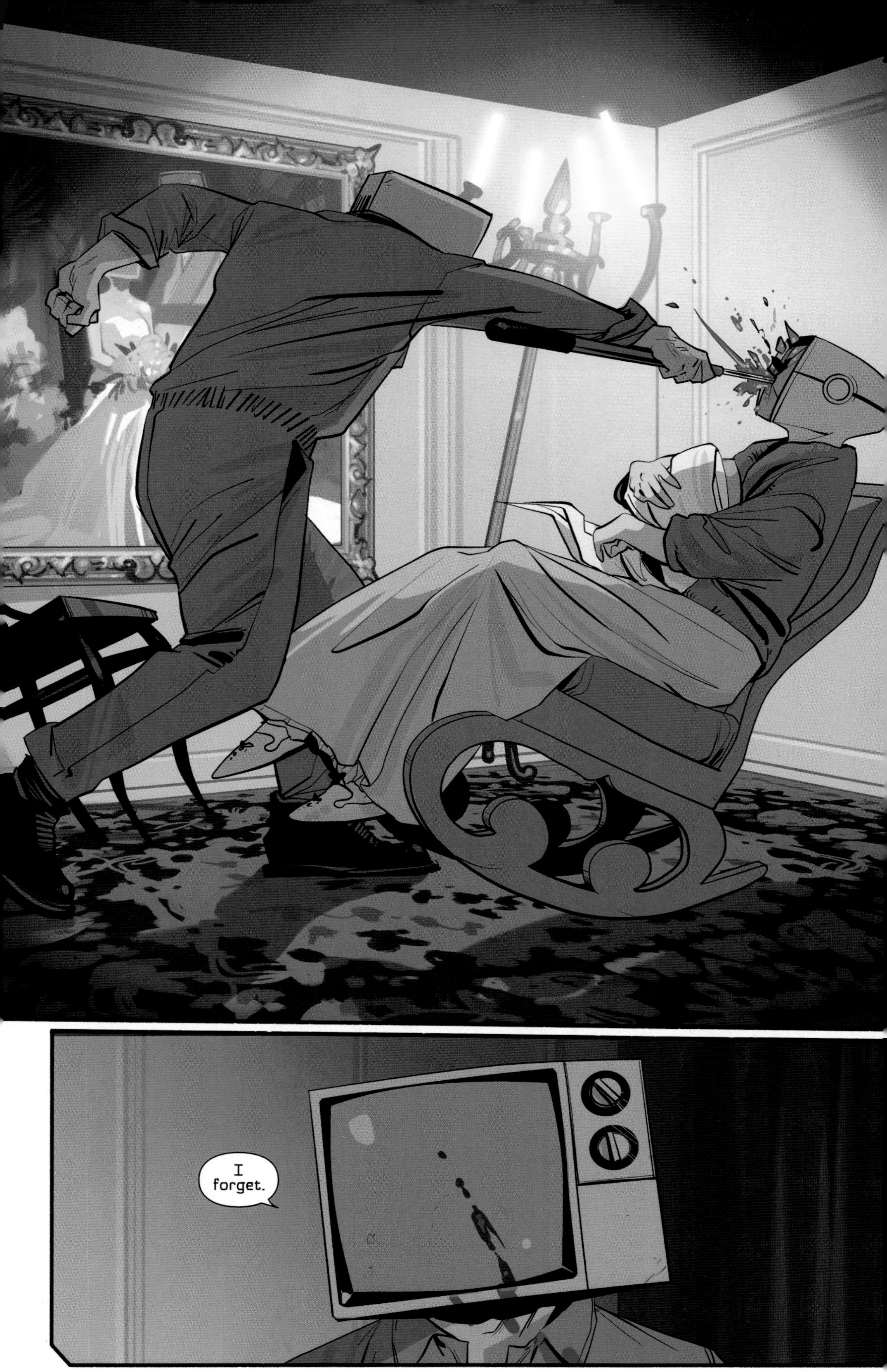
I forget.

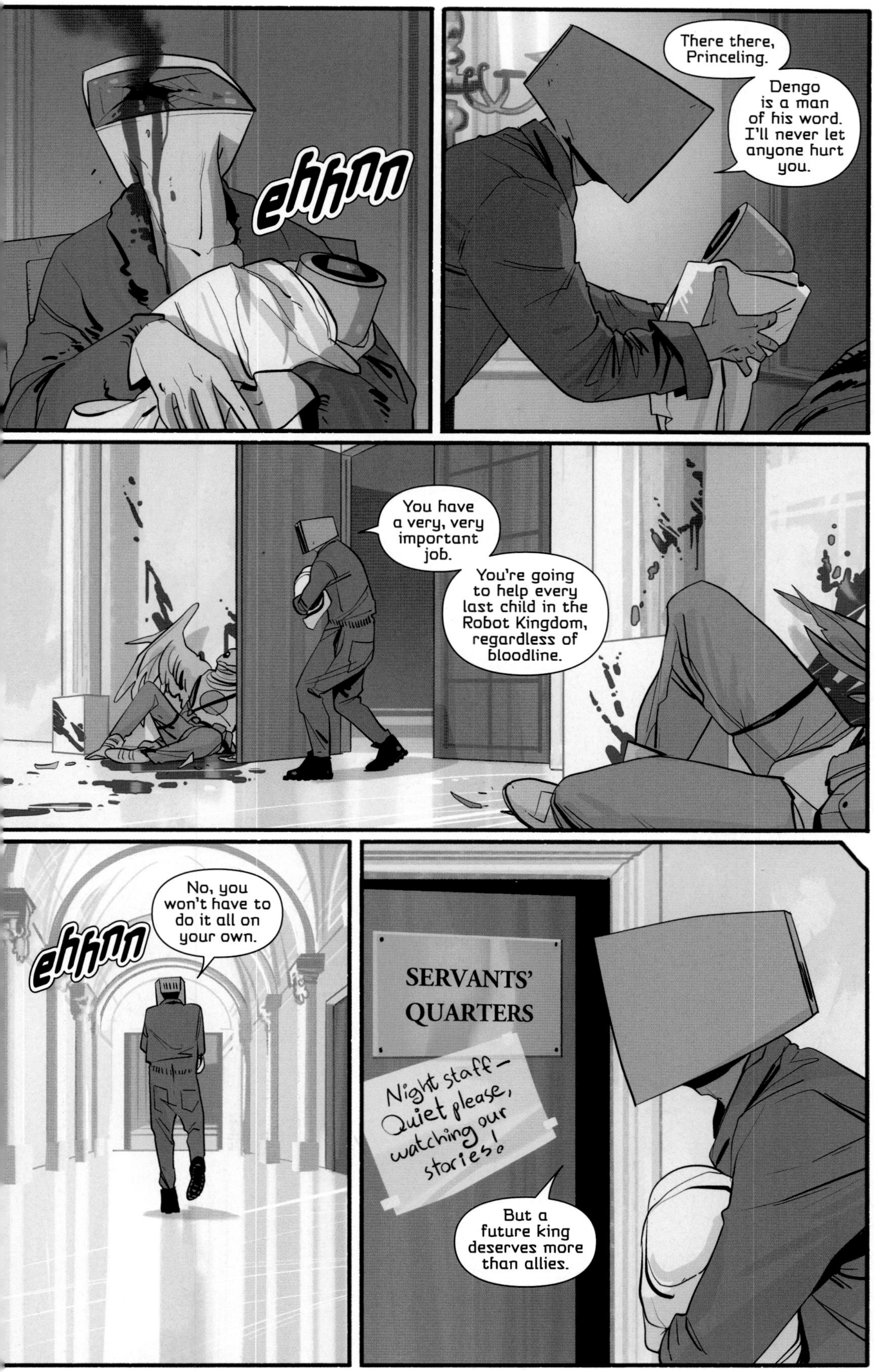
ehhnn
There there, Princeling.
Dengo is a man of his word. I'll never let anyone hurt you.
You have a very, very important job.
You're going to help every last child in the Robot Kingdom, regardless of bloodline.
ehhnn
No, you won't have to do it all on your own.
SERVANTS' QUARTERS
Night staff— Quiet please, watching our stories!
But a future king deserves more than allies.

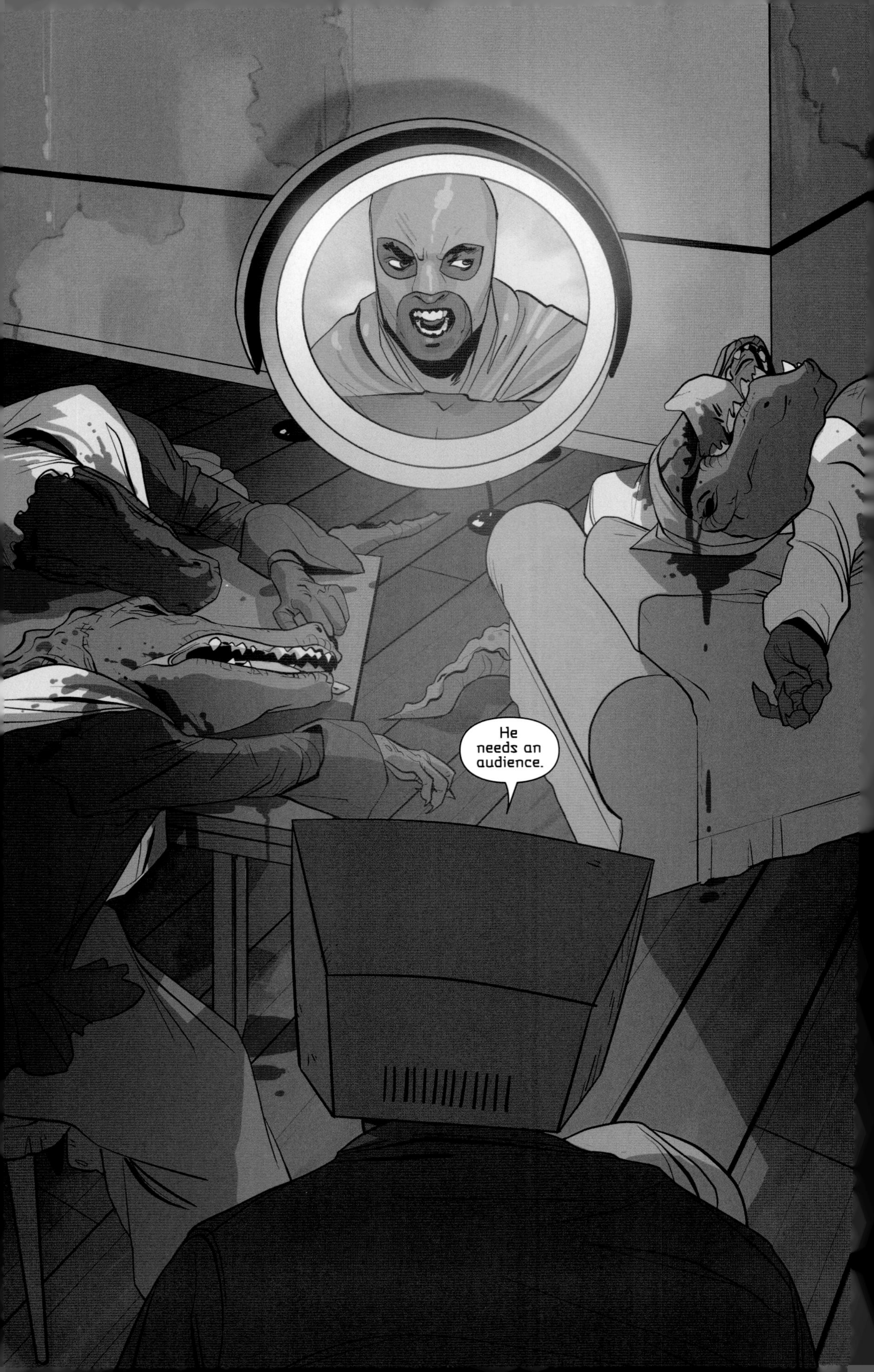
He needs an audience.

end chapter twenty

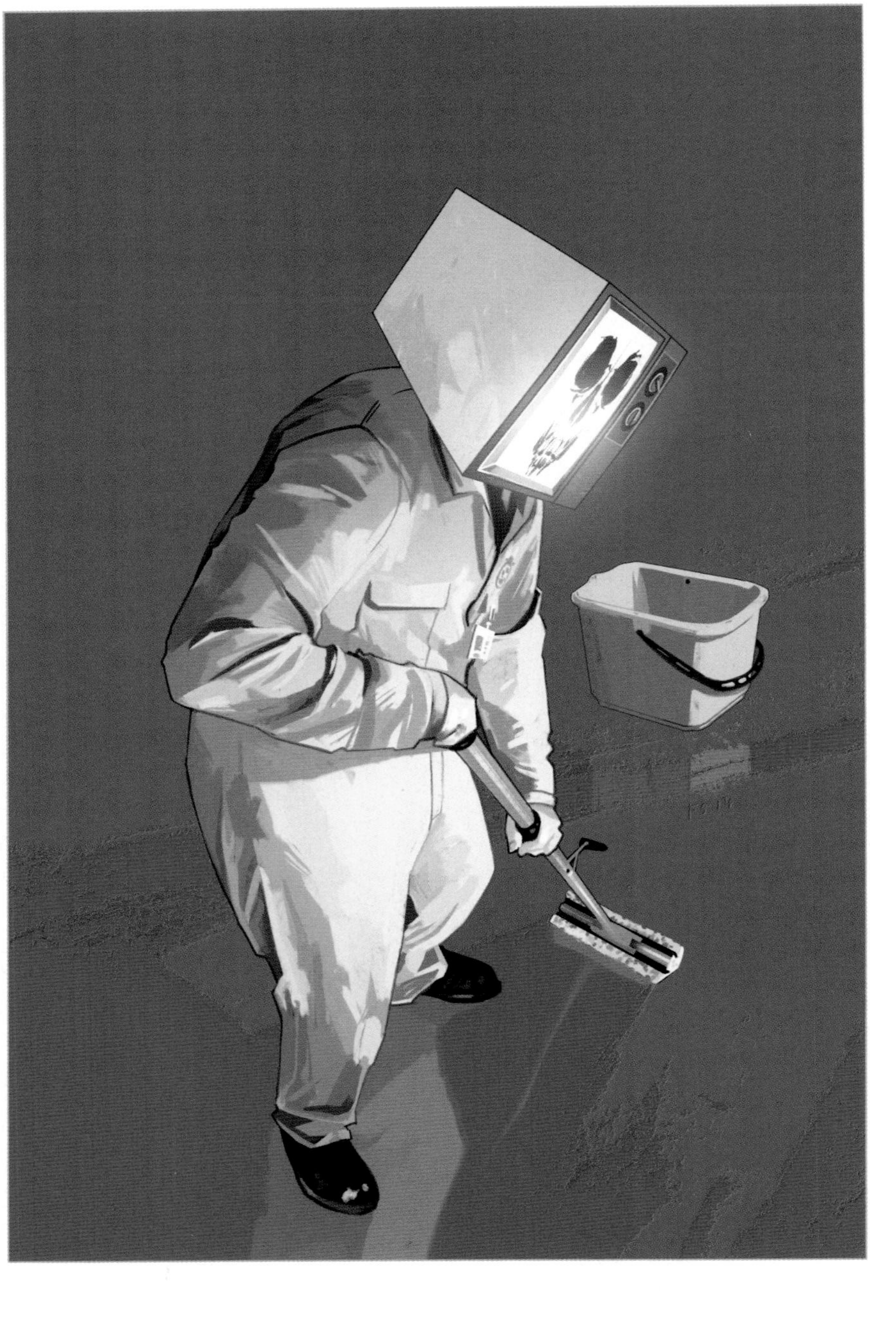

CHAPTER

TWENTY-ONE

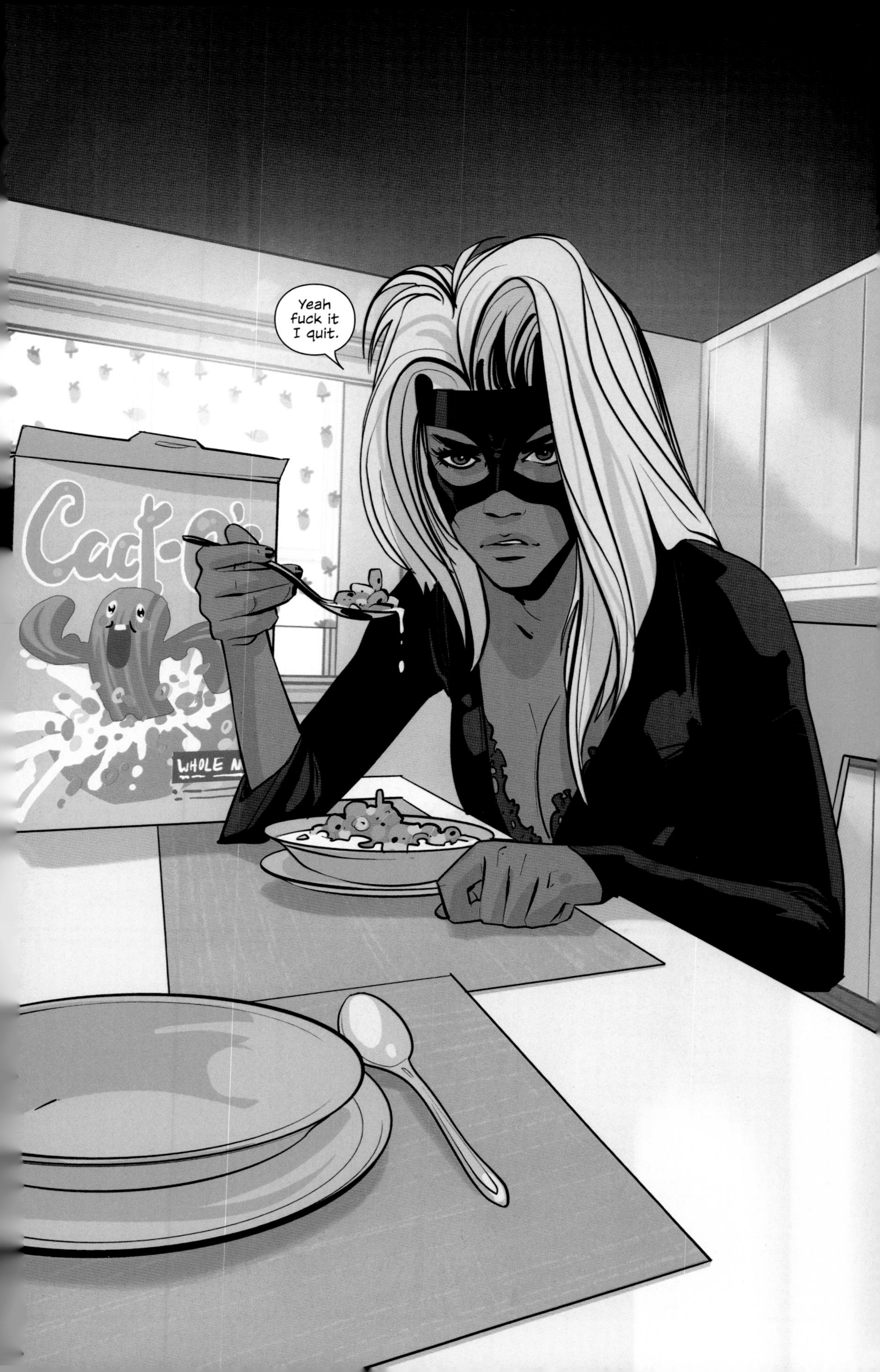
Yeah fuck it I quit.
Cact-O's
WHOLE

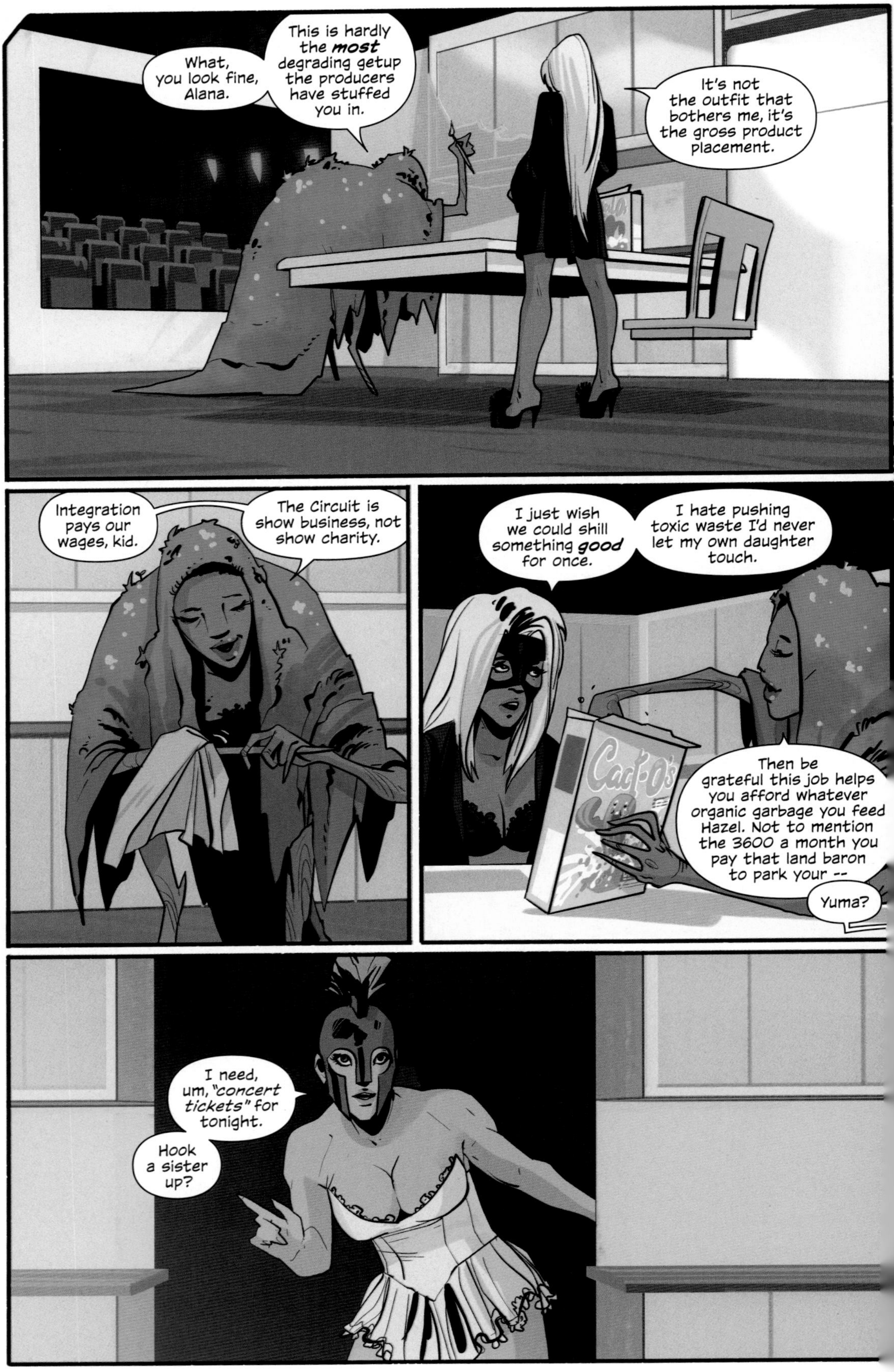
What, you look fine, Alana.
This is hardly the *most* degrading getup the producers have stuffed you in.
It's not the outfit that bothers me, it's the gross product placement.
Integration pays our wages, kid.
The Circuit is show business, not show charity.
I just wish we could shill something *good* for once.
I hate pushing toxic waste I'd never let my own daughter touch.
Cact-O's
Then be grateful this job helps you afford whatever organic garbage you feed Hazel. Not to mention the 3600 a month you pay that land baron to park your --
Yuma?
I need, um, *"concert tickets"* for tonight.
Hook a sister up?

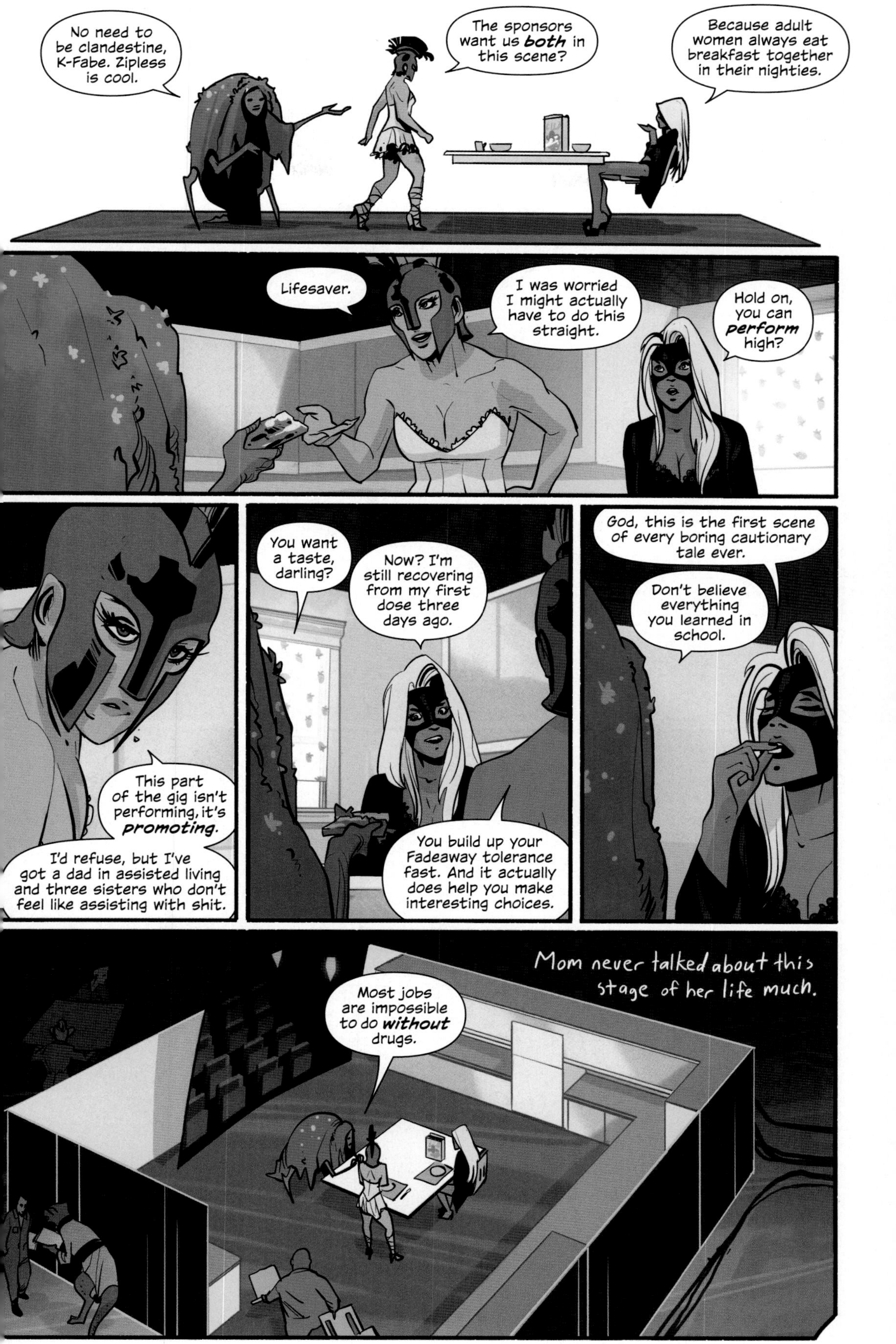

No need to be clandestine, K-Fabe. Zipless is cool.
The sponsors want us both in this scene?
Because adult women always eat breakfast together in their nighties.
Lifesaver.
I was worried I might actually have to do this straight.
Hold on, you can perform high?
This part of the gig isn't performing, it's promoting.
I'd refuse, but I've got a dad in assisted living and three sisters who don't feel like assisting with shit.
You want a taste, darling?
Now? I'm still recovering from my first dose three days ago.
You build up your Fadeaway tolerance fast. And it actually does help you make interesting choices.
God, this is the first scene of every boring cautionary tale ever.
Don't believe everything you learned in school.
Mom never talked about this stage of her life much.
Most jobs are impossible to do without drugs.

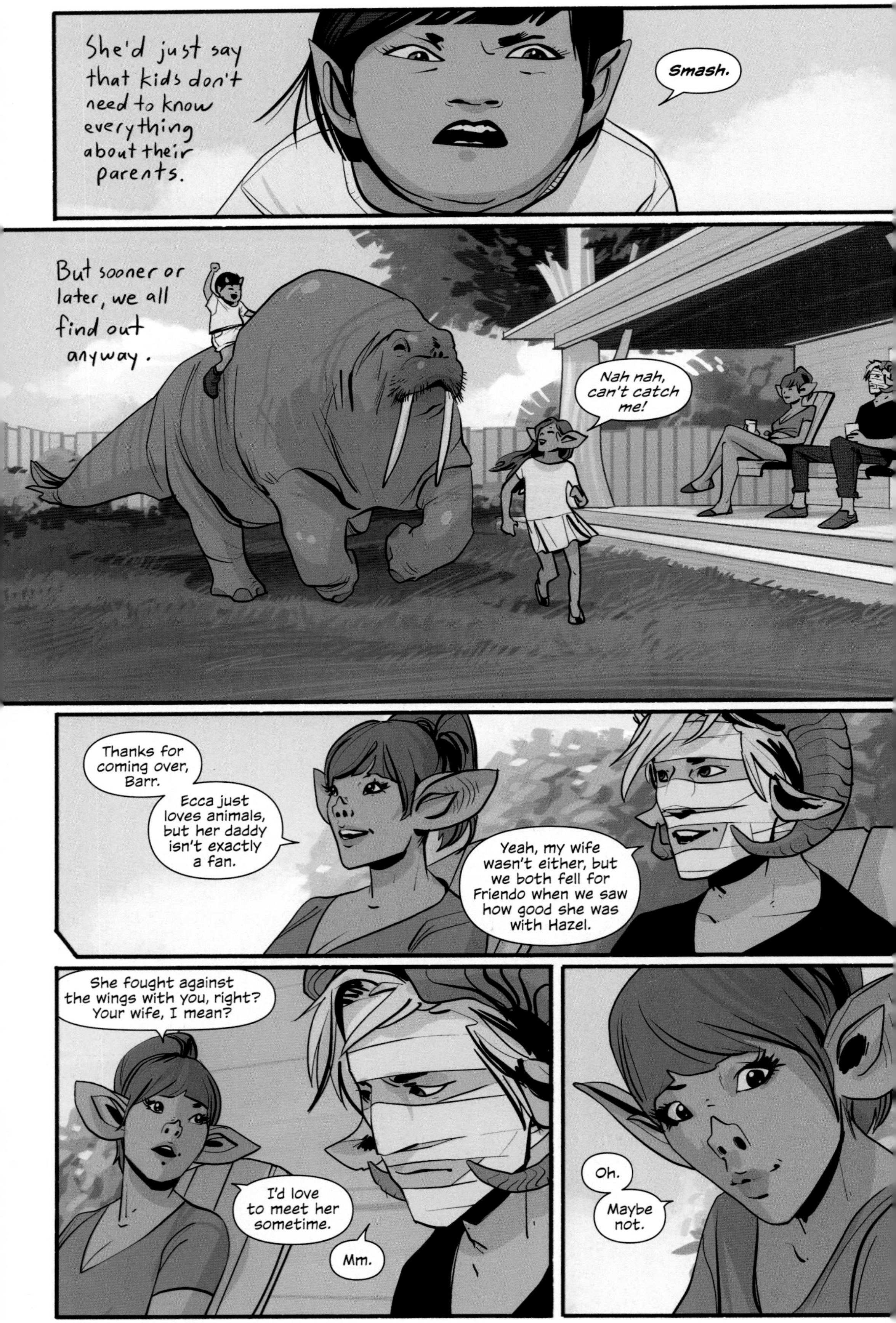

She'd just say that kids don't need to know everything about their parents.
Smash.
But sooner or later, we all find out anyway.
Nah nah, can't catch me!
Thanks for coming over, Barr.
Ecca just loves animals, but her daddy isn't exactly a fan.
Yeah, my wife wasn't either, but we both fell for Friendo when we saw how good she was with Hazel.
She fought against the wings with you, right? Your wife, I mean?
I'd love to meet her sometime.
Mm.
Oh.
Maybe not.

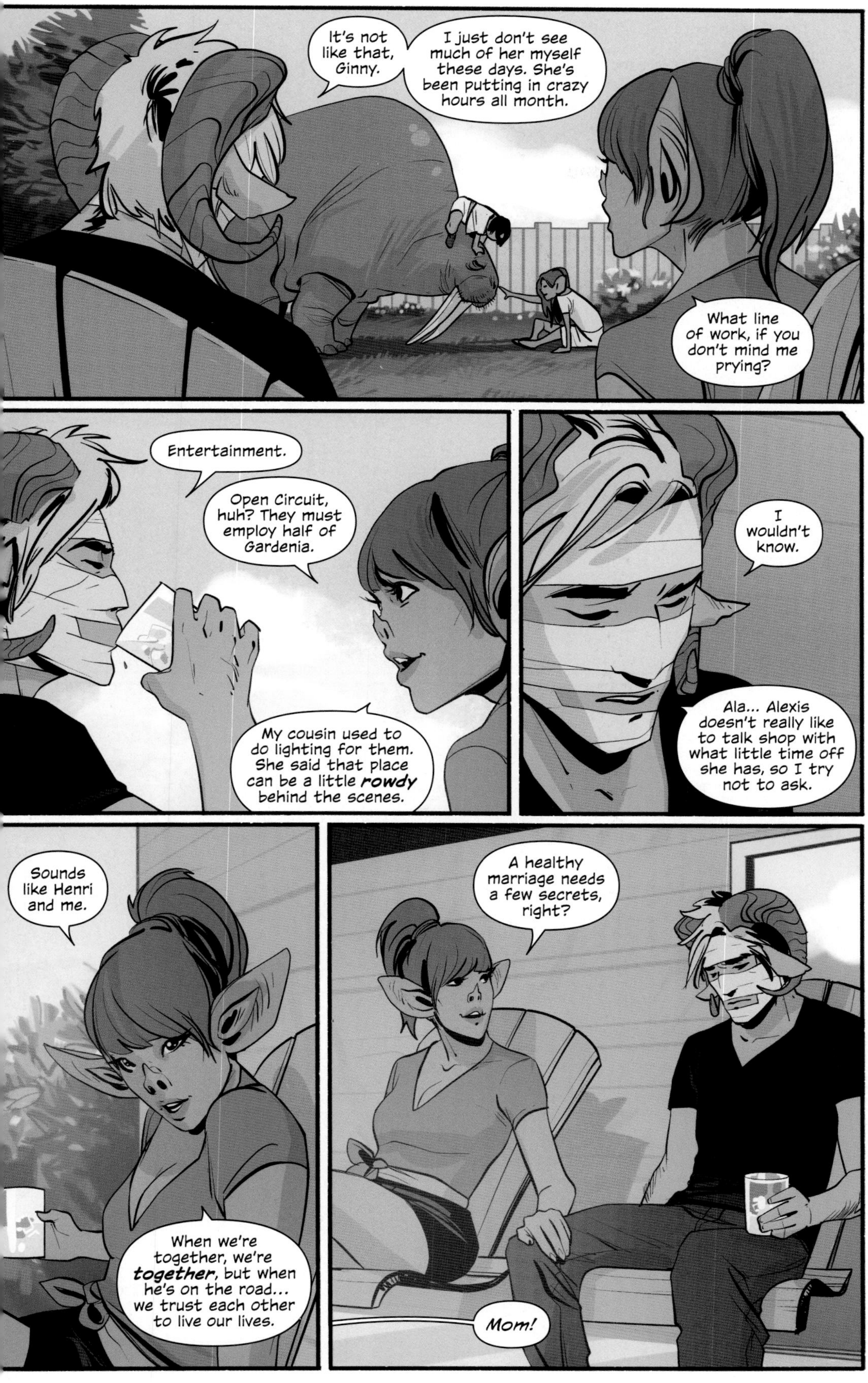
It's not like that, Ginny.
I just don't see much of her myself these days. She's been putting in crazy hours all month.
What line of work, if you don't mind me prying?
Entertainment.
Open Circuit, huh? They must employ half of Gardenia.
My cousin used to do lighting for them. She said that place can be a little *rowdy* behind the scenes.
I wouldn't know.
Ala... Alexis doesn't really like to talk shop with what little time off she has, so I try not to ask.
Sounds like Henri and me.
When we're together, we're *together*, but when he's on the road... we trust each other to live our lives.
A healthy marriage needs a few secrets, right?
Mom!

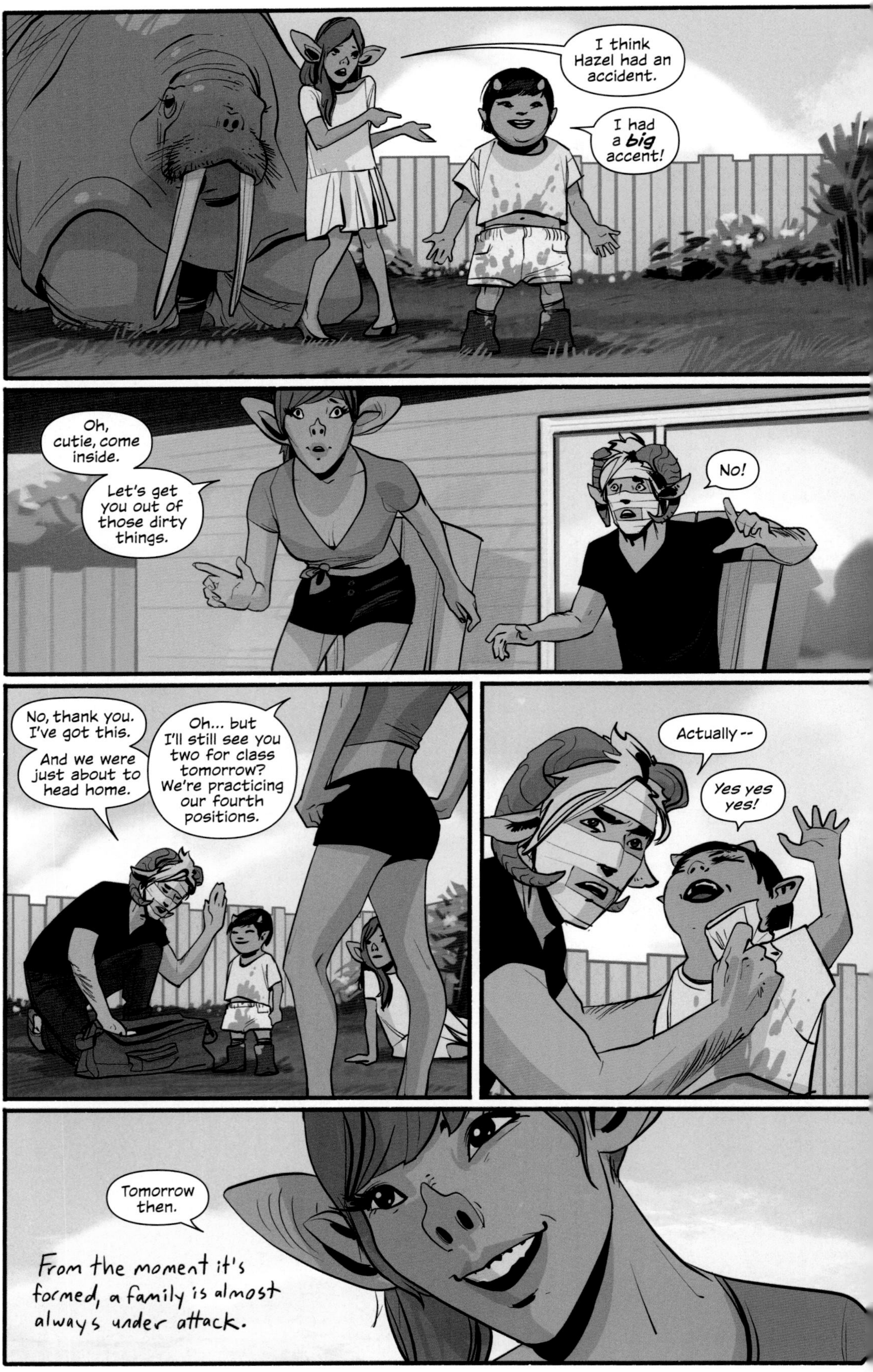
I think Hazel had an accident.
I had a **big** accent!
Oh, cutie, come inside.
Let's get you out of those dirty things.
No!
No, thank you. I've got this.
And we were just about to head home.
Oh... but I'll still see you two for class tomorrow? We're practicing our fourth positions.
Actually --
Yes yes yes!
Tomorrow then.
From the moment it's formed, a family is almost always under attack.

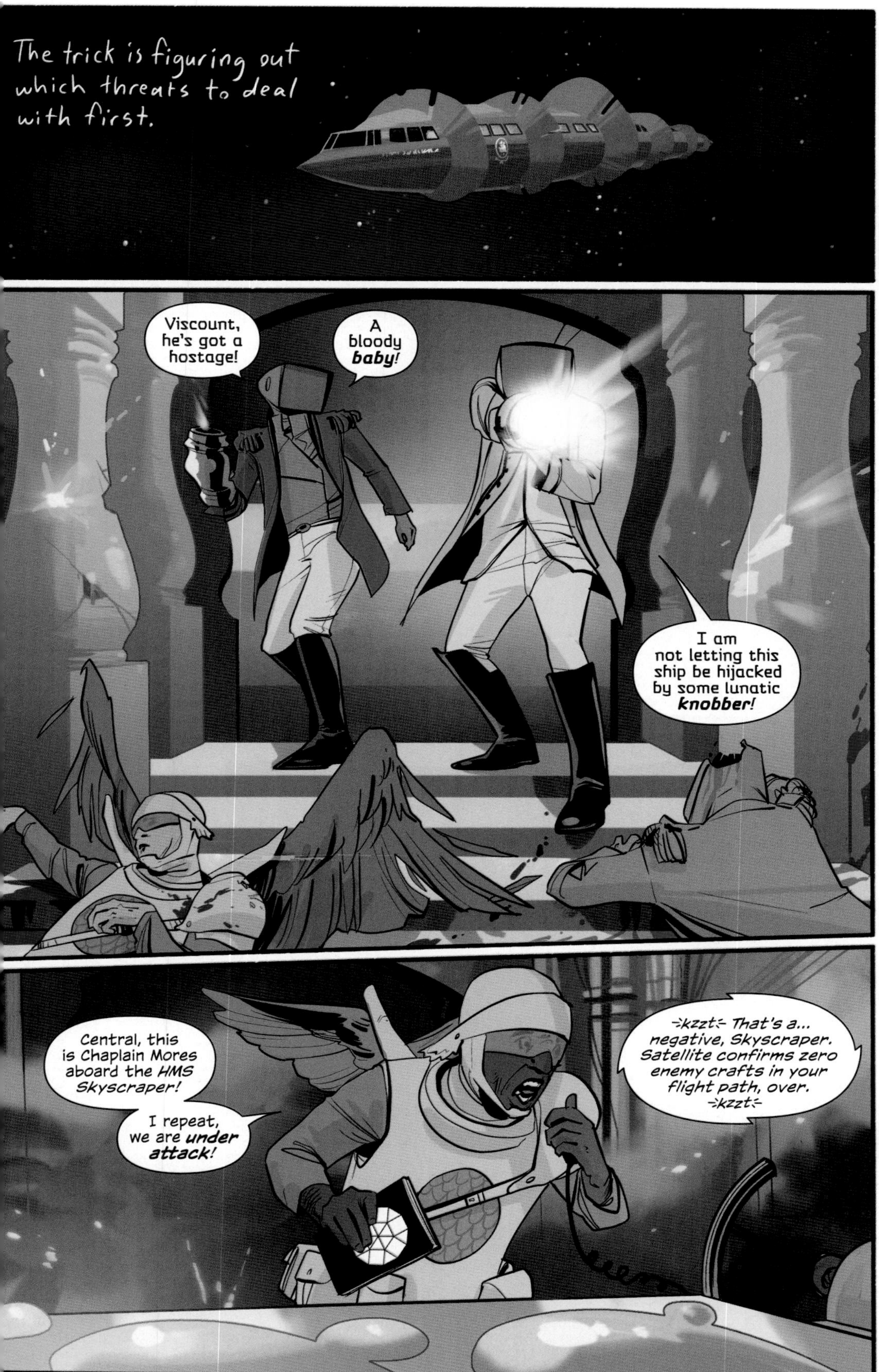
The trick is figuring out which threats to deal with first.
Viscount, he's got a hostage!
A bloody *baby*!
I am not letting this ship be hijacked by some lunatic ***knobber***!
Central, this is Chaplain Mores aboard the *HMS Skyscraper*!
I repeat, we are ***under attack***!
-kzzt- That's a... negative, Skyscraper. Satellite confirms zero enemy crafts in your flight path, over. -kzzt-

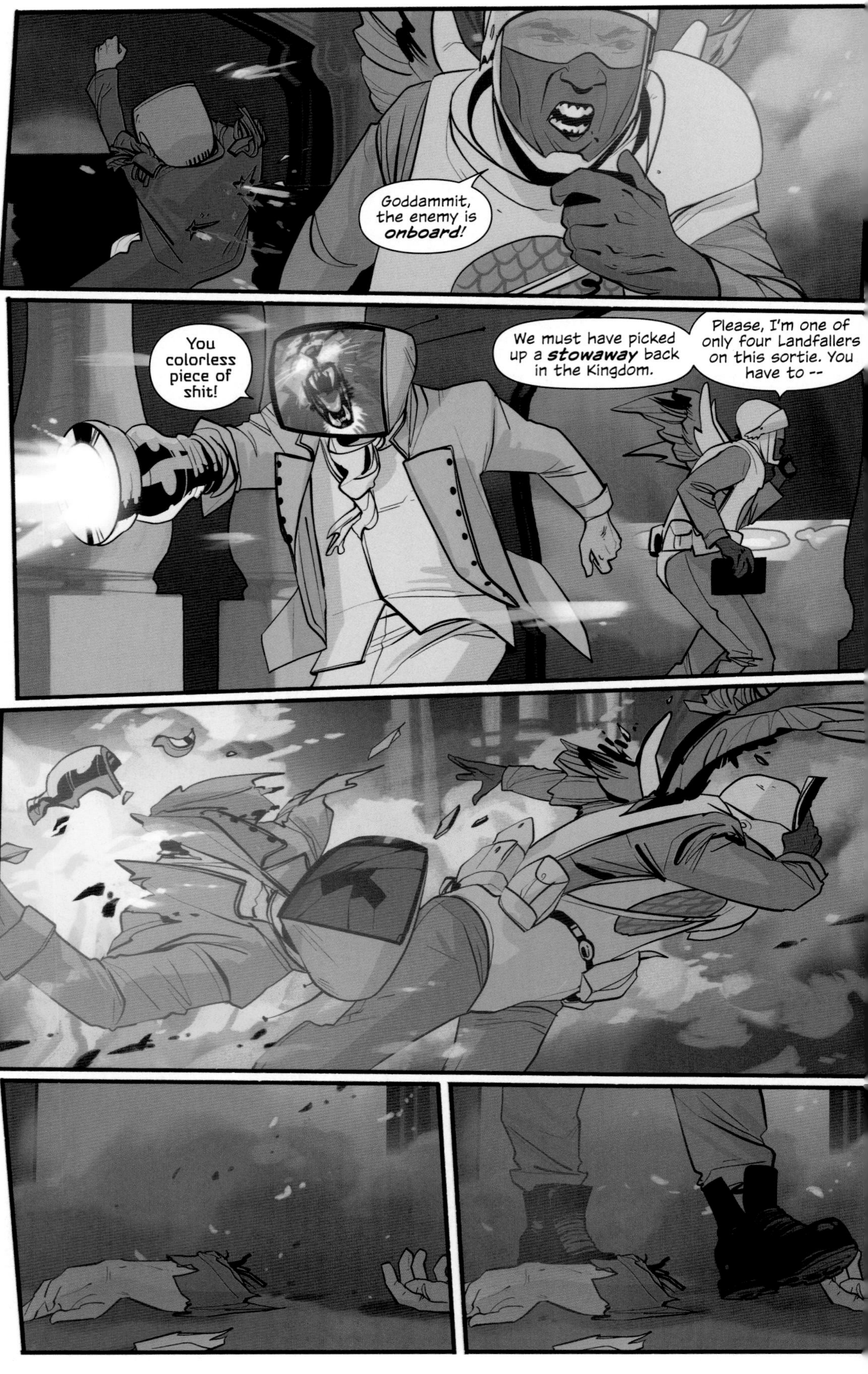
Goddammit, the enemy is **onboard!**
You colorless piece of shit!
We must have picked up a **stowaway** back in the Kingdom.
Please, I'm one of only four Landfallers on this sortie. You have to --

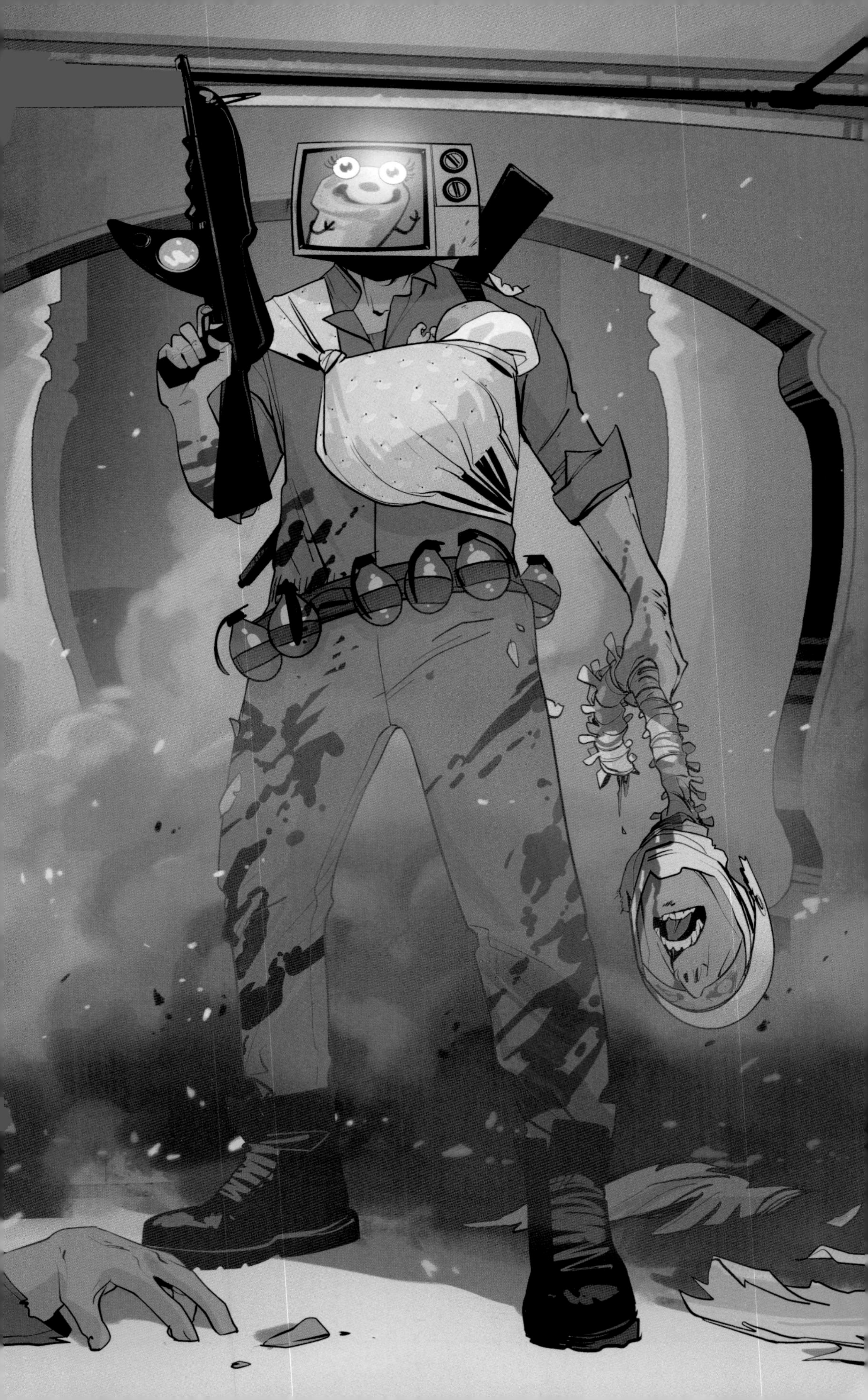

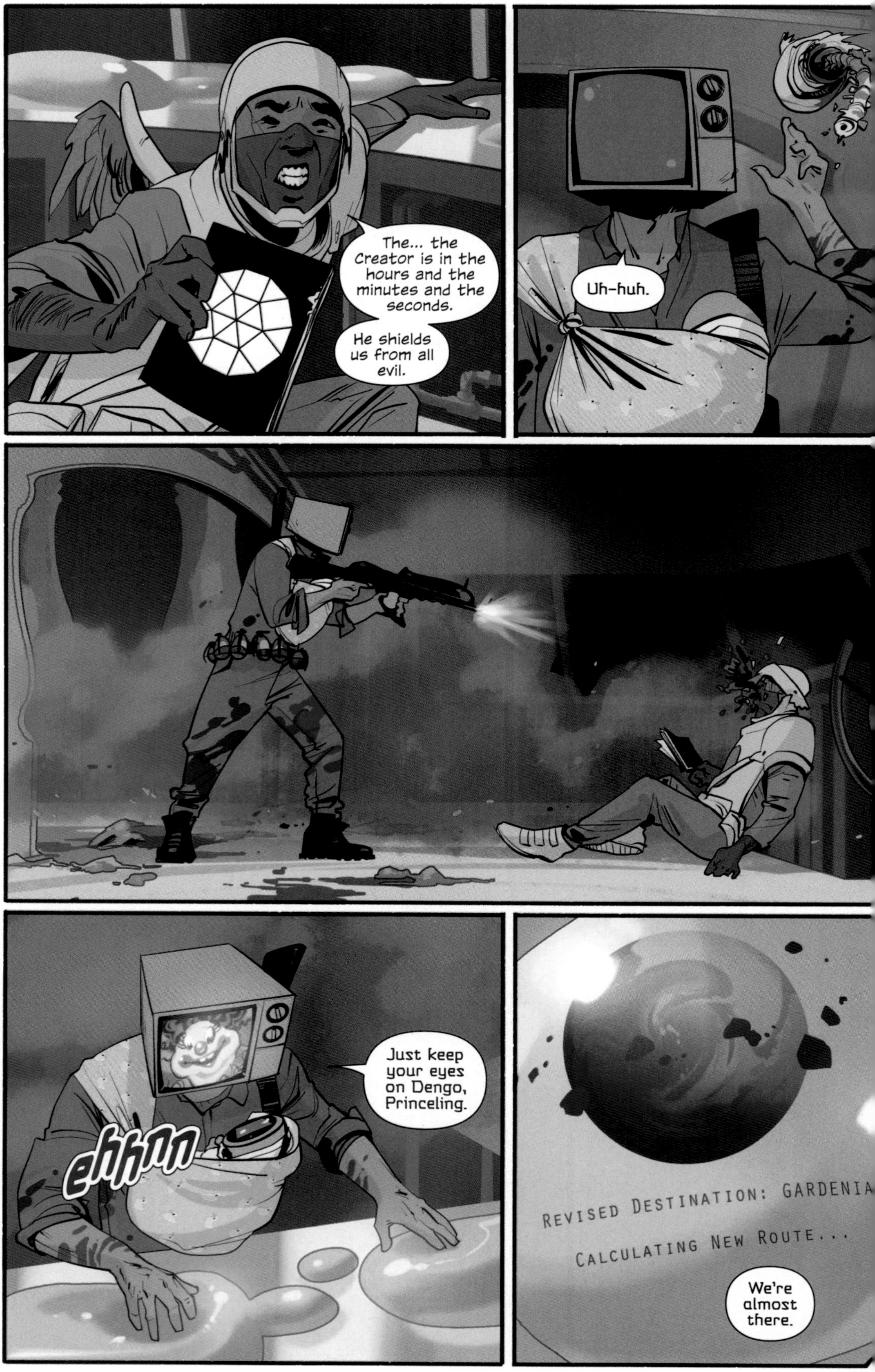
The... the Creator is in the hours and the minutes and the seconds.
He shields us from all evil.
Uh-huh.
Just keep your eyes on Dengo, Princeling.
ehhnn
REVISED DESTINATION: GARDENIA
CALCULATING NEW ROUTE...
We're almost there.

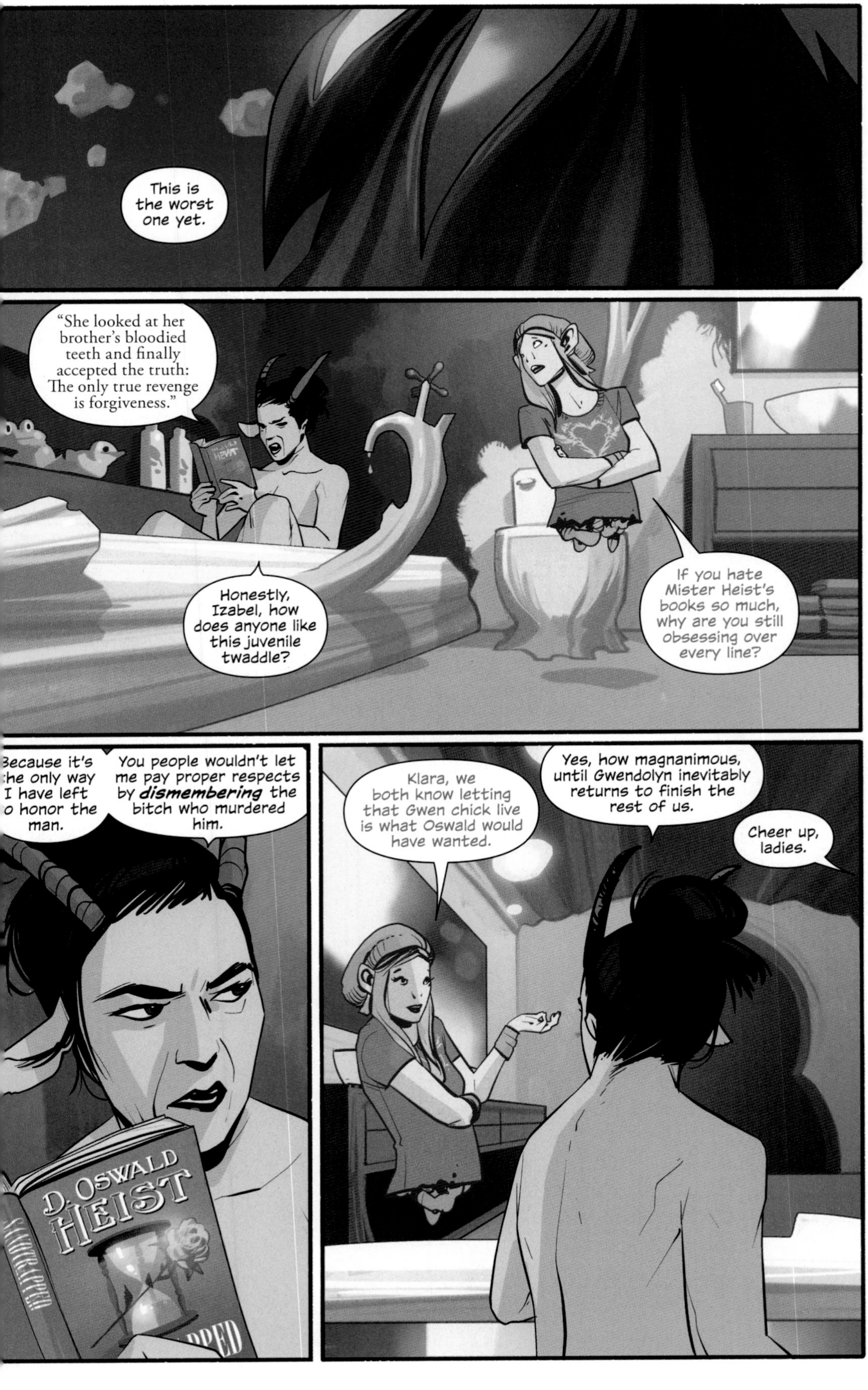
This is the worst one yet.
"She looked at her brother's bloodied teeth and finally accepted the truth: The only true revenge is forgiveness."
Honestly, Izabel, how does anyone like this juvenile twaddle?
If you hate Mister Heist's books so much, why are you still obsessing over every line?
Because it's the only way I have left to honor the man.
You people wouldn't let me pay proper respects by *dismembering* the bitch who murdered him.
Klara, we both know letting that Gwen chick live is what Oswald would have wanted.
Yes, how magnanimous, until Gwendolyn inevitably returns to finish the rest of us.
Cheer up, ladies.
D. OSWALD HEIST

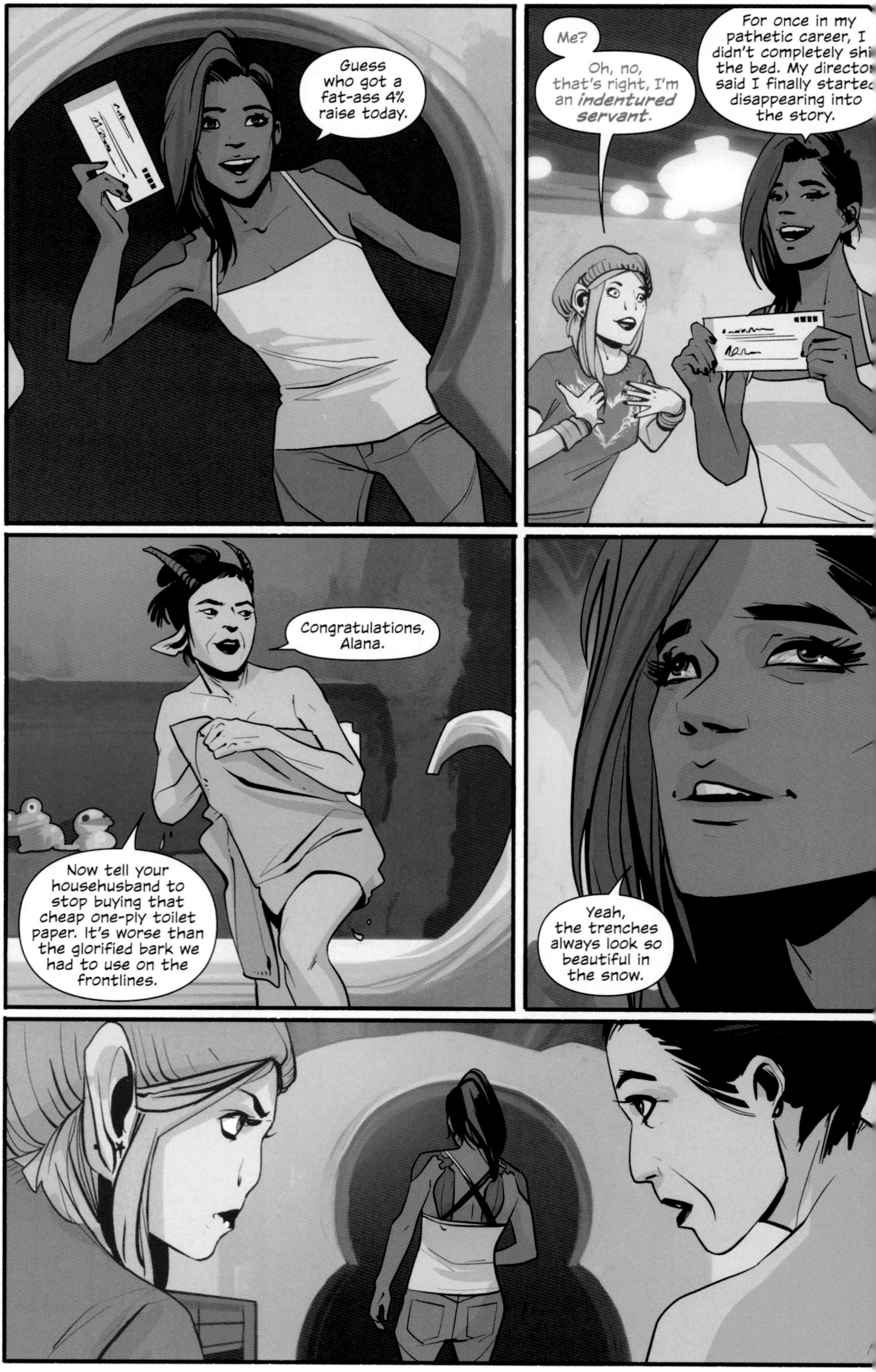
Guess who got a fat-ass 4% raise today.
Me?
Oh, no, that's right, I'm an *indentured servant*.
For once in my pathetic career, I didn't completely sh the bed. My directo said I finally starte disappearing into the story.
Congratulations, Alana.
Now tell your househusband to stop buying that cheap one-ply toilet paper. It's worse than the glorified bark we had to use on the frontlines.
Yeah, the trenches always look so beautiful in the snow.

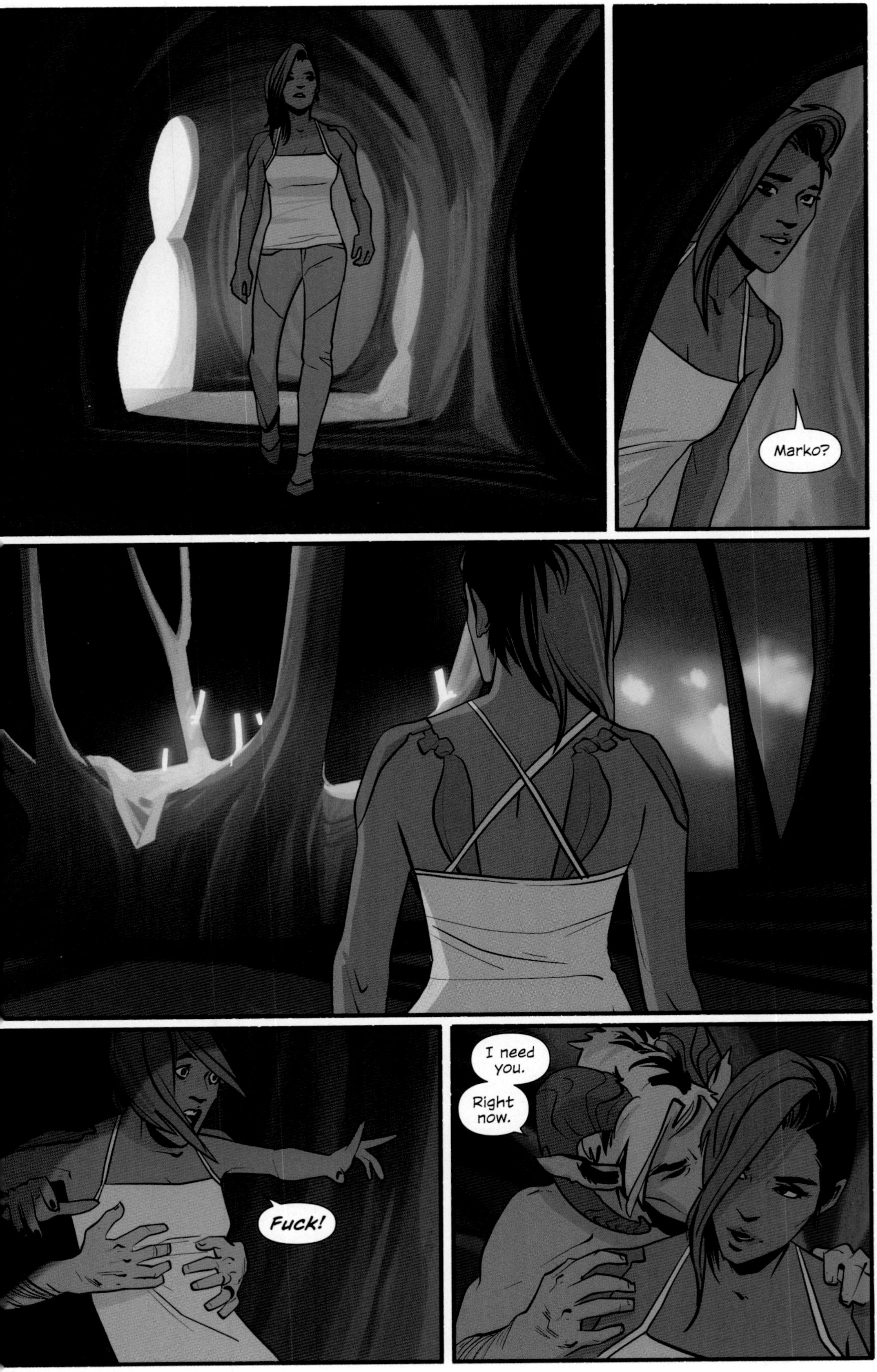
Marko?
Fuck!
I need you.
Right now.

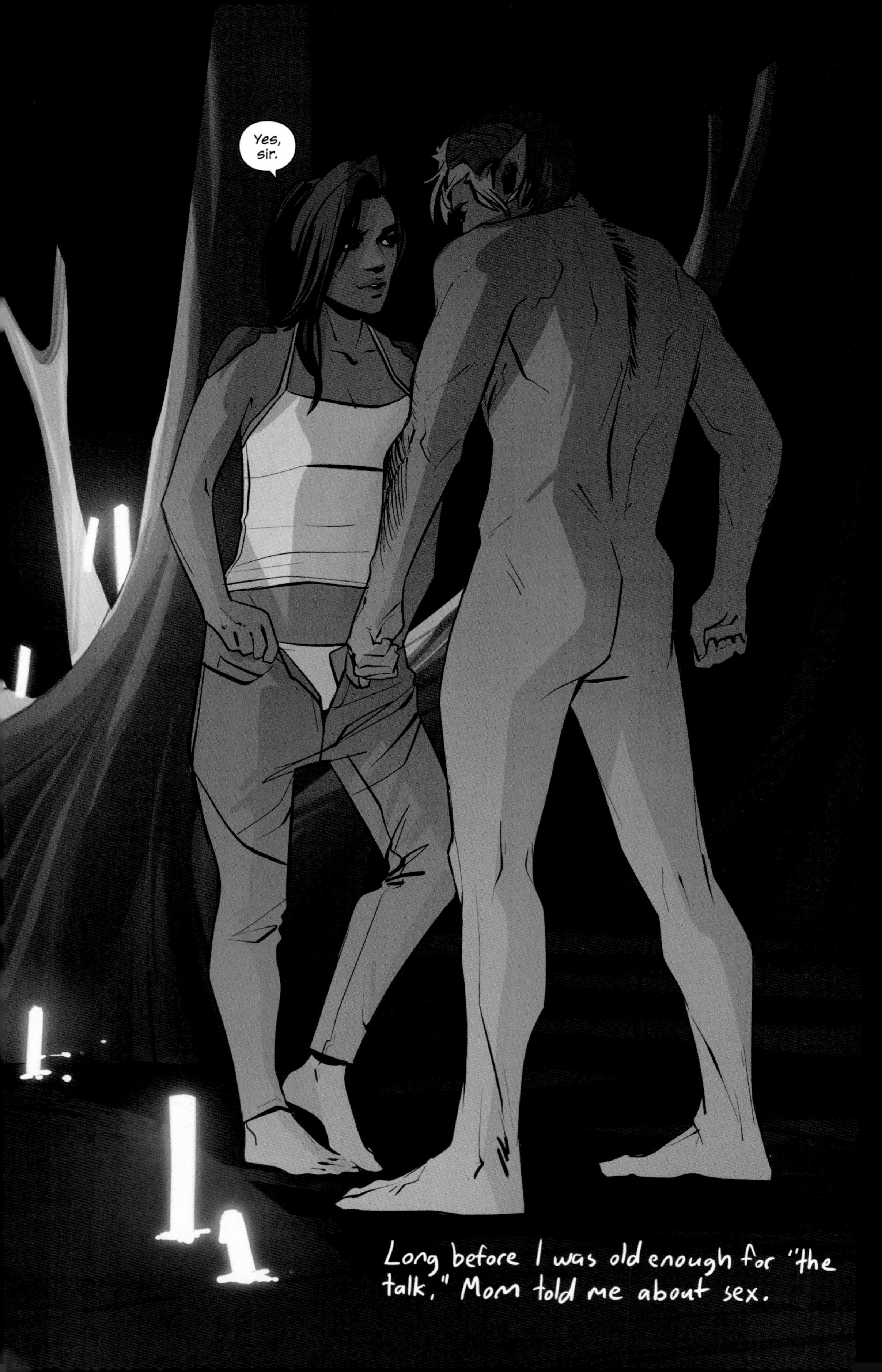
Yes, sir.
Long before I was old enough for "the talk," Mom told me about sex.

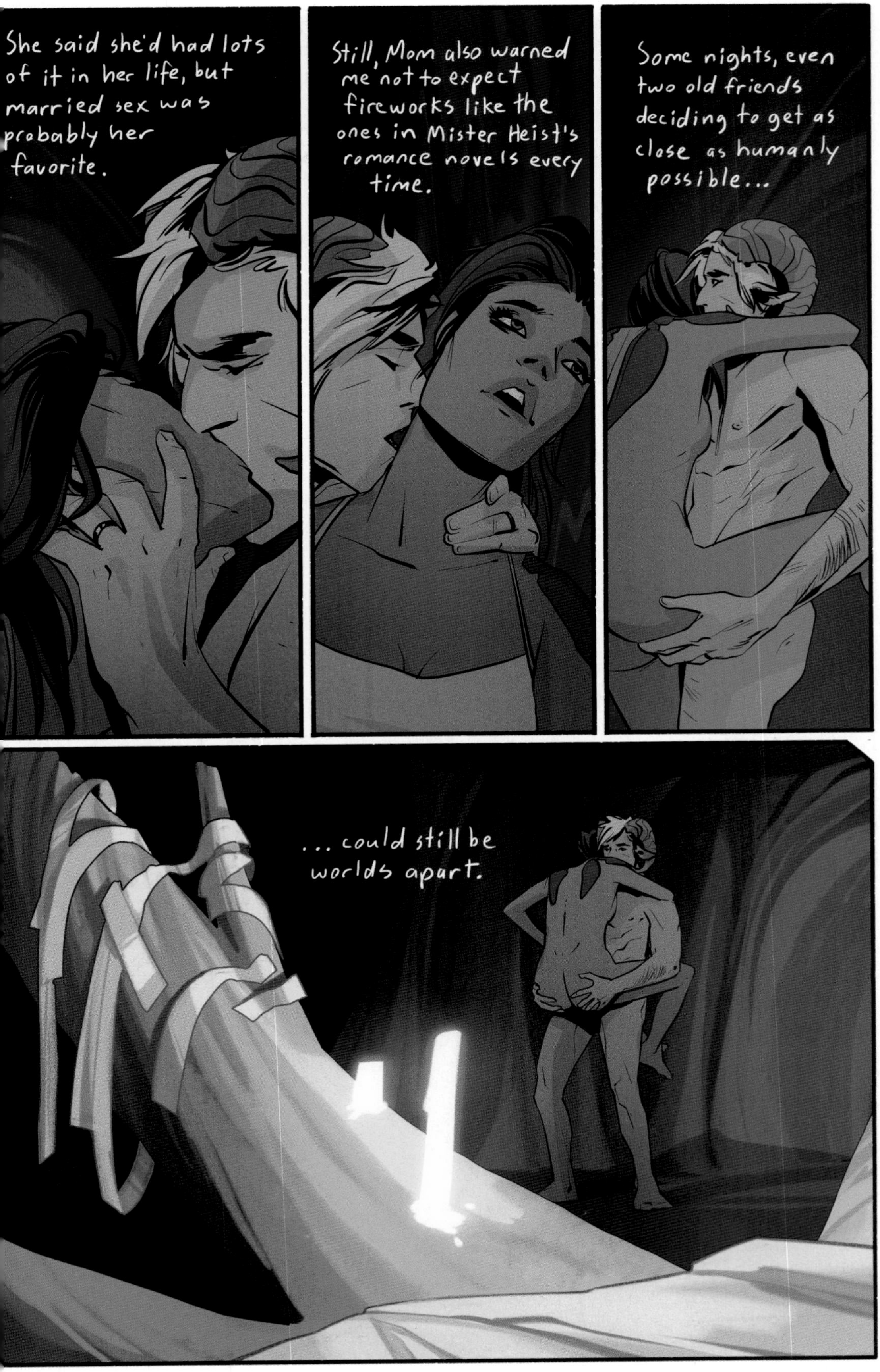
She said she'd had lots of it in her life, but married sex was probably her favorite.
Still, Mom also warned me not to expect fireworks like the ones in Mister Heist's romance novels every time.
Some nights, even two old friends deciding to get as close as humanly possible...
...could still be worlds apart.

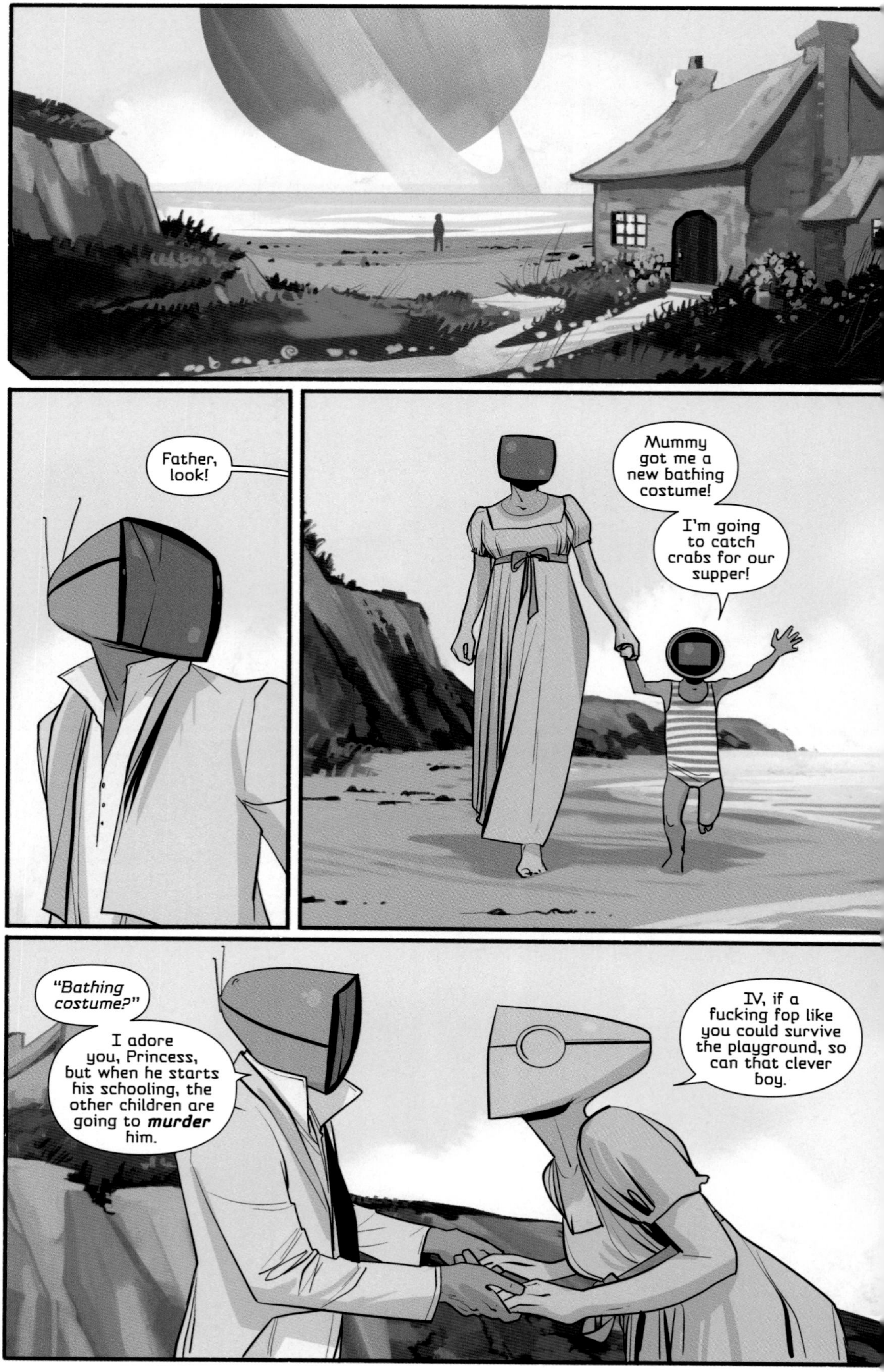
Father, look!
Mummy got me a new bathing costume!
I'm going to catch crabs for our supper!
"Bathing costume?"
I adore you, Princess, but when he starts his schooling, the other children are going to ***murder*** him.
IV, if a fucking fop like you could survive the playground, so can that clever boy.

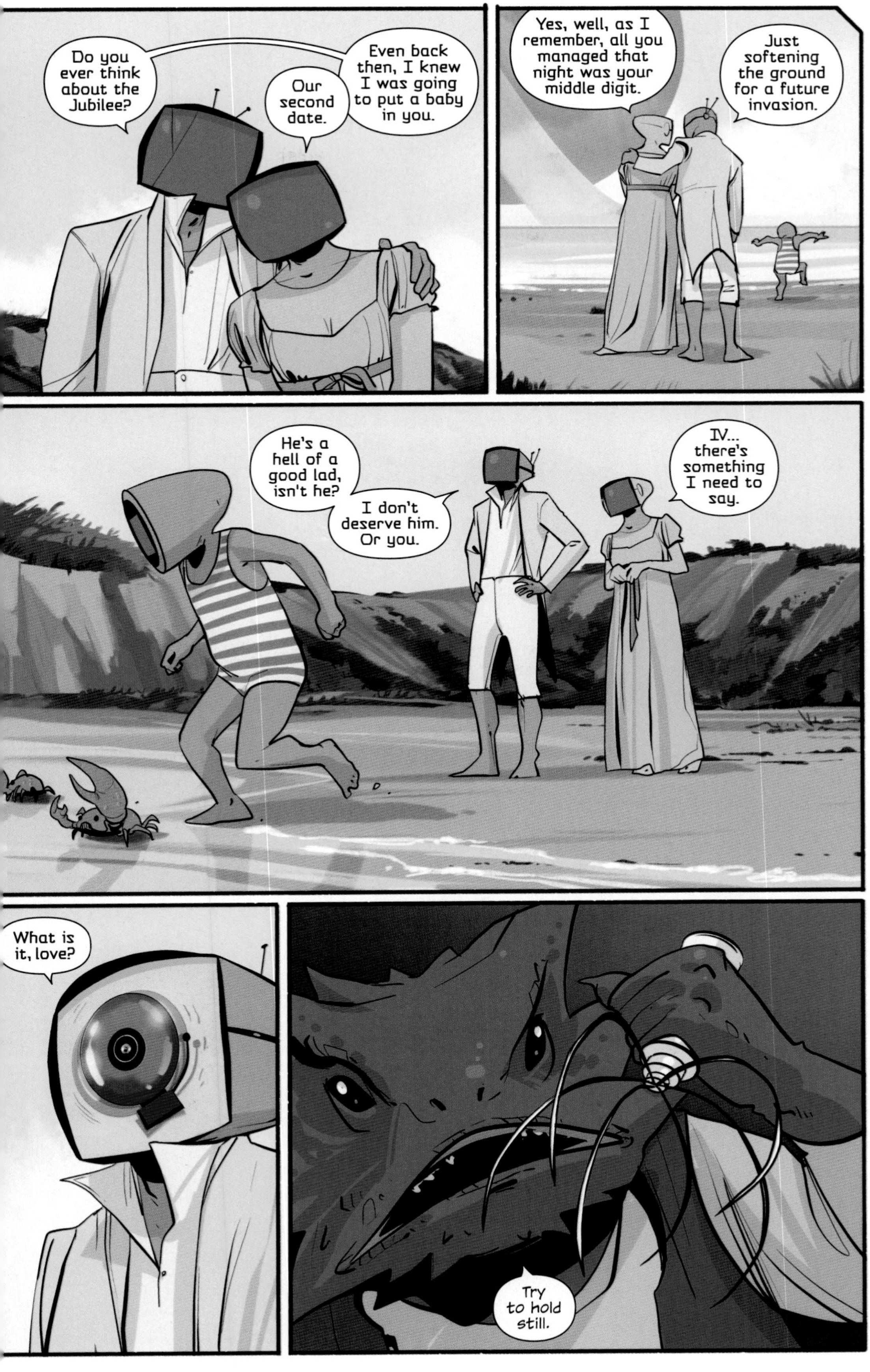
Do you ever think about the Jubilee?
Our second date.
Even back then, I knew I was going to put a baby in you.
Yes, well, as I remember, all you managed that night was your middle digit.
Just softening the ground for a future invasion.
He's a hell of a good lad, isn't he?
I don't deserve him. Or you.
IV... there's something I need to say.
What is it, love?
Try to hold still.

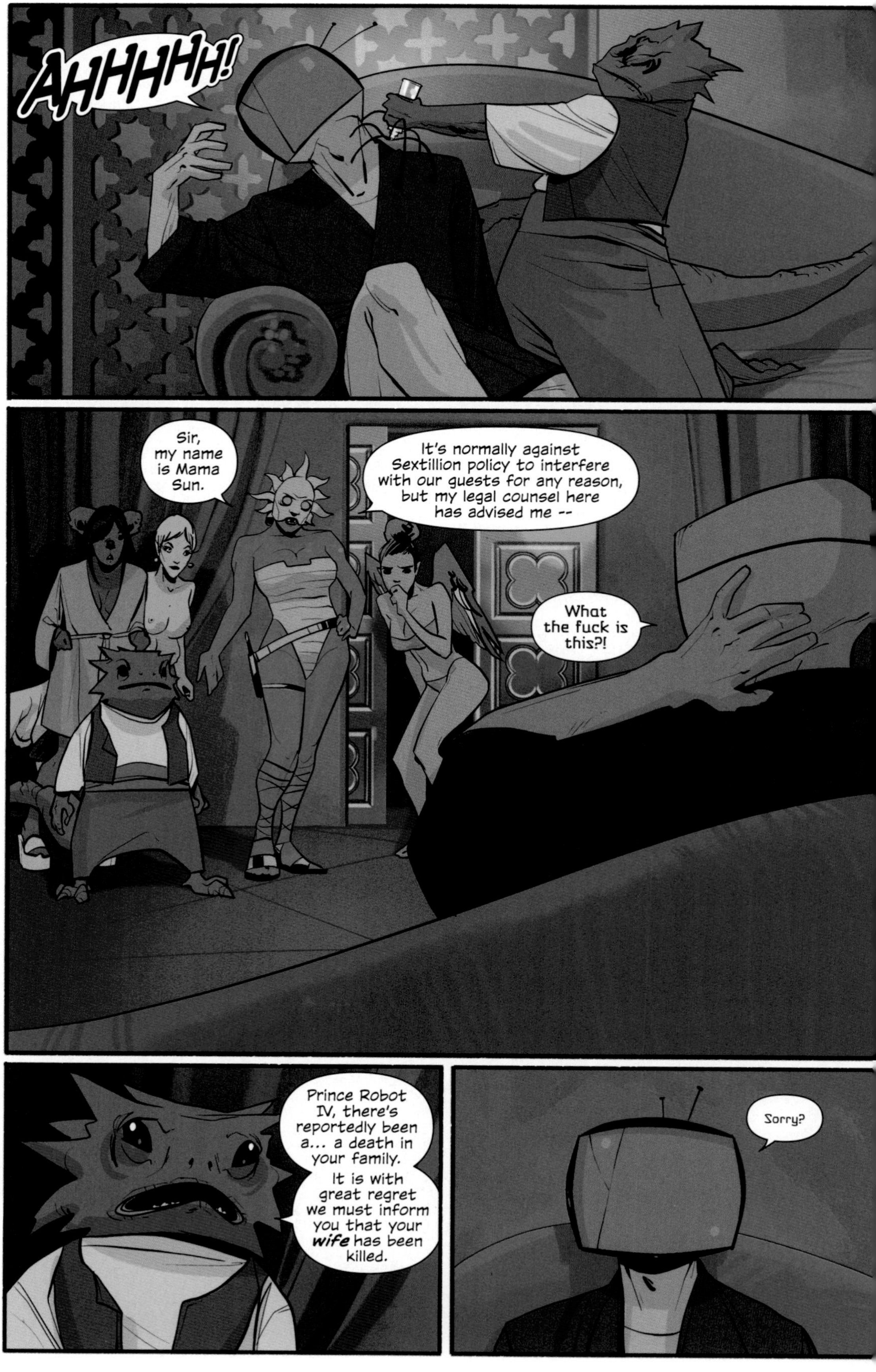
AHHHHH!
Sir, my name is Mama Sun.
It's normally against Sextillion policy to interfere with our guests for any reason, but my legal counsel here has advised me --
What the fuck is this?!
Prince Robot IV, there's reportedly been a... a death in your family.
It is with great regret we must inform you that your ***wife*** has been killed.
Sorry?

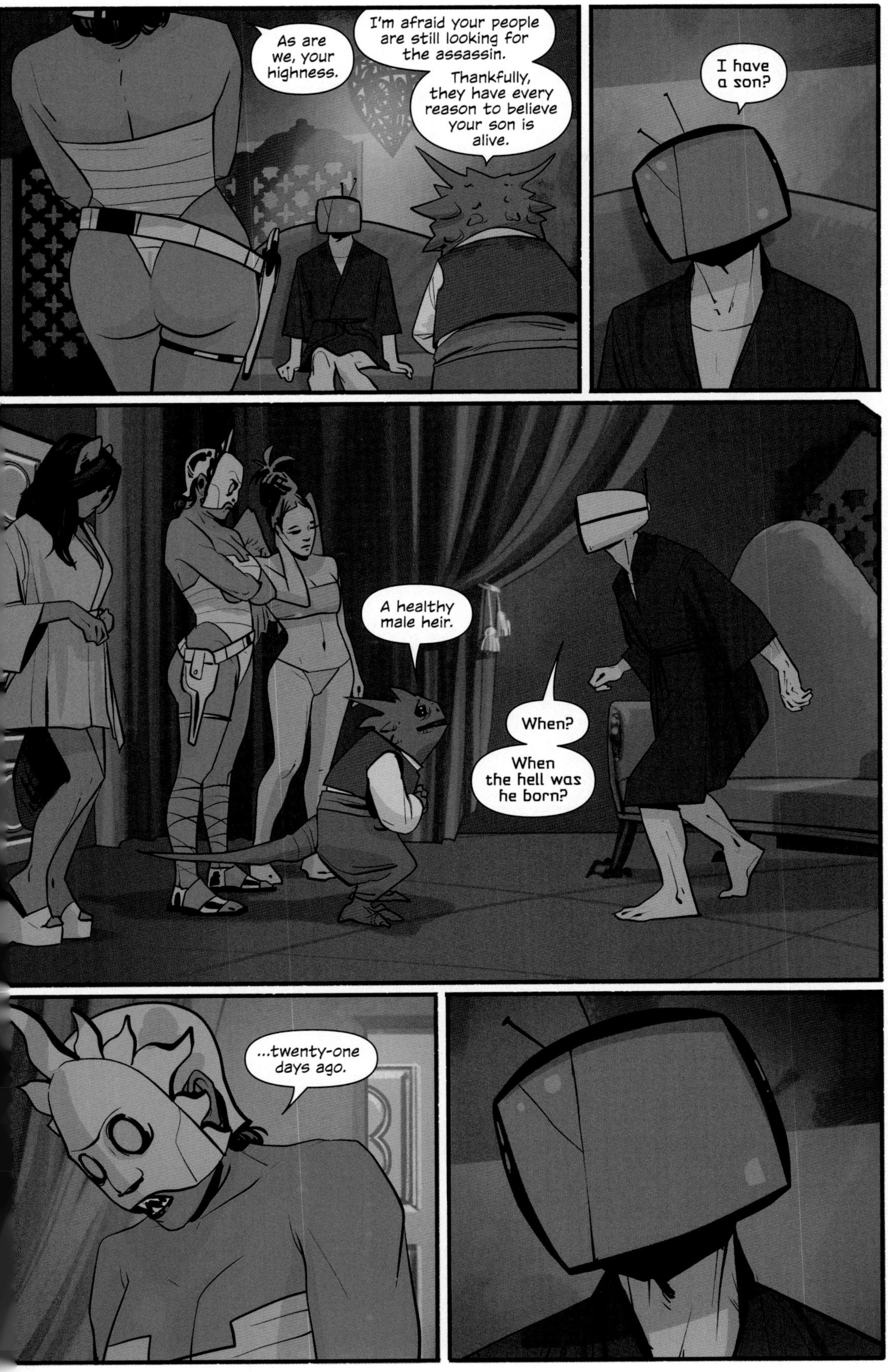

As are we, your highness.
I'm afraid your people are still looking for the assassin.
Thankfully, they have every reason to believe your son is alive.
I have a son?
A healthy male heir.
When?
When the hell was he born?
...twenty-one days ago.

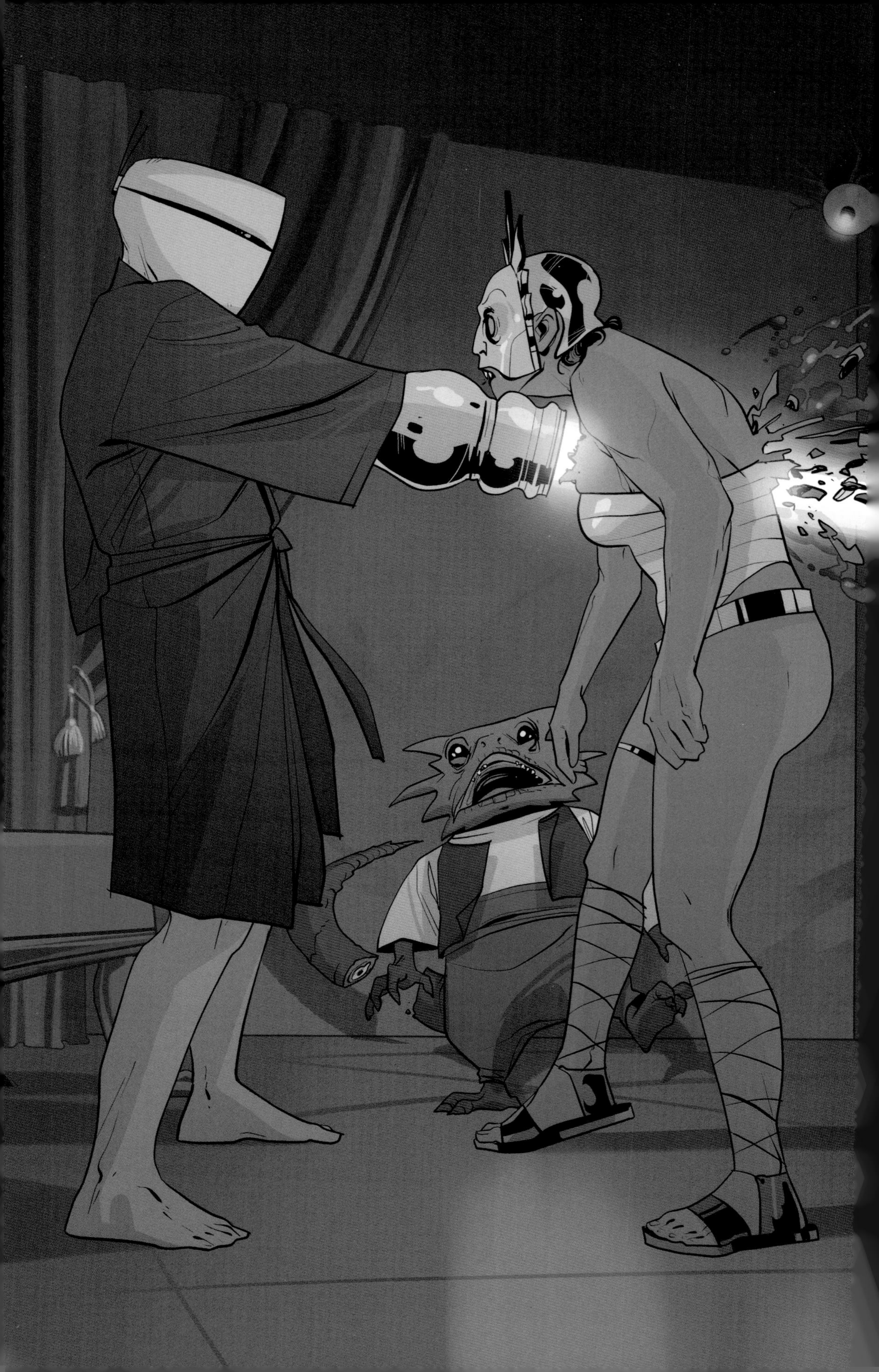

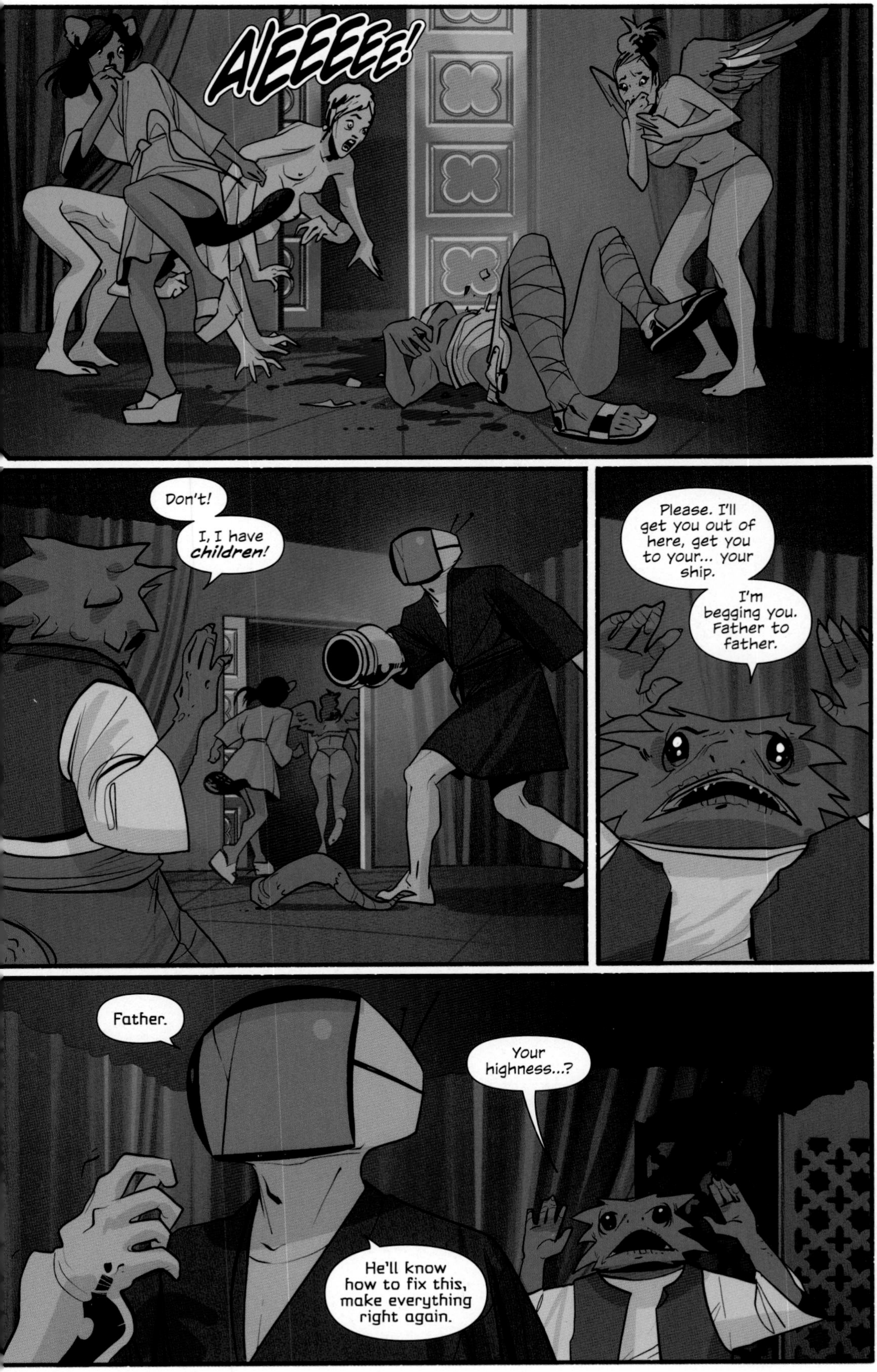
AIEEEEEE!
Don't!
I, I have *children!*
Please. I'll get you out of here, get you to your... your ship.
I'm begging you. Father to father.
Father.
Your highness...?
He'll know how to fix this, make everything right again.

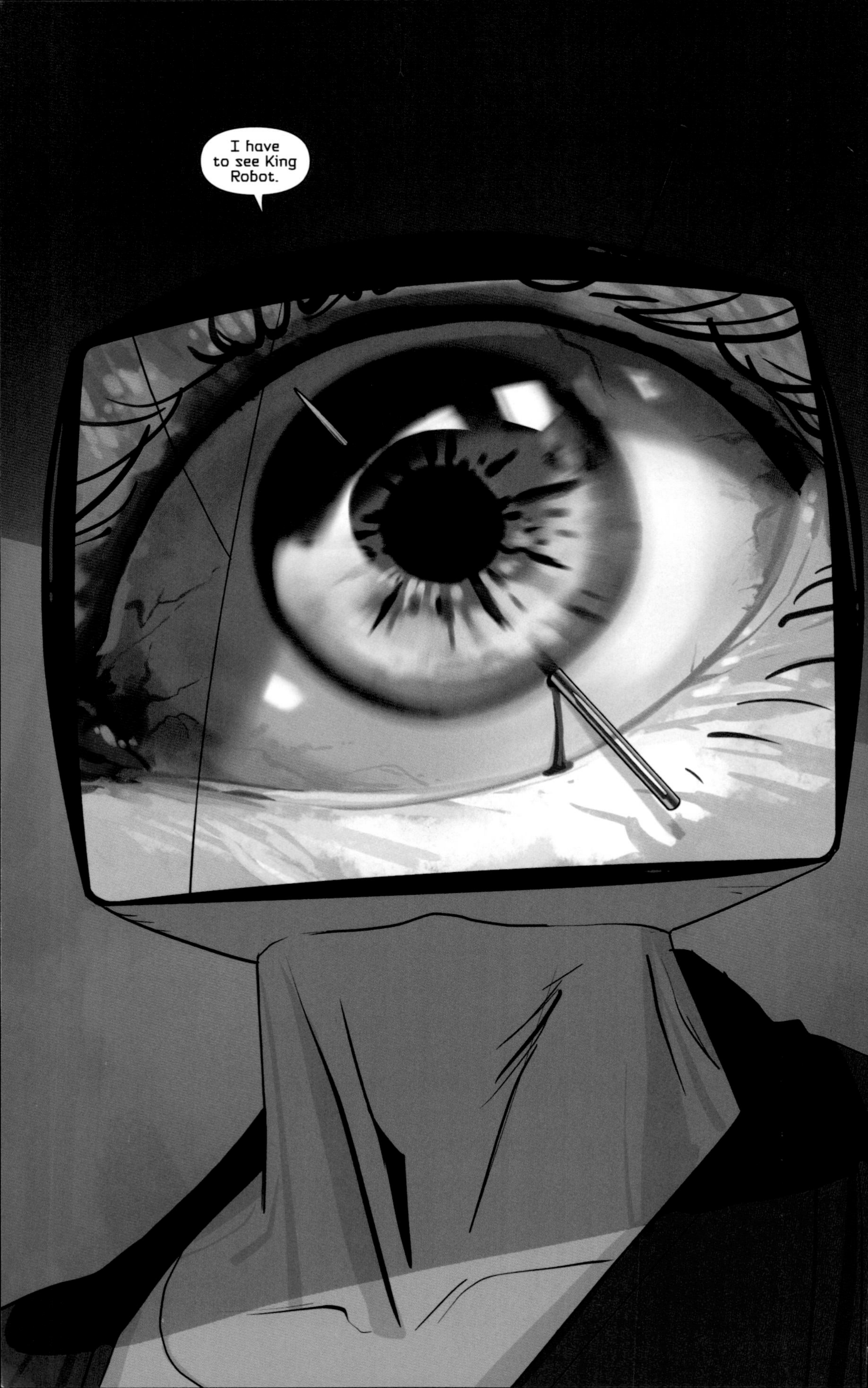
I have to see King Robot.

end chapter twenty-one

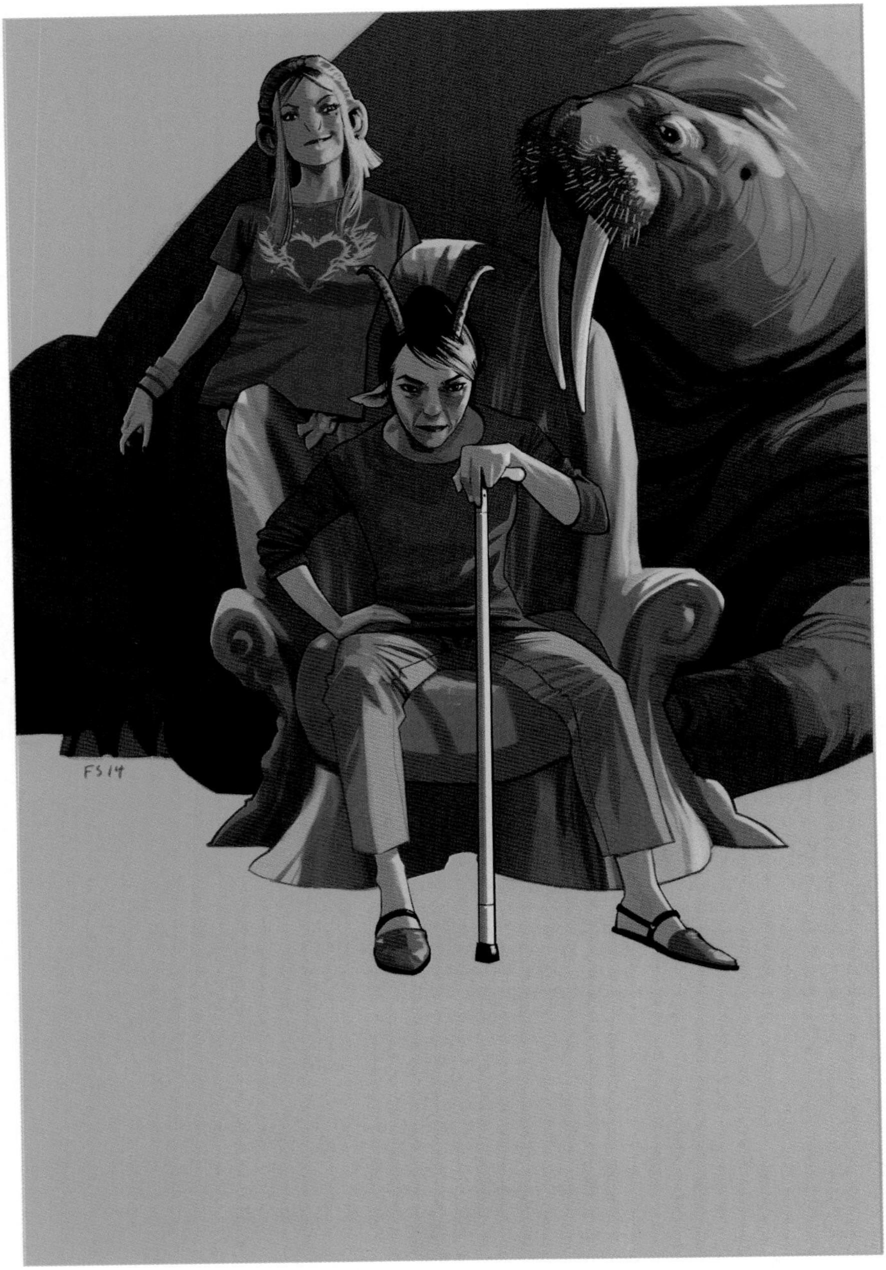
FS14

CHAPTER
TWENTY-TWO

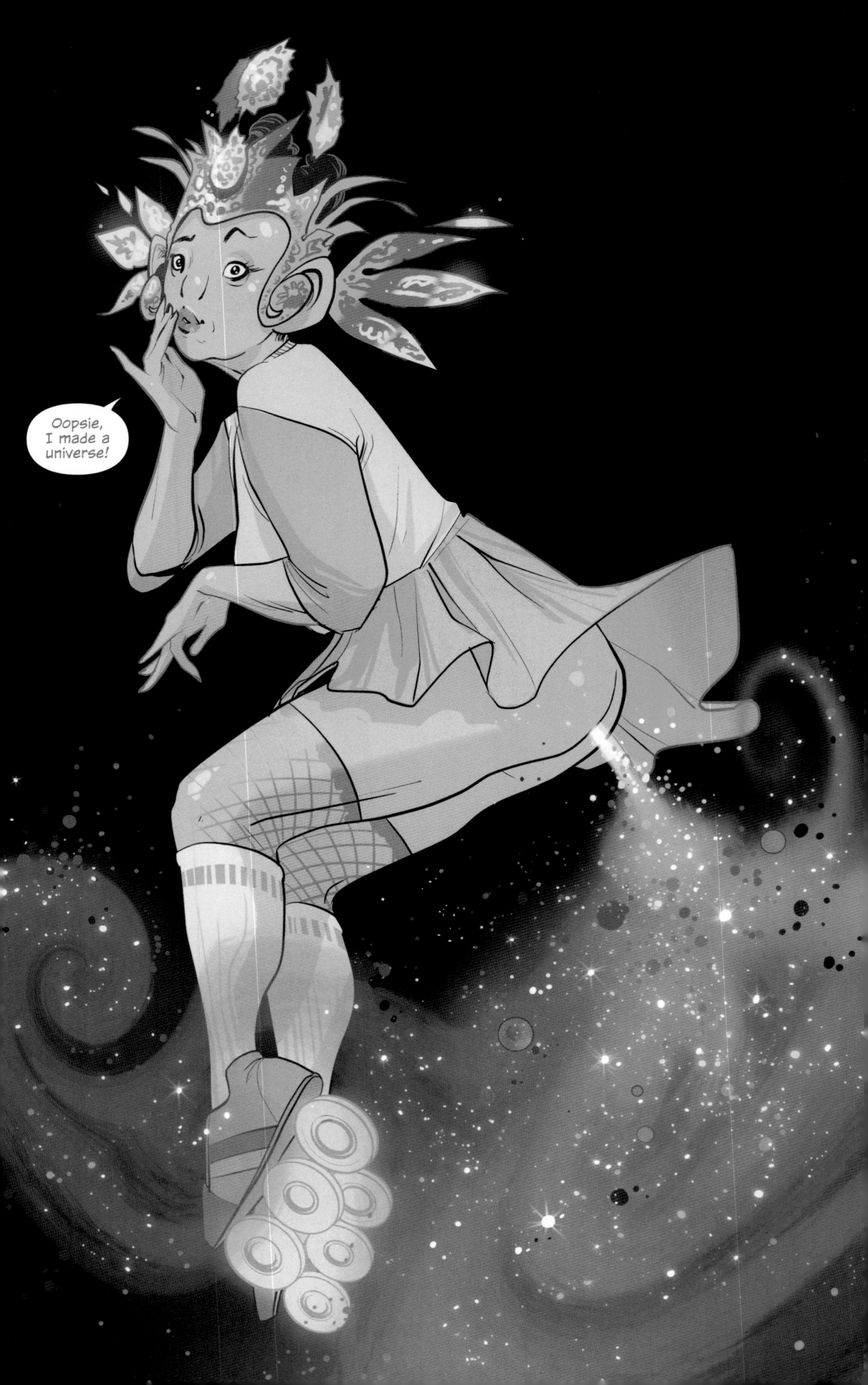
Oopsie, I made a universe!

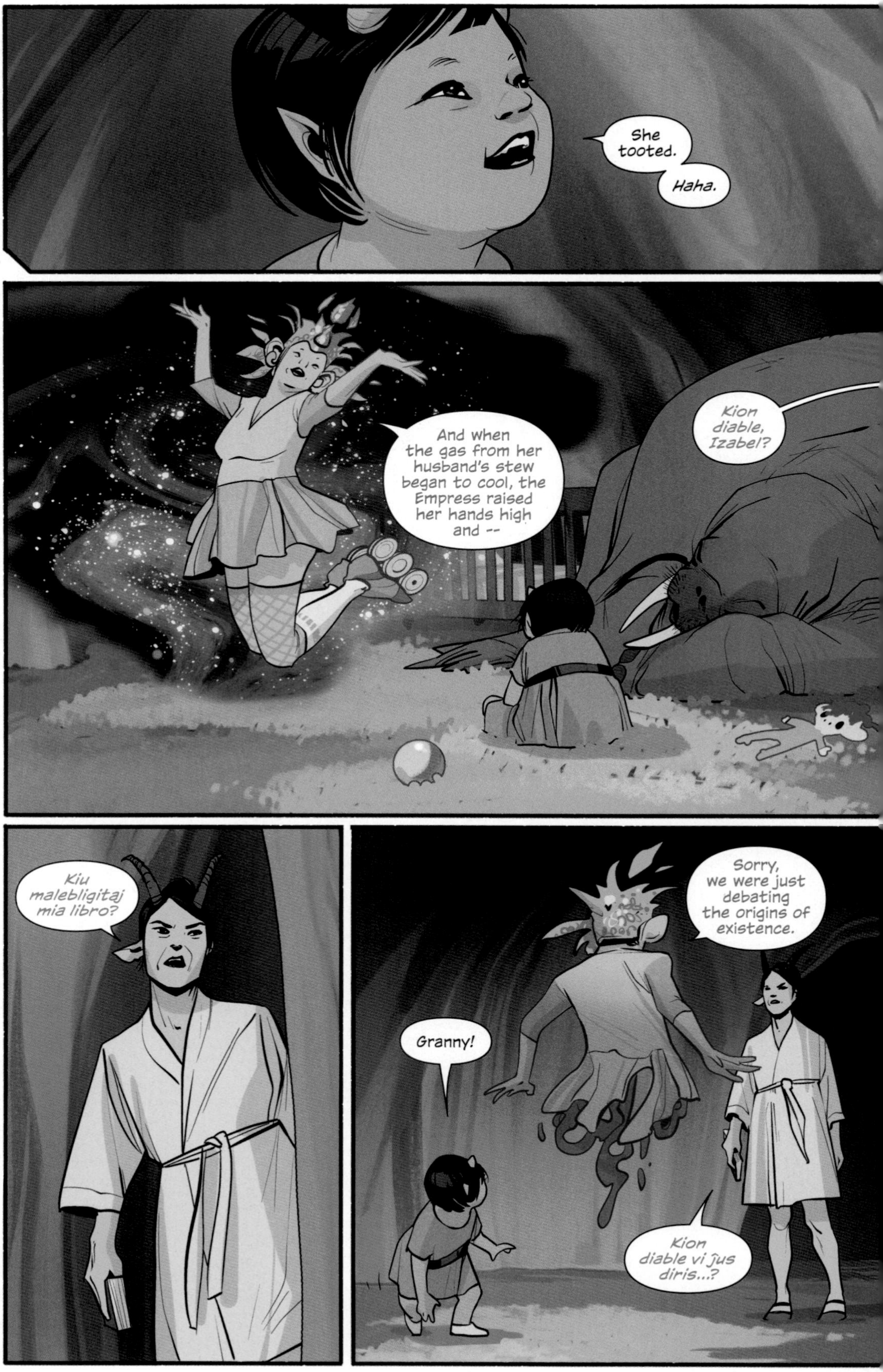

She tooted.
Haha.
And when the gas from her husband's stew began to cool, the Empress raised her hands high and --
Kion diable, Izabel?
Kiu malebligitaj mia libro?
Sorry, we were just debating the origins of existence.
Granny!
Kion diable vi ĵus diris...?

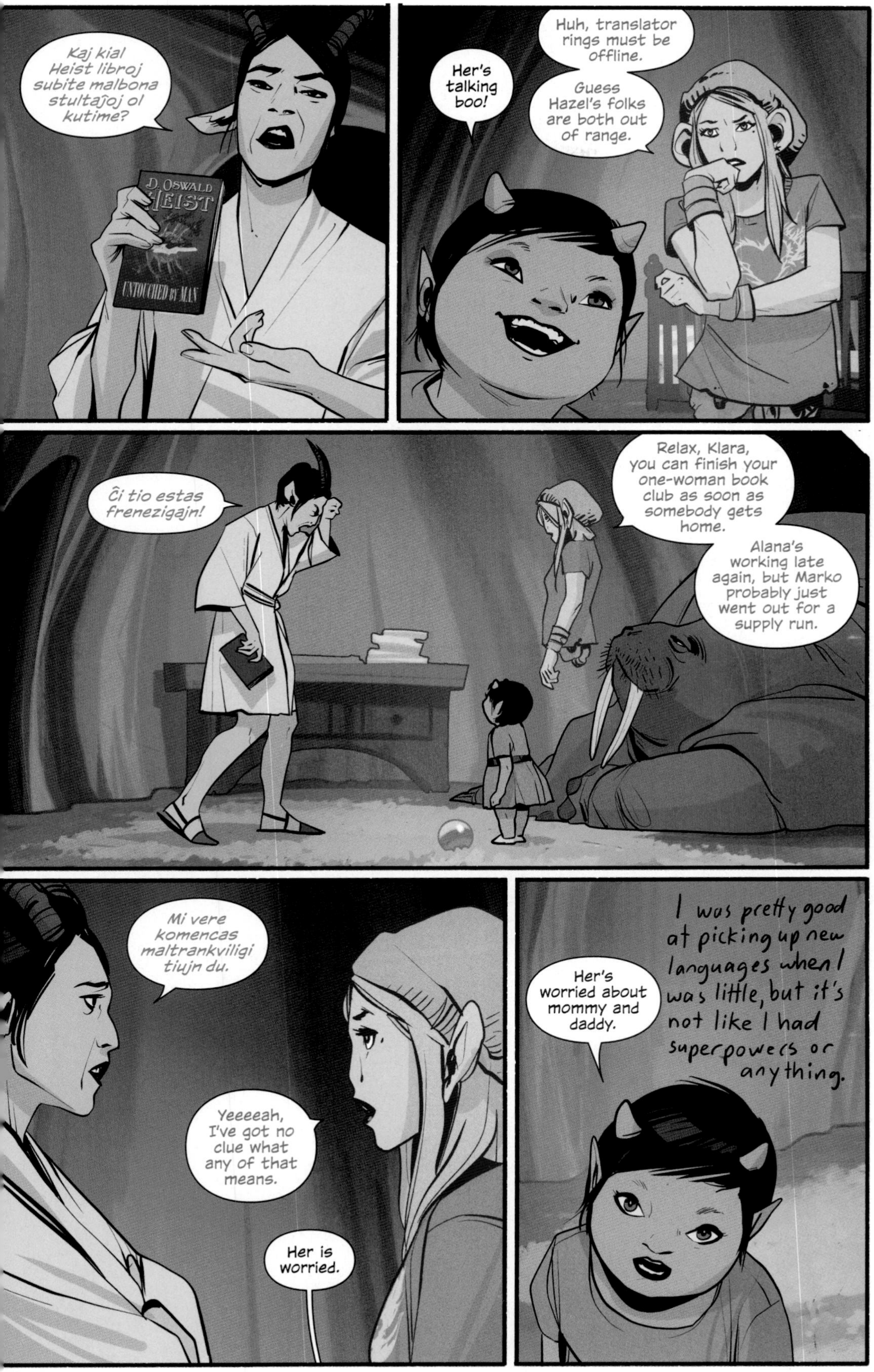
Kaj kial Heist libroj subite malbona stultaĵoj ol kutime?
D. OSWALD HEIST
UNTOUCHED BY MAN
Her's talking boo!
Huh, translator rings must be offline.
Guess Hazel's folks are both out of range.
Ĉi tio estas frenezigajn!
Relax, Klara, you can finish your one-woman book club as soon as somebody gets home.
Alana's working late again, but Marko probably just went out for a supply run.
Mi vere komencas maltrankviligi tiujn du.
Yeeeeah, I've got no clue what any of that means.
Her is worried.
I was pretty good at picking up new languages when I was little, but it's not like I had superpowers or anything.
Her's worried about mommy and daddy.

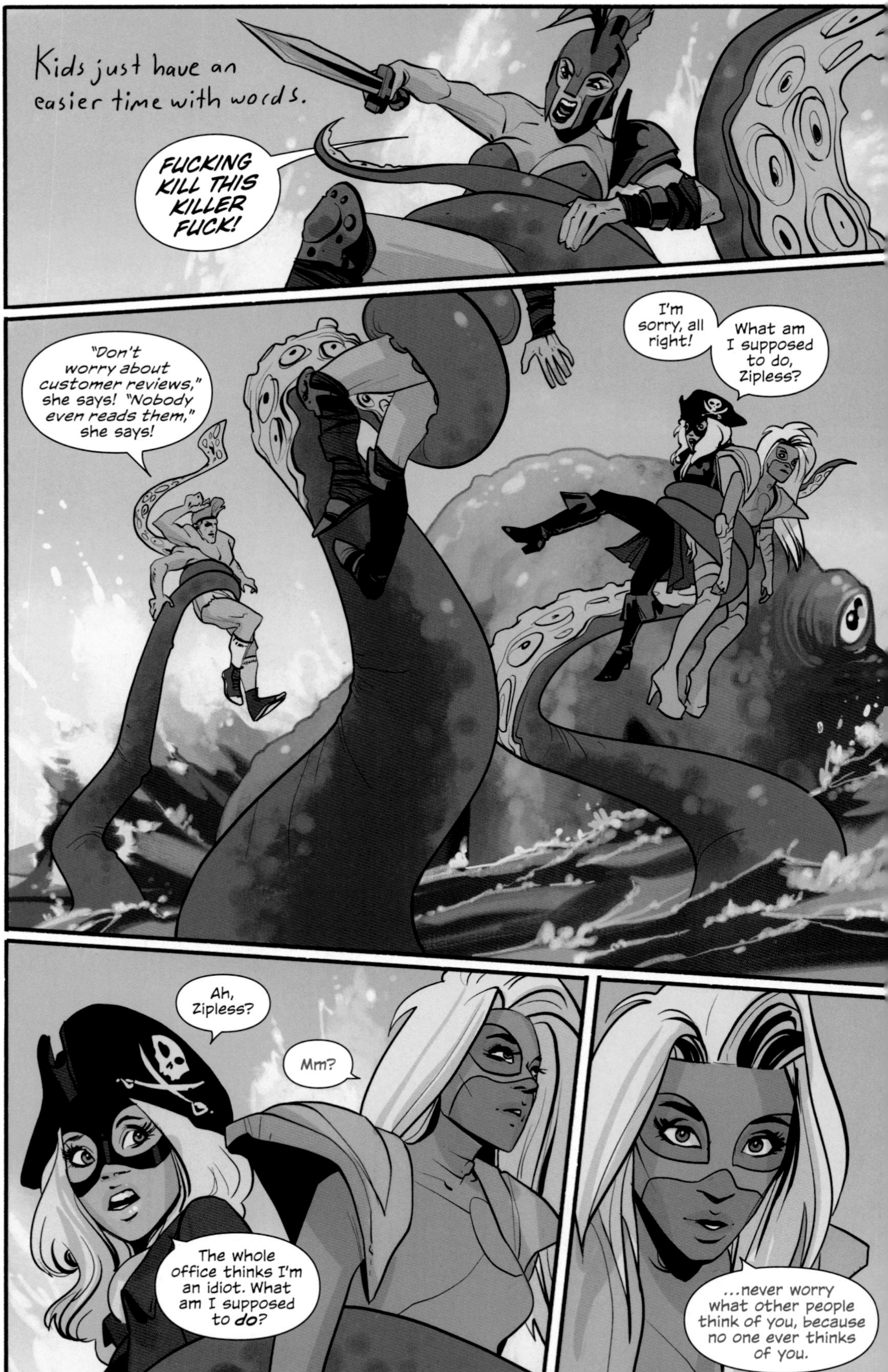

Kids just have an easier time with words.
FUCKING KILL THIS KILLER FUCK!
"Don't worry about customer reviews," she says! "Nobody even reads them," she says!
I'm sorry, all right!
What am I supposed to do, Zipless?
Ah, Zipless?
Mm?
The whole office thinks I'm an idiot. What am I supposed to *do*?
...never worry what other people think of you, because no one ever thinks of you.

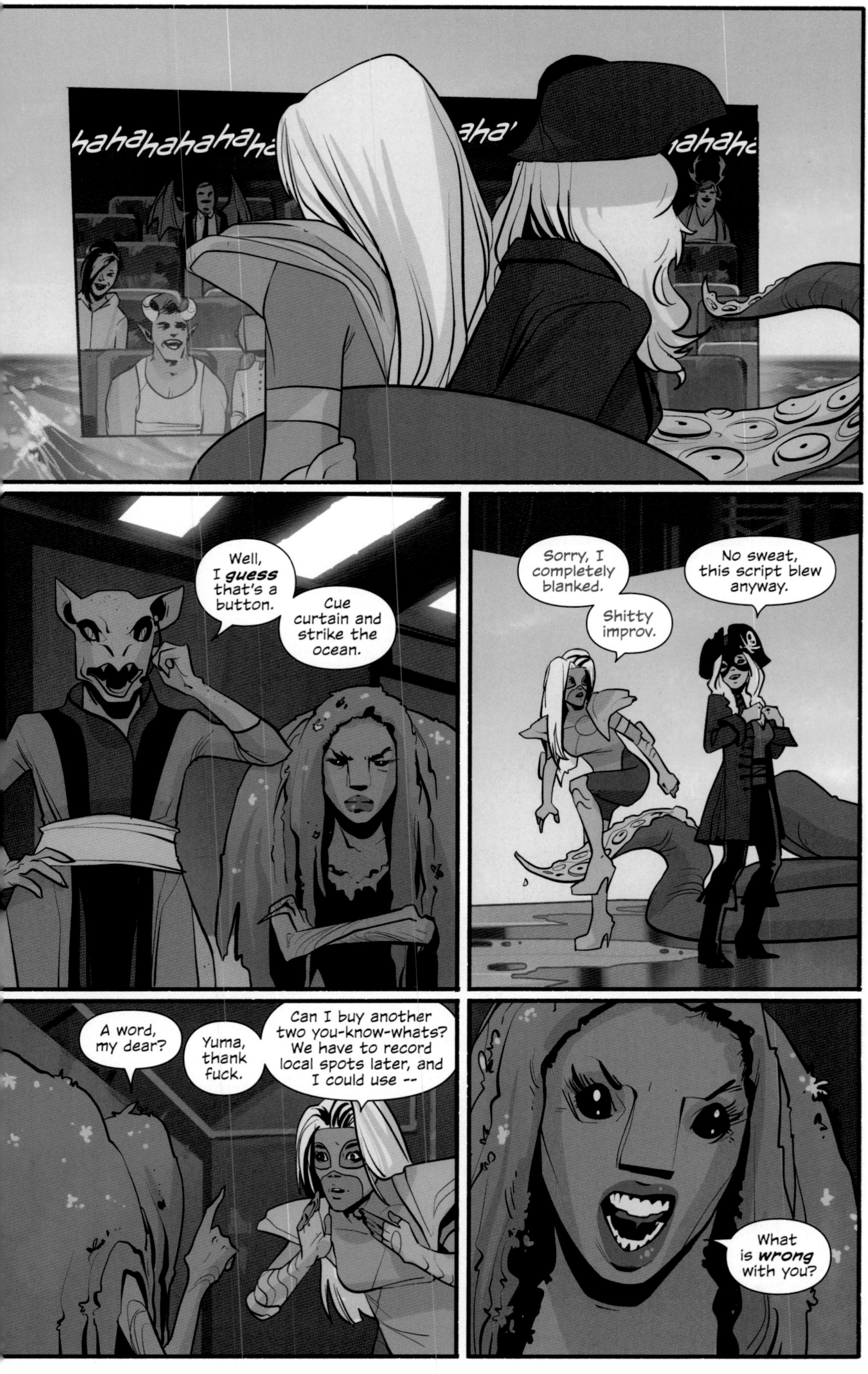
hahahahahaha
aha'
ahaha
Well, I guess that's a button.
Cue curtain and strike the ocean.
Sorry, I completely blanked.
Shitty improv.
No sweat, this script blew anyway.
A word, my dear?
Yuma, thank fuck.
Can I buy another two you-know-whats? We have to record local spots later, and I could use --
What is wrong with you?

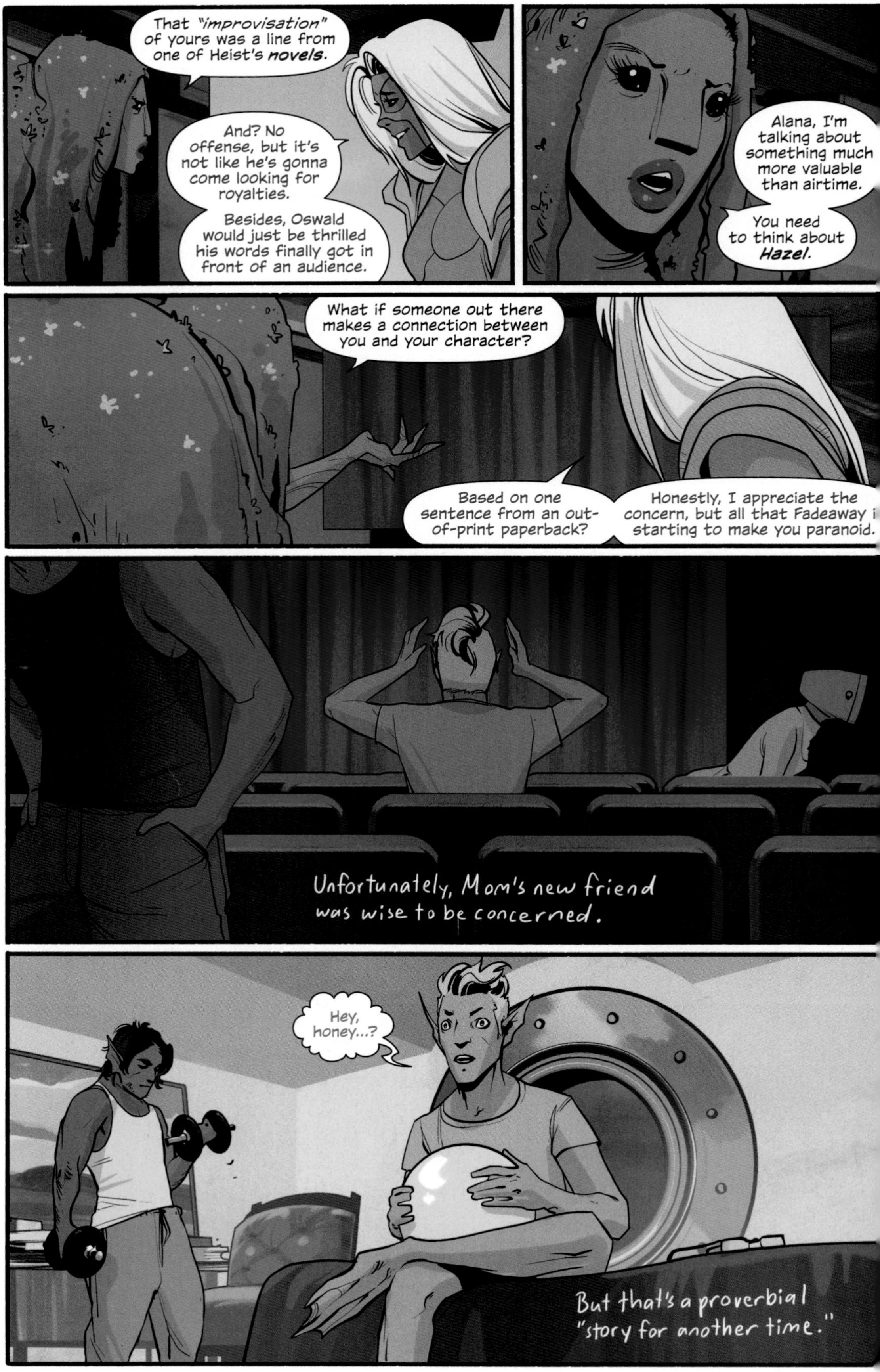

That "*improvisation*" of yours was a line from one of Heist's ***novels***.
And? No offense, but it's not like he's gonna come looking for royalties.
Besides, Oswald would just be thrilled his words finally got in front of an audience.
Alana, I'm talking about something much more valuable than airtime.
You need to think about ***Hazel***.
What if someone out there makes a connection between you and your character?
Based on one sentence from an out-of-print paperback?
Honestly, I appreciate the concern, but all that Fadeaway i starting to make you paranoid.
Unfortunately, Mom's new friend was wise to be concerned.
Hey, honey...?
But that's a proverbial "story for another time."

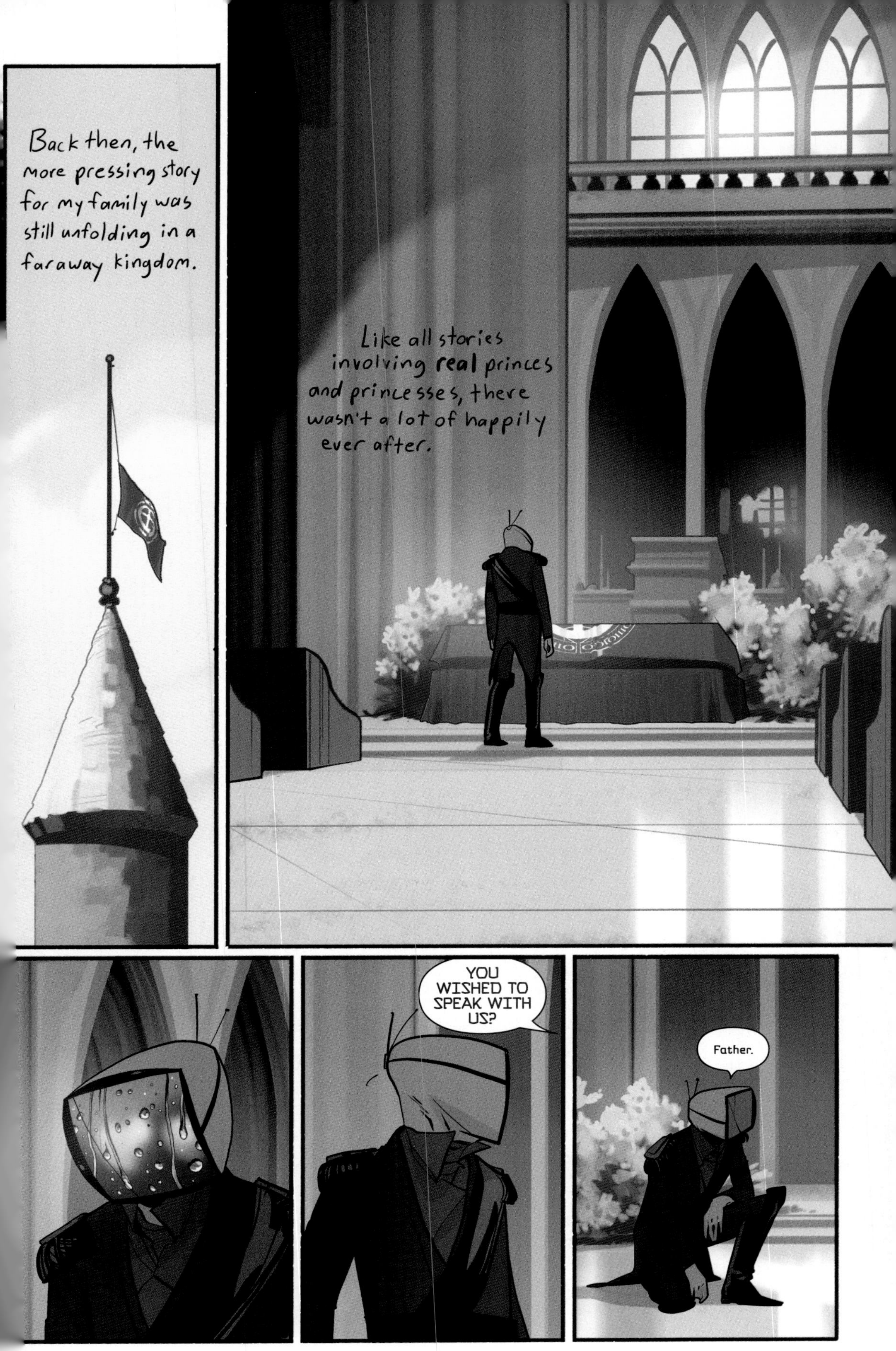
Back then, the more pressing story for my family was still unfolding in a faraway kingdom.
Like all stories involving **real** princes and princesses, there wasn't a lot of happily ever after.
YOU WISHED TO SPEAK WITH US?
Father.

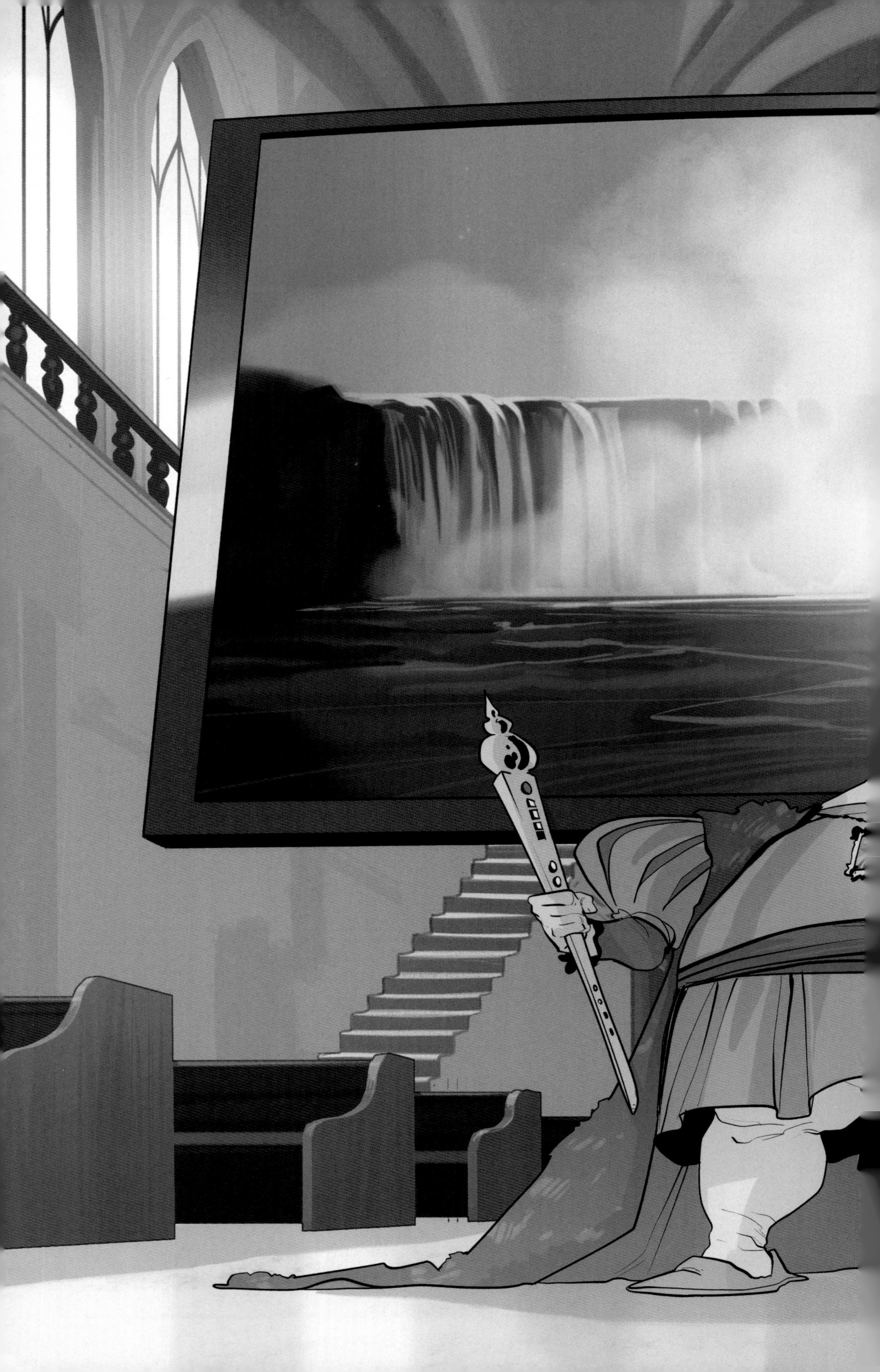

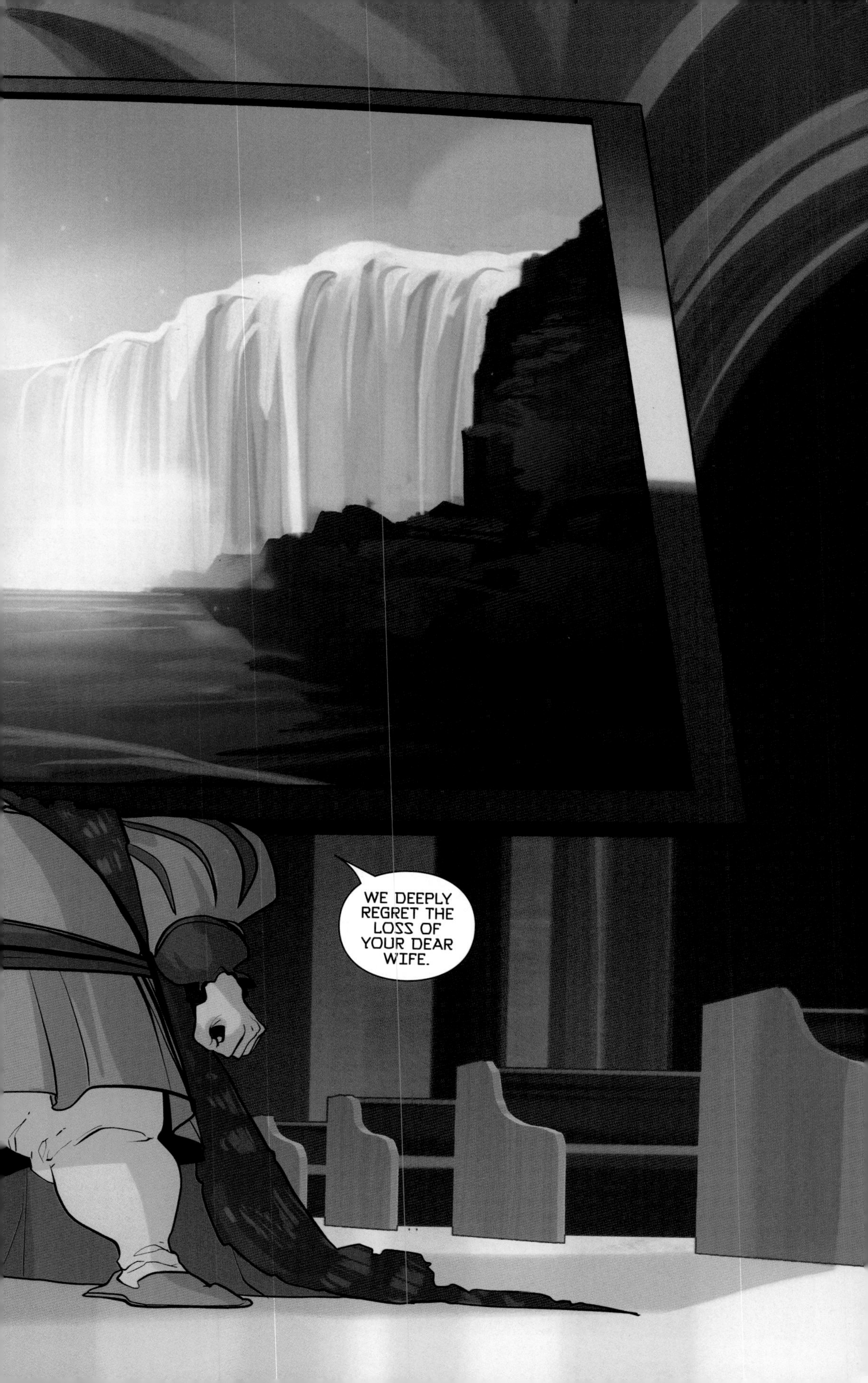
WE DEEPLY REGRET THE LOSS OF YOUR DEAR WIFE.

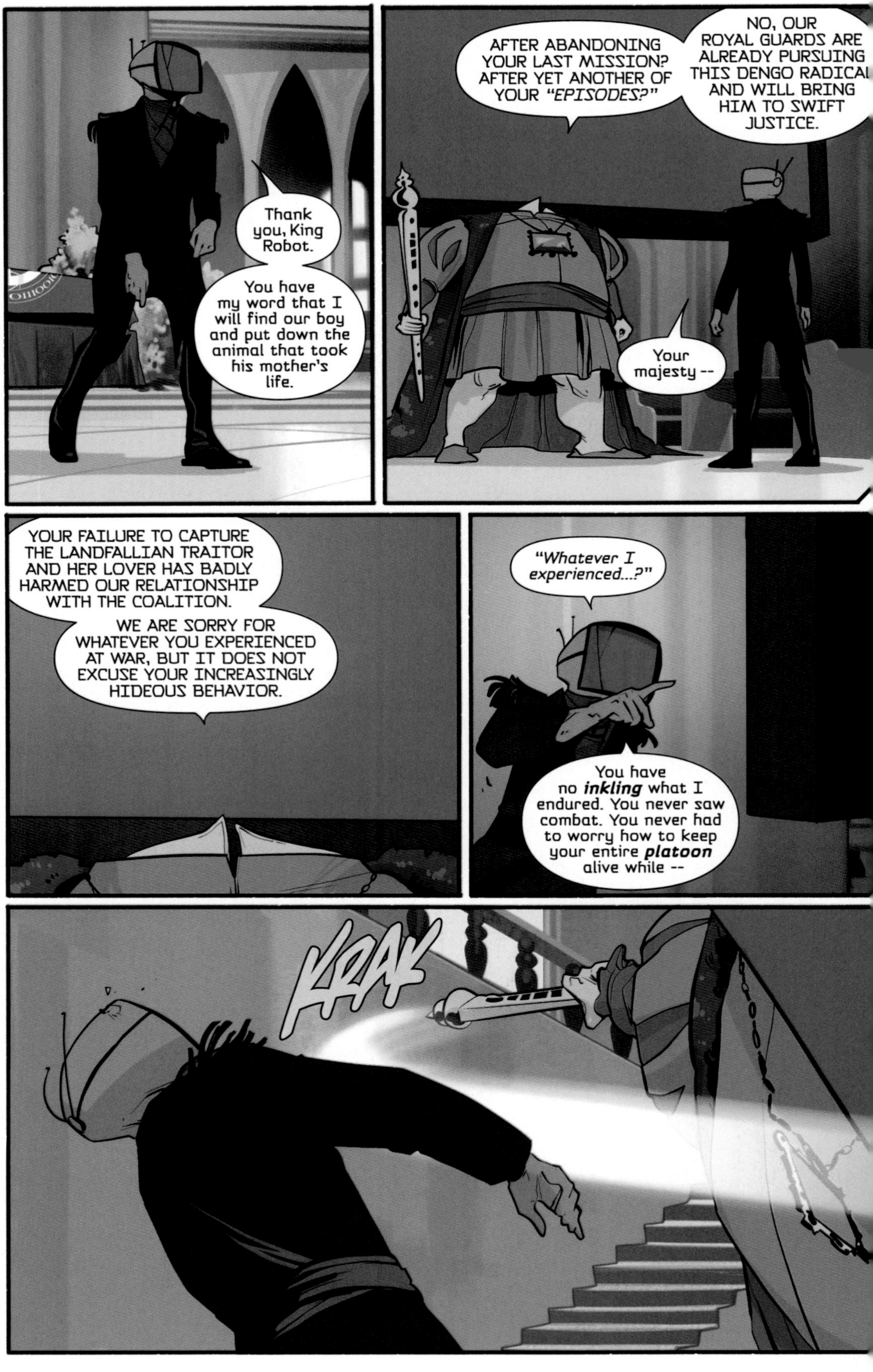
Thank you, King Robot.
You have my word that I will find our boy and put down the animal that took his mother's life.
AFTER ABANDONING YOUR LAST MISSION? AFTER YET ANOTHER OF YOUR "EPISODES?"
NO, OUR ROYAL GUARDS ARE ALREADY PURSUING THIS DENGO RADICAL AND WILL BRING HIM TO SWIFT JUSTICE.
Your majesty --
YOUR FAILURE TO CAPTURE THE LANDFALLIAN TRAITOR AND HER LOVER HAS BADLY HARMED OUR RELATIONSHIP WITH THE COALITION.
WE ARE SORRY FOR WHATEVER YOU EXPERIENCED AT WAR, BUT IT DOES NOT EXCUSE YOUR INCREASINGLY HIDEOUS BEHAVIOR.
"Whatever I experienced...?"
You have no inkling what I endured. You never saw combat. You never had to worry how to keep your entire platoon alive while --
KRAK

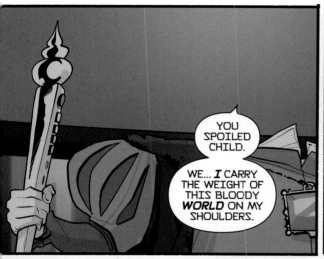

YOU SPOILED CHILD.

WE... *I* CARRY THE WEIGHT OF THIS BLOODY *WORLD* ON MY SHOULDERS.

YOU WERE A GOOD BOY ONCE.

WE WILL NEVER KNOW WHERE WE WENT WRONG.

YOU WILL CONVALESCE IN YOUR QUARTERS UNTIL THE PRINCESS IS TO BE ENTOMBED ALONGSIDE YOUR BROTHER.

You're... burying her next to *Duke?*

THE HIGHEST HONOR WE CAN GIVE YOUR LATE WIFE IS LAYING HER TO REST BY A TRUE CHAMPION OF THIS REALM.

Father, I'm begging you --

RETURN TO THRONE ROOM.

ba*beep*

GET BETTER, IV.

IF ONLY FOR YOUR *BOY*.

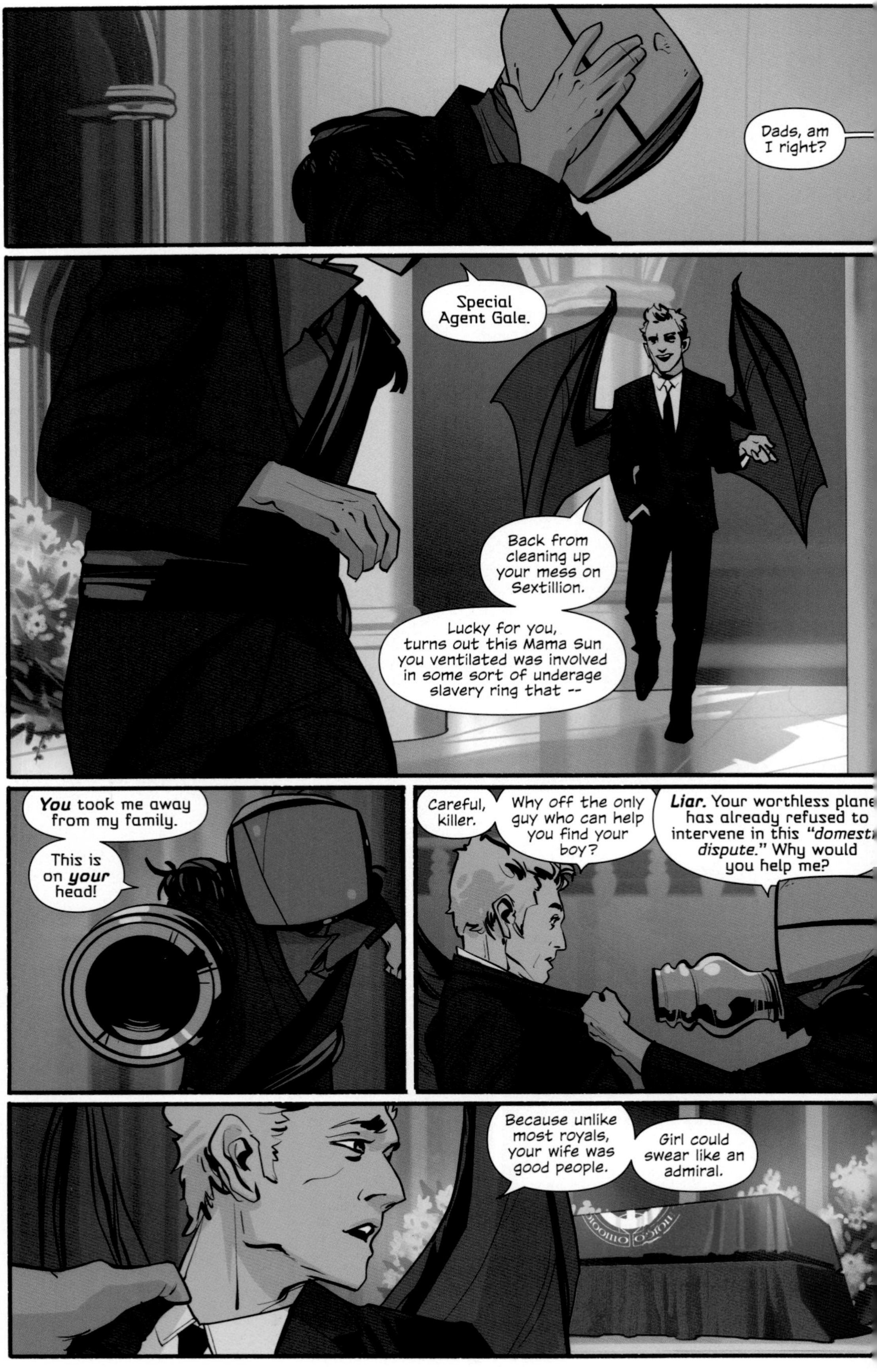

Dads, am I right?
Special Agent Gale.
Back from cleaning up your mess on Sextillion.
Lucky for you, turns out this Mama Sun you ventilated was involved in some sort of underage slavery ring that --
You took me away from my family.
This is on *your* head!
Careful, killer.
Why off the only guy who can help you find your boy?
Liar. Your worthless plane has already refused to intervene in this "*domesti dispute.*" Why would you help me?
Because unlike most royals, your wife was good people.
Girl could swear like an admiral.

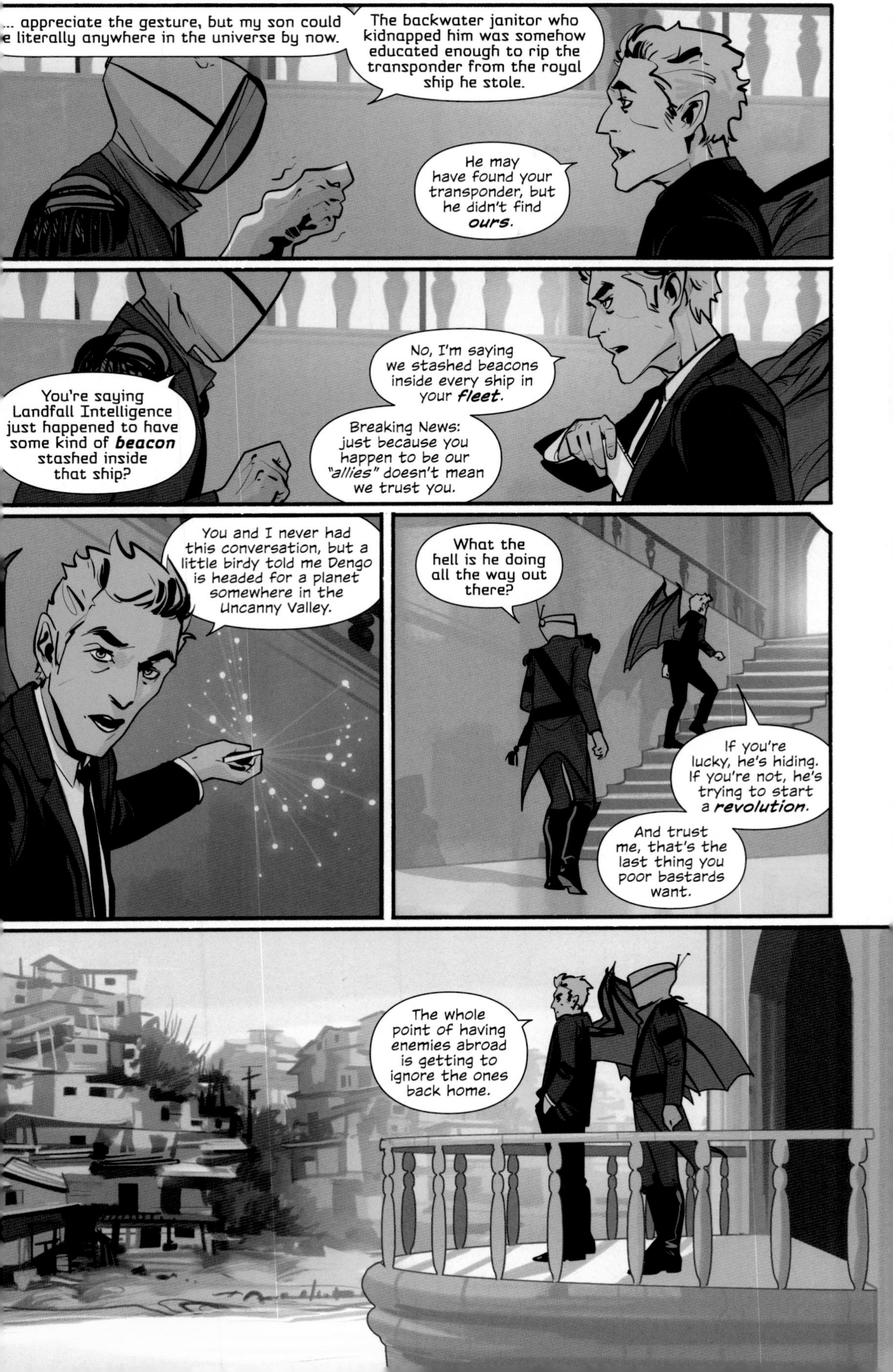
... appreciate the gesture, but my son could
e literally anywhere in the universe by now.
The backwater janitor who kidnapped him was somehow educated enough to rip the transponder from the royal ship he stole.
He may have found your transponder, but he didn't find ***ours***.
You're saying Landfall Intelligence just happened to have some kind of ***beacon*** stashed inside that ship?
No, I'm saying we stashed beacons inside every ship in your ***fleet***.
Breaking News: just because you happen to be our *"allies"* doesn't mean we trust you.
You and I never had this conversation, but a little birdy told me Dengo is headed for a planet somewhere in the Uncanny Valley.
What the hell is he doing all the way out there?
If you're lucky, he's hiding. If you're not, he's trying to start a ***revolution***.
And trust me, that's the last thing you poor bastards want.
The whole point of having enemies abroad is getting to ignore the ones back home.

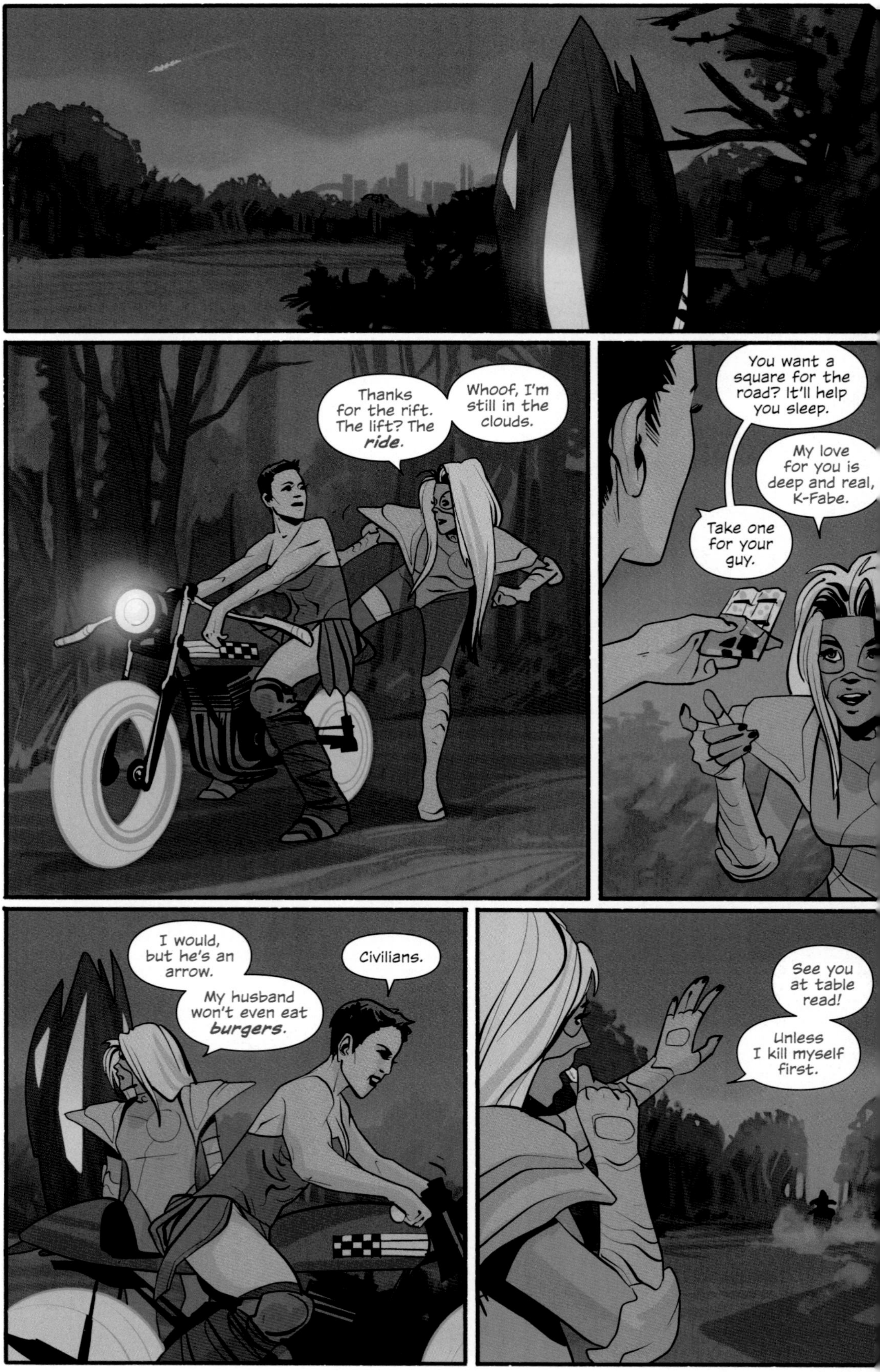

Thanks for the rift. The lift? The *ride*.
Whoof, I'm still in the clouds.
You want a square for the road? It'll help you sleep.
Take one for your guy.
My love for you is deep and real, K-Fabe.
I would, but he's an arrow.
My husband won't even eat *burgers*.
Civilians.
See you at table read!
Unless I kill myself first.

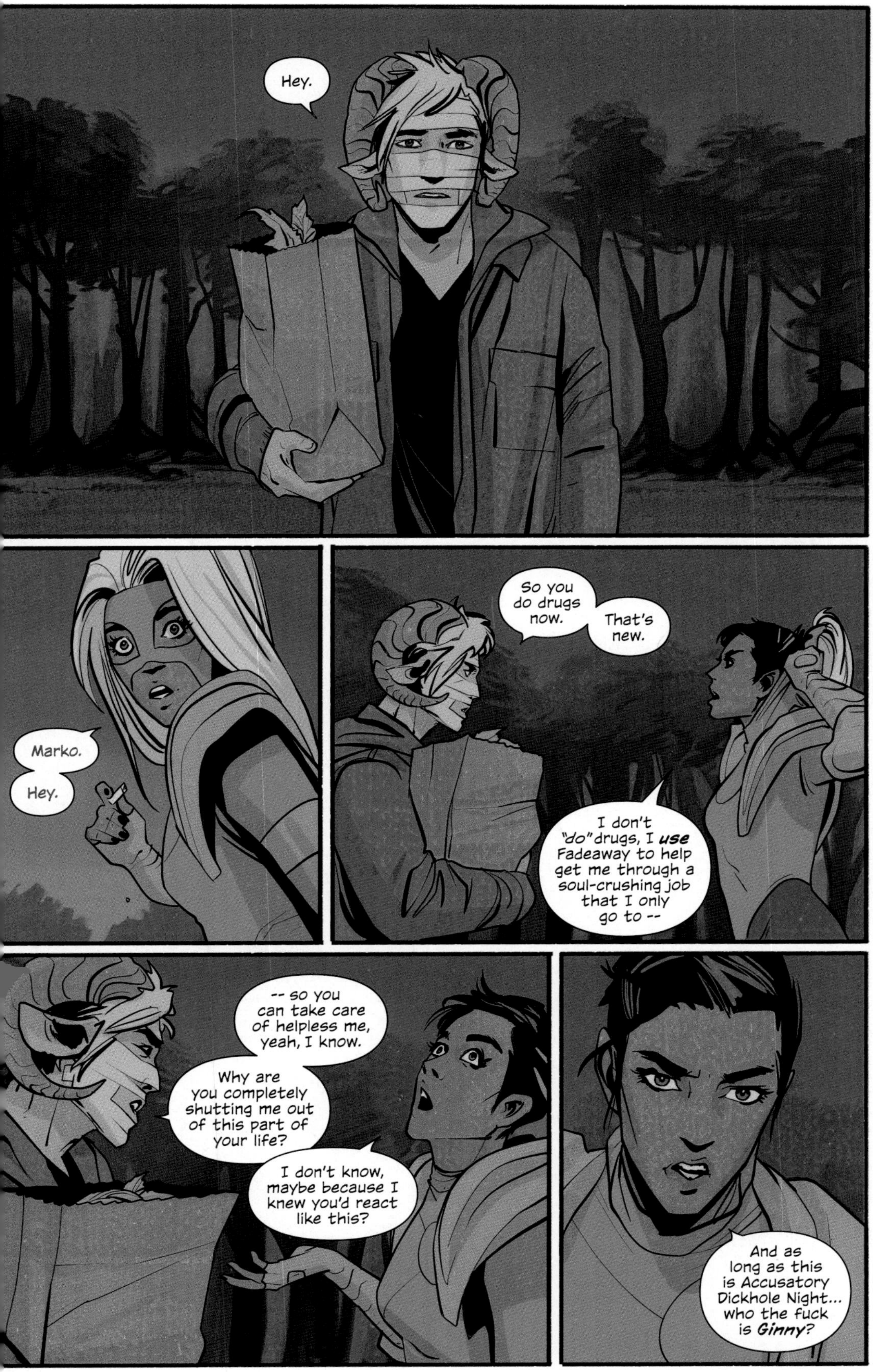
Hey.
Marko.
Hey.
So you do drugs now.
That's new.
I don't "do" drugs, I *use* Fadeaway to help get me through a soul-crushing job that I only go to --
-- so you can take care of helpless me, yeah, I know.
Why are you completely shutting me out of this part of your life?
I don't know, maybe because I knew you'd react like this?
And as long as this is Accusatory Dickhole Night... who the fuck is *Ginny*?

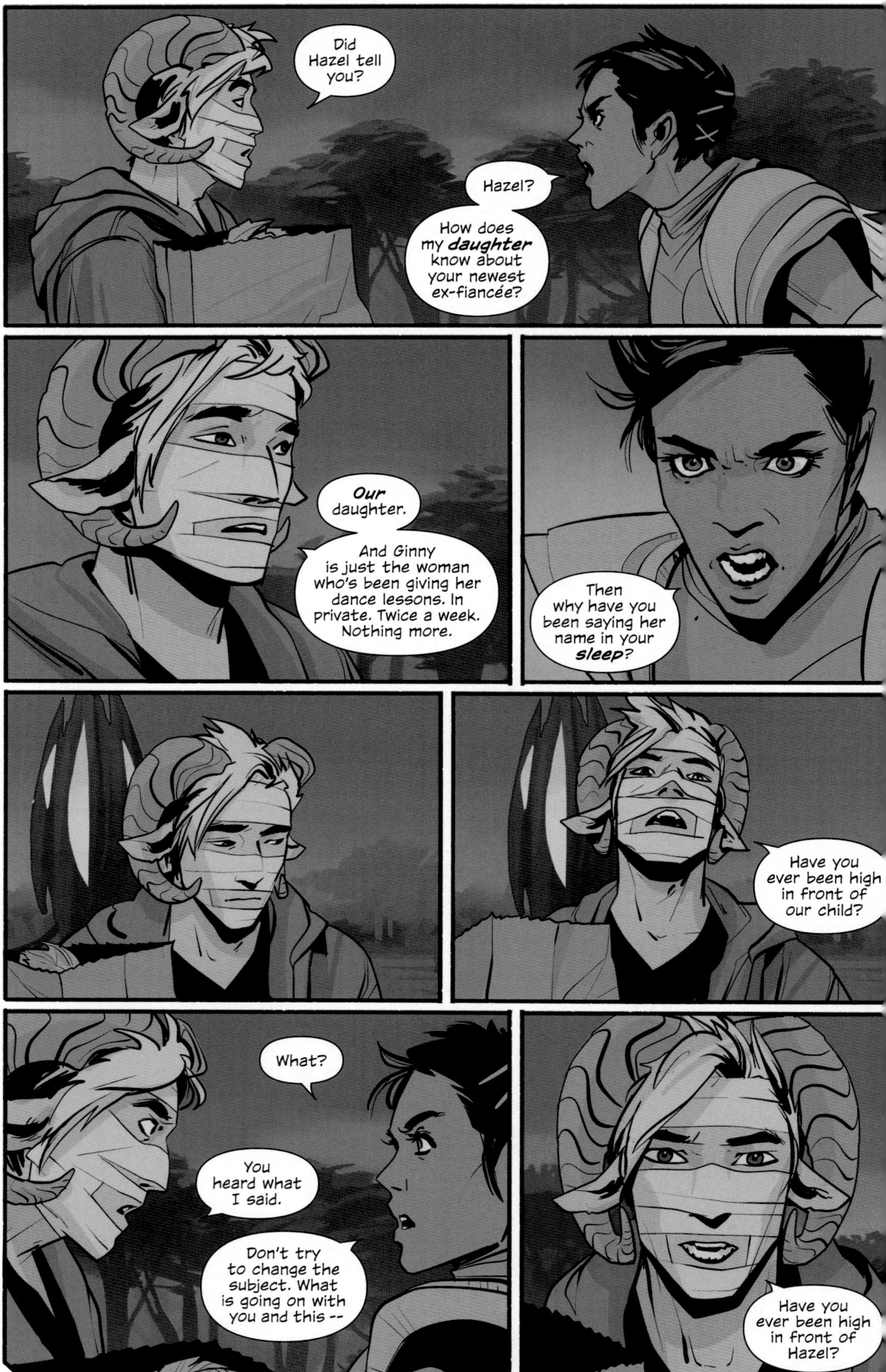
Did Hazel tell you?
Hazel?
How does my **daughter** know about your newest ex-fiancée?
Our daughter.
And Ginny is just the woman who's been giving her dance lessons. In private. Twice a week. Nothing more.
Then why have you been saying her name in your ***sleep***?
Have you ever been high in front of our child?
What?
You heard what I said.
Don't try to change the subject. What is going on with you and this --
Have you ever been high in front of Hazel?

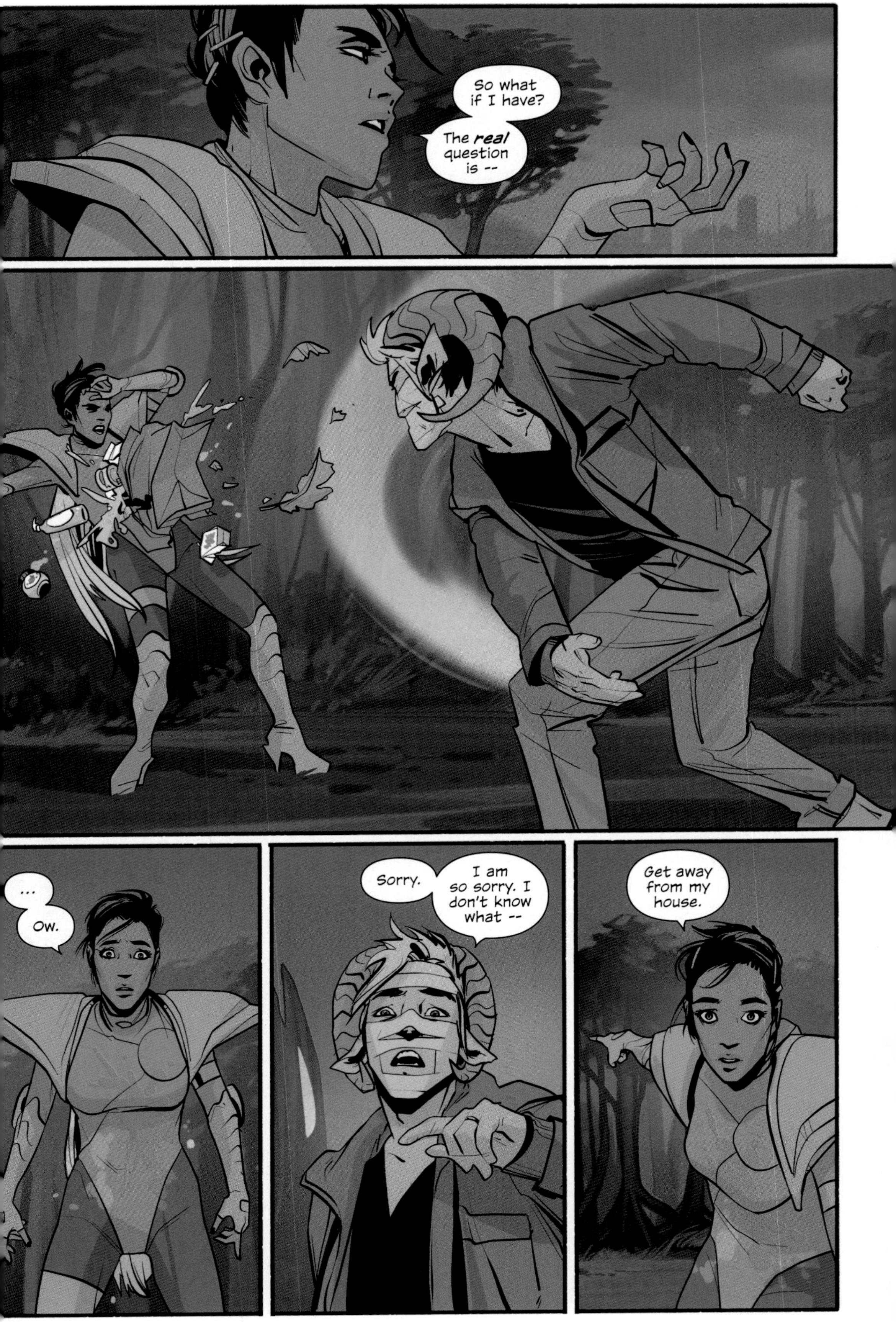
So what if I have?
The *real* question is --
...
Ow.
Sorry.
I am so sorry. I don't know what --
Get away from my house.

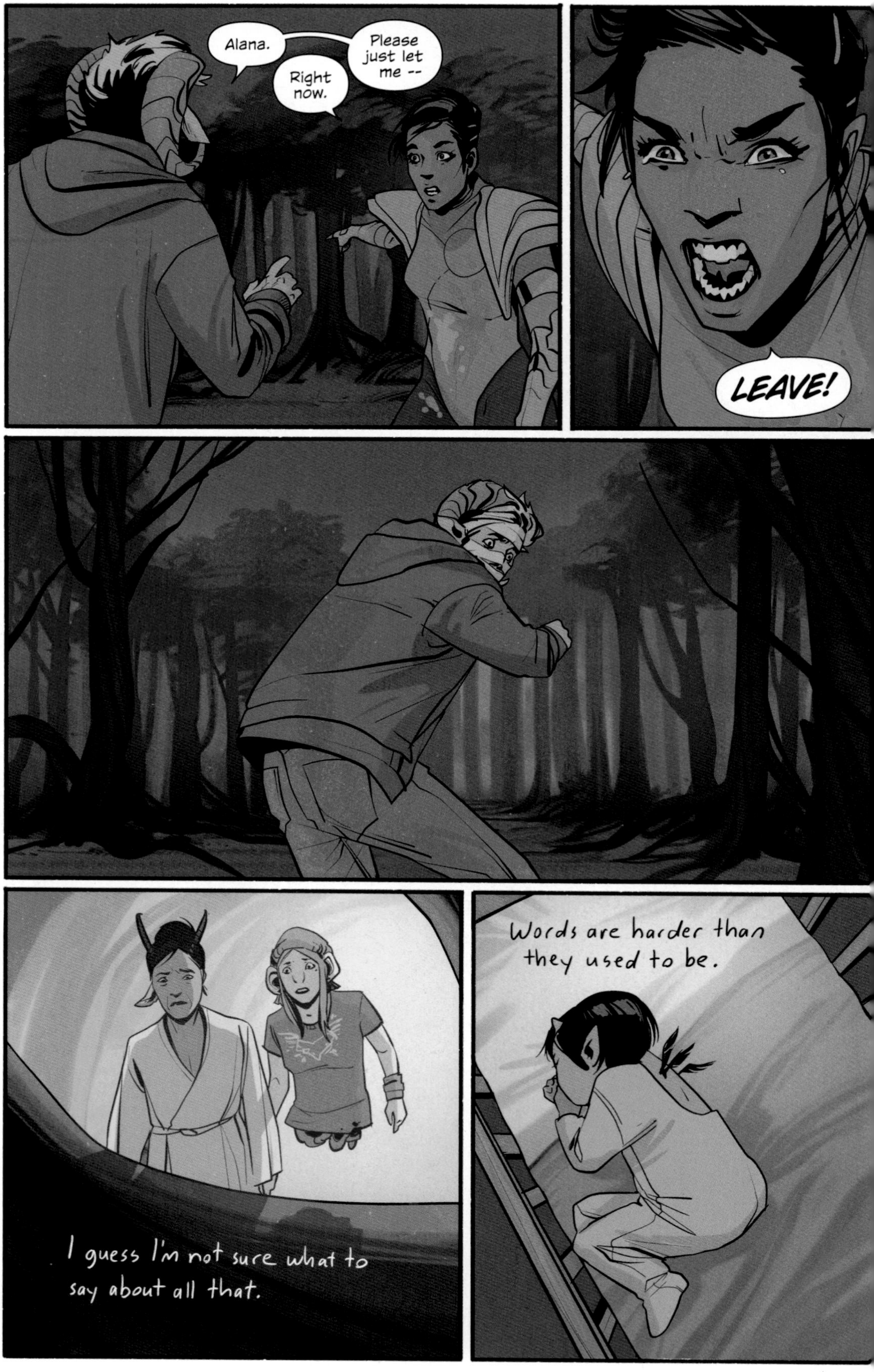
Alana.
Right now.
Please just let me --
LEAVE!
I guess I'm not sure what to say about all that.
Words are harder than they used to be.

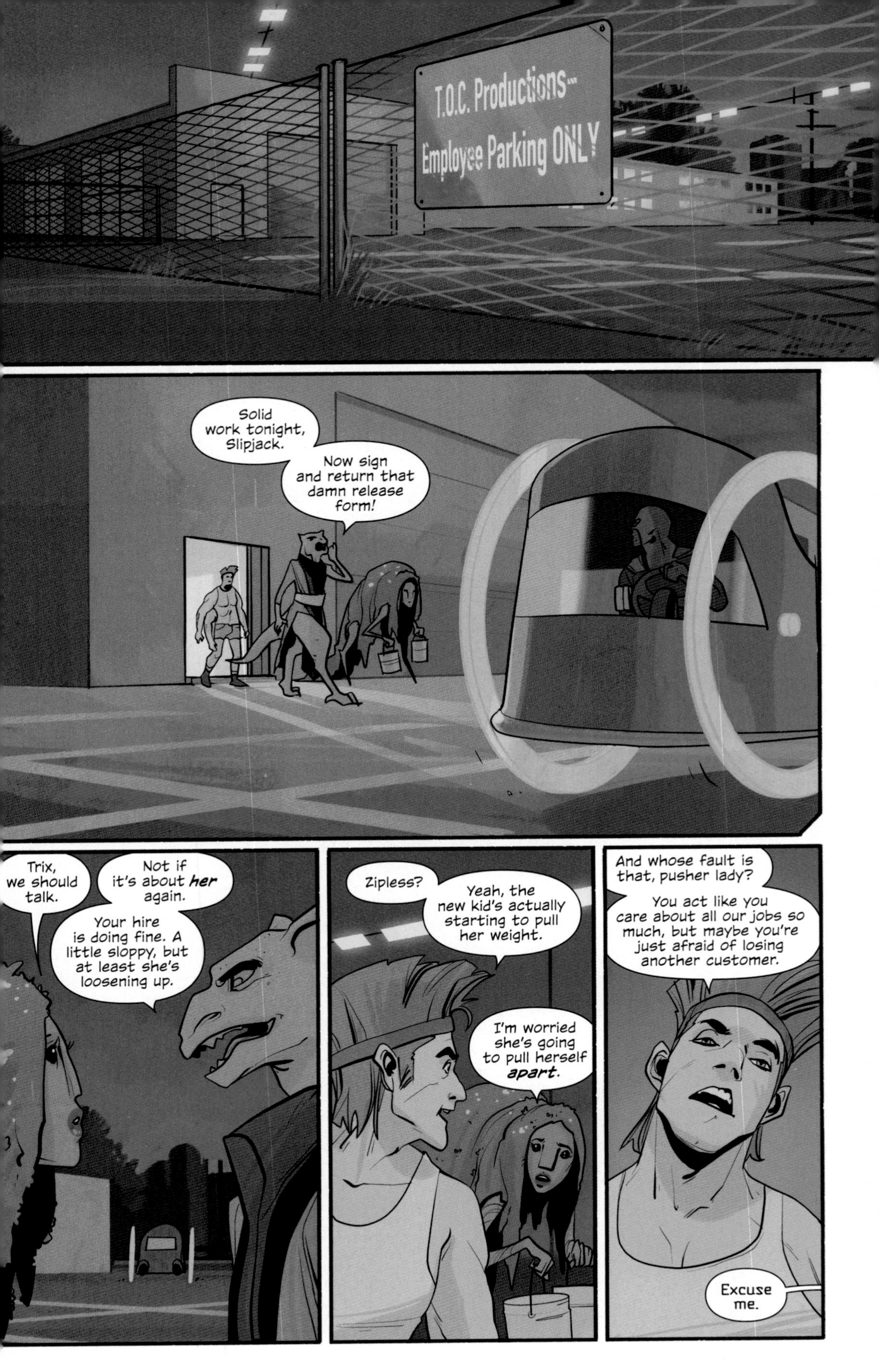
T.O.C. Productions—
Employee Parking ONLY
Solid work tonight, Slipjack.
Now sign and return that damn release form!
Trix, we should talk.
Not if it's about *her* again.
Your hire is doing fine. A little sloppy, but at least she's loosening up.
Zipless?
Yeah, the new kid's actually starting to pull her weight.
I'm worried she's going to pull herself ***apart***.
And whose fault is that, pusher lady?
You act like you care about all our jobs so much, but maybe you're just afraid of losing another customer.
Excuse me.

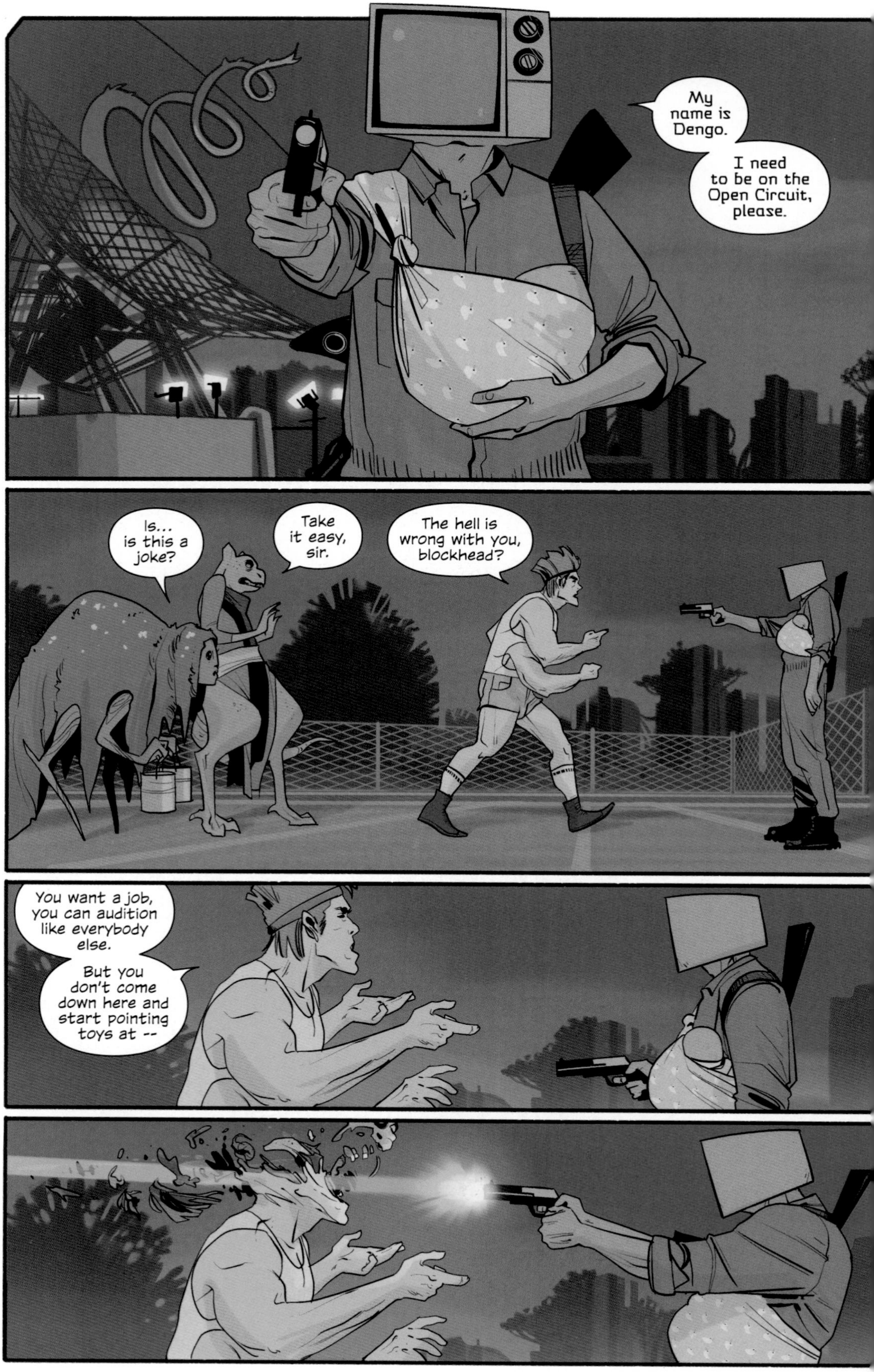
My name is Dengo.
I need to be on the Open Circuit, please.
Is... is this a joke?
Take it easy, sir.
The hell is wrong with you, blockhead?
You want a job, you can audition like everybody else.
But you don't come down here and start pointing toys at --

FUCK!

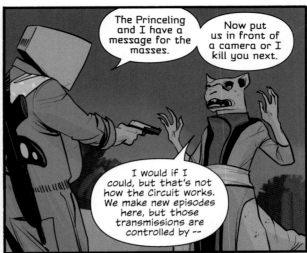

The Princeling and I have a message for the masses.

Now put us in front of a camera or I kill you next.

I would if I could, but that's not how the Circuit works. We make new episodes here, but those transmissions are controlled by --

God, please!

You, help me broadcast my speech to all stations right now or --

I can't! Nobody here can!

But if... if you let me *live*...

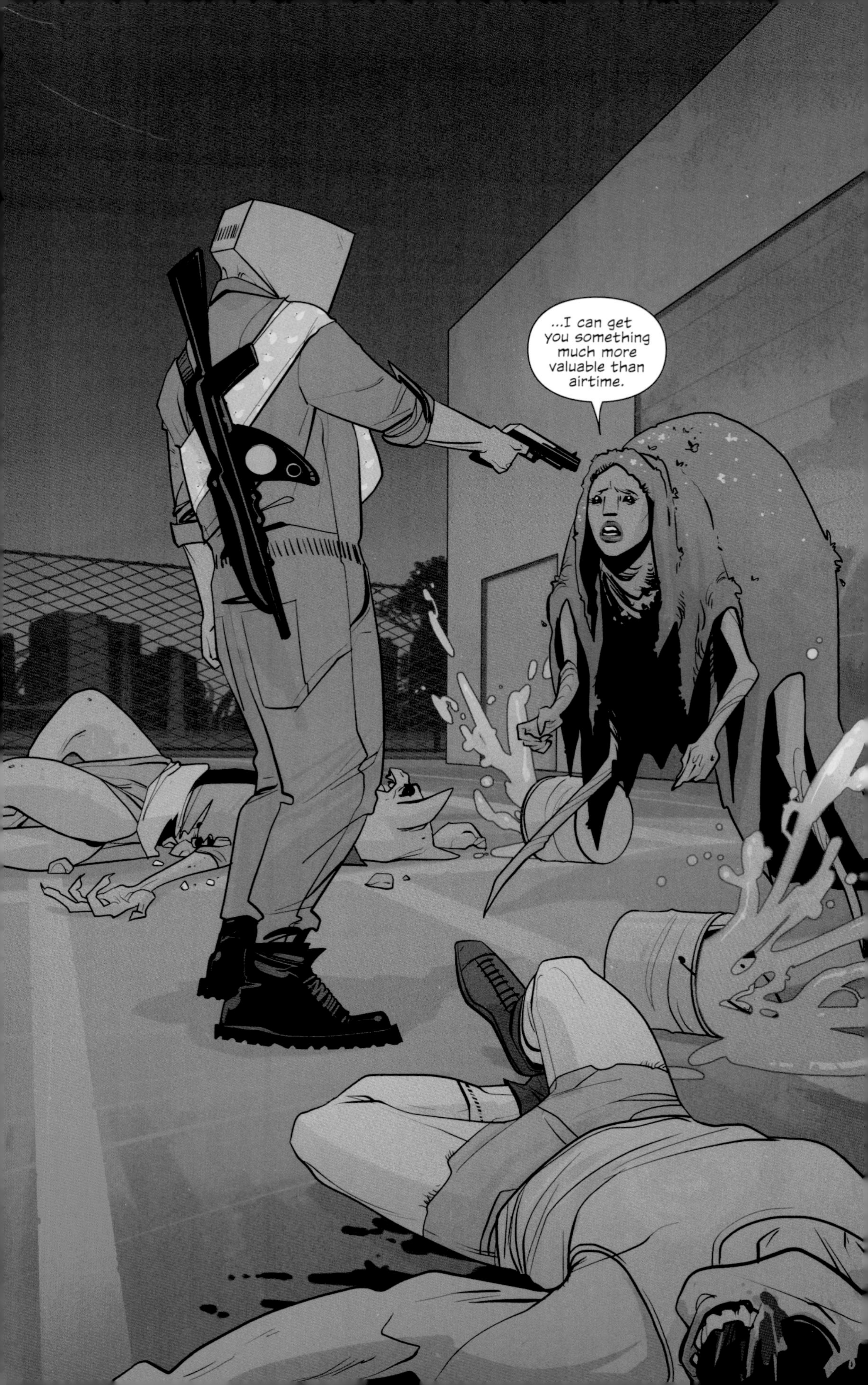
...I can get you something much more valuable than airtime.

end chapter twenty-two

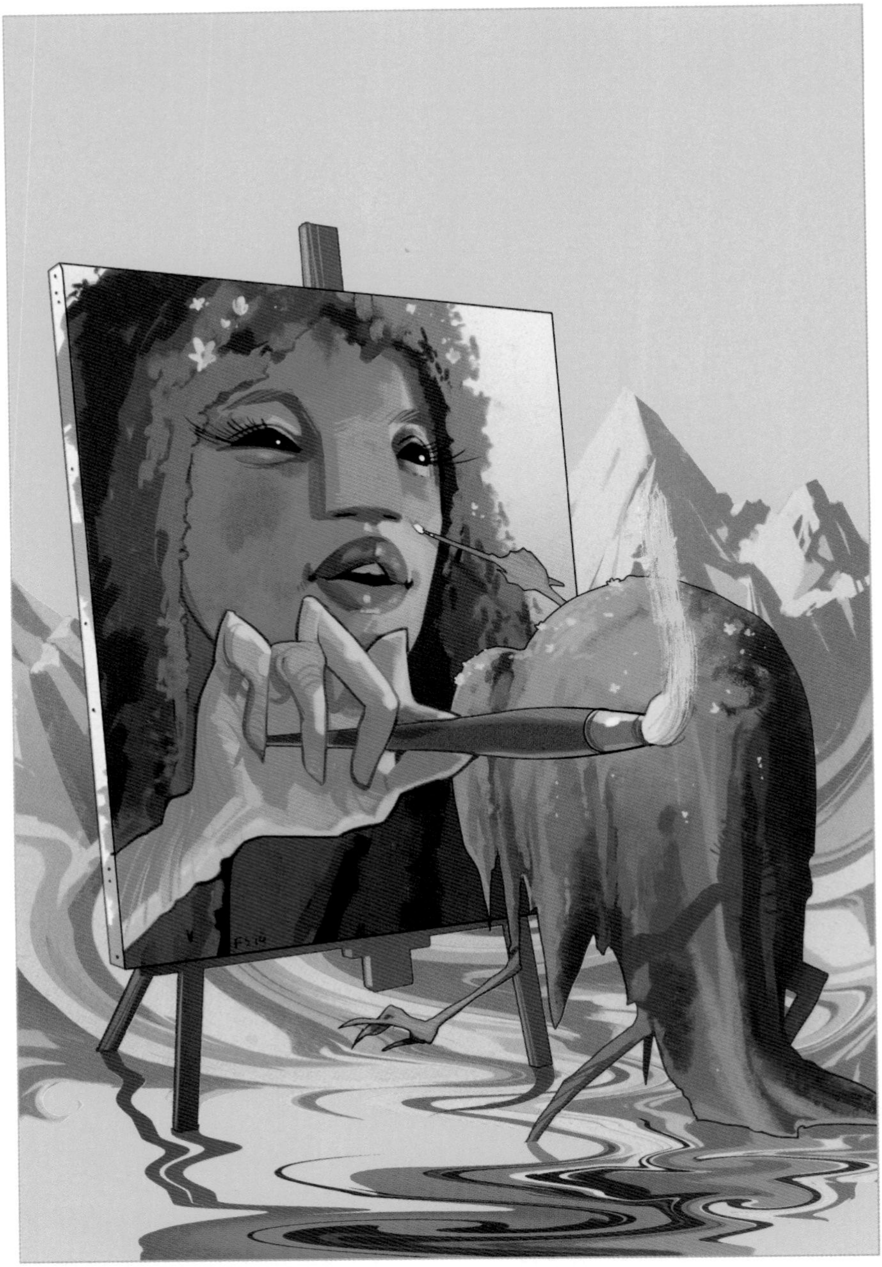

CHAPTER

TWENTY-THREE

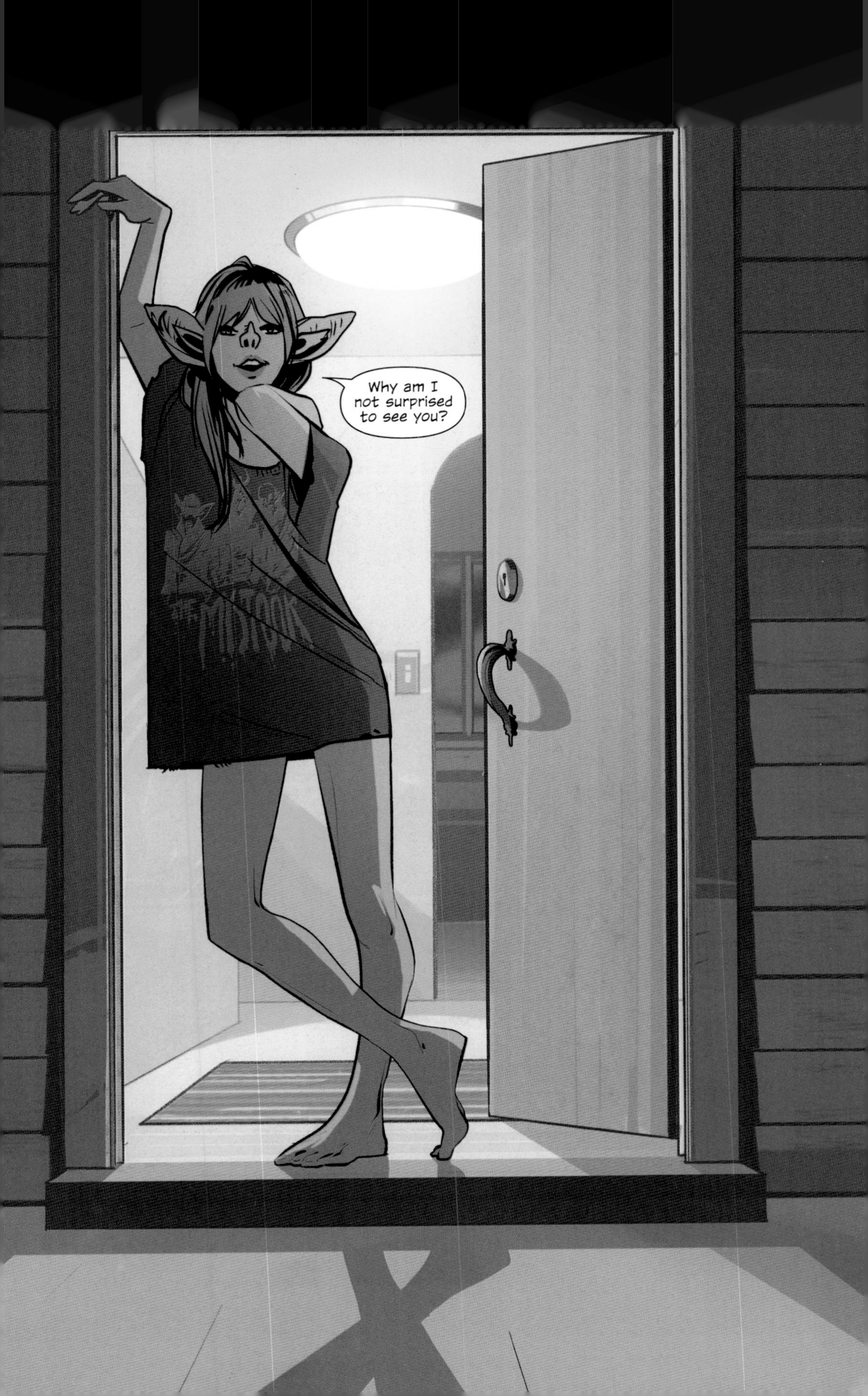
Why am I not surprised to see you?

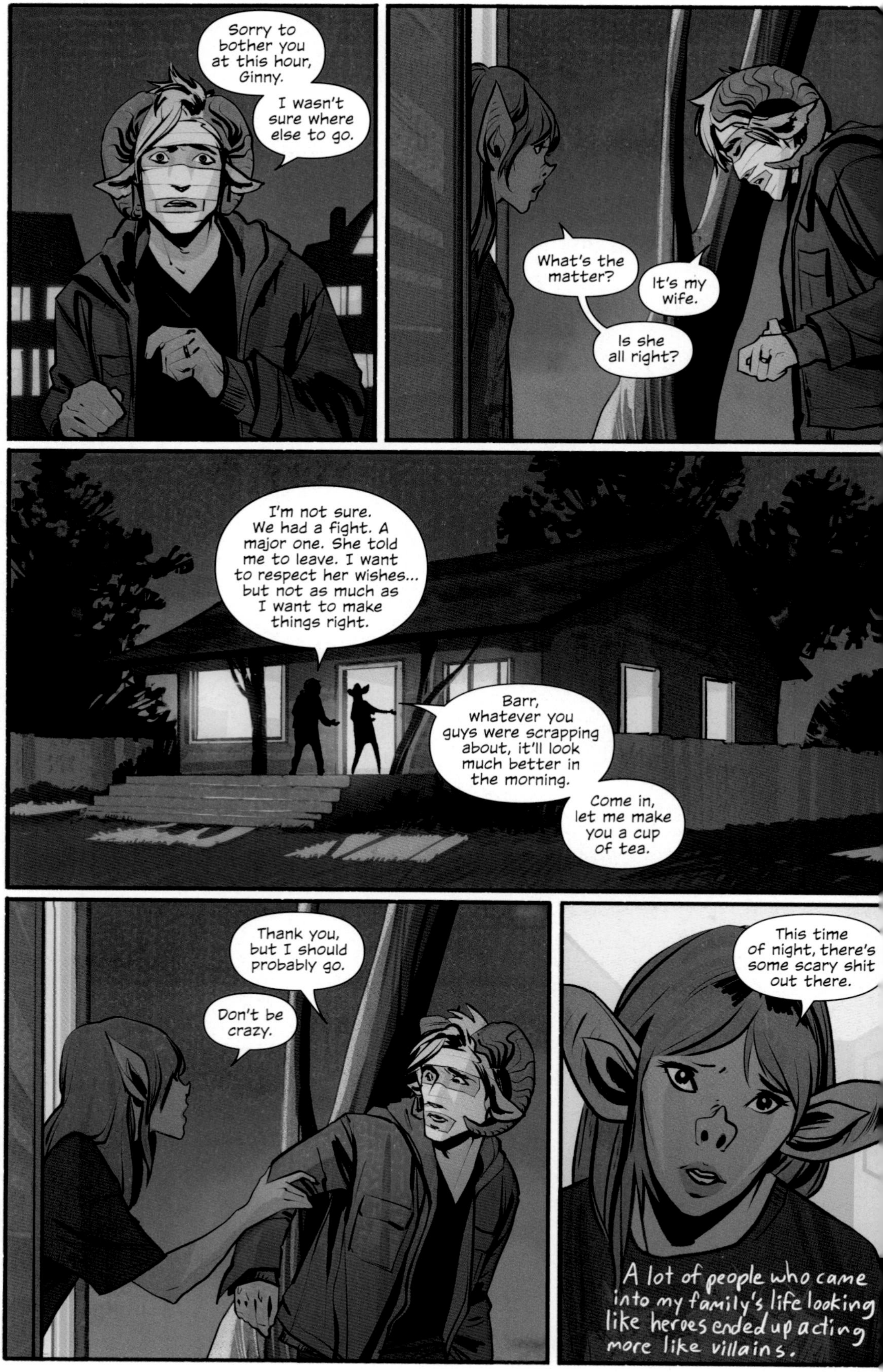
Sorry to bother you at this hour, Ginny.
I wasn't sure where else to go.
What's the matter?
It's my wife.
Is she all right?
I'm not sure. We had a fight. A major one. She told me to leave. I want to respect her wishes... but not as much as I want to make things right.
Barr, whatever you guys were scrapping about, it'll look much better in the morning.
Come in, let me make you a cup of tea.
Thank you, but I should probably go.
Don't be crazy.
This time of night, there's some scary shit out there.
A lot of people who came into my family's life looking like heroes ended up acting more like villains.

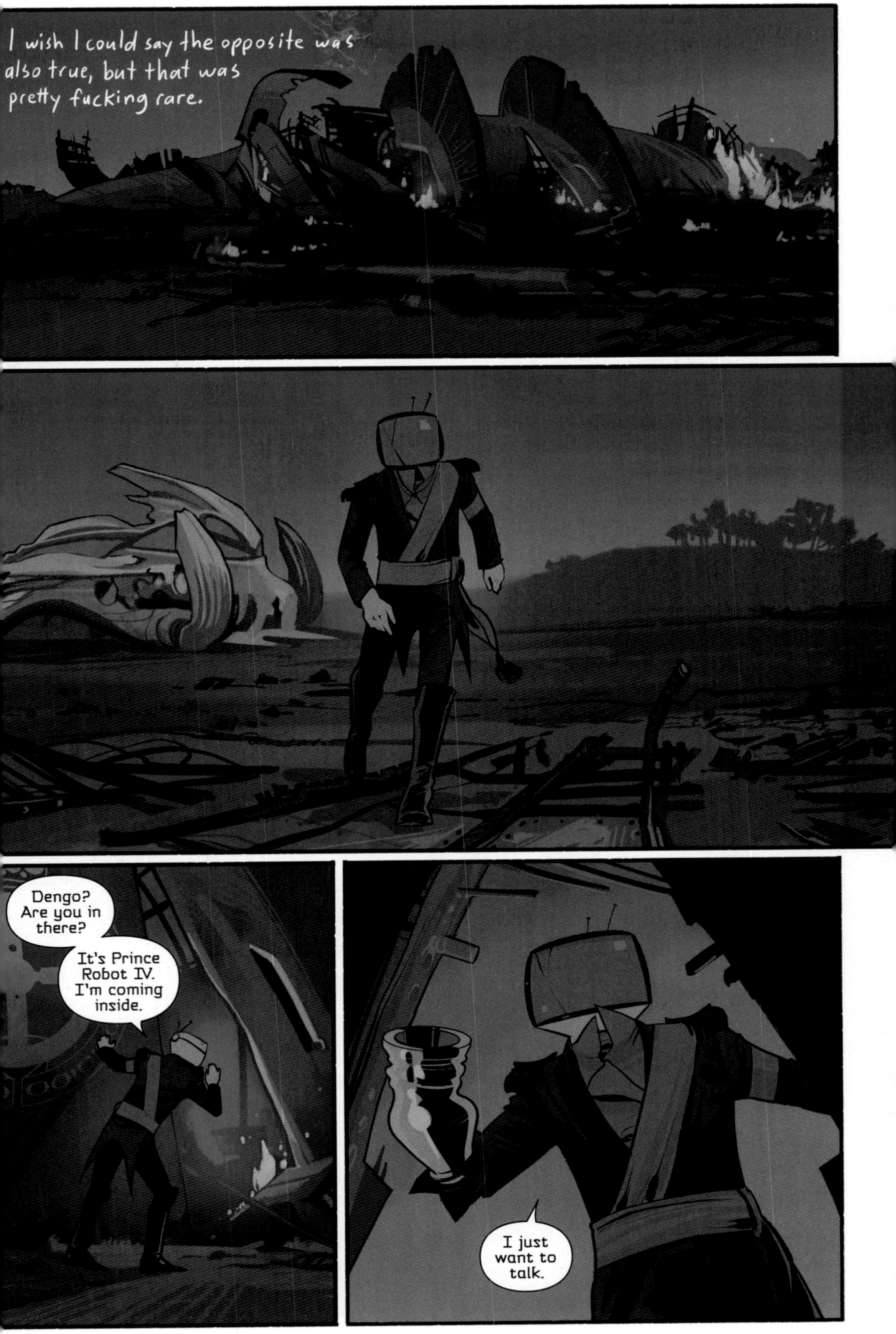
I wish I could say the opposite was also true, but that was pretty fucking rare.
Dengo? Are you in there?
It's Prince Robot IV. I'm coming inside.
I just want to talk.

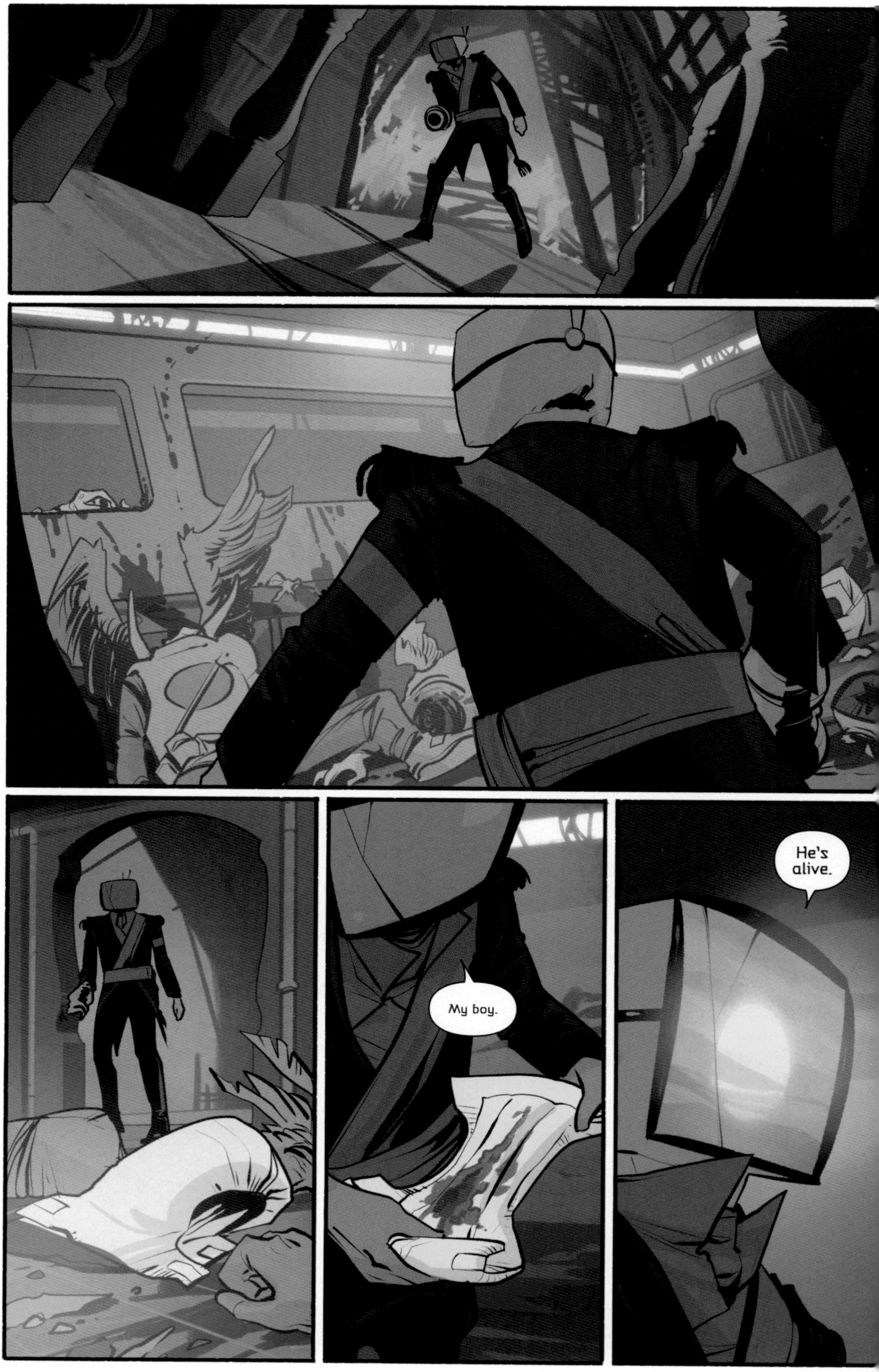
My boy.
He's alive.

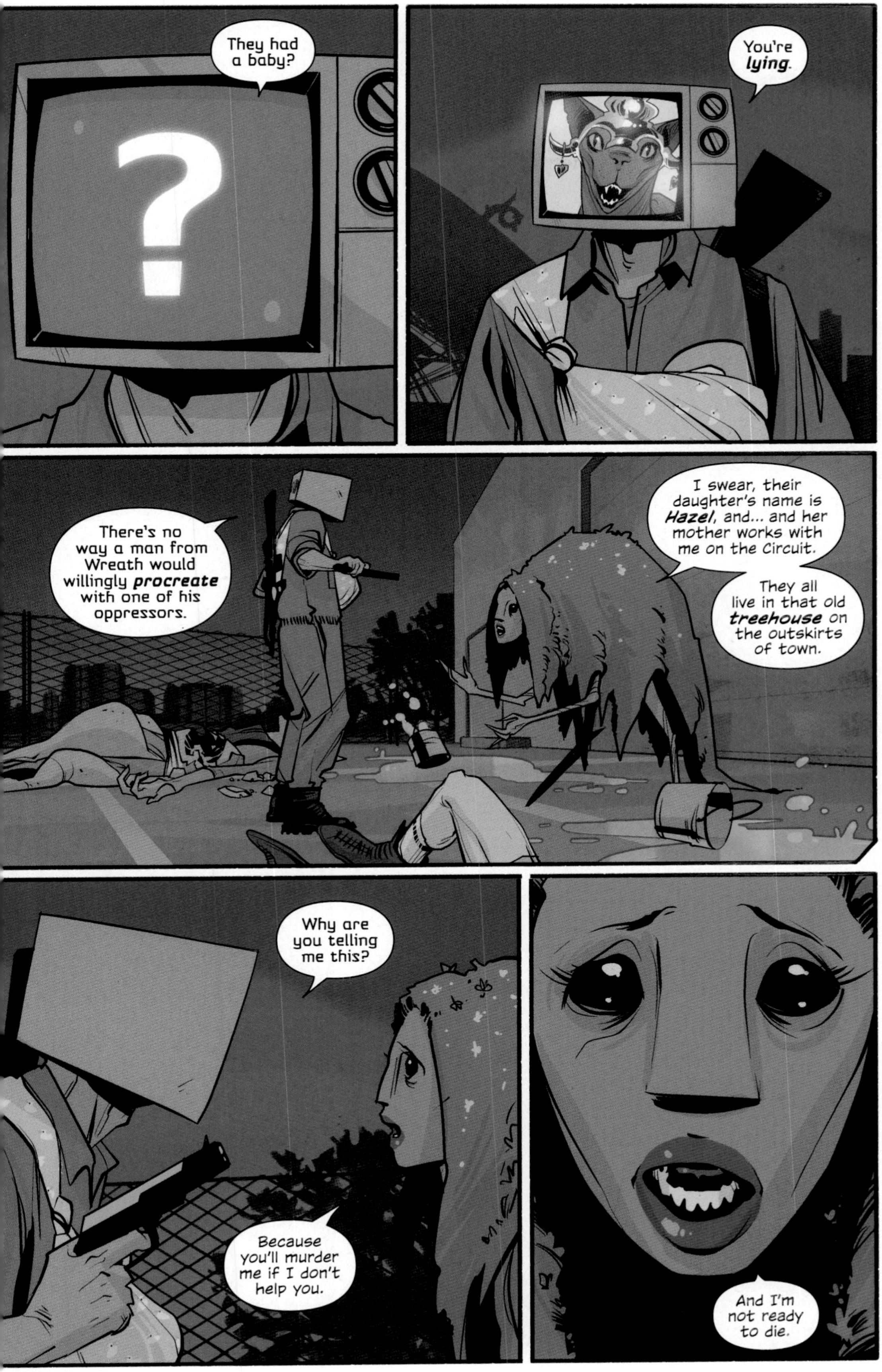
They had a baby?
You're *lying*.
There's no way a man from Wreath would willingly *procreate* with one of his oppressors.
I swear, their daughter's name is *Hazel*, and... and her mother works with me on the Circuit.
They all live in that old *treehouse* on the outskirts of town.
Why are you telling me this?
Because you'll murder me if I don't help you.
And I'm not ready to die.

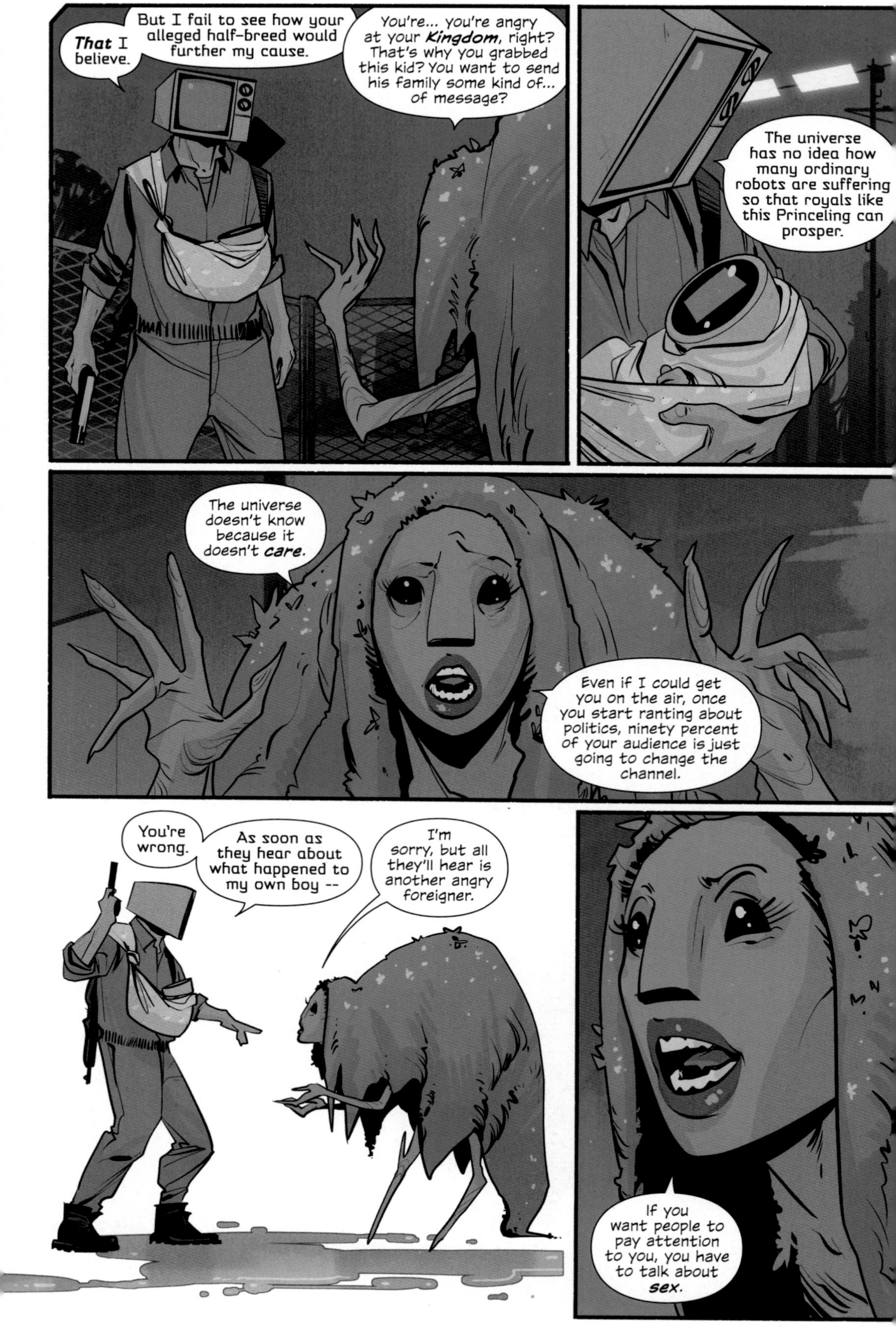
That I believe.
But I fail to see how your alleged half-breed would further my cause.
You're... you're angry at your Kingdom, right? That's why you grabbed this kid? You want to send his family some kind of... of message?
The universe has no idea how many ordinary robots are suffering so that royals like this Princeling can prosper.
The universe doesn't know because it doesn't care.
Even if I could get you on the air, once you start ranting about politics, ninety percent of your audience is just going to change the channel.
You're wrong.
As soon as they hear about what happened to my own boy --
I'm sorry, but all they'll hear is another angry foreigner.
If you want people to pay attention to you, you have to talk about sex.

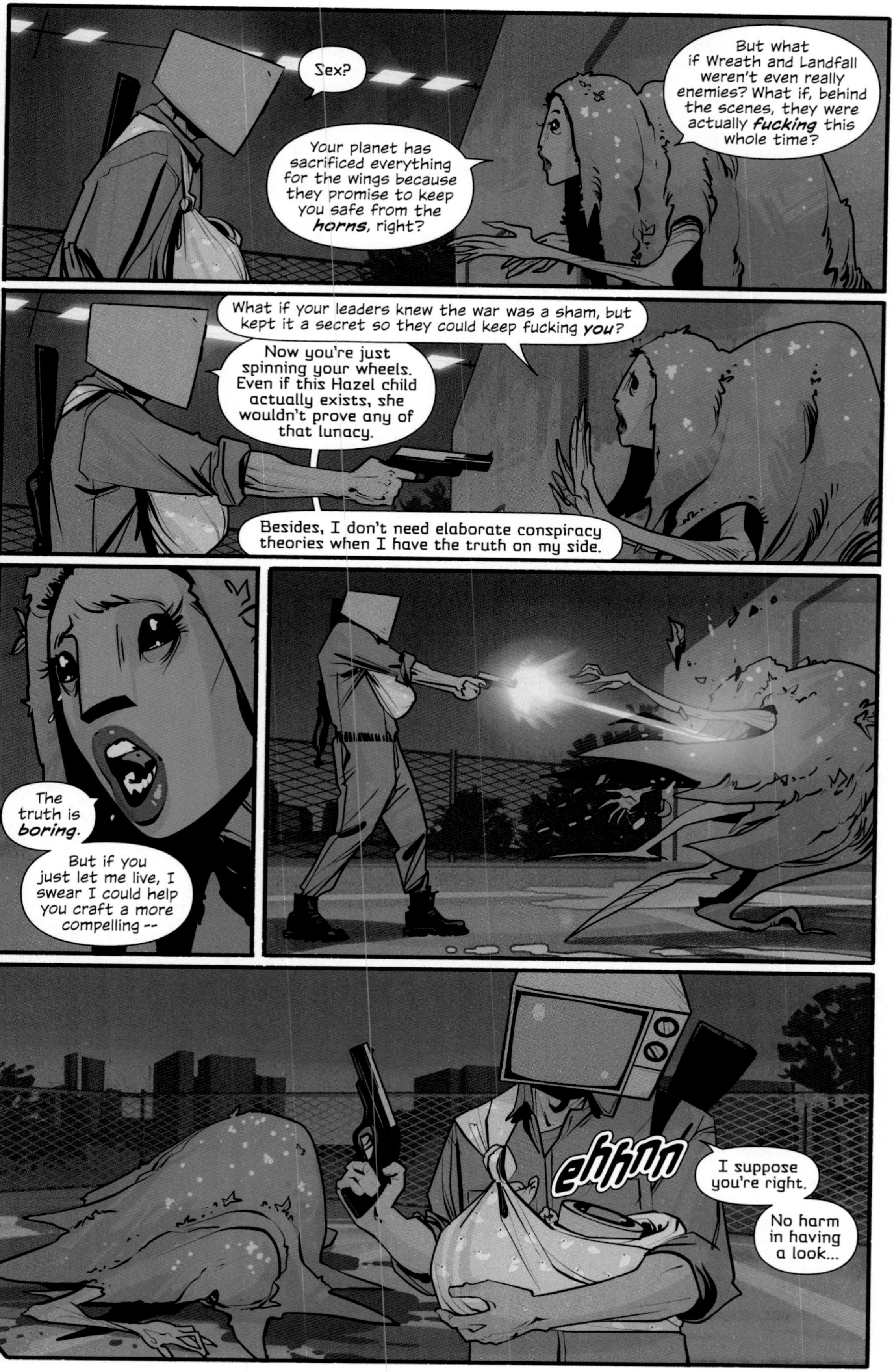
Sex?
But what if Wreath and Landfall weren't even really enemies? What if, behind the scenes, they were actually ***fucking*** this whole time?
Your planet has sacrificed everything for the wings because they promise to keep you safe from the ***horns***, right?
What if your leaders knew the war was a sham, but kept it a secret so they could keep fucking ***you***?
Now you're just spinning your wheels. Even if this Hazel child actually exists, she wouldn't prove any of that lunacy.
Besides, I don't need elaborate conspiracy theories when I have the truth on my side.
The truth is ***boring***.
But if you just let me live, I swear I could help you craft a more compelling --
ehhnn
I suppose you're right.
No harm in having a look...

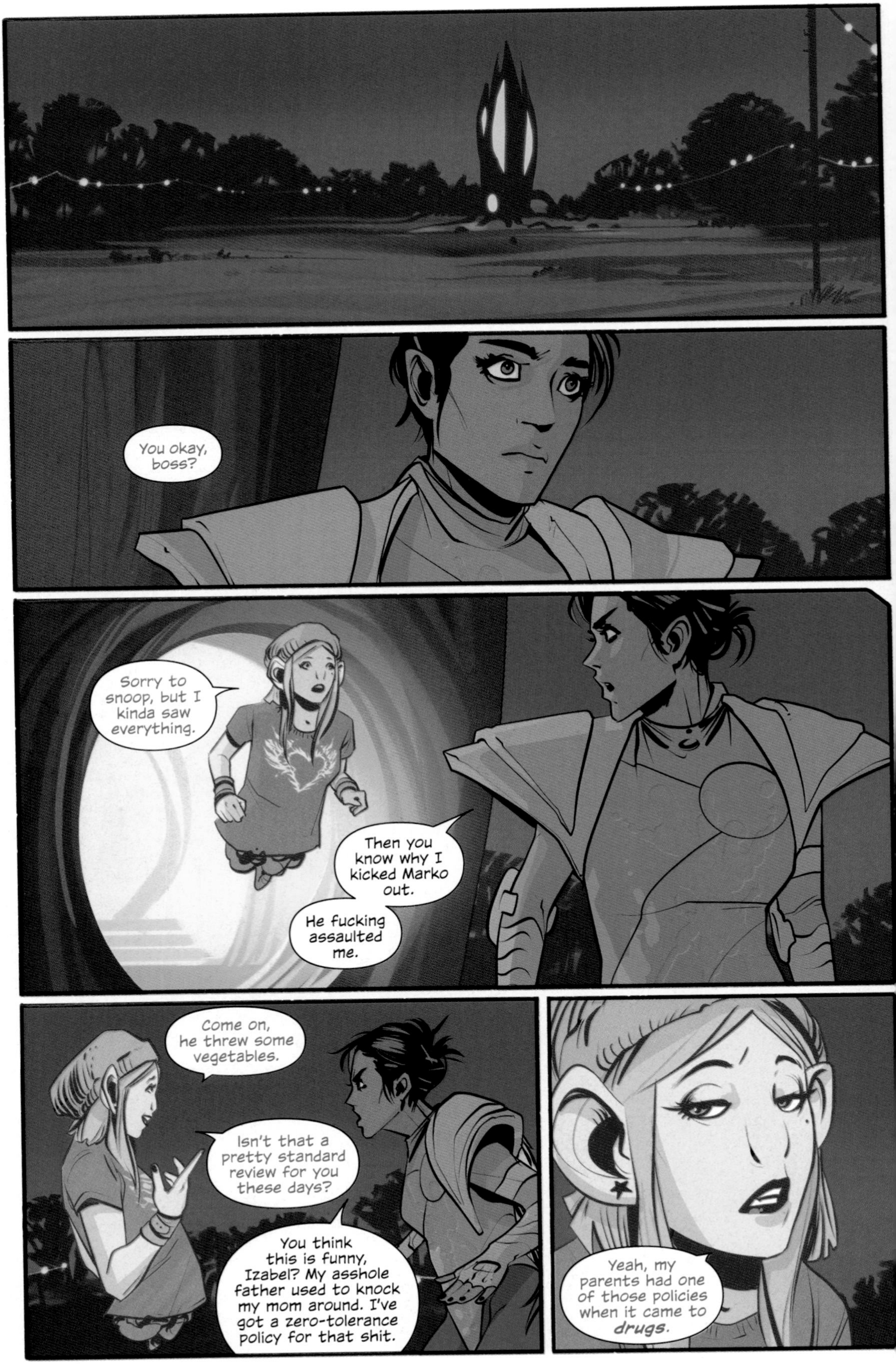

You okay, boss?
Sorry to snoop, but I kinda saw everything.
Then you know why I kicked Marko out.
He fucking assaulted me.
Come on, he threw some vegetables.
Isn't that a pretty standard review for you these days?
You think this is funny, Izabel? My asshole father used to knock my mom around. I've got a zero-tolerance policy for that shit.
Yeah, my parents had one of those policies when it came to *drugs*.

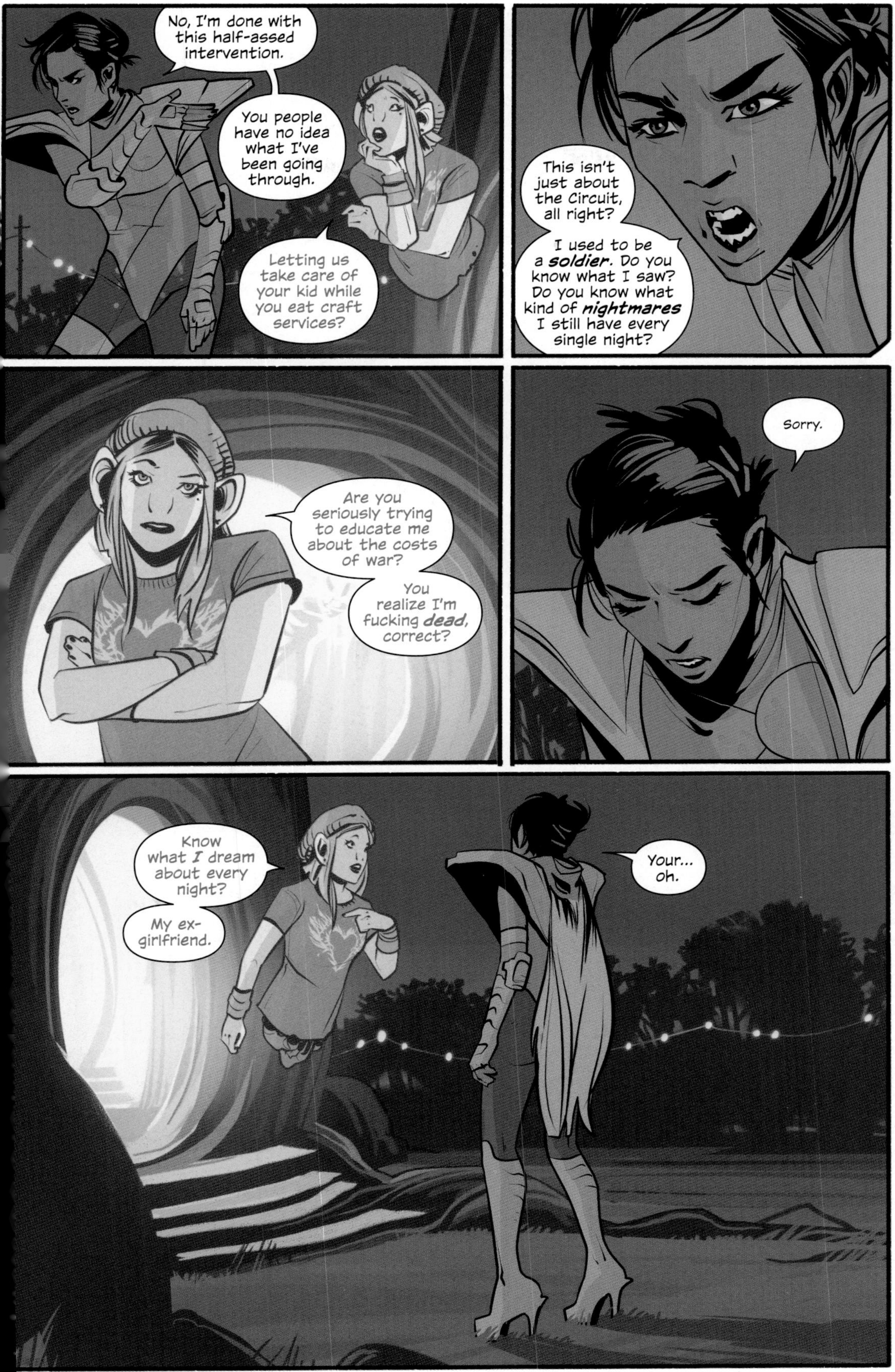
No, I'm done with this half-assed intervention.
You people have no idea what I've been going through.
Letting us take care of your kid while you eat craft services?
This isn't just about the Circuit, all right?
I used to be a **soldier**. Do you know what I saw? Do you know what kind of **nightmares** I still have every single night?
Are you seriously trying to educate me about the costs of war?
You realize I'm fucking **dead**, correct?
Sorry.
Know what **I** dream about every night?
My ex-girlfriend.
Your... oh.

Her name was Windy. We were just stupid kids.

She was smart and gorgeous and sweet to me, but she was also super into our planet's most judgy religion, so I eventually broke up with her.

Two days later, I stepped on whatever anti-personnel crap one of your sides buried in our backyard.

The whole time I was bleeding out, all I could think was, "Damn, I will never feel her breath on my neck again."

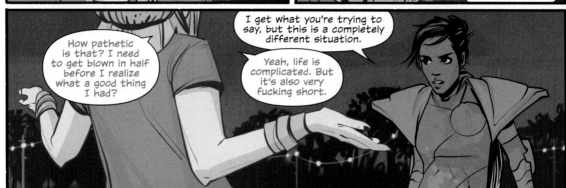

How pathetic is that? I need to get blown in half before I realize what a good thing I had?

I get what you're trying to say, but this is a completely different situation.

Yeah, life is complicated. But it's also very fucking short.

If you find someone who can forgive all your bullshit... the least you can do is try to forgive them.

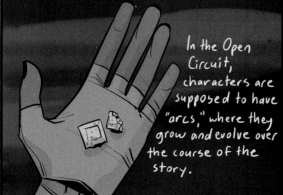

In the Open Circuit, characters are supposed to have "arcs," where they grow and evolve over the course of the story.

But Mom always thought that was nonsense.

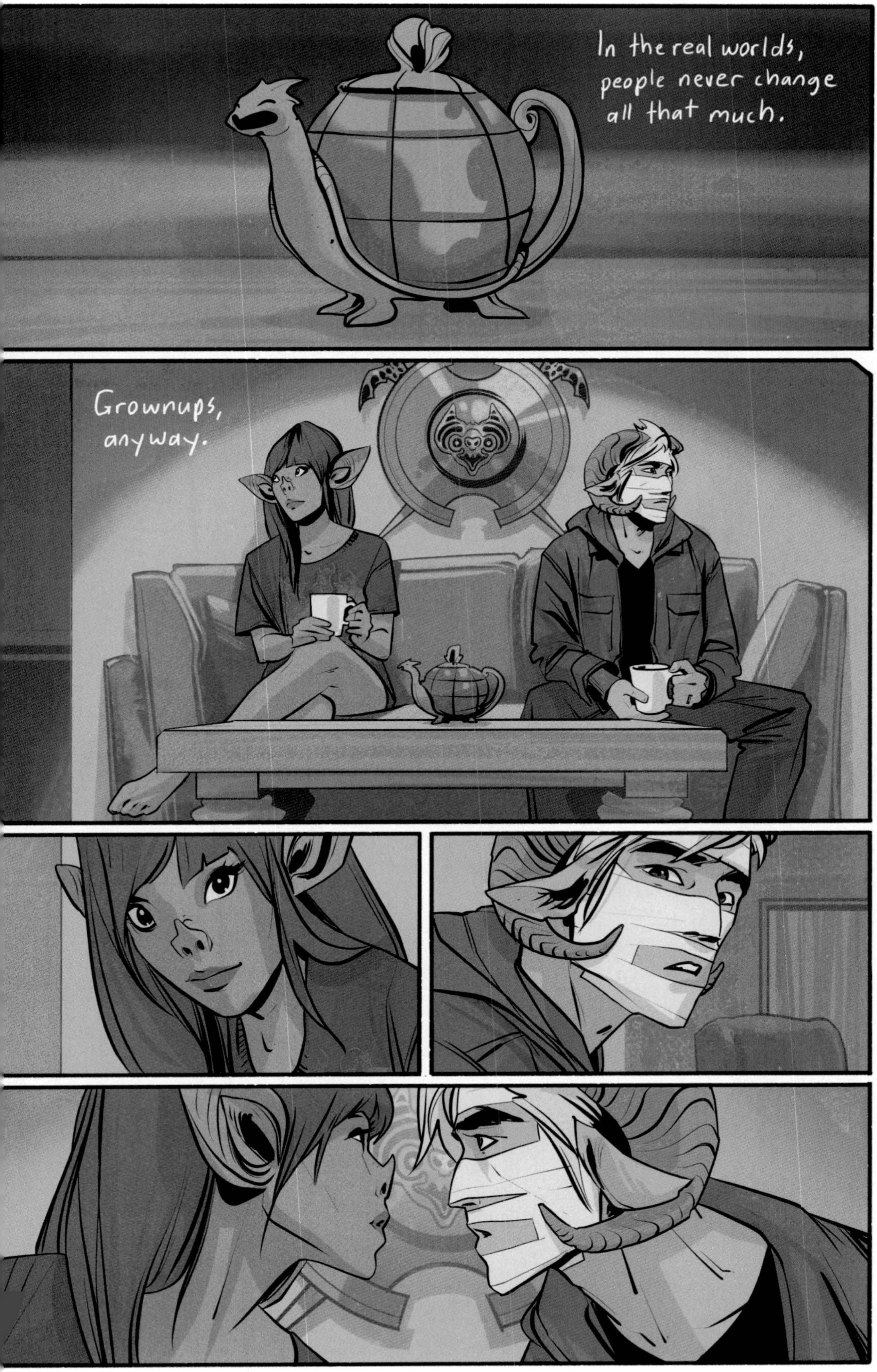
In the real worlds, people never change all that much.
Grownups, anyway.

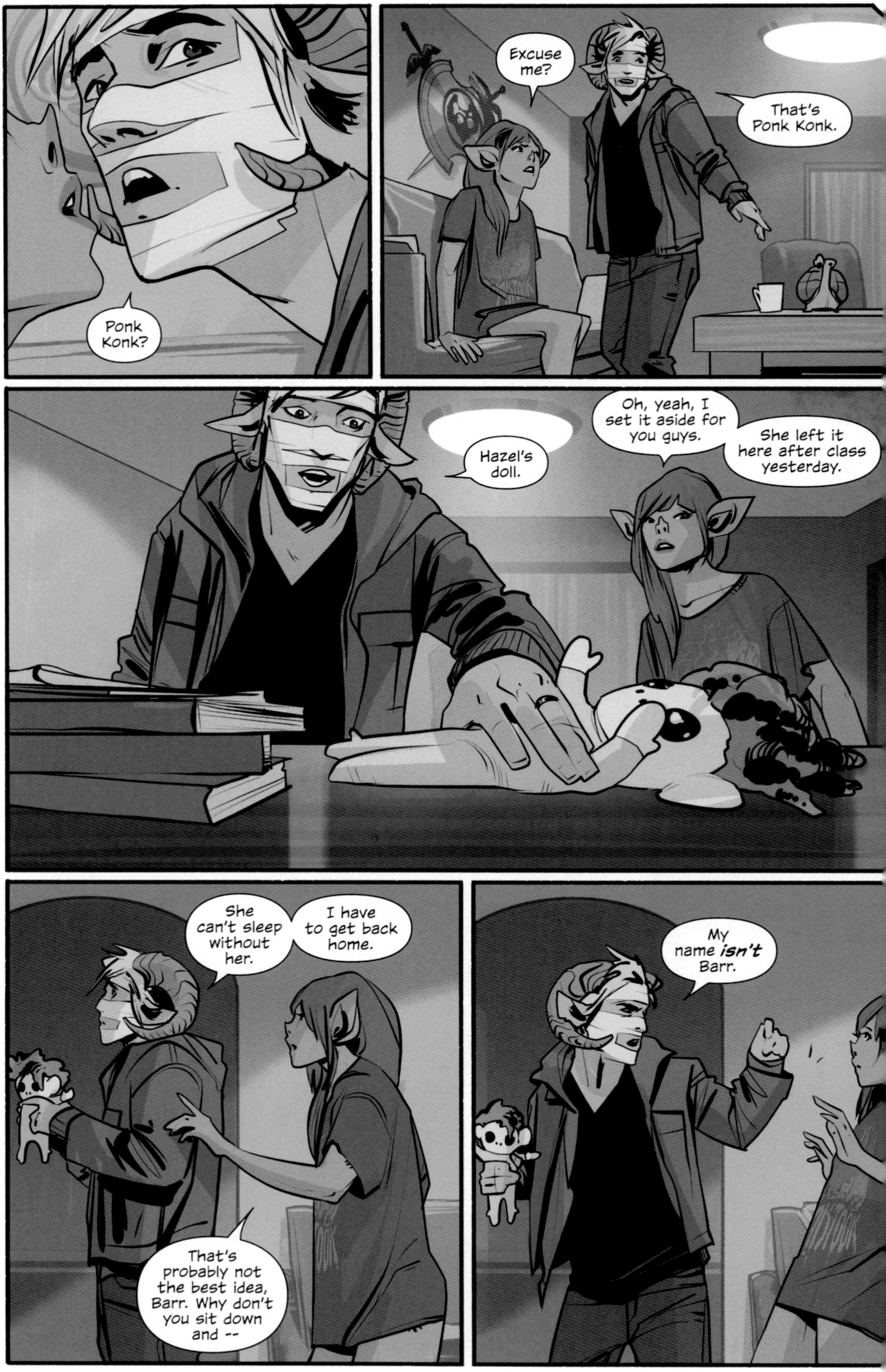
Ponk Konk?
Excuse me?
That's Ponk Konk.
Hazel's doll.
Oh, yeah, I set it aside for you guys.
She left it here after class yesterday.
She can't sleep without her.
I have to get back home.
That's probably not the best idea, Barr. Why don't you sit down and --
My name *isn't* Barr.

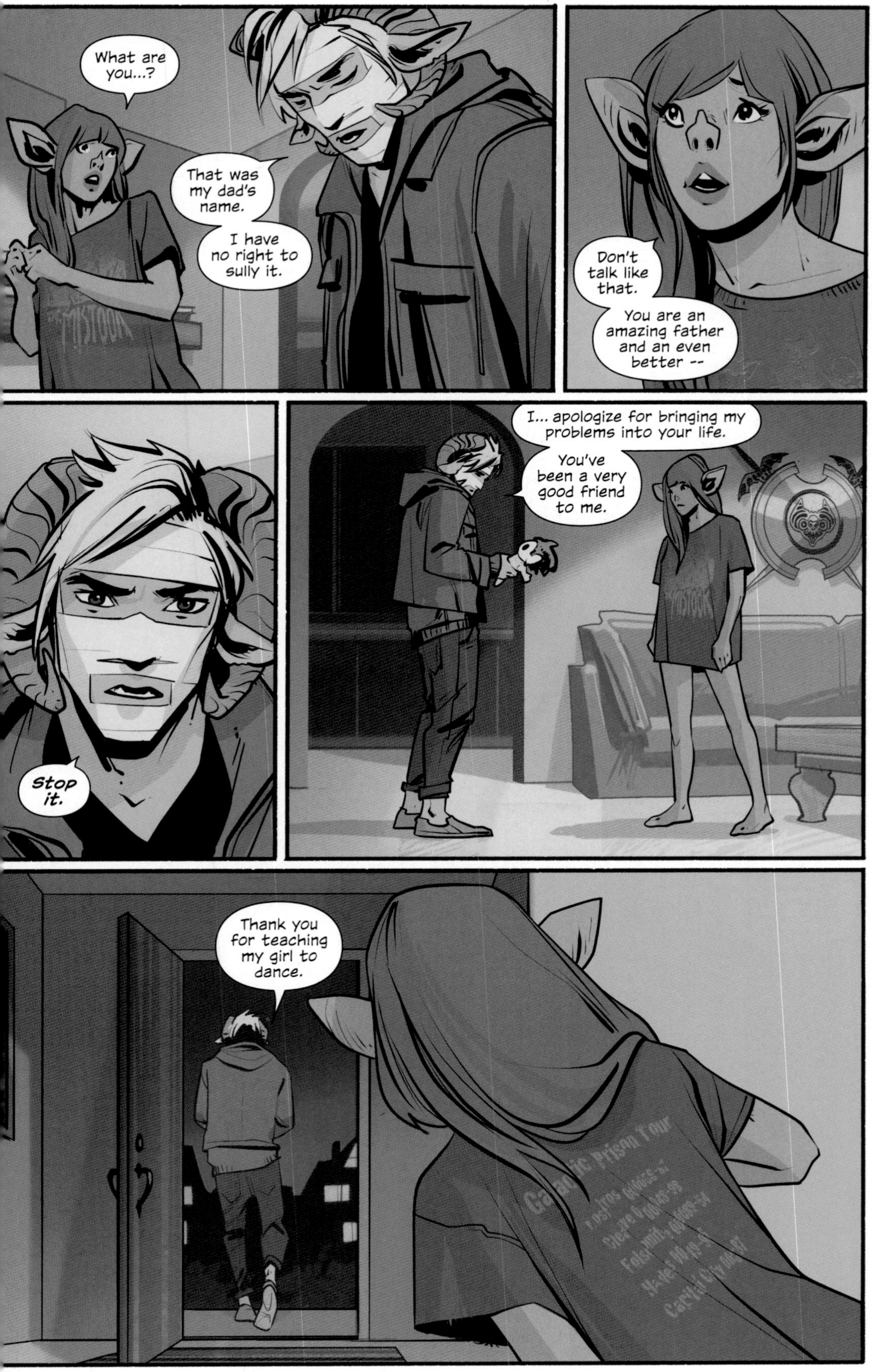
What are you...?
That was my dad's name.
I have no right to sully it.
Don't talk like that.
You are an amazing father and an even better --
Stop it.
I... apologize for bringing my problems into your life.
You've been a very good friend to me.
Thank you for teaching my girl to dance.

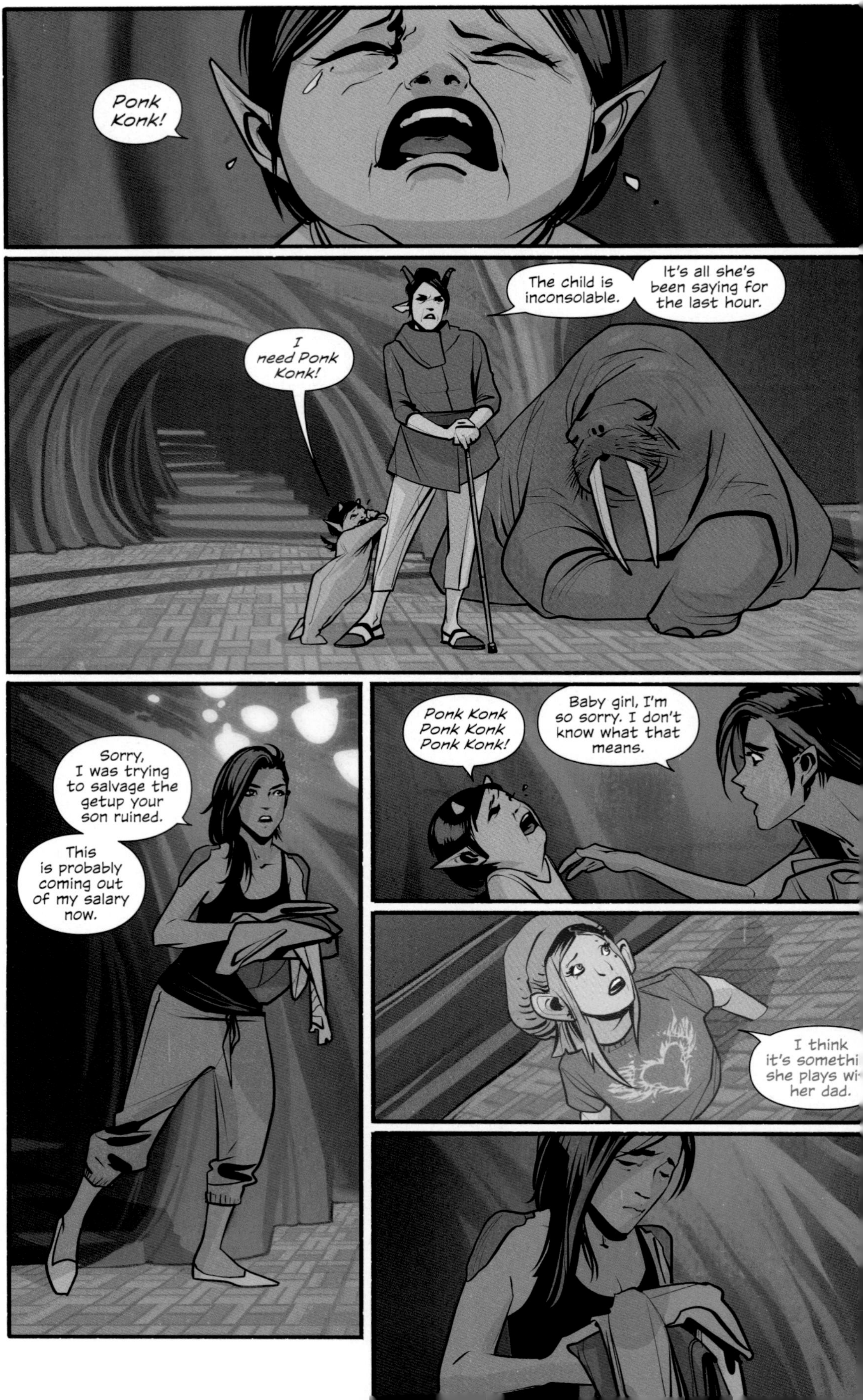
Ponk Konk!
The child is inconsolable.
It's all she's been saying for the last hour.
I need Ponk Konk!
Sorry, I was trying to salvage the getup your son ruined.
This is probably coming out of my salary now.
Ponk Konk Ponk Konk Ponk Konk!
Baby girl, I'm so sorry. I don't know what that means.
I think it's somethi she plays wi her dad.

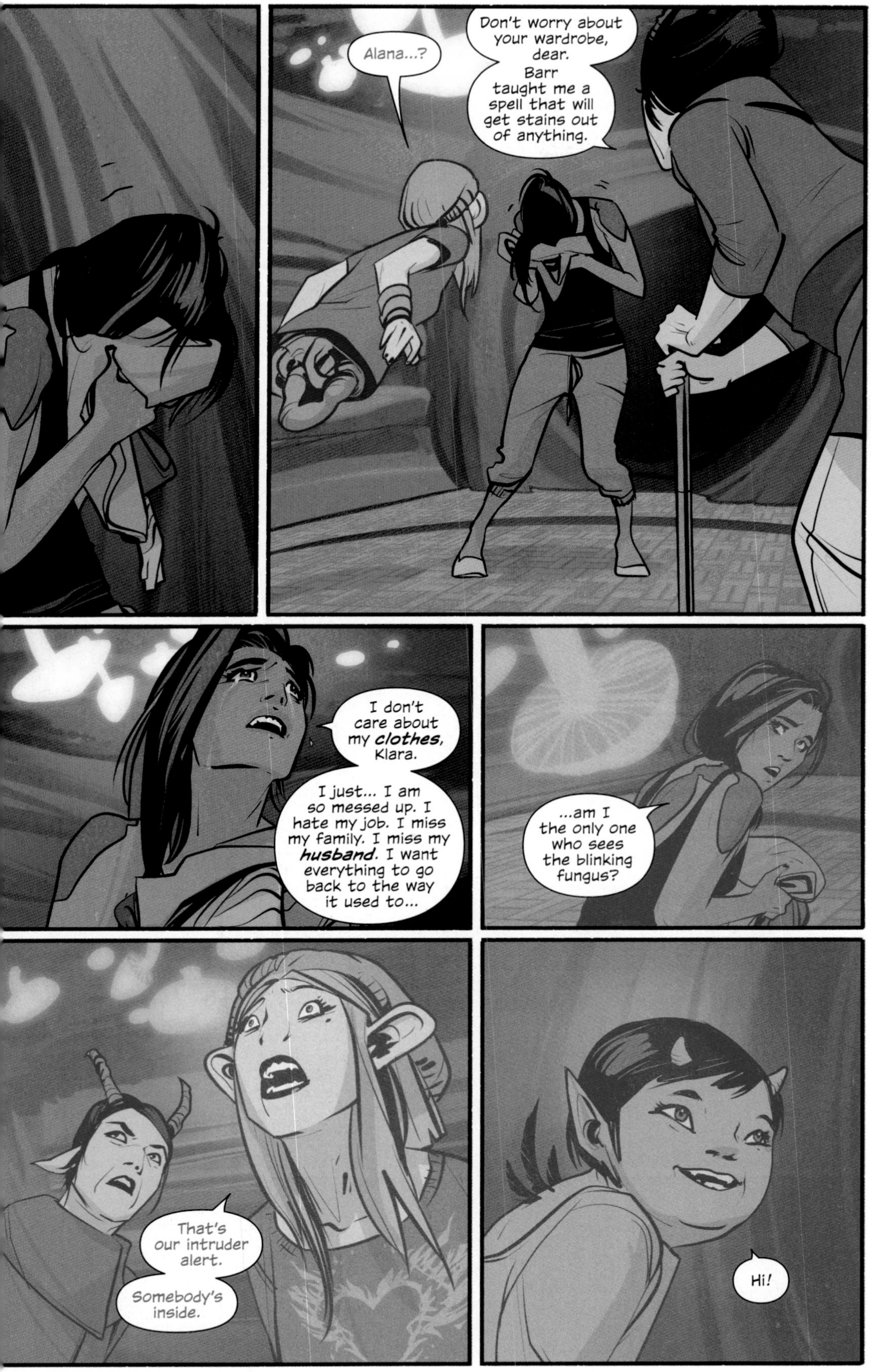

Alana...?
Don't worry about your wardrobe, dear.
Barr taught me a spell that will get stains out of anything.
I don't care about my *clothes*, Klara.
I just... I am so messed up. I hate my job. I miss my family. I miss my *husband*. I want everything to go back to the way it used to...
...am I the only one who sees the blinking fungus?
That's our intruder alert.
Somebody's inside.
Hi!

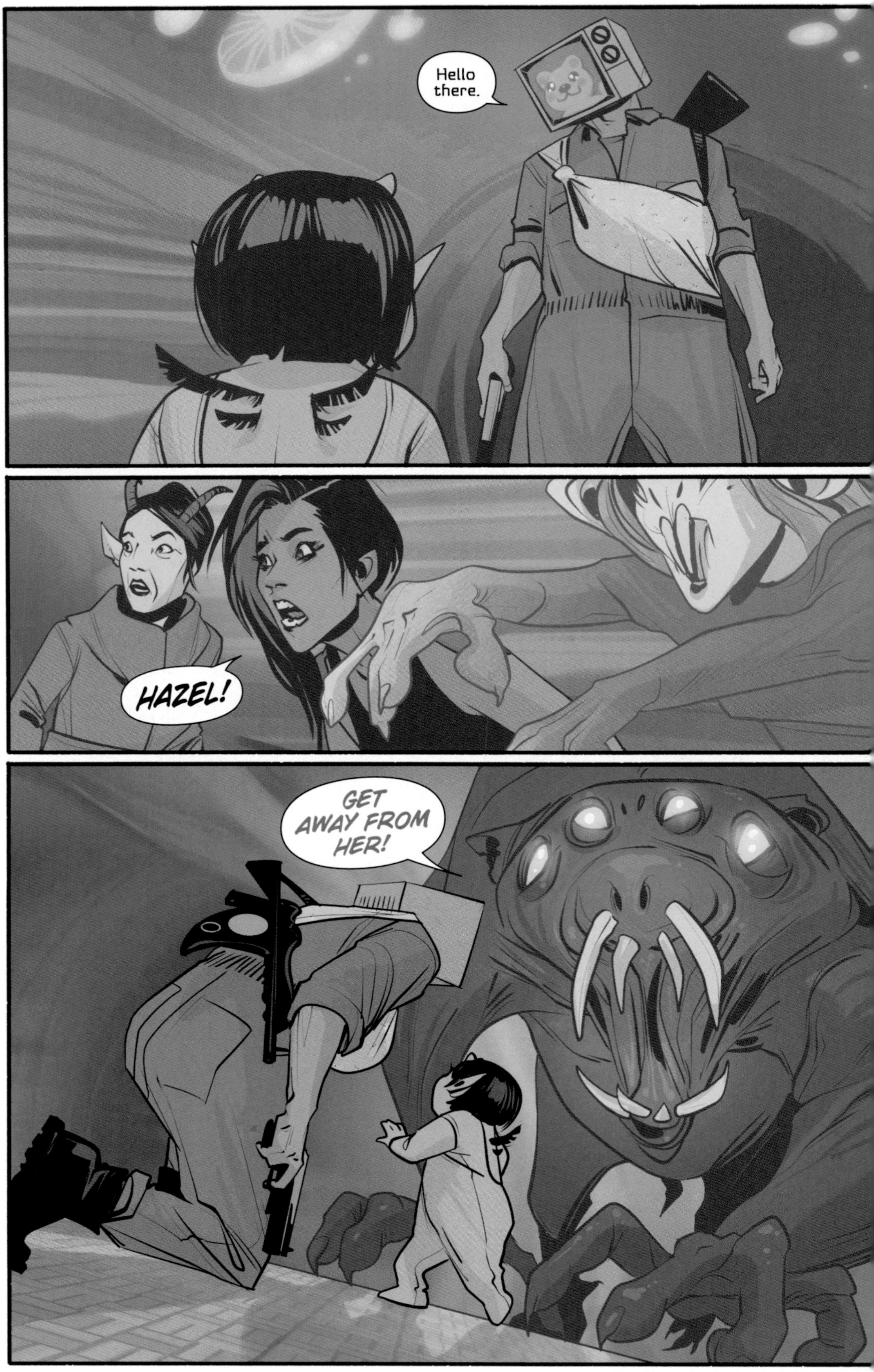
Hello there.
HAZEL!
GET AWAY FROM HER!

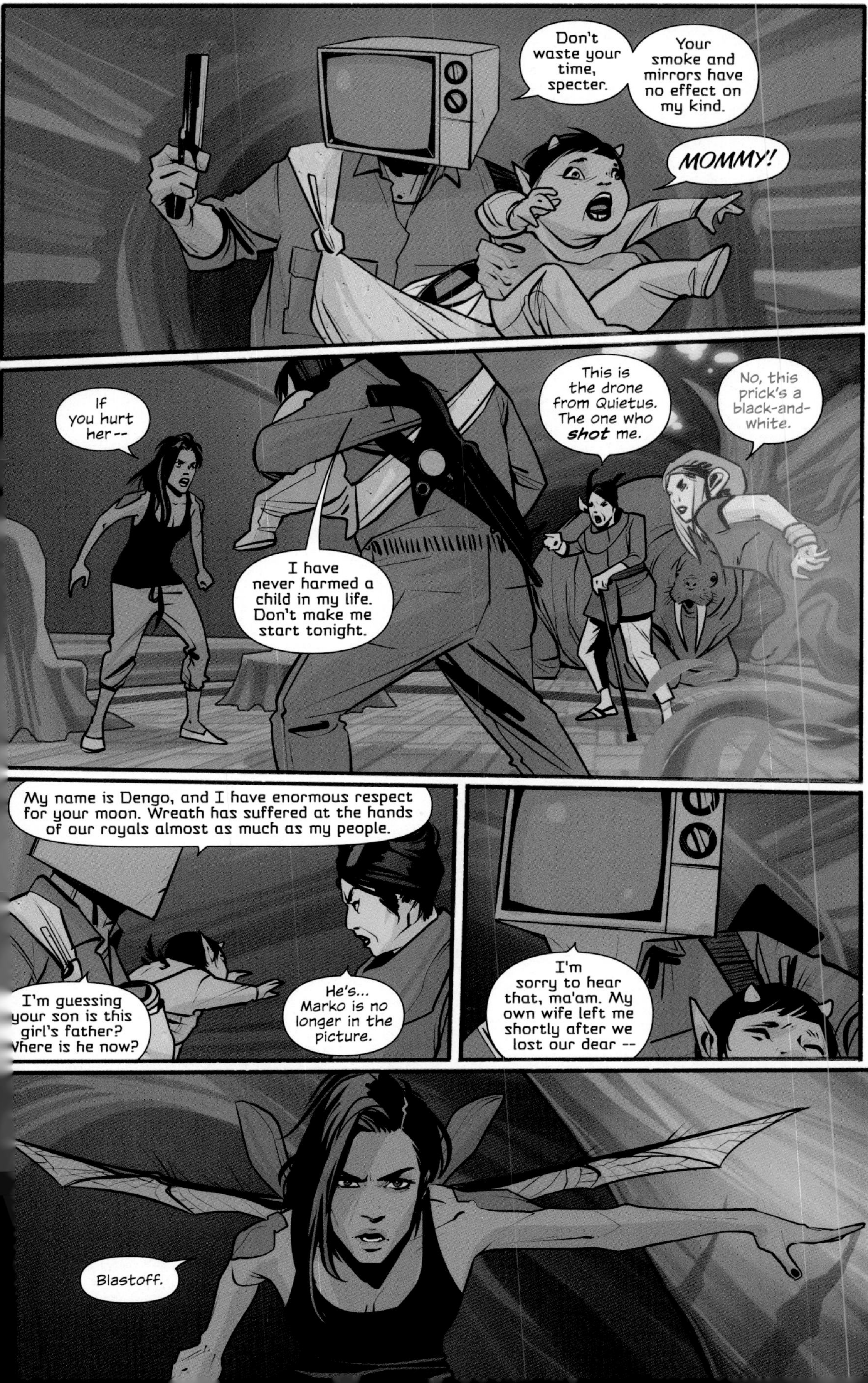
Don't waste your time, specter.
Your smoke and mirrors have no effect on my kind.
MOMMY!
If you hurt her --
This is the drone from Quietus. The one who **shot** me.
No, this prick's a black-and-white.
I have never harmed a child in my life. Don't make me start tonight.
My name is Dengo, and I have enormous respect for your moon. Wreath has suffered at the hands of our royals almost as much as my people.
I'm guessing your son is this girl's father? Where is he now?
He's... Marko is no longer in the picture.
I'm sorry to hear that, ma'am. My own wife left me shortly after we lost our dear --
Blastoff.

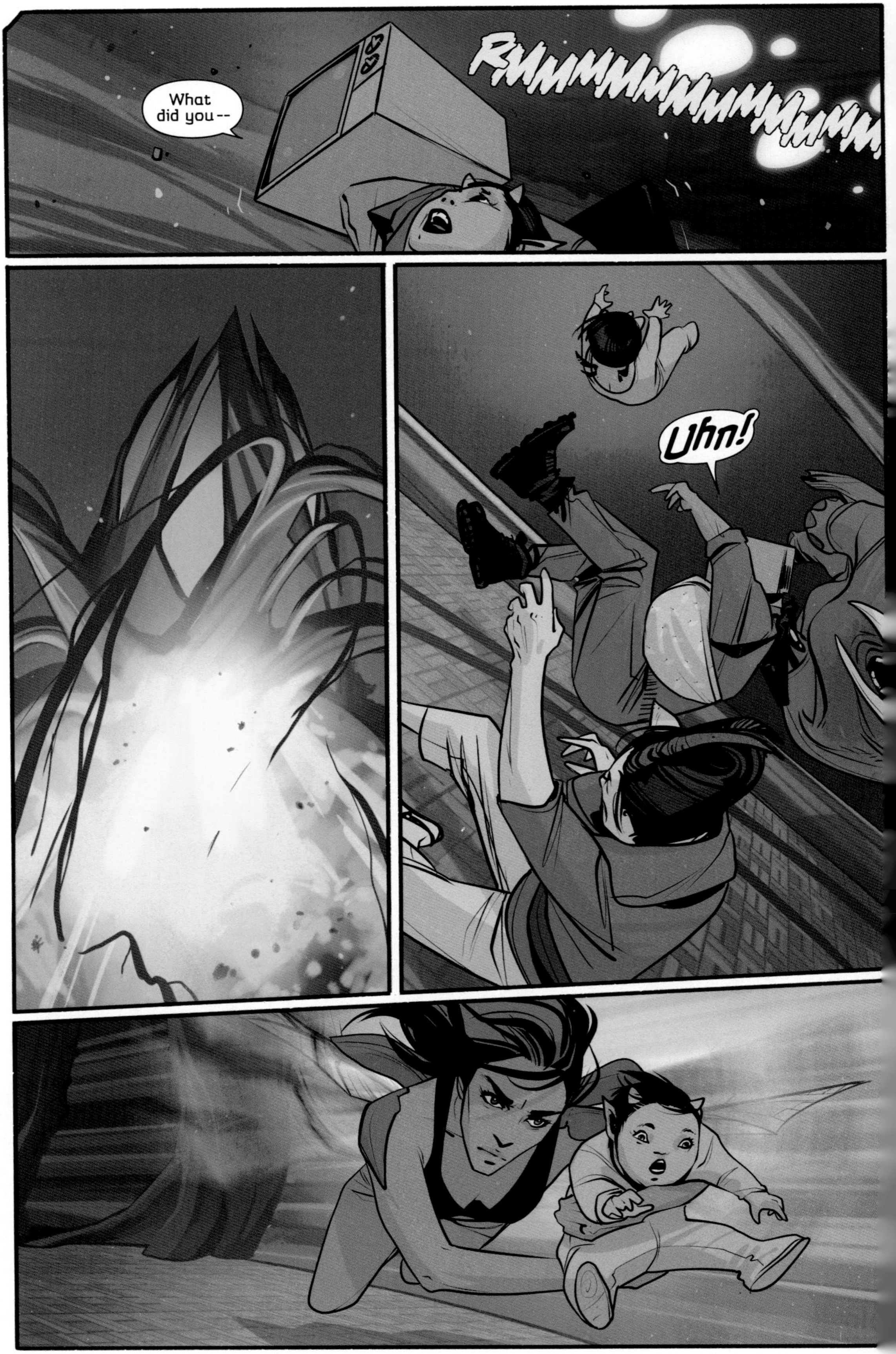
What did you --
RMMMMMMMMMMMM
Uhn!

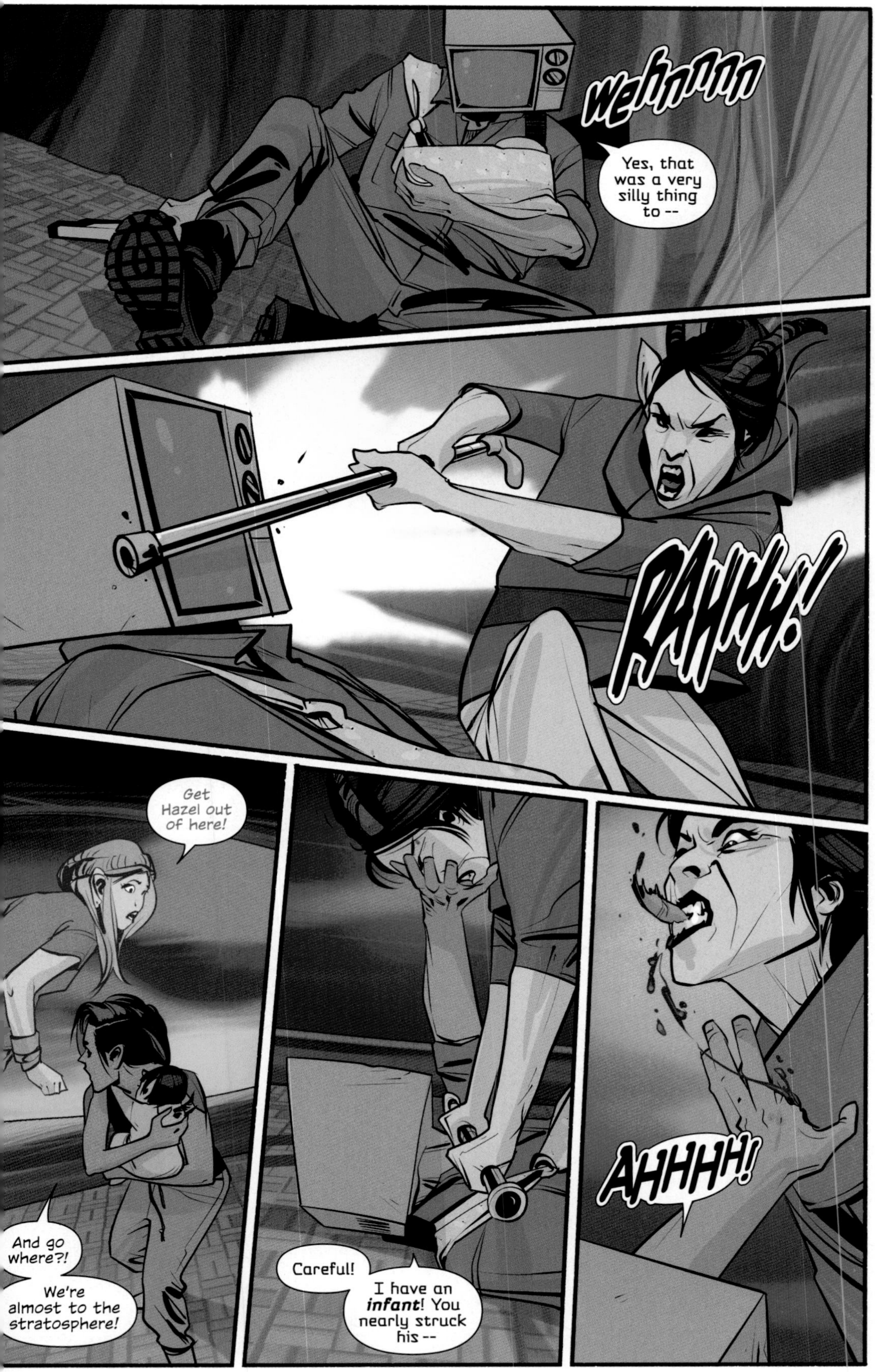
WEHNNNN
Yes, that was a very silly thing to --
RAHHHH!
Get Hazel out of here!
And go where?!
We're almost to the stratosphere!
Careful!
I have an ***infant***! You nearly struck his --
AHHHH!

ENOUGH!

Stop it!

Please!

I will.

After you people steer this craft to the exact coordinates I give you.

Don't listen to him, Alana.

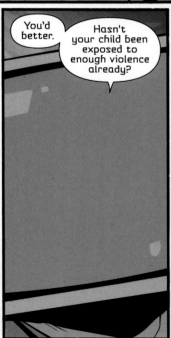

You'd better.

Hasn't your child been exposed to enough violence already?

Ponk Konk.

This was the story of how my parents split up.

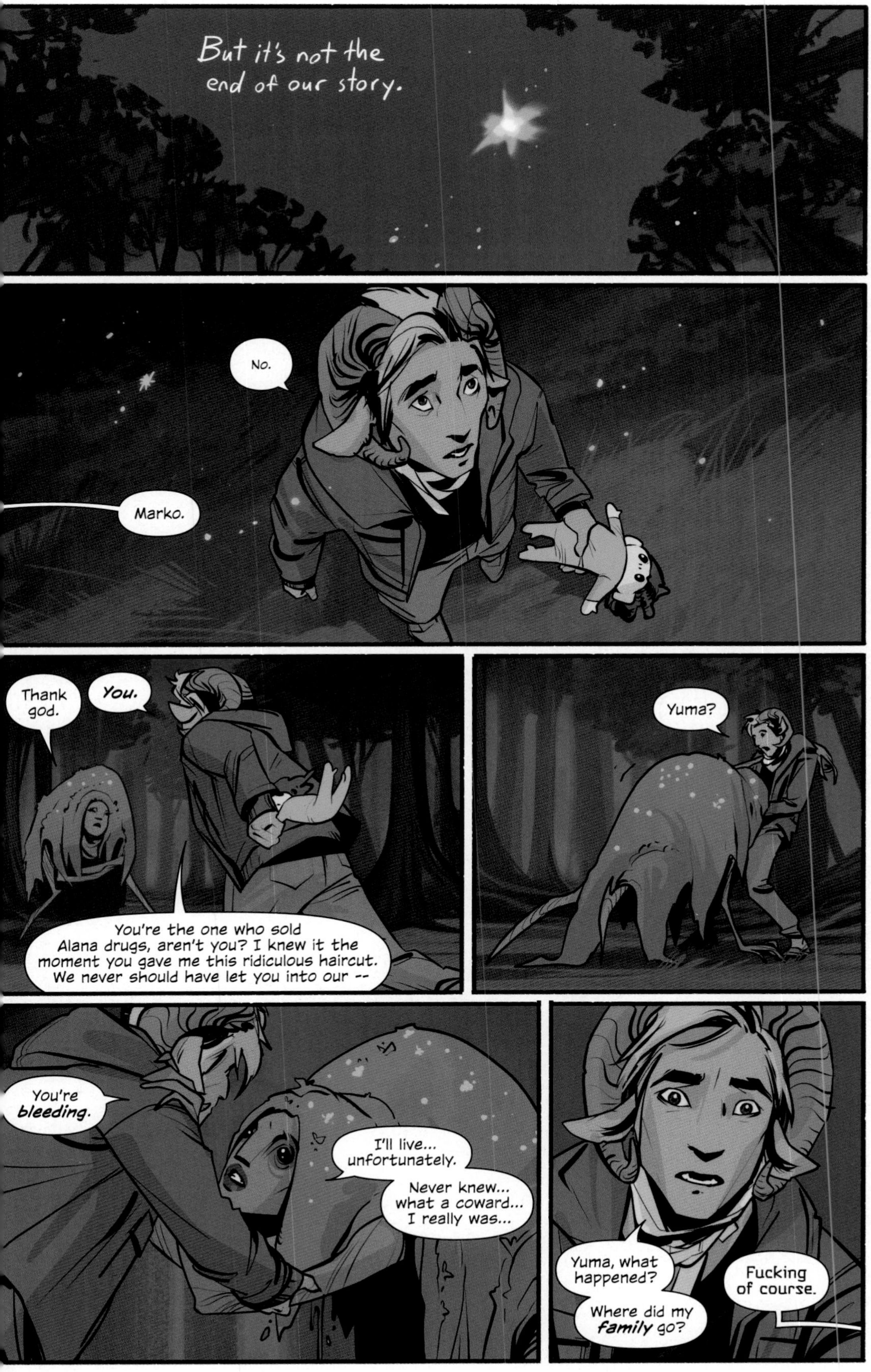
But it's not the end of our story.
No.
Marko.
Thank god.
You.
You're the one who sold Alana drugs, aren't you? I knew it the moment you gave me this ridiculous haircut. We never should have let you into our --
Yuma?
You're bleeding.
I'll live... unfortunately.
Never knew... what a coward... I really was...
Yuma, what happened?
Where did my family go?
Fucking of course.

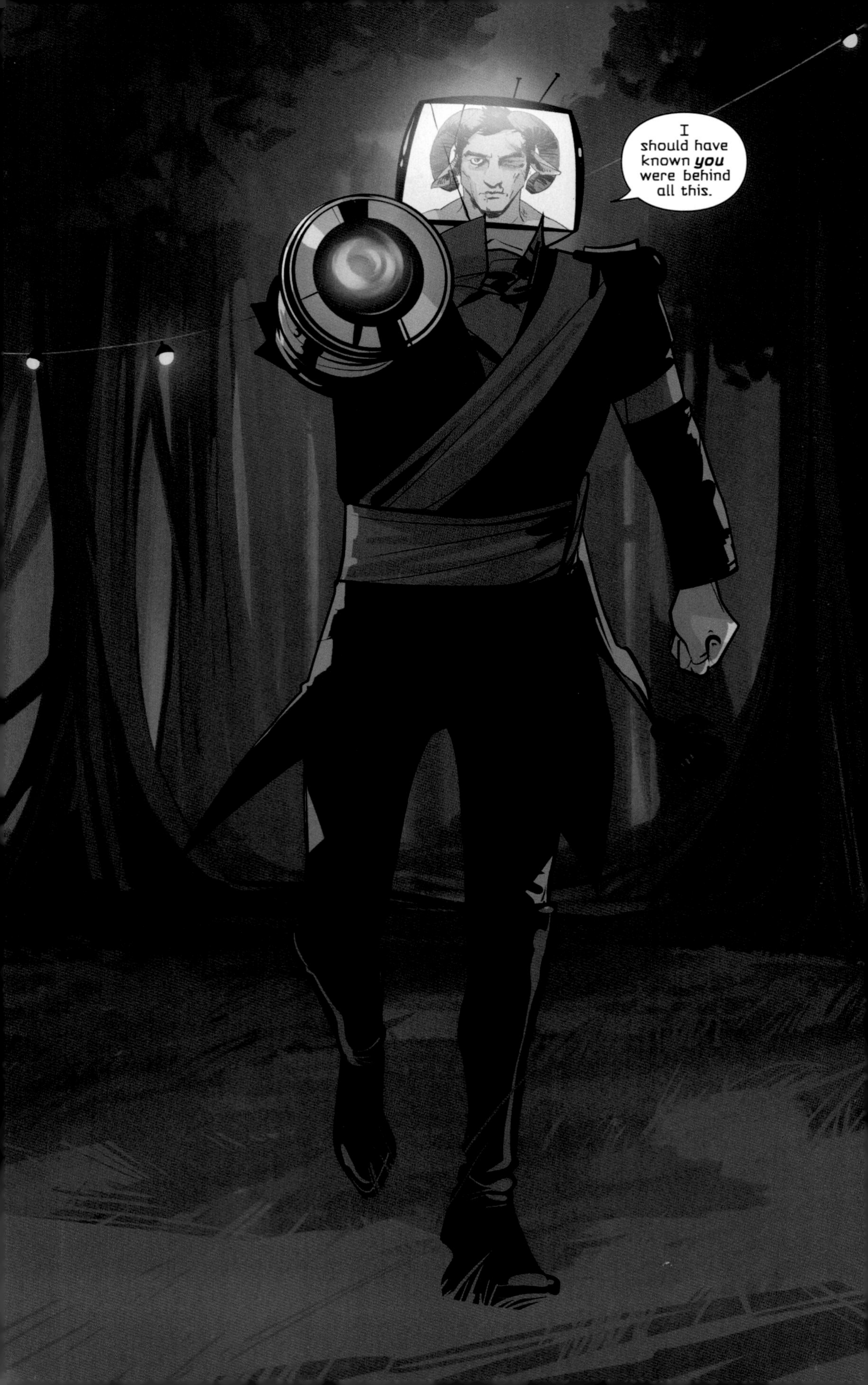
I should have known ***you*** were behind all this.

end chapter twenty-three

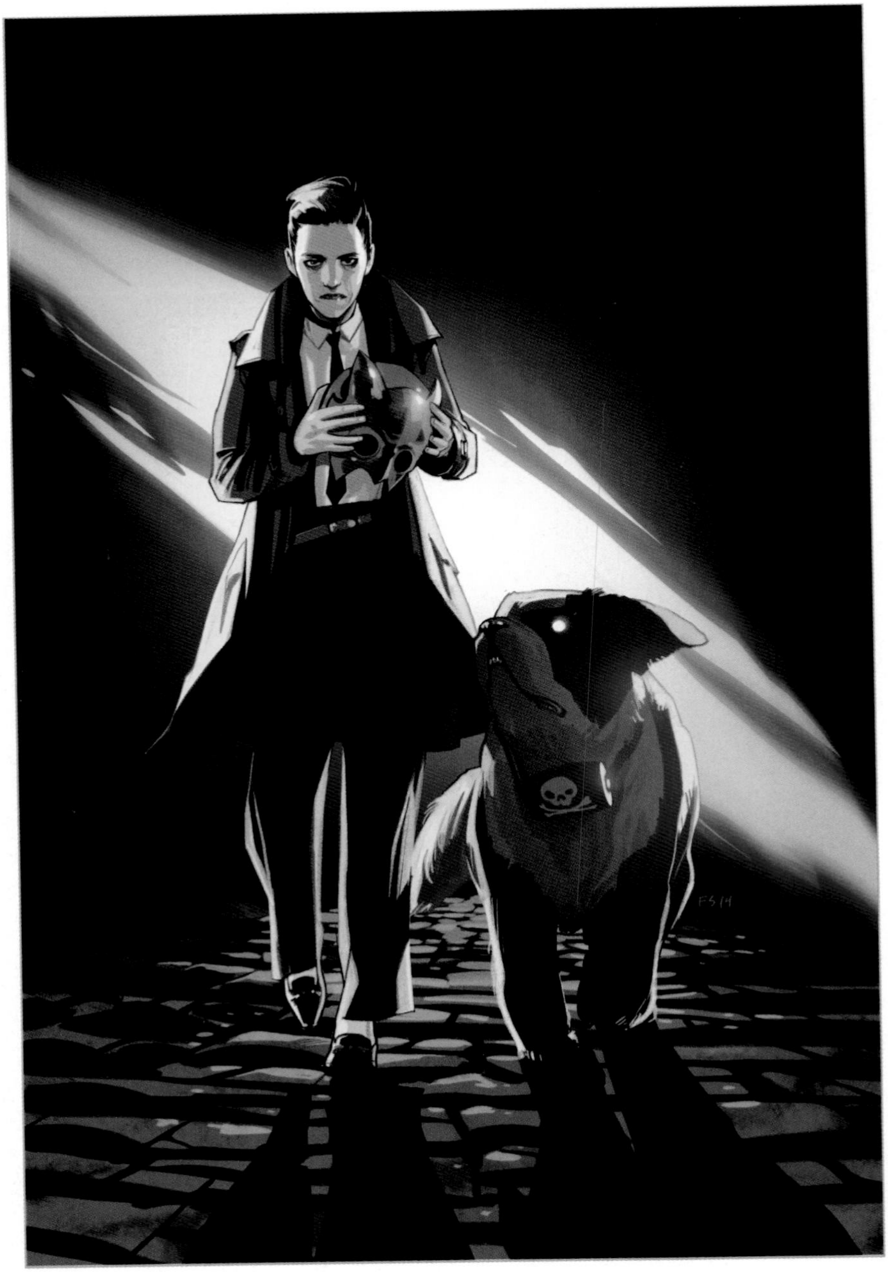

CHAPTER TWENTY-FOUR

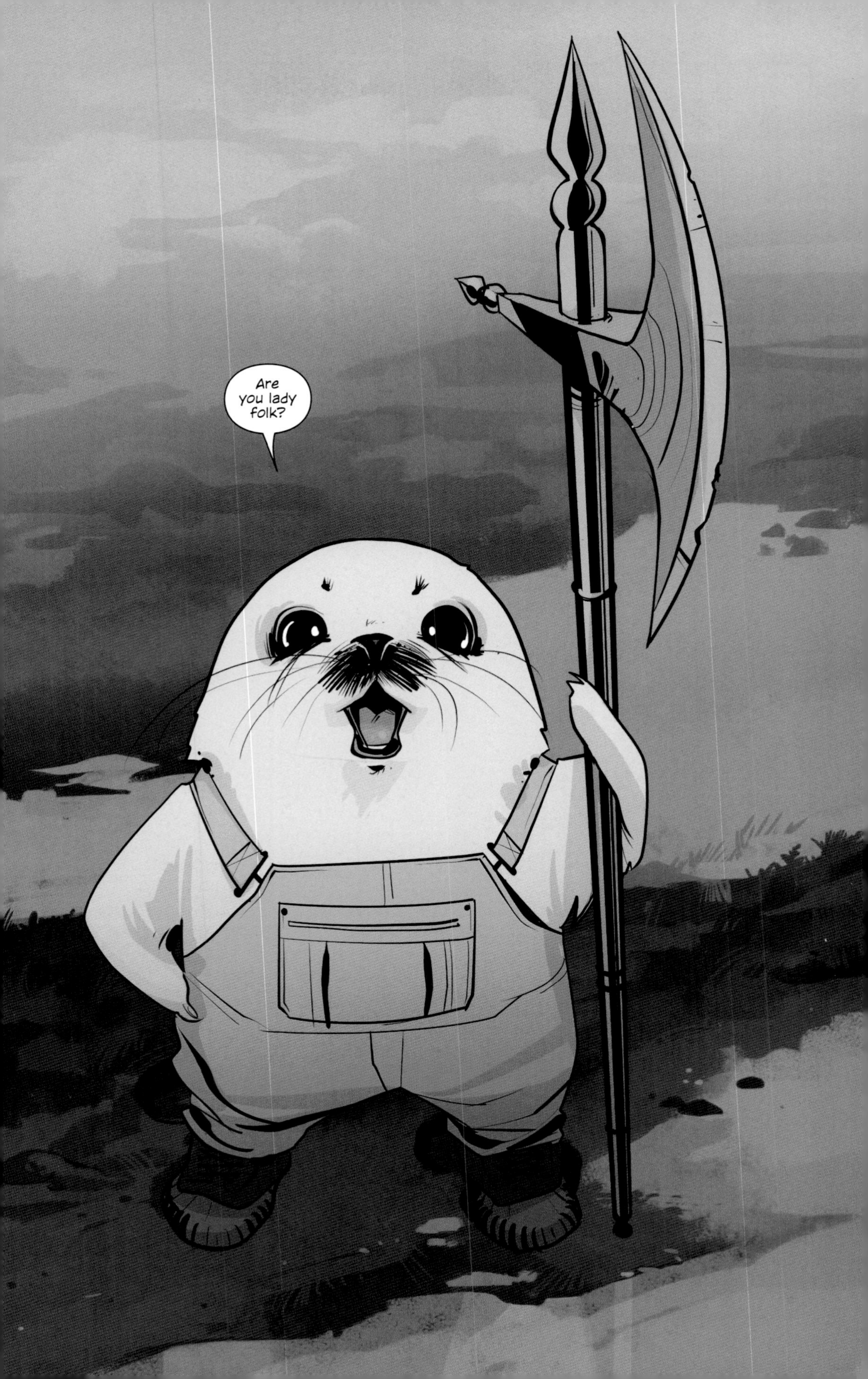
Are you lady folk?

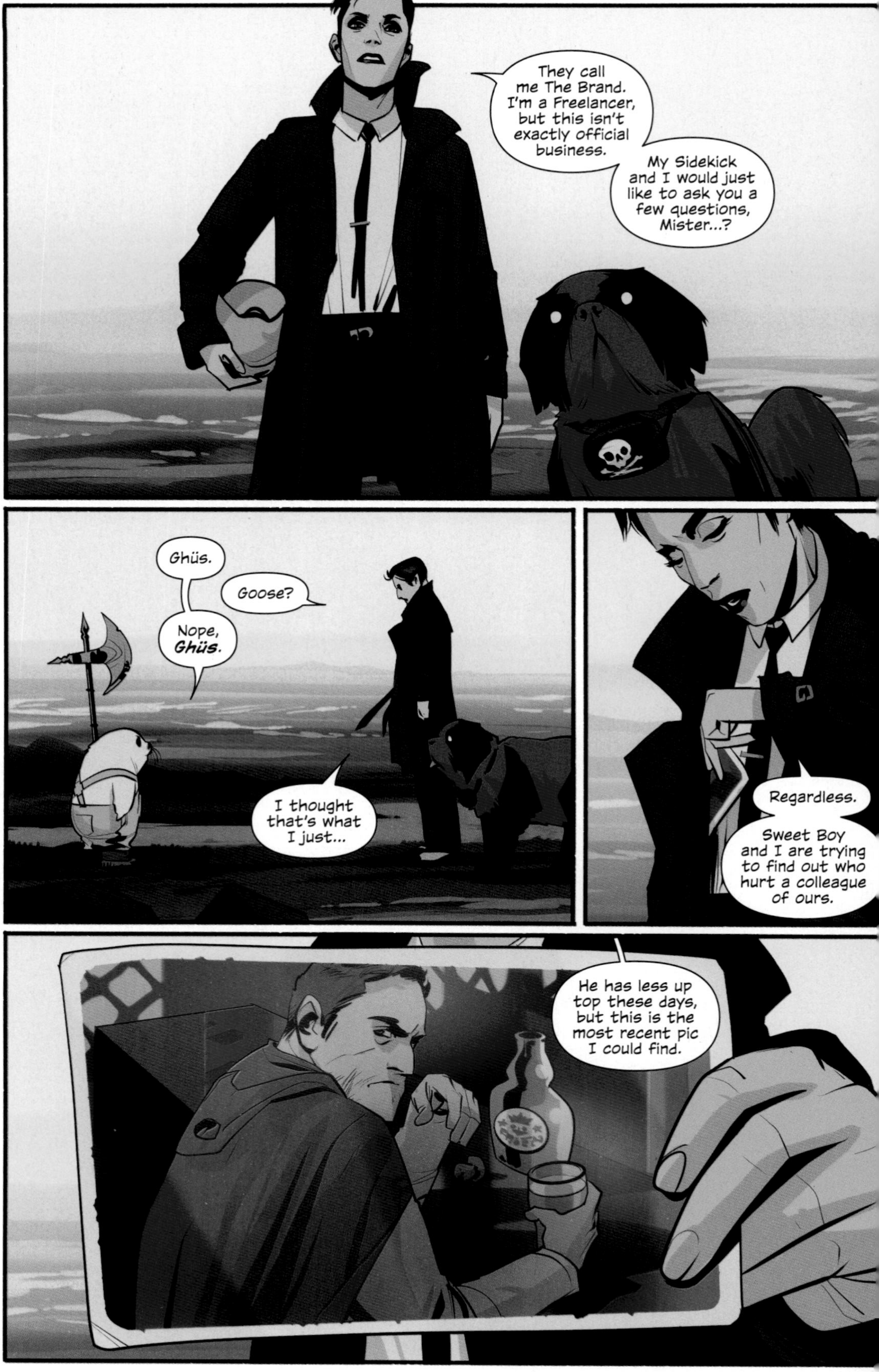
They call me The Brand. I'm a Freelancer, but this isn't exactly official business.
My Sidekick and I would just like to ask you a few questions, Mister...?
Ghüs.
Goose?
Nope, ***Ghüs***.
I thought that's what I just...
Regardless.
Sweet Boy and I are trying to find out who hurt a colleague of ours.
He has less up top these days, but this is the most recent pic I could find.

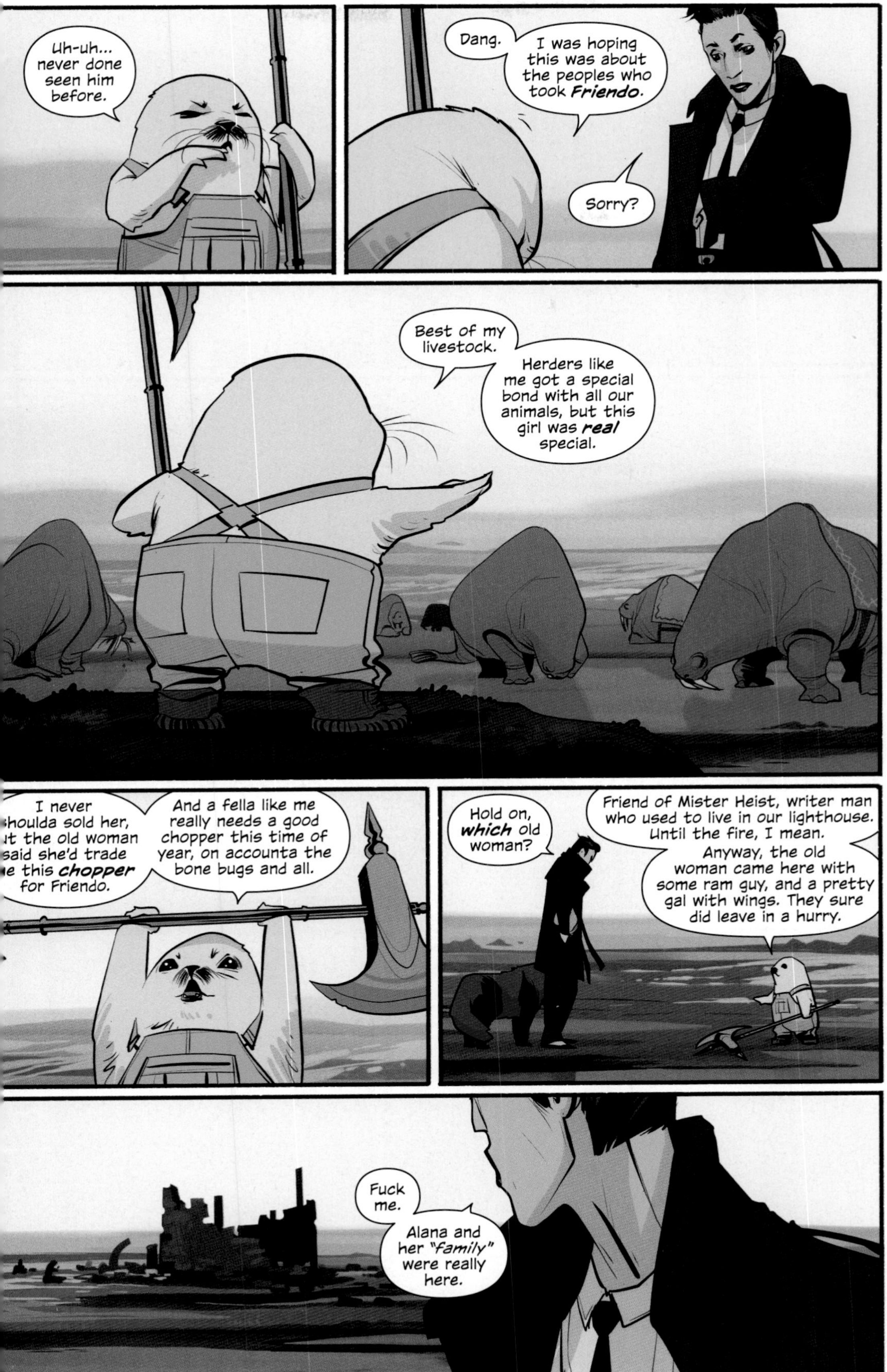
Uh-uh... never done seen him before.
Dang.
I was hoping this was about the peoples who took Friendo.
Sorry?
Best of my livestock.
Herders like me got a special bond with all our animals, but this girl was real special.
I never shoulda sold her, but the old woman said she'd trade me this chopper for Friendo.
And a fella like me really needs a good chopper this time of year, on accounta the bone bugs and all.
Hold on, which old woman?
Friend of Mister Heist, writer man who used to live in our lighthouse. Until the fire, I mean.
Anyway, the old woman came here with some ram guy, and a pretty gal with wings. They sure did leave in a hurry.
Fuck me.
Alana and her "family" were really here.

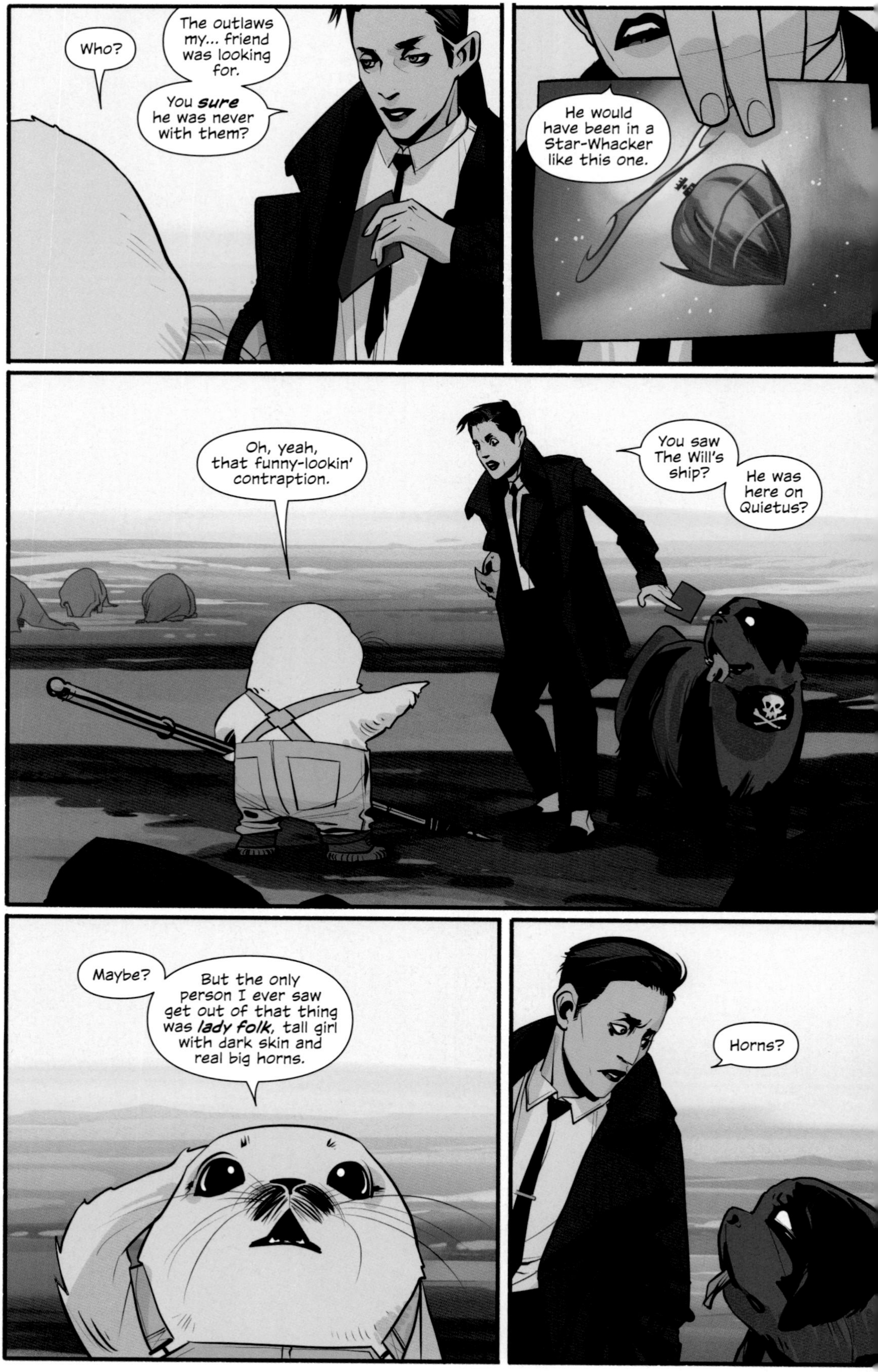

Who?
The outlaws my... friend was looking for.
You *sure* he was never with them?
He would have been in a Star-Whacker like this one.
Oh, yeah, that funny-lookin' contraption.
You saw The Will's ship?
He was here on Quietus?
Maybe?
But the only person I ever saw get out of that thing was *lady folk*, tall girl with dark skin and real big horns.
Horns?

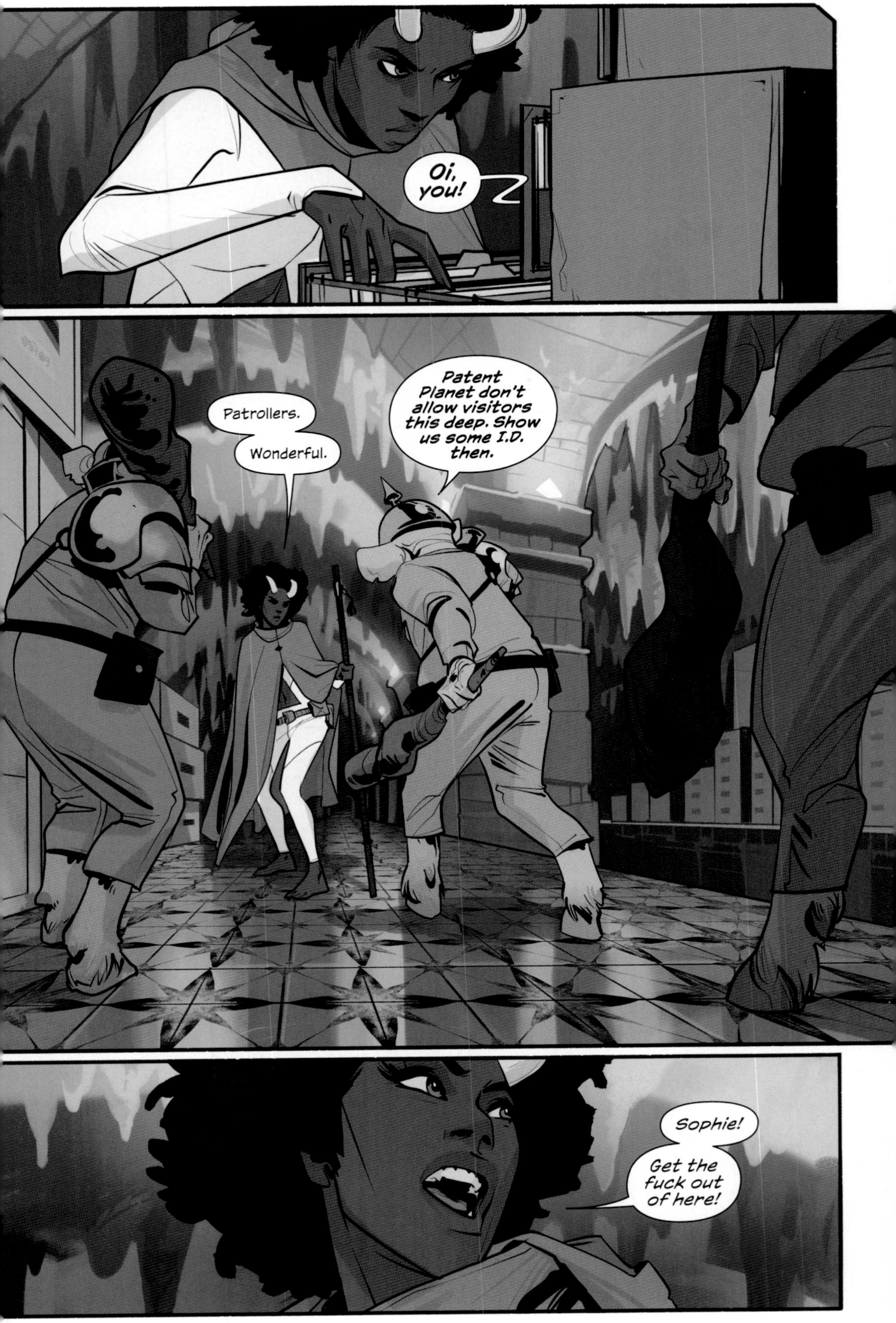
Oi, you!
Patrollers.
Wonderful.
Patent Planet don't allow visitors this deep. Show us some I.D. then.
Sophie!
Get the fuck out of here!

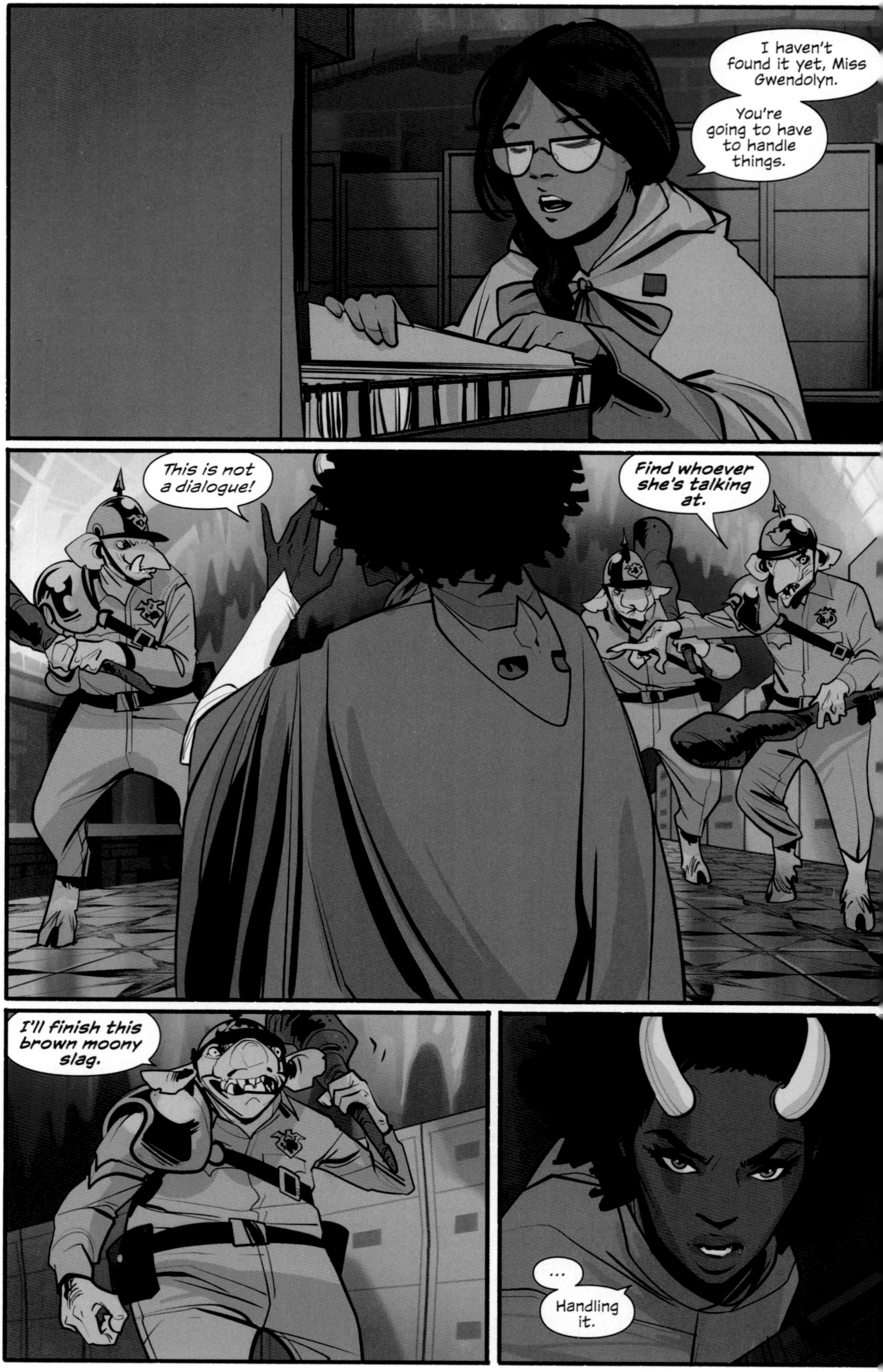

I haven't found it yet, Miss Gwendolyn.
You're going to have to handle things.
This is not a dialogue!
Find whoever she's talking at.
I'll finish this brown moony slag.
...
Handling it.

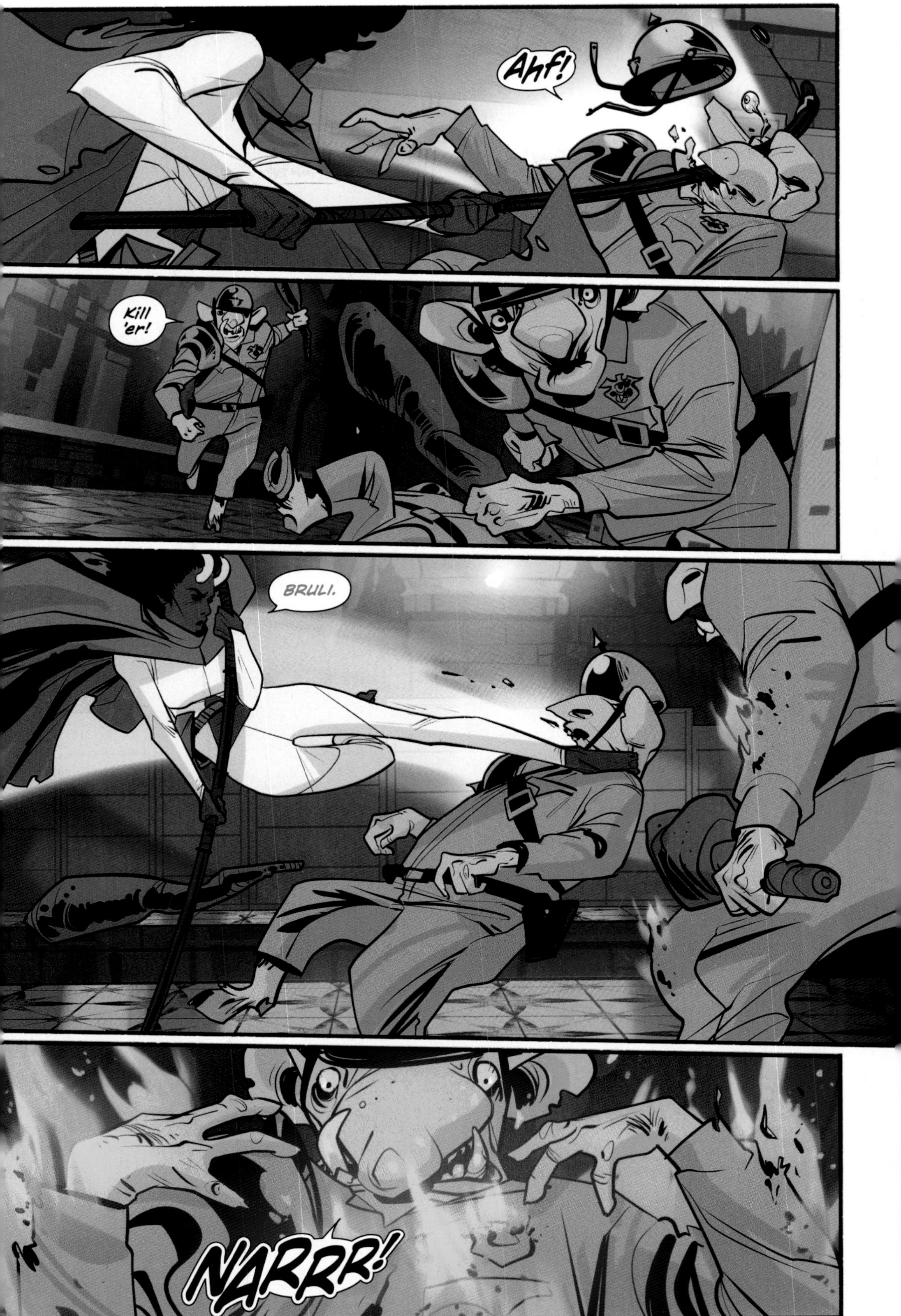
Ahf!
Kill 'er!
BRULI.
NARRR!

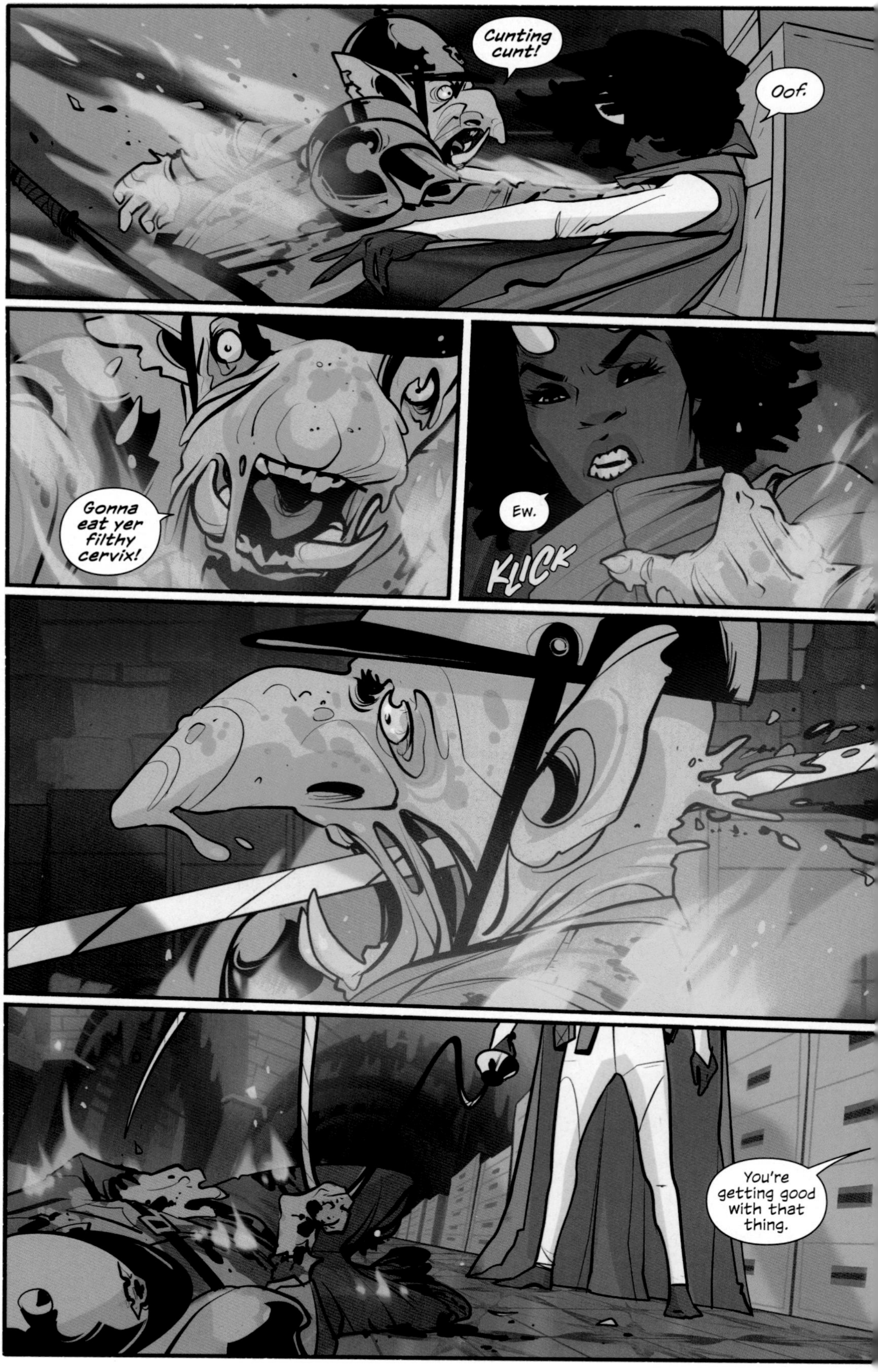
Cunting cunt!
Oof.
Gonna eat yer filthy cervix!
Ew.
KLICK
You're getting good with that thing.

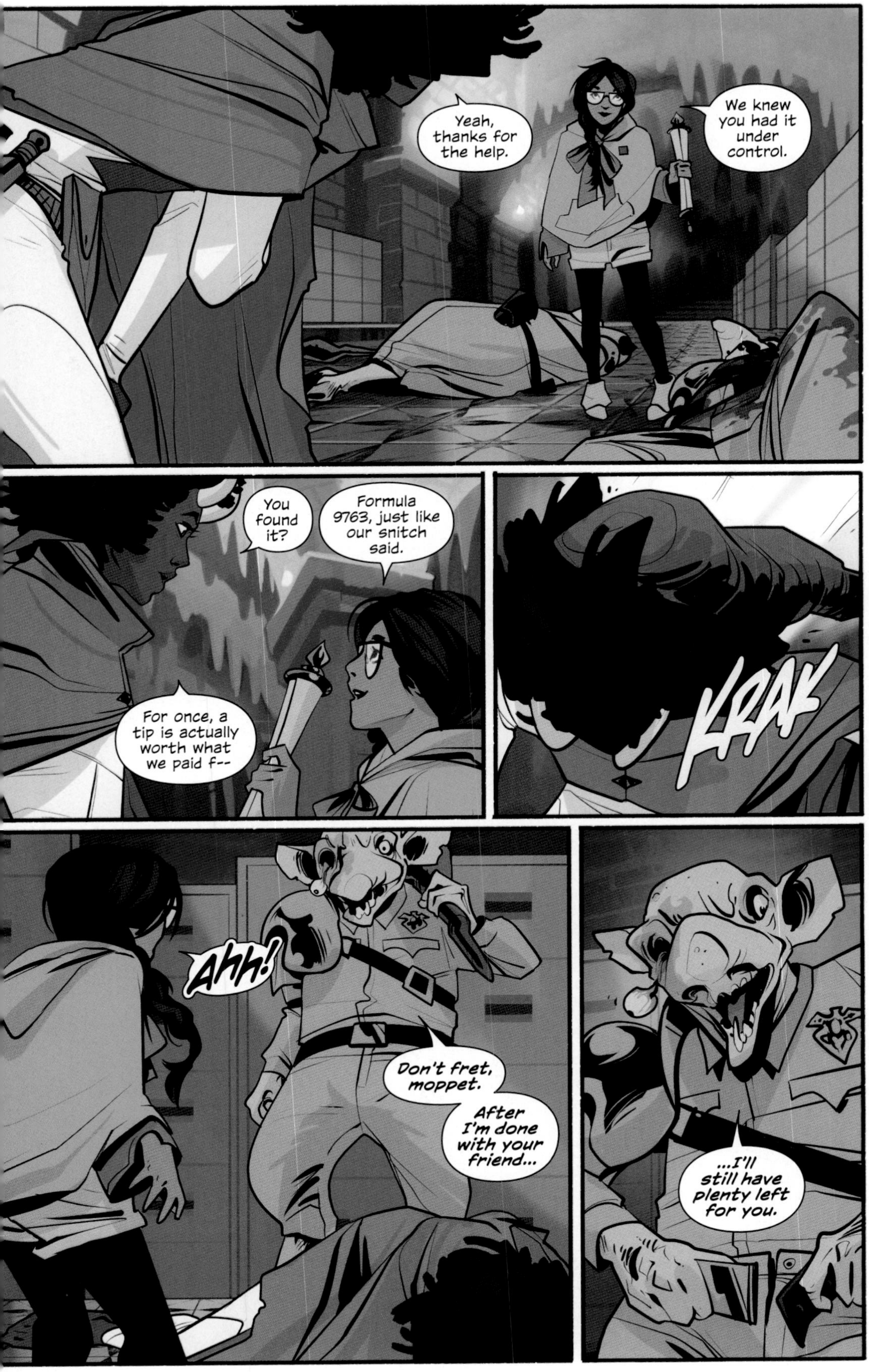

Yeah, thanks for the help.
We knew you had it under control.
You found it?
Formula 9763, just like our snitch said.
For once, a tip is actually worth what we paid f--
KRAK
Ahh!
Don't fret, moppet.
After I'm done with your friend...
...I'll still have plenty left for you.

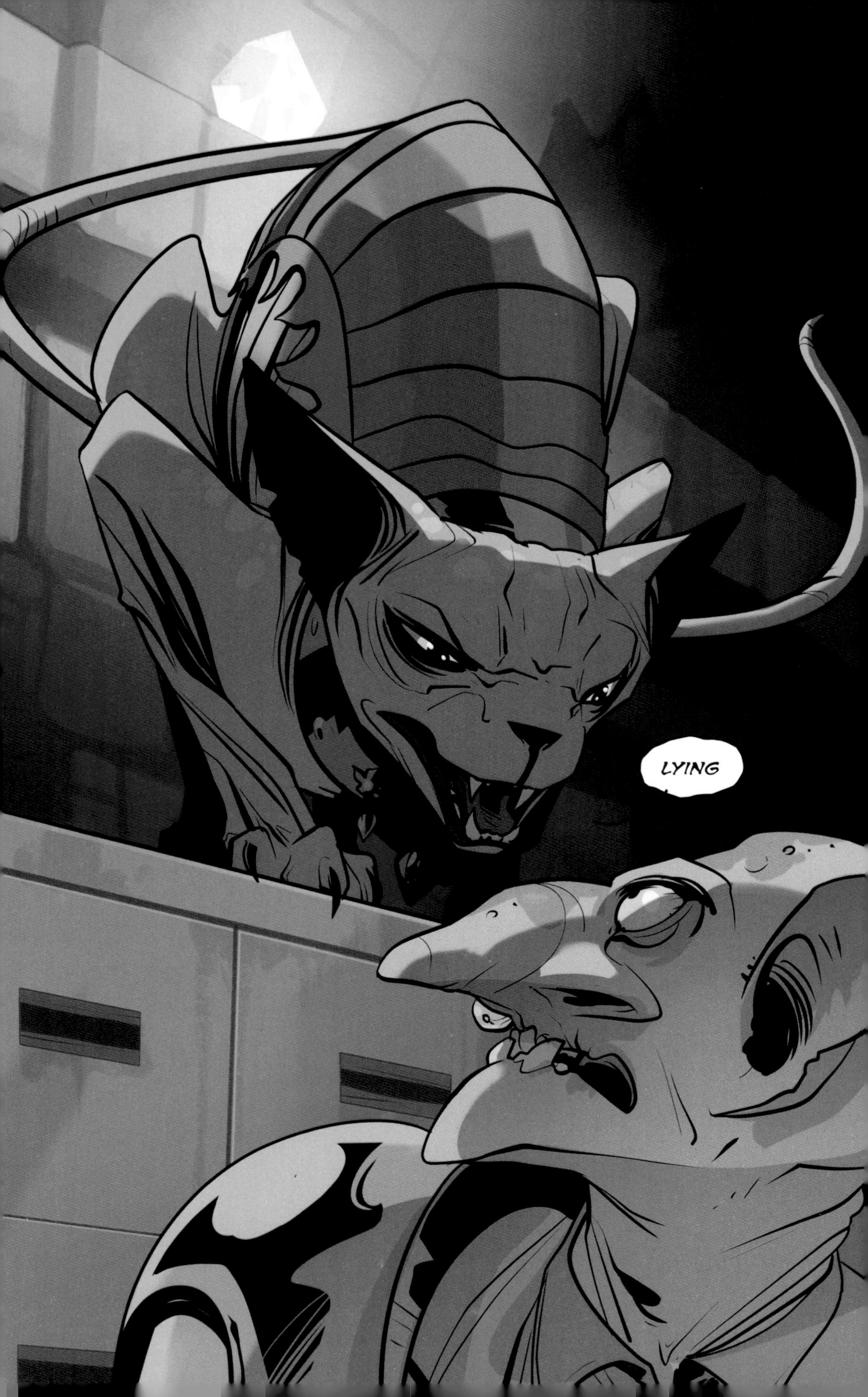
LYING

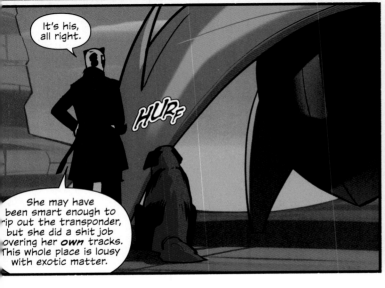

It's his, all right.

HURF

She may have been smart enough to rip out the transponder, but she did a shit job covering her *own* tracks. This whole place is lousy with exotic matter.

Billy, Billy, Billy... always getting mixed up with reckless broads.

It's unseemly!

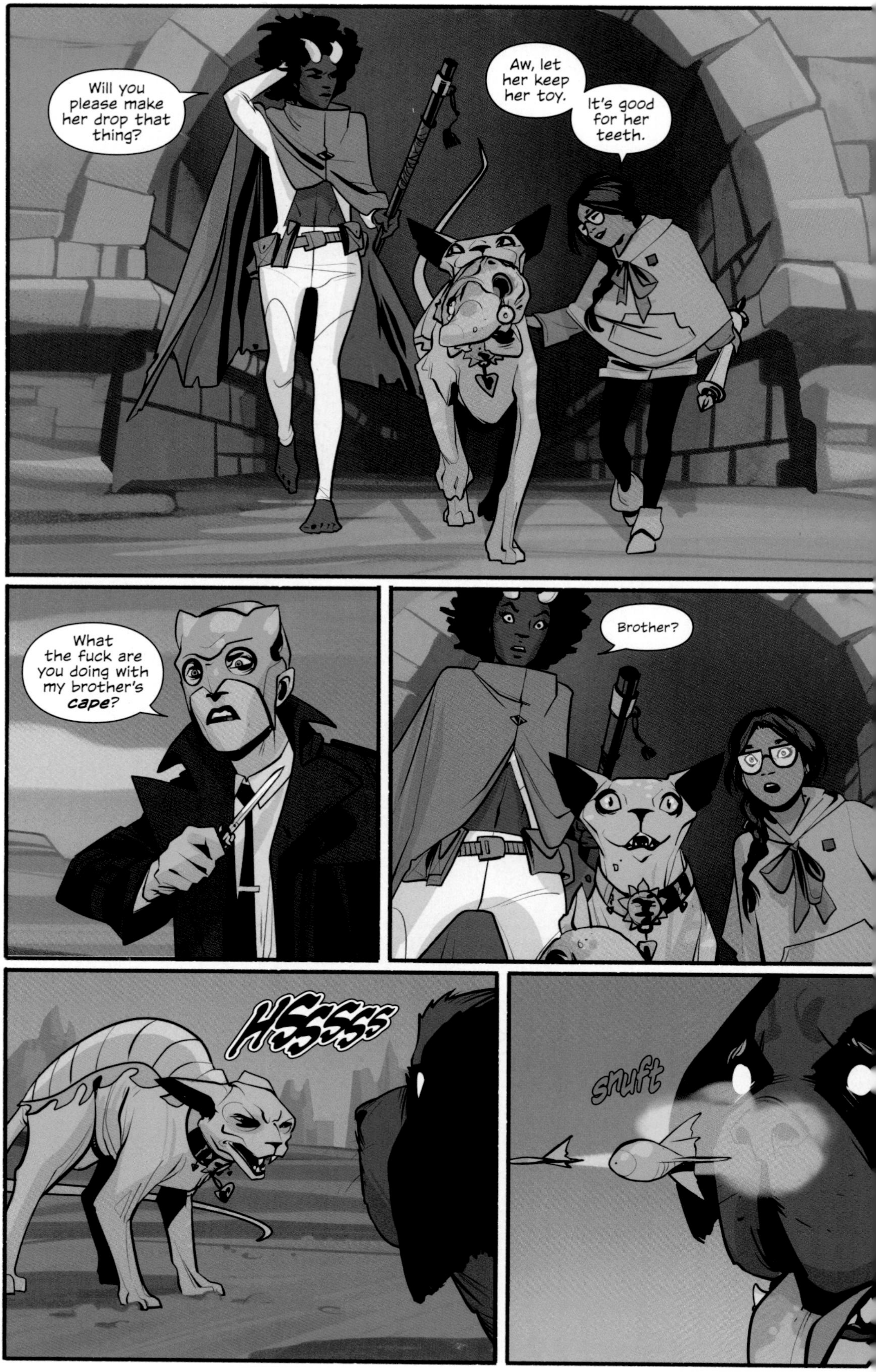

Will you please make her drop that thing?
Aw, let her keep her toy.
It's good for her teeth.
What the fuck are you doing with my brother's *cape*?
Brother?
HSSSSS
snuft

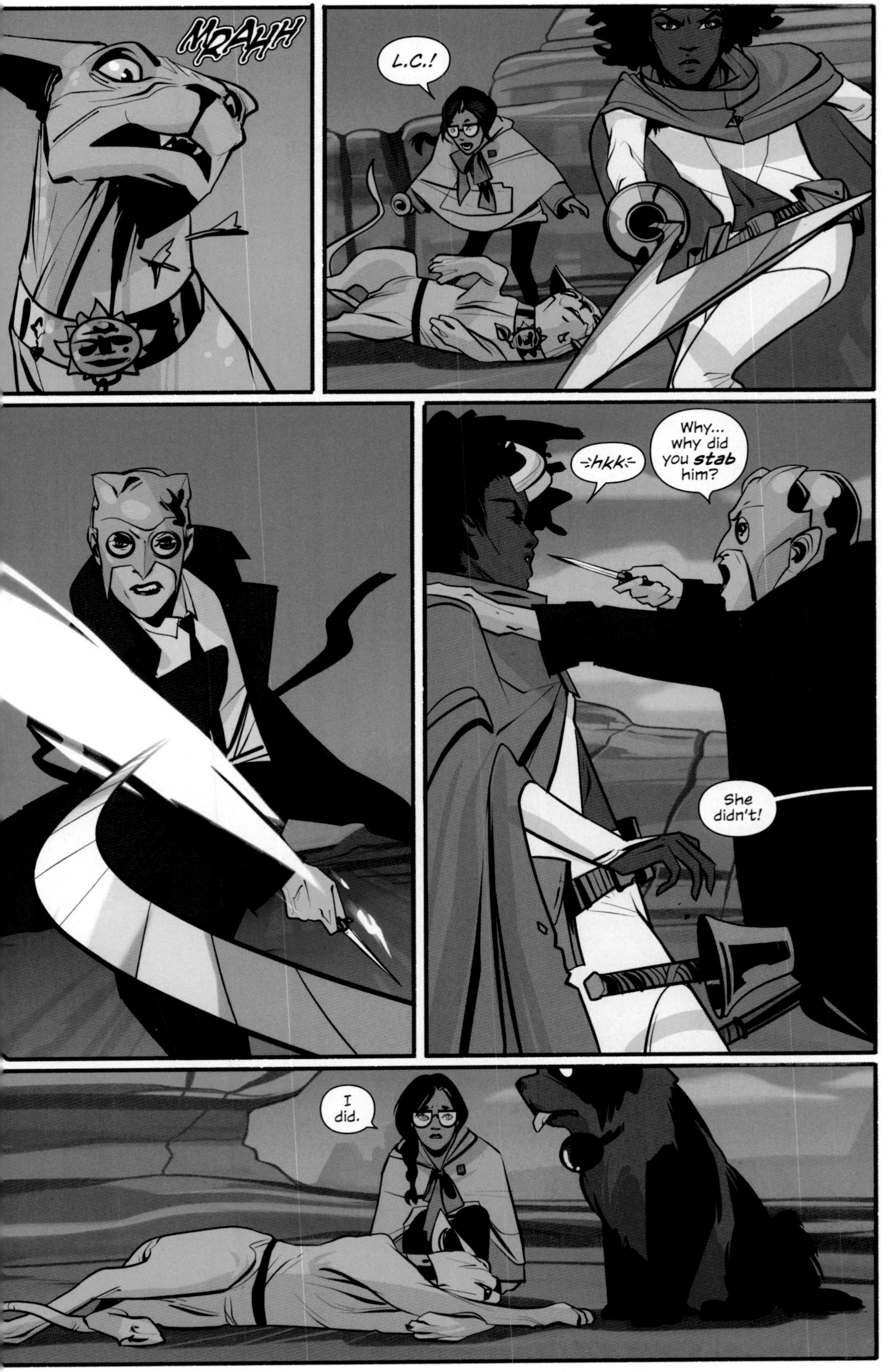
MRAHH
L.C.!
-hkk-
Why... why did you stab him?
She didn't!
I did.

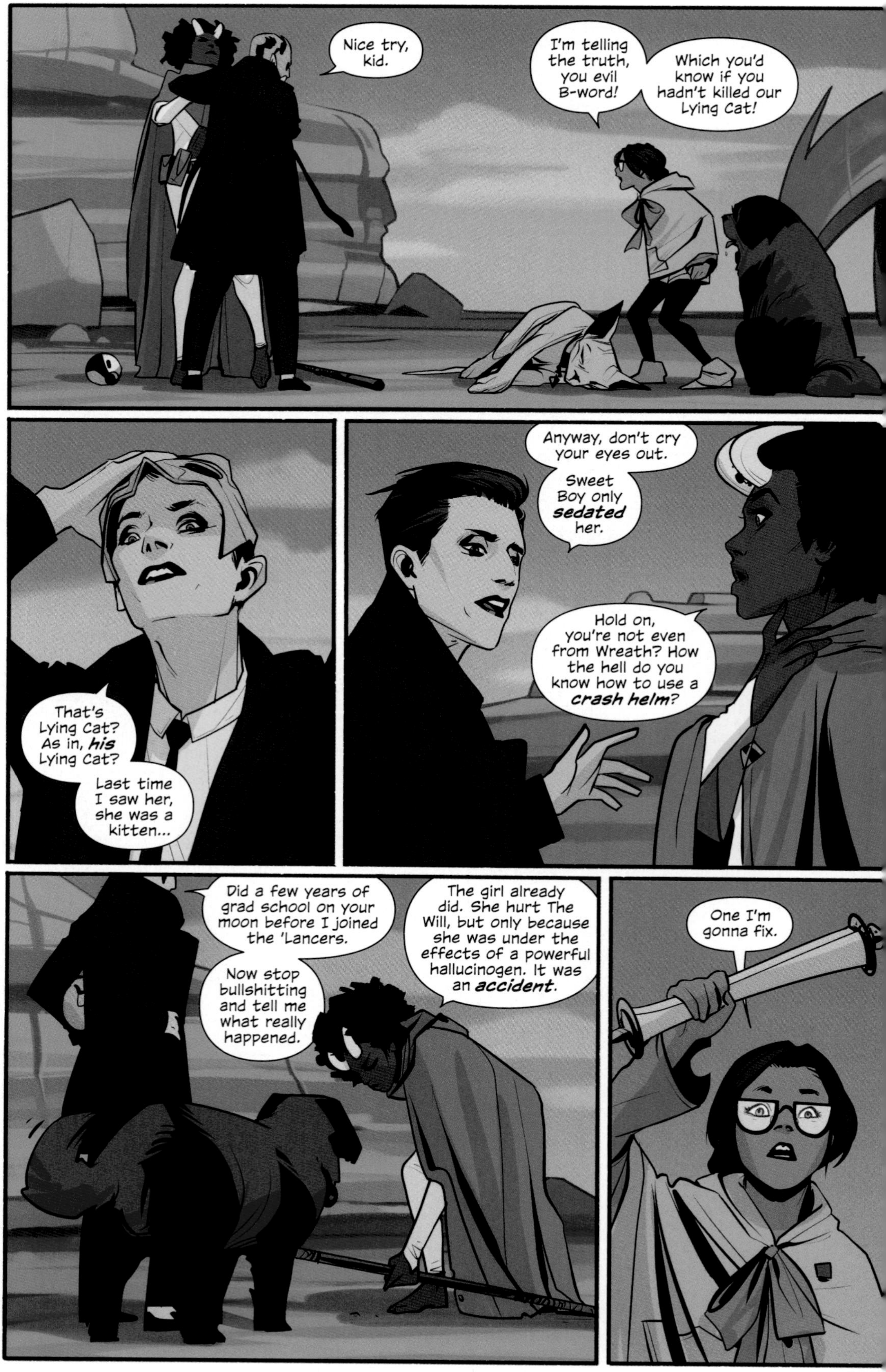
Nice try, kid.
I'm telling the truth, you evil B-word!
Which you'd know if you hadn't killed our Lying Cat!
That's Lying Cat? As in, his Lying Cat?
Last time I saw her, she was a kitten...
Anyway, don't cry your eyes out.
Sweet Boy only sedated her.
Hold on, you're not even from Wreath? How the hell do you know how to use a crash helm?
Did a few years of grad school on your moon before I joined the 'Lancers.
Now stop bullshitting and tell me what really happened.
The girl already did. She hurt The Will, but only because she was under the effects of a powerful hallucinogen. It was an accident.
One I'm gonna fix.

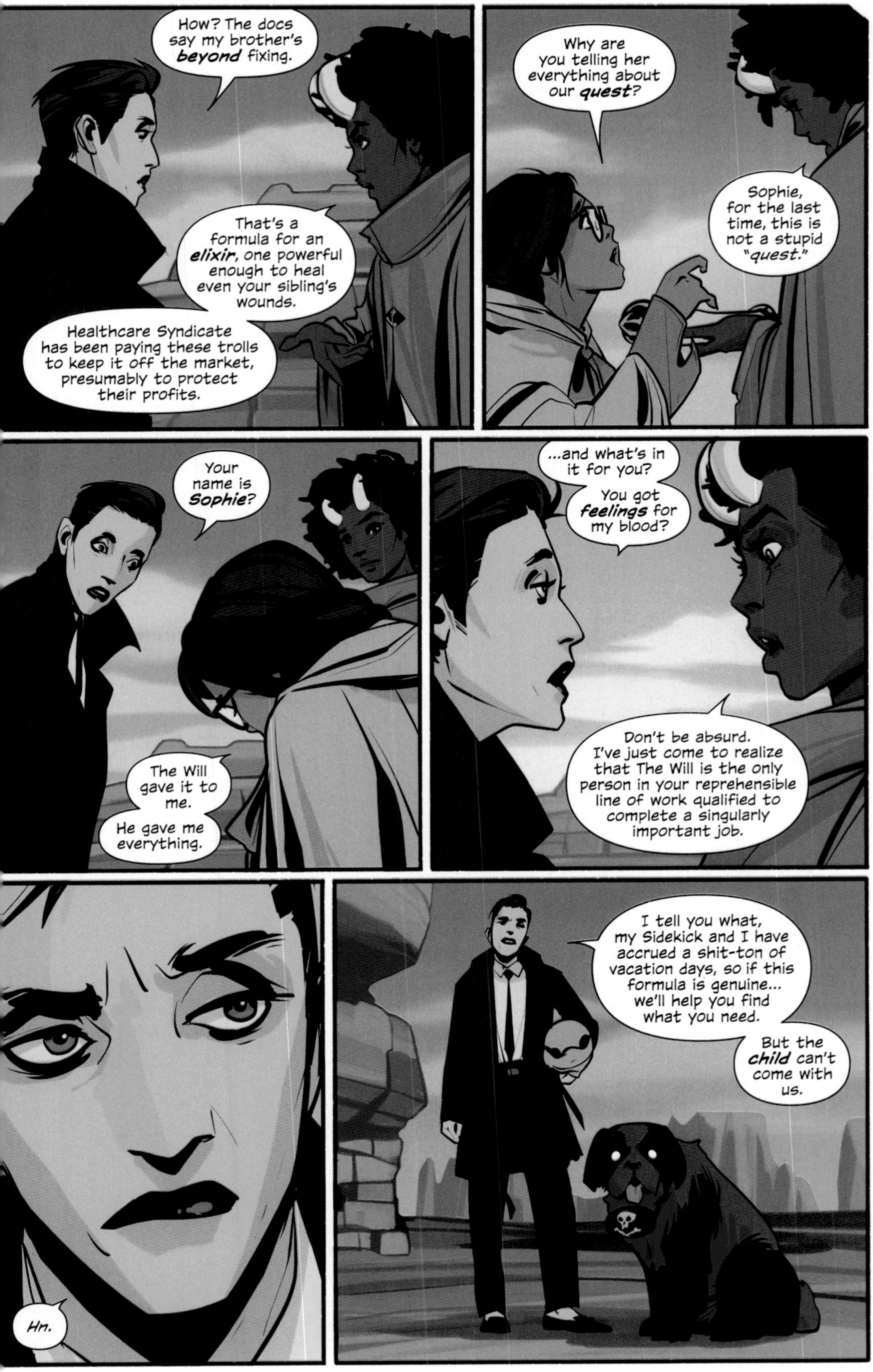
How? The docs say my brother's *beyond* fixing.
That's a formula for an *elixir*, one powerful enough to heal even your sibling's wounds.
Healthcare Syndicate has been paying these trolls to keep it off the market, presumably to protect their profits.
Why are you telling her everything about our *quest*?
Sophie, for the last time, this is not a stupid "*quest*."
Your name is *Sophie*?
The Will gave it to me.
He gave me everything.
...and what's in it for you?
You got *feelings* for my blood?
Don't be absurd. I've just come to realize that The Will is the only person in your reprehensible line of work qualified to complete a singularly important job.
Hn.
I tell you what, my Sidekick and I have accrued a shit-ton of vacation days, so if this formula is genuine... we'll help you find what you need.
But the *child* can't come with us.

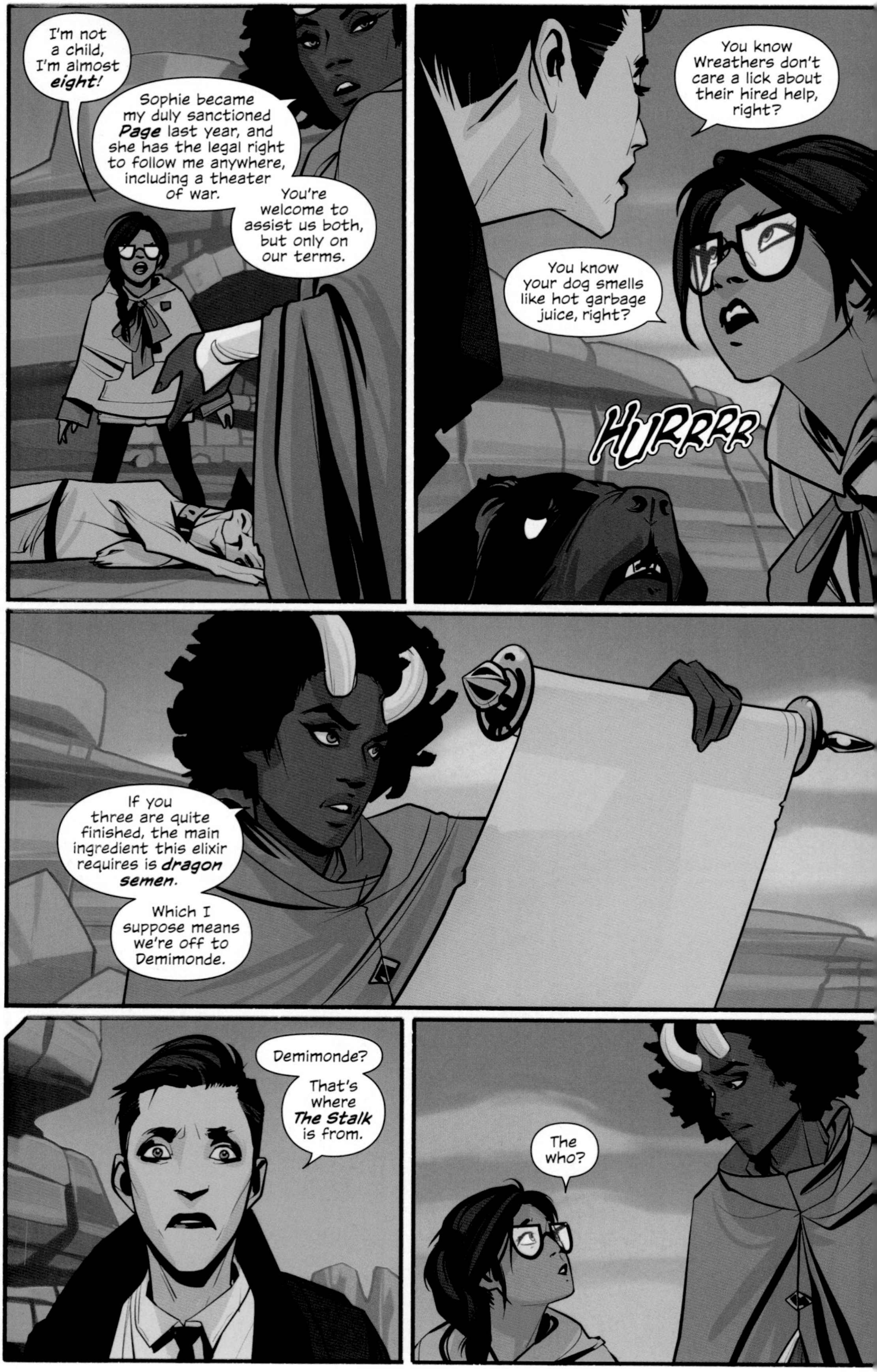
I'm not a child, I'm almost *eight*!
Sophie became my duly sanctioned *Page* last year, and she has the legal right to follow me anywhere, including a theater of war.
You're welcome to assist us both, but only on our terms.
You know Wreathers don't care a lick about their hired help, right?
You know your dog smells like hot garbage juice, right?
HURRRR
If you three are quite finished, the main ingredient this elixir requires is *dragon semen*.
Which I suppose means we're off to Demimonde.
Demimonde?
That's where *The Stalk* is from.
The who?

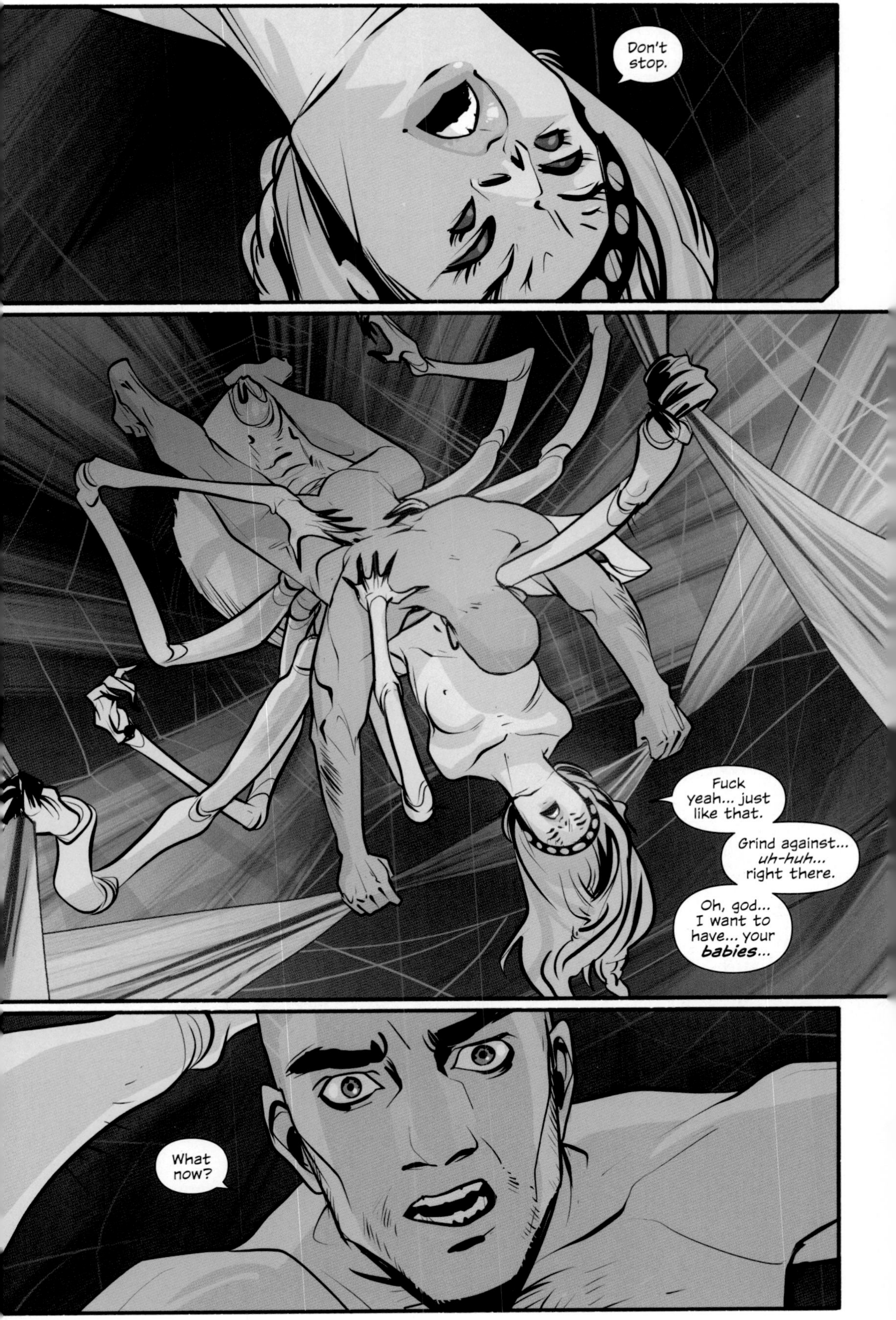
Don't stop.
Fuck yeah... just like that.
Grind against... *uh-huh...* right there.
Oh, god... I want to have... your ***babies...***
What now?

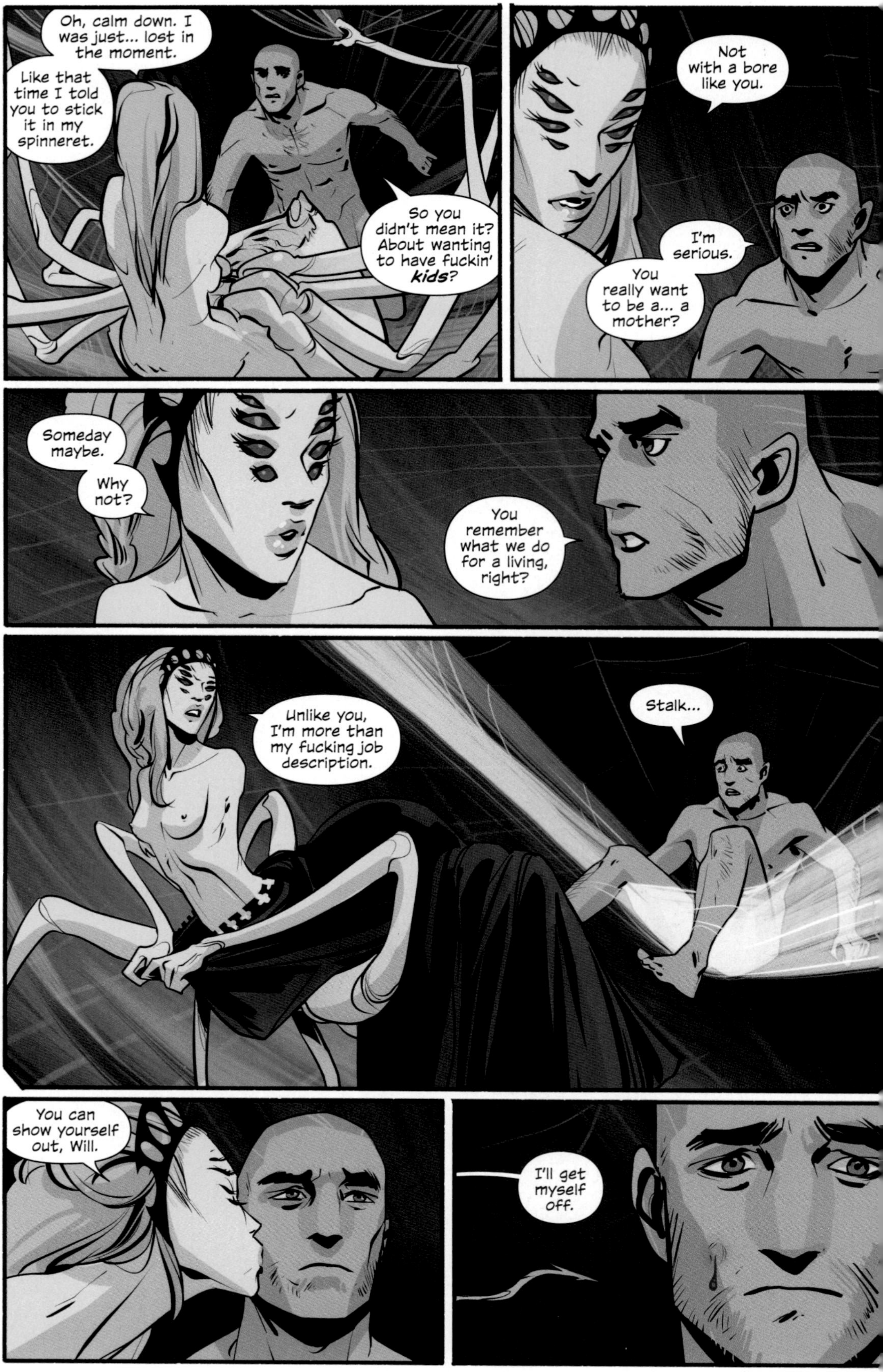
Oh, calm down. I was just... lost in the moment.
Like that time I told you to stick it in my spinneret.
So you didn't mean it? About wanting to have fuckin' *kids*?
Not with a bore like you.
I'm serious.
You really want to be a... a mother?
Someday maybe.
Why not?
You remember what we do for a living, right?
Unlike you, I'm more than my fucking job description.
Stalk...
You can show yourself out, Will.
I'll get myself off.

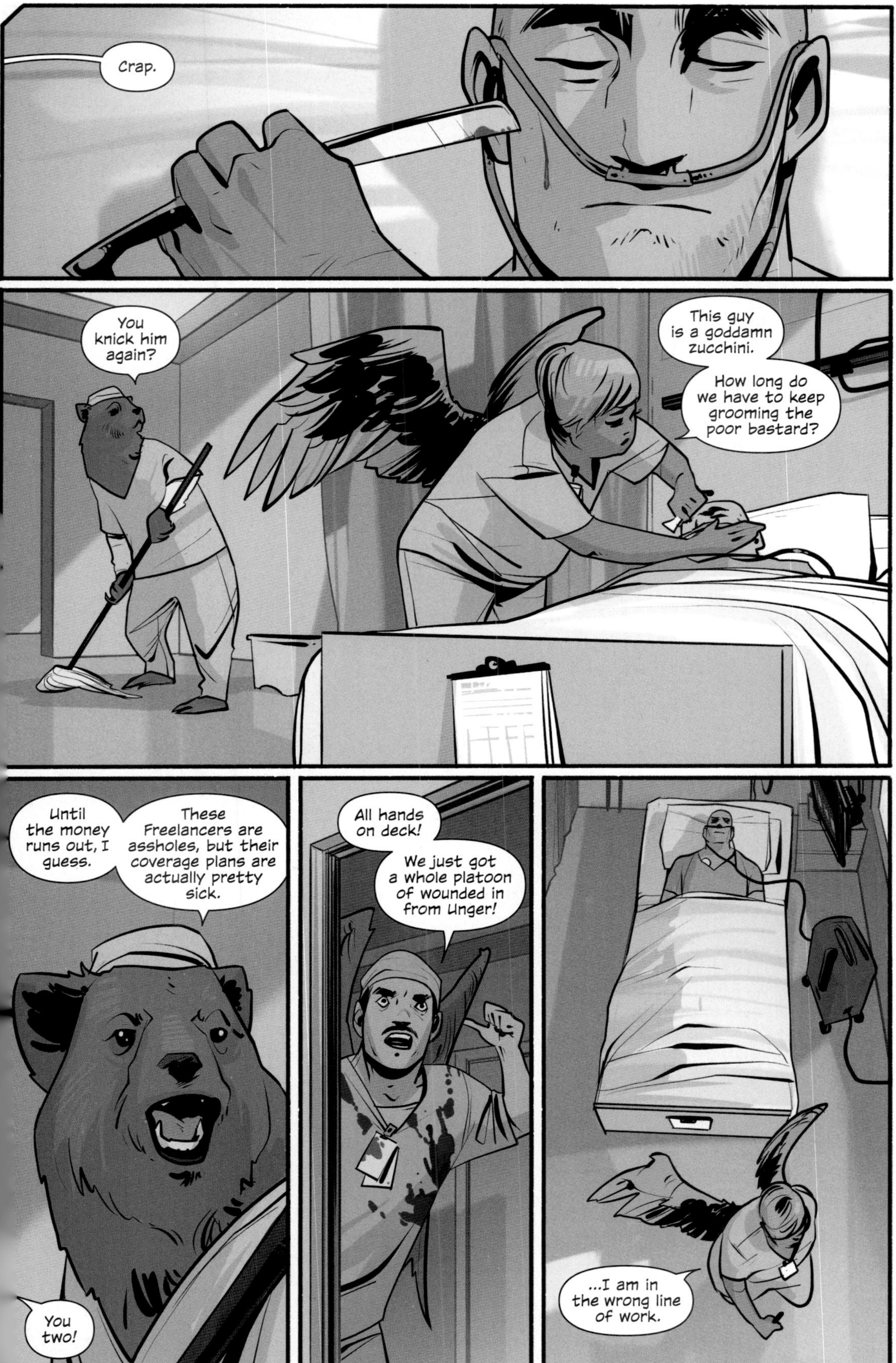
Crap.
You knick him again?
This guy is a goddamn zucchini.
How long do we have to keep grooming the poor bastard?
Until the money runs out, I guess.
These Freelancers are assholes, but their coverage plans are actually pretty sick.
You two!
All hands on deck!
We just got a whole platoon of wounded in from Unger!
...I am in the wrong line of work.

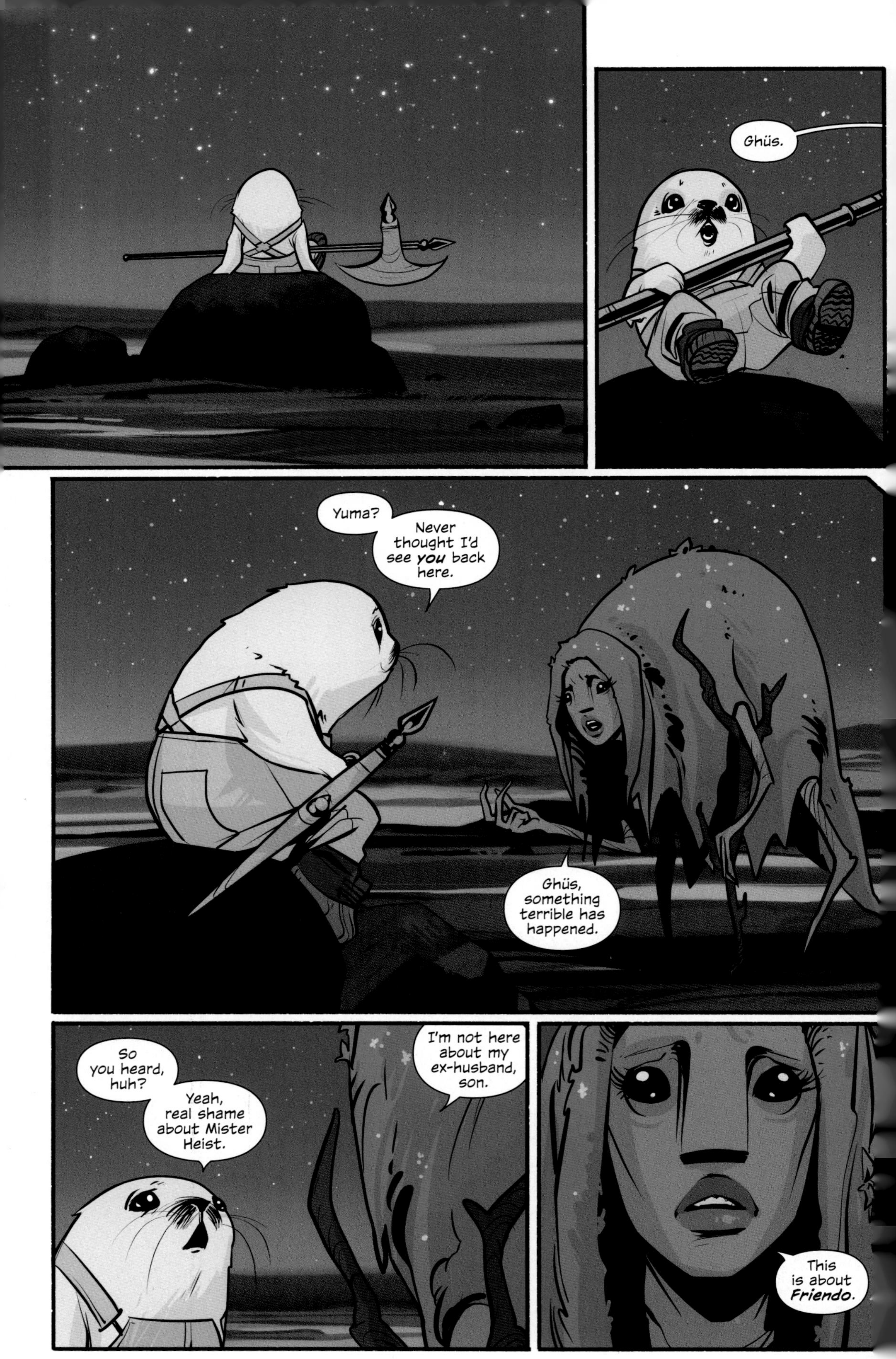

Ghüs.
Yuma?
Never thought I'd see *you* back here.
Ghüs, something terrible has happened.
So you heard, huh?
Yeah, real shame about Mister Heist.
I'm not here about my ex-husband, son.
This is about *Friendo*.

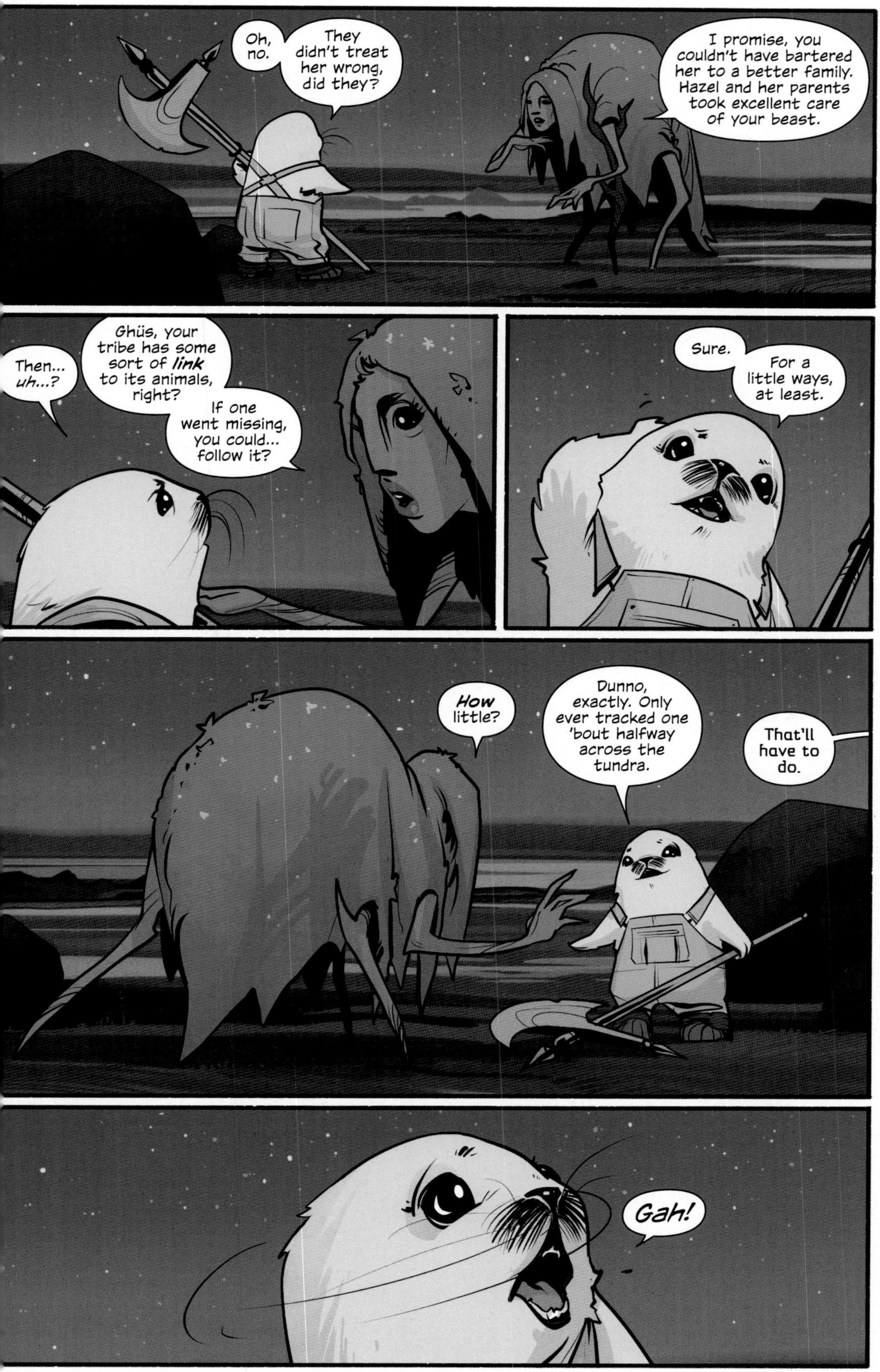
Oh, no.
They didn't treat her wrong, did they?
I promise, you couldn't have bartered her to a better family. Hazel and her parents took excellent care of your beast.
Then... *uh...*?
Ghüs, your tribe has some sort of ***link*** to its animals, right?
If one went missing, you could... follow it?
Sure.
For a little ways, at least.
How little?
Dunno, exactly. Only ever tracked one 'bout halfway across the tundra.
That'll have to do.
Gah!

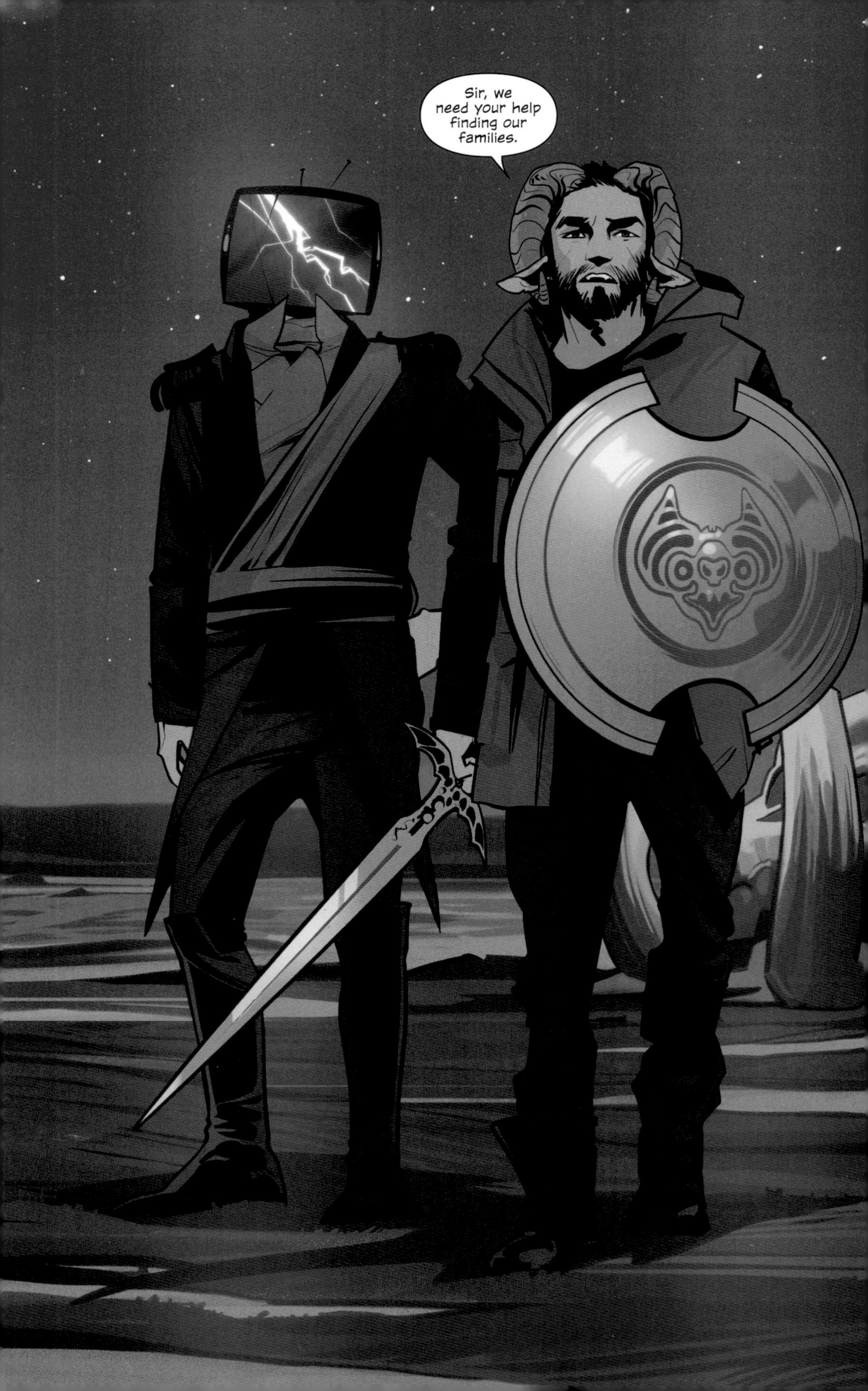
Sir, we need your help finding our families.

to be continued

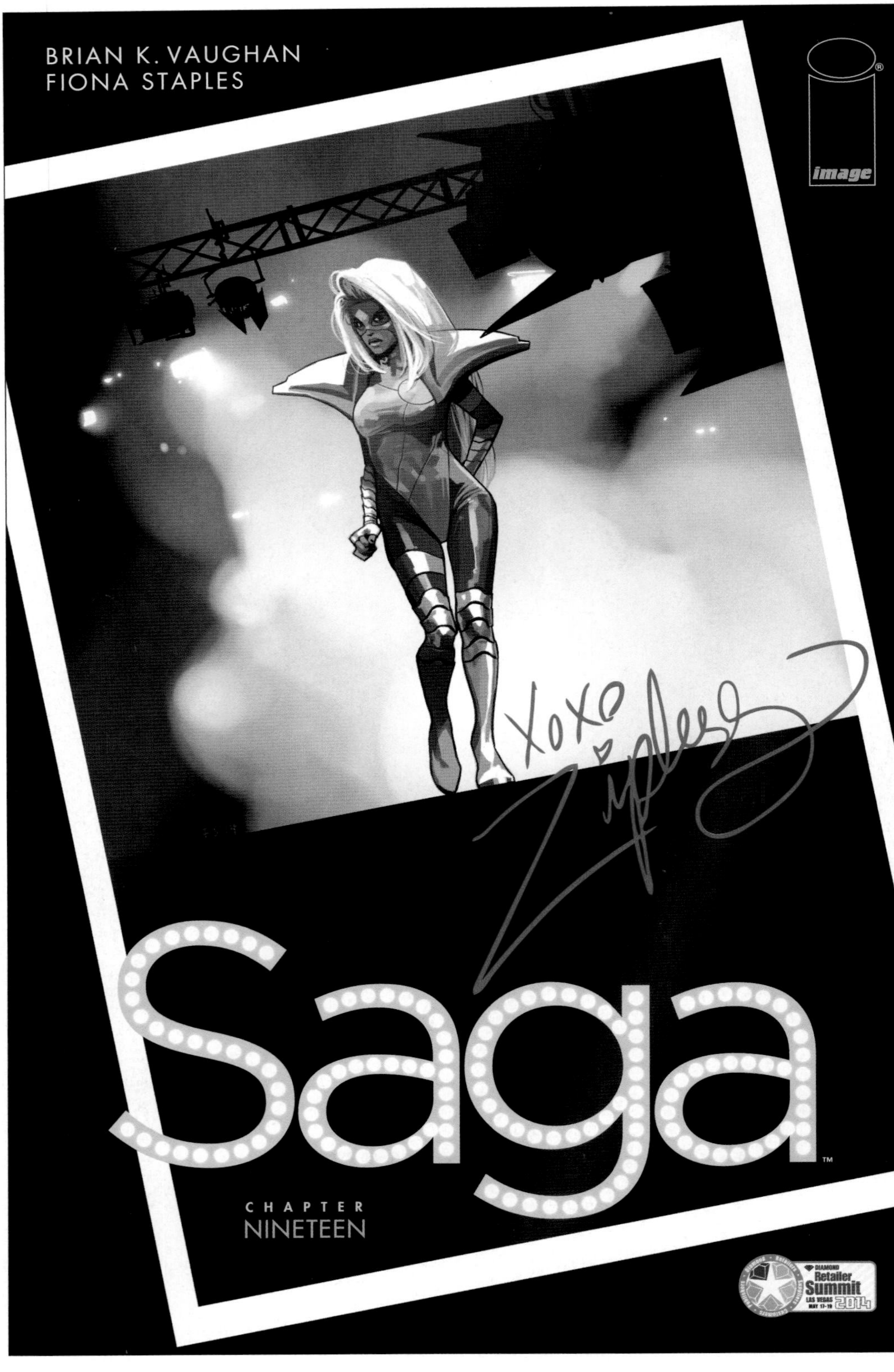
BRIAN K. VAUGHAN
FIONA STAPLES
image
Saga
CHAPTER
NINETEEN
Diamond Retailer Summit Las Vegas 2014

Chapter Nineteen variant cover for the Diamond Retailer Summit 2014

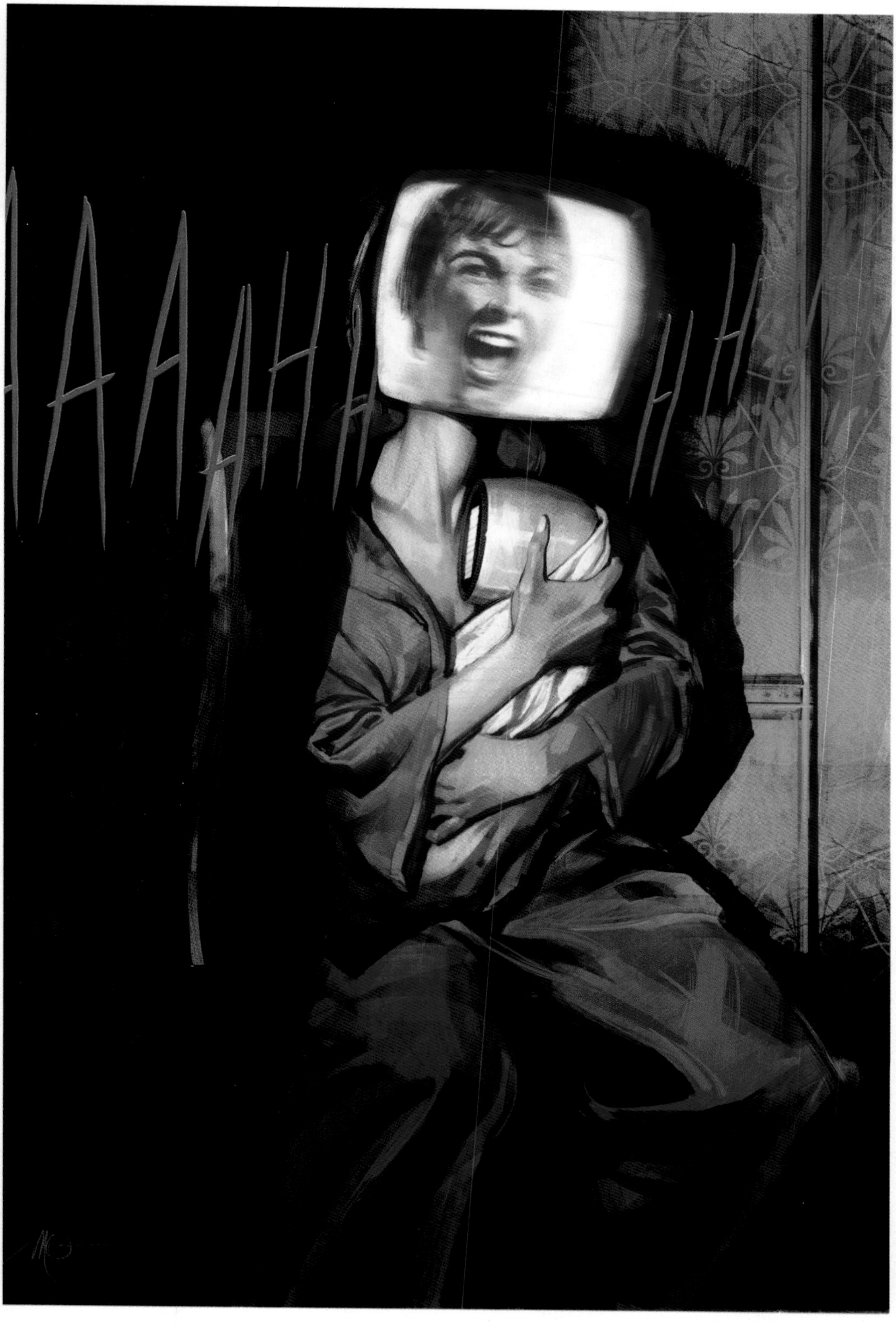

Variant cover by Massimo Carnevale for the Italian edition of Volume Four from BAO Publishing

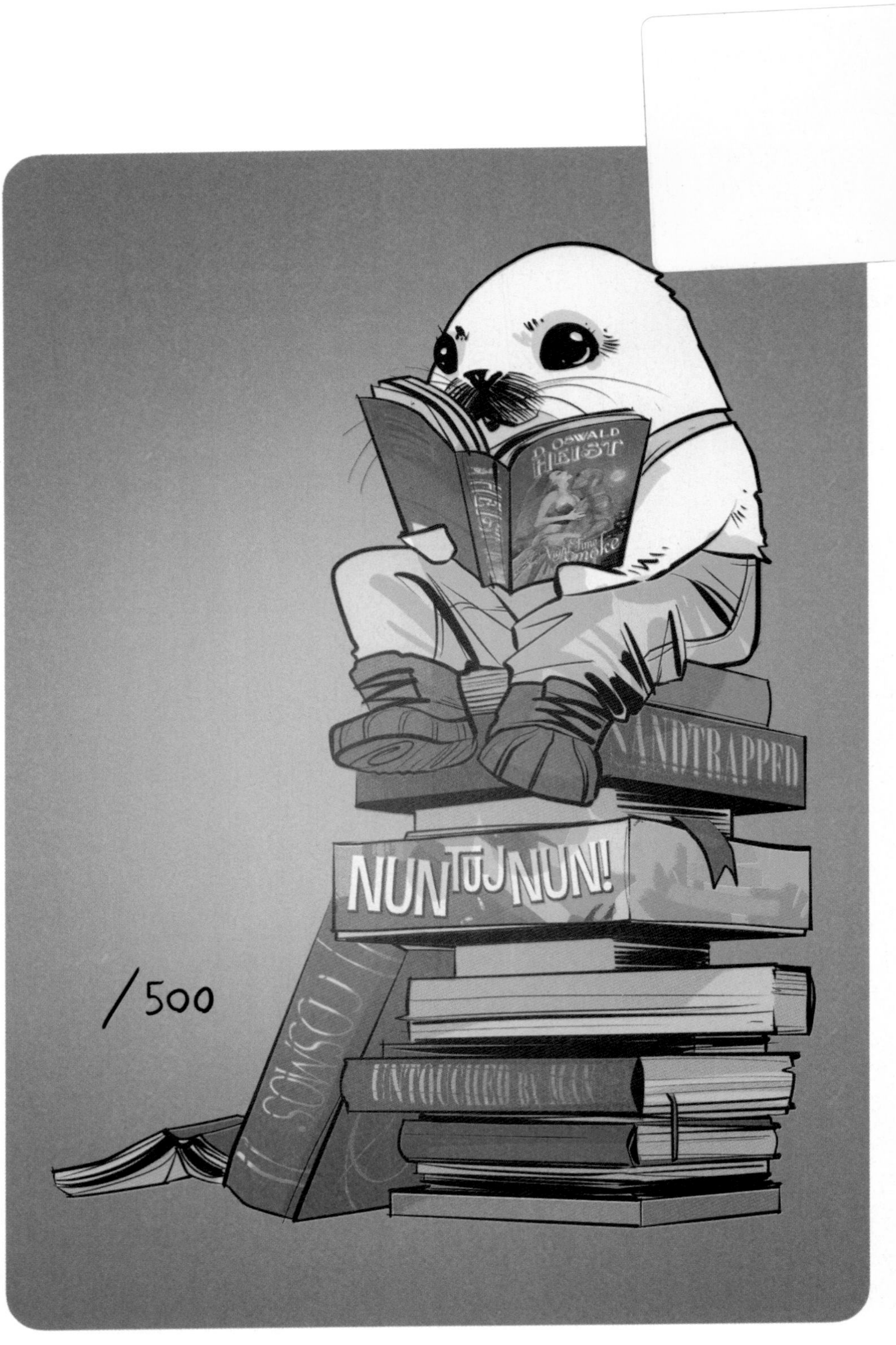
D. OSWALD
HEIST
NUN TUJ NUN!
UNTOUCHED BY MAN
/500

Limited edition bookplate for Forbidden Planet